Subject 37

Utopus, Book 1

Nathalie M.L. Römer

ISBN-13: 9789188459527

Emerentsia Publications
Marielundsvägen 9c
711 95 Gusselby
Sweden
emerentsiabooks.com

Ordering Information:

Orders by U.S. trade bookstores and wholesalers. Please contact Ingram: One Ingram Blvd., La Vergne, TN 37086 • 615.793.5000 or visit www.ingramcontent.com.

Independently printed as a Swedish publication.

Interior design and layout by Emerentsia Publications.

Official Website:
nathaliemlromer.com

Official Facebook Page:
facebook.com/nathaliemlromer

Official Twitter Account:
twitter.com/nathaliemlromer

Book website: nathaliemlromer.com/subject-37

For my loving partner Anders.

PART ONE

Past Paths

Subject 37

1.

FIFTEEN YEARS AGO

THEY HAD always called it—home. Their only home until they'd become adults, and things needed to change. And change they would everything. The youngest among us were the most acutely affected by the events of the next dozen years. They *were aware of* the things that were wrong with the society they were living in. They'd cause trouble for everyone in the place that was their home. Until things changed... one day... unexpectedly...

Utopus was the name of their home, and it was established many centuries ago because of the last war, which had destroyed most of the world and had killed so many people that only eighty million humans existed now because of this war. They'd learn that the war had happened 370 years ago, and it was called World War 3. After this war had ended - abruptly, and the people moved away from the regions affected by the poison spread by the weapons used in this war. These weapons were what would become the focus of a *few* people in Utopus and their efforts to cause change to to everyone's plight. As a part of this effort, they warned everyone to act like we were ignorant of the world, that no individual had any information of the world outside Utopus whose borders weren't even visible by demarcations. The borders were invisible and only ever visible in people's fear of the unknown. They were only ever marked as a border by the reactions from the residents whenever they would be too close to the border of Utopus and they'd have this irrational fear of outside, of things that *would* differ from their current life.

They were the youngest people living here, people now growing up in this city, and a *few* of us had discovered certain secrets that were seditious, dangerous and that had some sort of historical origin.

"This is *our* home," Steven would say often to Elisabet as he would try to convince her of his viewpoint as his knowledge of the world would increase as a consequence of the work he'd been doing with his father. "It's our only home, but it doesn't have to…"

Elisabet would just nod and then look away. Never answering his questions to give him *her* opinion of the situation. But she too would go along to get in trouble, which they did more while they were kids and not so much as adults, though he'd continue with these antics as more serious exploratory excursions which also were noticed by his father. Steven found that there was so much more going on with Utopus, and that it was more than a home. They established it at the end of a war that he had learnt about earlier in his life. It didn't take that many trips through the region, where Utopus was located, to discover that not all eighty million people of Earth - which was a guess based on what his father would talk about and a guess only, were living here. Also, Steven found out fast that nothing ever happened in this city by chance. The information and the things that happened hung over his entire life like a dark cloud…

So against this background, Steven observed his father and other scientists engage themselves in research that was supposedly leading them to answers; about what had happened in the past five hundred years, how our society should exist or not as it was now or in a different version, and why they lost so many people in the *last* war.

But enough about the world he was living in. This was our home and here he was going to tell everyone the story of how 'life' was for him and others. This wasn't about the lives of his father and the other scientists who were working on uncovering the evidence of what could have happened around the time this war had happened. They wanted better for us. We wanted to be normal teenagers or kids. They were busy fixing our world, so we'd be safe.

"Be careful *when* you do any stuff out there," father would say, "because it isn't safe out as you might hope for, or as it may appear." These were words Steven had heard since he was really young. "Keep an eye out for things that look odd," was the *new* thing his father had been adding for the past few years. "Watch also how people behave. You'll notice they behave a certain way…"

Steven noticed that everyone, including his father, was fearful of what were the invisible boundaries of their city, and there wasn't even anything that resembled a wall or fence or anything to mark outside as *outside*. They had *no* demarcations to keep us inside the city…

Outside—was Zone Zero, according to the paperwork which he saw in his father's office during the first time he had visited where he was working years ago. He'd often thought this as he'd investigated the definitely fortified city with the curiosity of a boy. Soon he'd discover the fortification was caused by fear rather than walls of fences.

As his father would say frequently: "Fear is a *wonderful* motivator to make people curious. It's also an excellent motivator to keep them from travelling or exploring."

With that comment repeated throughout my childhood, Steven would grow up to a boy of thirteen who'd watch on as people would leave. Not just when he was thirteen, but also five years earlier, and then again five years later. Apart from these unexplainable events, he had a relatively typical childhood, even if he had relatively few toys or books, not much in the way of clothing, and he'd been living for almost all his life in a small dwelling on the fourth floor of a grey building as far as he could remember…

Steven's life growing up wasn't that different from that of any other child or teen. It comprised being taught stuff every day and then, in his free time, he'd be exploring the old ruins interspersed between the stark, grey buildings of Utopus. Mostly with Elisabet, who was his unexpected friend from a very young age who was living in the building next his where his father and he had our small dwelling. She was the bravest of all my friends. However, she too wasn't willing to go into the underground structure he'd found one chilly morning, a few months before he turned thirteen, maybe three months after his mother had left to go somewhere. Steven visited the building perhaps five times in total and realised fast it was connected to Utopus in rather unexpected ways. It might have been where the earliest Utopus survivors of hundreds of years ago had lived.

Before he'd gone home again, he'd stared at the road ahead until his mother was out of sight. Steven would return there often over the next few years to check if she was returning. She never came back. And he would lead a tumultuous life in a city with many secrets, and other things, that would drive him to go on a journey unlike anything he had imagined of such a venture. The details of the entire journey were too boring for any discussion, so he just skipped ahead and talked about the discoveries he'd make during this endless life of living in a strange city and later making a trek through what once was called Europe.

I guess I should record, for future prosperity, the parts of this journey that matter and not tell of the entire journey until much later, Steven thought, *and I guess that the parts I tell them about, later, will sound fantastical and rather repetitive. I've read a few of the surviving books and often when the hero made a journey of some sort that would feel like a dreadful story to me, but then how I can even justify doing something similar?*

* * *

Steven knew he wasn't the only rebellious kid in the large community that resembled a city in a few places, even with most parts resembling ruins or tents, with certain of groups of people were being cramped in them when there were enough houses for everyone which confused me...

Because the young people knew that many of the houses were empty, they'd explored them, and in doing so, they were learning things that the adults wouldn't or couldn't teach us. Steven didn't know until years later this was what made his life in Utopus much more dangerous than it should have been. He'd look at the adults and wonder why they'd act all confused about our lives all the time, and assumed quickly it was all for show. That they'd do this to keep safe from the outsiders who'd arrive from time to time. As a boy, he didn't know who these outsiders were or where they came from, but he knew they were in the way. They were at his home. Even during his childhood, they were there...

"Elizabet, they're back," Steven had hissed at the girl beside him. "Do *you* know who they might be?"

"Sorry, no, never seen them before," the girl had whispered back. "My dad would want me to go home as he says they're dangerous."

"If we stay in the shadow unseen, we can slip by them and get to your home easily," Steven had said softly as he glanced over the undergrowth.

"Oh okay," she'd whispered. "How do we get past them? I don't want to go outside—"

By 'outside' she had meant 'outside Utopus'... they could go through the outskirts of Utopus, which was what the adults had designated as Zone Zero. Steven glanced in all directions, then he said plainly, "We can go there, which is close to a place I found. It's still dangerous but easier..."

Elizabet just nodded.

They walked single file through the taller undergrowth until reaching the path from which they'd arrived a few minutes earlier. Steven stopped the girl from walking on by lifting an arm in front of her. "Wait here, and I'll check the road," he said then stared around for a moment. "There's a patrol that passes here every hour," he whispered further. "It's soon time for them to pass..."

"Where did *you* discover this information?"

"Father told me to be mindful of what goes on around here," Steven answered as he glanced past a nearby tree trunk, which was luckily masking their presence from whoever might be out. "We need to be careful with how we do stuff but we can still search for answers. Haven't you ever wondered about how conveniently safe we are when they're here…"

"I've often watched them from my balcony with father's binoculars," Elizabet whispered, glancing each way, wanting to help him with checking for people in the road. "They—are strange. Always just staying near the open space in the middle of the city…"

"So you've seen them too, then?"

She just nodded as an answer.

Minutes later, they were watching two men as they walked past them without noticing they weren't actually alone in the desolate street. Each person was dressed in dark clothing of unknown origin - the two youngsters shook at one another silently to confirm that neither had recognised the clothing. Both youngsters then also noted that the individuals had their faces covered over with a head covering like neither of them had seen before. "I can see their face under the cloth," Elizabet whispered. "Why are they dressed like that?"

"I don't know," Steven whispered back. "We need to wait until they're gone. Once we cannot hear their footsteps anymore, it will be safe again. It takes about thirty minutes before we can go on…"

"My father will worry if I get home late," Elizabet said. "We need to go sooner. We shouldn't have been exploring like we did. It's too dangerous for that…"

"I'm aware of it," Steven said, "and my father has said as much. However, we've discovered more evidence that also matters because of it."

"You mean *you* did," Elizabet said. "I was only here with you because you're a friend and I don't think *any* of us should be walking around alone."

"Yet, we always do it anyway," Steven said matter of fact.

"I guess so…"

They were walking home silently almost two hours later, when dusk was settling over the sprawling city. They aimed their trek towards the pinpoints lighting up the housing towards the southwest where our two tall buildings were located. Among the buildings was the building that Elizabet would need to reach before it was too late in the evening, and opposite hers was the building that Steven would go to once the girl beside him was safely home with her father. In their part of the city, the lighting was absent in the crumbling streets and that always had bothered Steven, even more so when they got home this late…

"I'll be okay the rest of the way," Elizabet whispered.

"Are you certain?" Steven asked.

"Yes, I'm quite certain," she answered. "There are people walking around on the second floor. They're likely checking for vagrants right now. They've always been thorough. If they discover me, they'll escort me home…"

"I'll be waiting on my balcony," Steven said. "Go to yours now and I'll hurry to mine. If I don't see you on the balcony soon, I'm coming to your building…"

"Okay, even if it's not needed," Elizabet said, grinning mischievously for a moment.

Steven had watched after the girl as she'd rushed away. She was out of sight for a few minutes, then he saw her rushing up the left stairs of her building. After waving at her when she saw him standing on the dirt path, he turned and ran to the other building opposite. He rushed up, and was panting against the wall of the balcony only a few minutes later. He let himself slide down on the cold floor and had stared at the empty balcony on the other building where he'd seen the girl for the first time just a few months earlier. They'd sat staring at one another for the longest time before they had ever spoken or met up for what counted as play time in Utopus, which mostly meant rummaging through the ruins for interesting items to find from a distant past… Later they had gone for their first walk further away from their immediate community, somewhat outside the central areas that was where most people would generally gather, and they'd found a deep friendship blossoming between them soon after.

"Common, Eli, where are you?" Steven mumbled. It wasn't that often he'd refer to her by a shorter version of her name, mostly when he was worried about her. He jerked upright when there was a loud bang that echoed from across him. A moment later, Elizabet stood at the wall on her balcony and he could see her heaving from breathing in the dim moonlight that was bathing her balcony. "Are you okay?" he called out, knowing that she'd hear him as his voice would echo against the buildings.

"Yes, but I'll tell you tomorrow, okay?" Elizabet called back. Or I can try to come to the balcony if you're there later…"

Steven nodded plainly…

2.

STEVEN FROWNED WITH CONFUSION WHEN she turned abruptly and walked back inside her small dwelling so fast. Normally, they'd talk until it was late in the evening. He sat there, studying her building for a long time, and was dismayed when almost all the lights would go out in the next hour, when normally most people in both buildings would sit on their balconies. He glanced at his own building and saw it was also almost completely darkened.

He got up and glanced down at the dirt path in case there was something there of interest, then he frowned when a group of men were departing Elizabet's building unexpectedly. Then to add to his shock, Steven startled when a hand from behind him pulled him away from the edge, towards the darkest part of the small balcony, then after another moment he'd been dragged inside their dwelling in a matter of seconds, so much so that Steven felt unsteady on his feet and fell back onto the sofa with a loud thud.

"You're home! Good," his father hissed into Steven's ear rather coldly. "WE need to mind our step…"

"They cannot spot you here…"

Steven stared confused at his father, then he asked, "Who are they, father? Why can't they—"

"I warned you enough times about being cautious about how people are behaving around here," his father grunted as the only answer Steven knew he'd get.

"But I was careful," Steven protested. "I was careful all day…"

"Then why were you looking at them on the balcony?" his father said, "and if they'd seen you they might be flooding this building right now…"

"I was curious about why all the lights are out over there," Steven replied, "and Eli told me she's okay but didn't want to talk and that's unusual."

"Best that you don't mention any of this when your mother is home," his father hissed. "You know how she is—since—"

Without saying another word, his father had pulled Steven back into their small dwelling. The boy had landed hard on the sofa in the living room, and while fighting back tears had glared at his father. Father and son had a closeness that was uncommon in the harshness that was Utopus. Steven had always loved his father, and they generally had a good relationship.

Two men marching through their district would shatter this illusion until the boy was almost two decades older. The clatters of boots had faded in the distance a few minutes later, replaced by an oppressive silence for several minutes, but a few minutes later the distant sounds restarted. Steven noticed that at hearing each sound his father had flinched…

* * *

A half hour went by with them not speaking and just sitting on either side of the small room. Each male glanced towards the back of this room that had to pass as a living room and kitchen when the outer door of their dwelling opened then and this door opening cut off anything else that either male might have wanted to say…

Steven saw a frown on his father's face, when he glanced, and noticed from this that the frown was a waning for the boy. He was being told to comply with his father's previous warning. Then his father's gaze shifted, and following this gaze, Steven found himself staring at the door at the back of the room, that was hidden by the slight darkness there, made more acute by the light in the room diminishing from the meagre six candles to just two.

Steven glances around when the room darkened and caught the motion of his father straightening up. It wasn't by accident the minimal amount of light in the room had partially vanished. Steven eyed the window, and Utopus was somehow more visible than it had been with all candles lit up.

Steven was distracted from checking what might be the reasons for the sounds that were sounding out in the distance when a woman walked then into the room, and she was evidently out of breath. She was staring with obvious relief at the two males after showing a momentary frown…

Steven felt relief when he realised that none other than his mother had got home. "What has happened?" she whispered at his father, ignoring her son for now. "He needs to know what's going on," she said, nodding once at the boy.

"He's too young for the knowledge," his father said. "My father never wanted either of us to know the truth until we were old enough to know…"

Steven glanced at each parent, confused over how cold they sound. Their usual hugging didn't happen today. They almost sounded angry at one another. The only time that his father had spoken to him today was to tell him off for being outside. And then he'd been angry at him for an unknown reason. Still seemed angry at him right now.

"What's the matter, father?" Steven whispered. "Mama, why do sound so sad…?"

No answers except for his parents changing the topic, even doing something to distract him from their current situation.

"We're eating soup," his father said. "We'll figure out what to do later when we have more news."

Steven gaped after his father as neither behaved in a way he recognised. Both parents seemed scared. Nervous. Tired. Then he noticed his mother's eyes were bright red like she'd been crying. She was biting her lip, constantly glancing at the window, especially when the distant thudding sounds rung out. His father frowned at each such sound.

"We need to stay inside until we hear whether it's safe," his father said softly, "and that means no going out until a few days have passed, okay, son?"

Steven jerked when suddenly it seemed that his father was addressing him instead of his mother. He had plainly nodded…

"I can slip past them to find out if Eli and her father are okay," his mother whispered, "and I know it's unsafe right now, but I owe him this bit of help for what he did for me all those years ago, okay."

Steven stared confused at his mother. This was the first time ever she'd indicated to *know* either Elizabet or her father when he'd only been friends with the girl for the past three months. Elizabet has said they'd lived there for four months. How could his mother know them from years ago?

This wouldn't be a question Steven would ever find any question for. At least certainly *not* until the boy was a man and close to the end of his long life…

Steven's father had glanced at the boy beside him when the boy's mother had walked into the dwelling, and who'd nodded at him to show that, in fact, he understood the full meaning of his father's warning. The events of that evening would keep haunting Steven for the rest of his life, though he didn't know it, yet, in what way. These events would gnaw at his mind and they would urge him onto a path that might lead to a resolution later on, at a moment when he could sit down only slowly from advancing age, and a path of danger that he hadn't known about until that day…

That night we sat silently as a small family, or what might marginally resemble such a thing in a broken world, around a small table, all of us eating from a nondescript warm soup, and all of us were listening to the distant sounds coming from another part of the city. Both his parents frowned from time to time. Normally, their evening meal would be filled with us chatting until Steven would go sit on the balcony for talks with Elizabet.

The sounds disturbed Steven. Each one sounded louder than the previous one. They sounded like no other sound he'd ever heard in the few years he'd been in the world, and at seven years he was not understanding any of it. Each time he would begin to attempt to ask either parent what was going on, he'd see his father with a finger over his lips, while at the same time his mother stared towards the window…

Steven also glances that direction.

The windows, which were just a thick sheet of plastic rather than anything more solid and resistant against the cold seeping into their dwelling, would move at each moment that the sounds came. Steven tried to stare through the material and only barely saw the faint orange light flickering where he knew was another dwelling. Another child, a girl, sitting there with just her father, eating soup or something else. Likely feeling as worried as him about the sounds.

I hope Eli is okay, Steven thought as he stared back at his plate to hide the frown that had appeared on his face while he was glancing outside. He'd jerked somewhat when another sound rung out, which was more a booming sound than the more rhythmic sounds that had been happening ever since his father had dragged him inside.

Steven felt hand on his shoulder, and glancing up saw his father staring at him. A quick dart with only his eyes and the boy realised his mother wasn't in her seat anymore.

"She's gone to check on them," Steven's father said gently. "She saw how you stared that way."

A quick nod towards the window.

"Oh, right," Steven said sheepishly. Again another quick glance outside, and now it seemed that the lights in Elizabet's house were extinguished. *Is she sleeping already?* Steven thought and feeling a bit angry but to be honest to himself he had no reason to be angry. She had promised she'd tell him 'tomorrow' —*whatever it was going to be she needed to tell him.* What had started with an exciting trek of exploration with him puffing up and showing a shy girl how much he knew of the 'old places' had fast spiraled into a whirlwind of strange sounds, frightened parents, his friend acting out of character, and him with being confused, scared and annoyed.

Steven jerked upright when the outer door is shut with a loud bang. He stared up. To see Elizabet, her father and mother all standing at the door. Steven and Elizabet stare at one another, both confused.
"I needed them to stay here for this night just in case," his mother hissed. "Half their building has been emptied. It may not be safe for him here anymore…"
Elizabet stared up at Steven's mother as confused as Steven.
"What's going on, Papa?" Elizabet's whispered.
"I cannot tell you, child," he answered her, and was refusing to answer as Steven's parents had done with him. After that night, Steven would never see him ever again, and Elizabet went to live with her grandmother. No one ever spoke about her father again…

Except for Elizabet and him when they were far away from anyone else…

A possible story for why her father had gone away came later, but never with any explanation or confirmation.

When it was morning and Steven woke up, Elizabet and her father were gone, and when Steven walked in the living room his parents sat side by side on the sofa, each staring another direction, neither talking. When his father noticed that Steven standing in the room he just nodded towards the outer door, and recognising the gesture the boy rushed away…

*** * ***

The following few evenings, Steven had gone out alone, and stood outside so as soon as he'd eaten the little soup we had available as a meal, though eating as a morning meal felt weird to the boy. Steven walked to behind a heavy drape supposedly would pass for a wall, and he dropped onto the pile of old rugs that were supposedly a bed for me. He lay there, staring up at the ceiling. A day of adventure and exploring had turned into a dangerous day of them, Steven and Elizabet, constantly hiding behind the undergrowth quite often, and then rushing from one ruined building to the other to get home safely…

"This is the last time I'm going anywhere with you," Elizabet had hissed angrily at him.

However, they'd been located many hours from home when the last dangerous men had passed them by, so the pair had to trek back through a sprawling city stretching over a longer distance that, in the past, would have taken someone to travel only in a matter of a few hours rather than most of the day and that was there and back.

"Those people don't belong here," Steven said. "They're making it dangerous for us all—for everyone here and maybe even other places I'm guessing…"

"Hmm, if you say so," she'd grunted.

Steven knew there was something about 'those people' that he'd now seen eight times, with Elizabet seeing them three times. He didn't know how these people fitted in yet, but they were who or what his father had warned him about. He realised he was growing up because of this knowledge, and maybe faster than he should. He was discovering a dangerous adult world…

Maybe too soon, Steven thought, *but I guess I can adapt… but what about Elizabet? She's too young still…*

Steven lay awake on his makeshift bed for many hours, thinking about everything he'd seen already during his brief life. After about three hours, he rose from the bed and tiptoed to the living room. There he stopped for a moment to listen. He smiled for a short moment then glanced at the door to the balcony. He could hear his parents in the tiny adjoining room where his father lay snoring rather loudly. He slipped onto the balcony and sat down beside the back wall which was his usual spot there, and he stared across the fissure between the buildings towards the other empty balcony and he wondered what his friend was going to tell him later in the day…

* * *

In her own dwelling, opposite of Steven's dwelling, Elizabet had been sitting beside her window, awake and thoughtfully staring at the sky until the first pinks and oranges in the sky drove her to her bed. However, she'd dived down quickly when she'd glimpsed a familiar figure on the balcony of the other building…

She lay down. She had decisions to make. About how to behave and act around her friend. About the future. About how to handle the boy's enthusiasm, seemingly, for danger which felt wrong at times to her but who had shown her a different sort of world than she'd imagined. Elizabet had always regarded the world around her as odd, maybe also messy and certainly quite unfriendly, especially after what had happened yesterday and last night. Until now, she'd never assumed the world was dangerous.

Her father regarded them, her friend and his parents, as odd, she thought as she had glanced up at the window, fighting the temptation to glance out one more time. However, despite her father's misgivings he'd allowed her to be friends with the boy on the other balcony. Sometimes she could almost imagine him as some sort of investigator like in the book under her bed. Sometimes he was just a boy with an over-imaginative mind. *But not today. He wanted me to discover the wrong things about this place and then we had spotted those men in their dark clothing. I saw more of them in this building as I was coming up the stairs, and they were all behaving like they were searching for something… or someone…*

"Come, eat some breakfast."

Elizabet glanced up surprised, and she wondered *why* breakfast was so early…

3.

TEN YEARS AGO

ELIZABET WASN'T certain if she should go to Steven's building after she'd glimpsed the men with dark clothing inside her building. She wasn't certain of who these men were, but she'd heard the whispers about them. Those whispers combined with the obsession from the boy across in the other building had made her more cautious than most girls of her age would be in such similar situations.

But her friendship with the boy she'd waved shyly who had been sitting across of her on the other balcony had changed her. The boy showed her that bravery and courage didn't need to come from otherworldly deeds or from massive conquest.

She wasn't certain how she was influencing the boy, but she hoped they'd be friends for life. She saw him also like an older brother really. She only had her father. Having travelled with him from one district to the next, with them always trying to find a place to fit in. She her place when the boy showed an acceptance of her. Showed that love, friendship and loyalty are the core of everything that was humankind…

Even when she was angry, Elizabet couldn't stay angry *that* long with her friend…

"Elizabet, your grandmother is waiting for you," a gentle voice called out. The girl recognised her grandmother's neighbour who had obviously been sent to find the girl, and knew she'd usually find her in her old home, where would lie on her old bed, pining for a father who was gone from her life…

The neighbour had been told her father had died, and her grandmother had sternly demanded that the girl would repeat this explanation to everyone.

"No one can *know* where he has gone," was the repeated warning.

The girl glanced up on hearing the voice. It was the first time since she'd gone to live with her grandmother she felt like her world felt like it could be alright. She was still missing her Papa. She didn't know where he'd gone. Even after pressing her grandmother for more information after the boy had gone back home had resulted in only head shakes. Even though her grandmother shared so much knowledge and secrets about Utopus with her granddaughter, she could never tell about the girl's father, her only son.

Elizabet walked up the stairs and rushed through a long corridor before skidding to a halt in front of a blue-painted door, which was the result of Steven wanting to prove to his friend's 'new parent' that he was reliable and trustworthy. And so her grandmother had accepted him, and a renewed round of her going for lengthy treks began...

Elizabet opened the door, and she heard people talking softly, then stop speaking as she closed the outer door. Walking into the kitchen, she finds her grandmother, Steven and Steven's father sitting there. Steven was crying, his cheeks were covered with streaks where it seems that dirt and tears had mixed, his eyes were bright red and looked like someone had inserted a little bubble of water in each of them. Elizabet looked around, expecting his mother to be somewhere in the room but the four of them are the only people in the two-room dwelling.

Elizabet wanted to speak when she noticed that her grandmother had motioned for her not to speak. "Eli, why don't you take Steven with you to your normal play area," her grandmother says softly, "and you'll be able to talk. He'll need it..."

Immediately, Steven's father lifts the boy beside onto his feet roughly, then pushes him towards the girl. Steven jerked to a halt at an arm's length from Elizabet. Both youngsters go bright red when her grandmother's soft chuckle echoed through the kitchen...

Elizabet grabbed hold of Steven's hand and pulled him with her to the outer door. Within minutes they were both gone, and after another five minutes they were at her old home, sitting side by side in the corner of her balcony, in the shade so no one would notice them there from the opposite building.

"I'm sorry for ignoring you for the past few years," Elizabet said. "I've missed our adventures…"

"Me too," Steven said with a small voice, followed by a suppressed hiccup.

"Maybe we need to find out who they are really," she whispered, leaning in then placing her head gently on his shoulder, which was an action she'd repeat often until their last visit would happen.

"Isn't that too dangerous?" he whispered back, but there was a hint of a smirk on his face. "You said it was too dangerous and you weren't going anywhere with me anymore, Eli…"

Elizabet glanced at him and rolled her eyes, then she shrugged. "I don't know," she said, "but you told me they don't belong here, so if that's the case we need to know why, and if it's possible we need to do something about it. Us and all our friends really…"

* * *

Five Years Before Selection

The conversation of five years earlier that had caused the long treks to resume had a purpose now for the boy as he stood waiting in a ditch, waiting for Elizabet to return from her 'mission' of getting something that would help them with their endeavour of finding information about the black structure on the opposite side of the stream. For the past sixteen days it had stood there unmoving, rather than being that mysterious structure that would appear and disappear…

"Did you find it?" Steven asked when Elizabet dropped down in the ditch beside him.

"I found much more," she answered. "Also, Perri helped me with part of it. He was there and wanted to know what I was doing in the Academic Institute and we actually argued a bit because he claimed that I had told him I wanted to join the University. So, I told him about your plan… I hope that was okay… But anyway, he wants to help too, and he knows a few others who would do the same…"

"Ah right," Steven said, smiling weakly for a few moments. "We'll all have a year then to convince the 'adults' that we want to do this, however, my idea is a round about way really. You know scientists join the

University, so we'll become scientists… all of us… then I'll convince my father I'll help him with his work, and make it so so obvious that they cannot do their work without me, or us, they let us work in the Academic Institute despite us being scientists…"

"What's the goal for this?"

"I want to find my mother," Steven answered, "and if I can also find your father too…"

Elizabet had glanced down at the mention of her father. It had been a decade since he had vanished without a trace. She'd lived with her grandmother until she had died from advancing age, and now for the past four years Elizabet had been living alone in her old dwelling once more, and had resumed the game of sitting on the balcony opposite of his one for lengthy discussions. Always shaking her head whenever Steven offered the idea of living with him and his father instead…

"I miss Papa," Elizabet whispered. "I wonder so often what has happened to him."

"To be honest, I wonder about it too," Steven said flatly, "and what had happened also to my Mama. I've wondered for ten years now what she had meant—errr…there was something that had happened near here, well, close enough to here, after you went to your grandmother's home. Remember the massive explosion near the river…?"

"I don't really," Elizabet said softly. "Hmm, maybe I was too young to really remember any of it. I can hardly remember Papa let alone other things of that long ago…"

"I was seven when we stood on the balcony. All three of us stood there and father and mother never would visit it before or after the explosion happened, and it means you were maybe *too* young to really remember it," Steven said. "If I was seven you were almost five at the time, and yes, you might *not* remember it well. However, it all had happened only literally a few hours after you left to go to your grandmother's home. I'm certain I specifically heard my parents say something weird. Papa and Mama were playing a game with me, then I heard the loud sounds and my parents rushed to the balcony, and Papa never goes there… I'm certain I heard them say that 'something' had started, but then the three of us went back inside because of the fires— but I cannot remember anything else, and I'm also not certain I remember it correctly…"

"Maybe what I've found might help you remember more about the event, or more precisely it's what Perri got for me when he got a chance to look around—there," Elizabet whispered. "He could go inside because he had already selected… and it's funny, but he chose to be a Scientist already. He's going to try to find more interesting information… I guess *he* wants to be nice too."

"Good, the more people who are able to *help* us with everything we're working on, the better it will be for the plan we've been working on so far," Steven said somewhat flatly while he also looked away for a moment to hide that he felt flustered at the idea that Elizabet was getting on well with another man but he speaks on before she might notice his behaviour, "but now what I'll need to *do* is to get them to choose me as the next Subject during the selection in five years time. For that part of the plan to be successful I need to get out of Utopus, and I need to find out more what goes on in Zone Zero… Are *you* certain that you won't come with me to the place I've found there recently…?"

"Errr… nope," Elizabet said softly, pulling up her nose for a moment, "and I'm okay with this stuff we're doing *here* but I feel rather icky at the idea of rummaging around a polluted place. I think you shouldn't go…"

"I should be going there, even if I'm going there alone," Steven said. "I'm certain I *may* find answers there that could help us with our current mystery…"

"Hmm, okay, it's your loss if some sort of monster lives in Zone Zero," Elizabet said, "like someone in District 5-C had told me years ago—"

"That was where you lived before coming to this district, right? Before we 'met' on our opposite balconies," Steven asked. "Eli, you *do* realise you were like three years old when that person had told you that stuff. They might have been teasing you, or trying to cause you trouble…"

"Hmm, I hadn't thought of it in that way. Never thought up to now they were trying to scare me or tease me or whatever was their intention," Elizabet said, sounding a little angry. She sighed for a moment, then was frowning for a moment. She glanced around and then she turned around to allow herself to sit down on the nearby stone slab, facing away from the vista of the black structure and the other buildings flanking it that were known to them as the University and the Academic Institute. She glanced at Steven before she said, "Anyway, do you want to see what Perri found…?"

"Sure," Steven said abruptly. He shrugged somewhat. He was feeling jealous of his friend now for entirely other reasons. Perri had already selected a career as a scientist. He already knew some of what was really going on. He could find the answers that Steven was only guessing at, even if he'd been able to go to both buildings secretly with his father a few times, but this had only ever resulted in closed doors, and mostly waiting in the long corridors…

Steven sighed and realised that five years was a long time to wait, then he glances glumly at Elizabet again then over his shoulder towards the nearby buildings and doing this mostly to check if a certain building is located behind him, and he shrugs, then after a lengthy pause he grunted, "Show me what you got…"

∗ ∗ ∗

Two Years Before Selection

The fathers of the past, at least according to something that Steven's grandfather had always said, would commonly come home with a gift for any children whose parent they might be. This old world of plenty had disappeared a long time ago. So his grandfather often told his son, Steven's father, that the only gift 'they' couldn't take away from anyone was the gift of wisdom.

The day for his father to put into practice what his father had done came in two parts. The first part happened to him soon after he'd been a child and had encountered the men marching alongside with Elizabet by his side. Those men had looked so out of place it had caused them both to feel scared. Even Steven who'd been an explorer of the region pretty much since he could walk had not ventured out much afterwards.

His grandfather, as Steven would so often recall in later years, had been the gift of wisdom, as he'd stated at the end of his story, and this was a tradition that his own father, Dr Burgard, would soon enough continue with his own son…

4.

STEVEN HAD FELT SURPRISED WHEN the thick drape dividing the sparse living room and his even sparser bedroom was pushed aside and his father stood towering beside him.

"We need to talk," his father had said plainly, and then he'd just dropped the drape without checking if Steven was complying with his request. —*Or was that a demand?* Steven thought. He wasn't going to question whatever his father wanted from him. Not now at least. Not when the plan of being the next Subject had gone to plan so far…

"What's up?" Steven grunted as he dropped onto the sofa beside his father.

"Please, listen to what I'm going to tell you," Steven's father said. "It—it will be important later…" Steven glanced sidelong at his father, who sat slumped in the seating beside him, looking lost in thought and seemingly searching for his next words to say. Steven saw him attempting to speak several times. When he finally spoke the comment surprised Steven…

"There was a time when a father could promise a son so much more than what this world offers now," his father said. "There is one thing you need to promise me and don't ever ask me what I mean with these words. There is… there's someone you need to find, and I cannot tell you how, why or where. Do you understand what I'm saying?"

Steven stared ahead for a moment then he nodded, feeling both confused and angry that there was such an obvious mystery being pushed on him. He wondered if his father had found out about his plans but as no letters had arrived nor had his father burst into the house venting his anger at a son over things done neither was the case. He wondered then when such a letter would arrive but he couldn't ask…

"There are lessons to learned from how our society appears, and before you choose your career path… the little amount that exists in reality of such a thing… you need to learn certain things," his father said. "There are these two books I've kept safe just my father did before me, and at least five generations before him. There was a time before when books were plentiful, but five hundred has lost us much…"

"What do you mean..?" Steven asked, now feeling even more confused, glancing quickly at his father. He looked at the floor when he noticed that his father was staring ahead with a chiseled stare, lacking any emotion in his face. As far as the boy could see in the few seconds that he looked towards his father.

"I know you explore, and perhaps even outside Utopus," his father said plainly, "but why you do it or what you're looking for… well, I guess that's your business. I've given up many years ago on deciding for you what you do with your life. Not since…" His father sighed deeply but before Steven could say something the monotone talk continued. "— These are two books you'll want to read before you choose your career. Read them, and I'll be back in an few hours…" His father pushed two books into Steven's hands. "—when I'm back I'll discuss a few specific things that my father wanted me to learn and that I want you learn right now. Also, we'll discuss a few other things…"

Dr Burgard had got up from the sofa and was gone from the dwelling before Steven could say or ask anything. Steven stared at the outer door for several minutes, waiting for his father to walk inside. But the familiar footsteps had faded away quickly, followed by silence everywhere…

* * *

Steven glanced at the two books lying on his lap that his father had so hastily dropped there. He'd always had an interest in finding books whenever he was exploring the old ruins of the city that had existed before Utopus had been built. Books showed pictures of the old world, and the text described things he could only imagine what they might look like.

He lifted the top book finding then that it was only part of a book, or more precisely a third of a book. The cover was too damaged to find out what the name of the book might have been, or who had written it. He opened it to the first page where usually he might find the title repeated, but it was missing.

Hmm, someone tore the page out, Steven thought, *why and who…? Maybe the person who decided to tell each next generation about this book did it and that means it was missing when father and grandfather had it in their possession. I can only guess…*

Steven ran a hand over the first sheet of paper which felt fragile to the touch. It felt rather old and dry, like the paper had been kept dry purposefully. *Someone did this on purpose*, Steven thought. *Perhaps grandfather, or his father, or others before him…*

"Father had mentioned *them* before he left," Steven mumbled. "I'm wondering if knowing this specific information is in any way important for me to know…"

Steven glanced up and stared towards the outer door to listen if his father had returned at all. But it was all silent everywhere.

Even outside, Steven thought glumly, *and maybe even too silent.*

"Those who cannot remember the past are condemned to repeat it…" Steven mumbled, staring at the first page and the words someone had underlined, and it also seemed that this person or someone else had intentionally traced over each letter. He ran a finger over the paper, and it was clear that a pen had been used for tracing. Pens were almost impossible to find in recent decades according to Steven's father…

Steven studied the words written there. *Written and not words that were in this book originally*, Steven thought. *Who wrote this in this book…? Not the person who wrote it here, but it seems that person had copied it from somewhere else…*

Steven turned the pages in the book, or at least the part of the book that was still intact, to check what else the text in the book may contain. The text spoke about events, people and ideas that were foreign to Steven, or the parts he could read. Where something important was being said it had been traced as before. A name was underlined in a page that was virtually blank of any text.

"Who is this Martin anyway…?" Steven mumbled. "Why is *this* name important?"

On a later page, another word was underlined. *Freedom.* Then on another page the words underlined were, *remember the past,* and below at the bottom of the same page, the future belongs to our children. Steven frowned and contemplated over the things he had been reading. The words seemed to convey a message that someone had wanted to remember, tell others, teach someone, make certain they were read inside a book of mostly faded text. There was other pieces of text he'd been reading, somewhat, but these words had been accentuated to stand out. It seemed to him that this might have been the intent of his father, for his son to work out find out what was going on. From knowledge he needed to learn for himself… it seemed.

Steven picked up the second book, consisting of the top half of the original book with the cover missing entirely. Steven grunted from annoyance. There was no name or title for this book, however more of the text was visible. As he reads, Steven pales. The text wasn't a descriptive text has the other book had been, but clearly a story someone was telling about a future that took place hundreds of years from when the story had been written.

In the story, or the parts Steven was able to glean, something had happened to cause people not to like books. *They're burning all the books they can find*, Steven thought, *and I wonder if this stuff isn't so different from how we live now where books seem to be a rare thing. Something about why this book, even if only half of it exists is supposed to demonstrate that nothing is as it seems. But I already knew that. It's why I want to be a scientist, and attempt to get chosen as a Subject… Why are books banned whichever version of the history was happening? Whether it was this one or the real one that I can see from the window. That means I need to search for a place where someone secretly stored books that might still be intact and read them all…*

Steven glanced from the window, towards the north, where a decade ago, at the young age of seven, Steven had stood with his parents with them staring over the remains of the river at something that had been happening there. He had felt his mother's hand tremble in his own. He had heard his father's voice break under the pain of being unable to shield a son and wife from the sight. Whatever they'd been seeing that day had been the catalyst for change. His father began explaining more about the world, his mother than had vanished from the son's world, the constant words of warning about the dangers had persisted to this day, the mystery of the contrast between blatant lie of being told everything was fine and the reality had deepened…

* * *

A Month Before Selection

Steven walked from the University, finally, with a self-satisfied grin on his face. He glanced around to check for anyone in his vicinity but the large clearing in front of the building was devoid of people, more so than usual. Not even any of his friends were anywhere to be seen. She shrugged, then began his trek home which was a familiar route past the stream that once, long ago, might have been a deep river which would have divided the northern and southern parts of the old city Stockholm. He'd recently found a sign that had been disregarded by someone. Turning it over he noted that there was a name faintly visible under the thick layer of rust. The name turned out to be Stockholm…

He took his time to get home knowing his father was currently inside the Academic Institute, and in a heated discussion with other Academists. He knew because his father gone there particularly early… for something. So he took the opportunity as given for him to go to the University to apply there.

"So I guess I'll know in the next few weeks if I've been selected," Steven muttered as he glanced over his shoulder towards the building he'd visited, "and I hope father won't discover this too early and stops it."

However, fifteen years of planning and searching for answers was so close to getting fulfilled. Now there was just a final visit to the place just south of Utopus to make before he was hopefully leaving as the Subject. He needed to go to make a plan of how to get inside it as up to now he hadn't been able do this. He just wished he was able to convince Elizabet to come with him, but she'd fervently refused to go…

"You can go," she had said somewhat angrily. "I'll go work in the University in the meantime…"

Steven had barely reached the path outside the building where he had been sharing a dwelling with his father; his mother had departed from there a decade earlier, and now Steven realised that in a month his father would have to endure a second round of pain of the loss of someone he loved. This time it could be a son he'd lose…

He felt a shiver go down his spine as he glanced up at the two buildings in turn. He recalled acutely when he had stood watching a few men marching away. *They had looked so very much out of place that night,* Steven thought, *and I'm still no closer to finding out who they were…*

He stopped, and felt like someone was out to go after him. Like a dozen of those men in their dark clothes would suddenly rush at him and drag him off to somewhere. Perhaps to the third structure that he'd seen as he entered the University, and was gone when he'd walked out…

Steven rushed home and only a few minutes later stood leaning against the outer door, panting loudly.

"Best to lay low for the next month, or at least until the decision is made," Steven mumbled.

* * *

After reading the letters that Steven had discovered months ago inside his father's desk, and while his father hadn't been home, Steven had a few hard decisions to make about what he'd need to do with the knowledge that he now possessed about Utopus and other things. However, he was clueless just then that it would be only a couple of years before he'd be forced to confront the knowledge up front. That knowing this, and what was coming, would alter his entire adult life…

The moment of the opportunity to get things into action had come that evening…

Steven had been sitting in his usual place on the balcony. When he'd finally had found the courage to venture out to his favourite place on the balcony. He'd stared for a moment across to the next door building but he knew Elizabet wouldn't be in her home. He sat down, and stared blankly. He had nothing else to do than to wait now for the inevitable, whether it came as a decision that would have him walking south or that he'd be a scientist for possibly the remainder of his life…

He sensed this was a moment where he might have some solace instead of the worry he'd had up to this day or that might face afterwards. This moment of calm was what he needed to quell the nervousness that was overwhelming him right now.

"Another month and then I'll go south," Stephen mumbled. "Then a journey begins to find out who had built Utopus, why they had done it, and what the others and me can do to create a better future for all of us…" He glanced in a southerly direction, then he sighed for a moment. "—I will find you, Mama, and bring you back home with me…"

Steven thought about the letters more. They'd given him the proof the entire world was in danger. After reading them, he'd replaced them precisely where he found them. Got up. Walked onto the balcony. Sat down…

"Two final things," Steven mumbles. "A goodbye to my father and Elizabet, and help him for the remainder of the time I got here…"

Suddenly, Steven felt certain he was travelling south soon. South, towards another existence…

33

PART TWO

Present Day

Subject 37

5.

So this farewell, departing so abruptly from Utopus, came in rather unexpected ways and with a whimper. Or, that was how Steven had wanted to remember it afterwards…

No one was there to say goodbye, like when his mother had departed a decade earlier. Yes, perhaps, his father was there, but only at a distance.

* * *

Although, going by the information in the remnants of books that they'd found together, the people of an earlier part of history had always thought the destruction of their world, would come as *'nuclear bombs'* - whatever they were. If there had been a *'third version'* of such a war, it made him wonder what these first and second wars had even been like. *Were those ones as destructive as the third war had been, as we still lived with the consequences from it in our society?*

His father had pointed at a sinister metal covering, some eighty kilometres outside Utopus, which he'd showed him on an early spring morning last year. Then, his father had found an object in an abandoned building quite recently, which would let us look at the distant parts of the area outside Utopus with no need to step outside Utopus. As a boy, Steven was always uncertain what this object was called but later understood it was a binocular.

When Steven had suggested checking out the metal covering up close by travelling to it, his father had reacted just like everyone else did in the city whenever such a suggestion was made.

His father had refused to go the ancient building that was located so tantalisingly close to Utopus. But the boy *did* go there…

The boy had left secretly in the darkest part of night, when no person in Utopus might have seen him do this stuff. Then he'd returned before the bleak northern sun rose in the east…

* * *

The first time there, Steven had stared at the structure for well over an hour before he'd dared to figure out a way to get inside it.

The undamaged covering had pointed at an event that had been so sudden that the people in control of the coverings hadn't have had the time to activate whatever the large metallic devices inside the stone enclosure might be. They'd appeared to Steven like devices with the capability to cause even more damage than how the world got destroyed, if they ever were opened, but he doubted that there was any person anywhere who understood their workings. And what he found out during the nightly treks were things he wasn't ever going to share even with his father.

Rumours had circulated frequently that the war of 370 years ago got started by other methods though. More nefarious methods. Methods that tricked the world into believing it was safe…

The names of the people who'd caused the devastation, which still affected the world Steven was growing up in, were long forgotten by everyone. Whatever they'd fought for—or fought against was long gone and irrelevant now.

An uncovered document, one of the few still in existence, and found about twenty years before Steven was born, was still interesting enough even for a boy like him every time he'd secretly look at it. He'd studied the document for a last time about an hour before they had come to tell him that they'd selected him as a Subject…

His father had said that the contents of this paperwork was the proof that the war of 370 years ago was waged with chemicals, and the people of five hundred years ago had called these processes of technology either 'bioengineering' or *'genetic engineering.'* Something drastic had happened that had caused everything to go wrong. No one living in my own era really had any abilities to perceive the true nature of what these technologies might have been.

Most scientists simply didn't understand these technologies as all the information about them had got destroyed, or was simply lost. Even if they, of all people here, would again understand what they were it may not help us.

Steven was certain from reading the information in the papers, as he understood their content, that the skills of the scientists in Utopus didn't resemble any of the skills of scientists living five centuries ago, and the knowledge we were perceiving as *'science'* was just a small portion of what they may have known before the war.

This was the reality we had to deal with every day. This reality was everywhere; inside Utopus, outside its invisible boundaries, and was felt by us every day. That didn't even include the environmental conditions, such as the daily dust clouds on the horizons that would hide anything that could yield answers for why we had a broken world. And that was what the other thirty-six Subjects were sent to investigate. As none of them ever returned did it mean they'd failed?

***

Steven glanced south for the dust clouds he'd seen in the morning after he'd been sitting as he'd done so regularly for the past fifteen years or longer, and which he'd done with more frequency to keep an eye on Elizabet's balcony for her safety, and with them discussing this way the possible ideas of why things were the way they were, and what they and their friends could do about everything going on…

"We have only few choices," Elizabet would tell him as she'd stare at him with sorrowful eyes.
"I know, but I need to try," he'd always replied.
So now Steven decided that he needed to travel south where currently the passage further into Zone Zero was blocked by the storm. He stared at it with the binoculars, or distance-looker he'd also had called it affectionately since childhood; and even though he knew its proper name now as an adult. Now he was glad that his father had found the device.
As Steven had busied with packing a rucksack with the minimal number of items needed that he could bring with him on his journey, he'd placed the device on the pile of items he was discarding as not-so-important for his journey. His father, who'd had sat watching him pack from across the room, had risen to his feet and picked it up. "This is yours now," he stated plainly to Steven. "It will help you discover things more easily without—"

His father had turned and he'd never completed the sentence however Steven was quite capable to guess what the next words might have been. He'd suggested it would help with his intended task so Steven had packed the device. Whatever was out there he needed to discover it and fast. Or whoever…

Before storing the binoculars inside his rucksack, Steven had checked it over as it had seemed rather old suddenly, and possibly as old as the metal covering at the nearby bunker. It could easily have been used by the people who'd used the abandoned building, out there in the nearby fields before everything became Zone Zero - the name for everything located outside Utopus. Using the binoculars made it clear rather quickly how different the level of maintenance was inside and out there. Outside was a bleak, forgotten landscape. Nothing seemed to live in it…

As Steven had walked from the dwelling, glancing back just once as he'd hoisted the rucksack in place on his back, it was so clear suddenly that the bleakness from outside had been seeping into Utopus for a long time already. However, someone made certain that the illusion of Utopus being a green, lush area was kept up at all times. It was supposedly a place of prosperity, good housing, good health, happy people…

Steven had stopped at the doorway. Realising that from here he could see what his mother might have seen a long time ago. A boy and a man pretending everything was normal, that they were a happy family. Not a care in the world. *Yeah right*, Steven thought, *they were just like everyone else, pretending they had not a care in the world…*

"So much for the world being any good," Steven mumbled angrily. "None of them are a Subject. They don't know how that feels really. My mother did, and she couldn't even stare her only son in the eye after she chose that destiny…"

But I'm a Subject, Steven thought, frowning for a moment then he turned and walked outside to meet up with whoever would want to bid him farewell, *and tomorrow I'll start my journey south properly. First I need to check the bunker more thoroughly. After that I'll find out more information about Zone Zero…*

* * *

Steven and his father had been studying as many maps as they could find in the weeks preceding the departure. He'd grabbed a pencil from the drawer of the table and on the largest of the maps he drew a large outline. He made an effort to draw the line really thoroughly, and part of the line went past the edge of Utopus. The bunker was outside the line.

"Everything inside this line is Utopus," his father had stated rather bluntly. "Everything outside this line is fair game for you to explore, dissect, turn upside down… whatever it is you got planned out there."

Steven glanced at his father and received what had almost seemed a dismissive shrug before the older man had glanced down, then had placed a spread-out palm over the area he'd outlined.

"This isn't open for exploring," he continued. "It would be too dangerous to pretend to live here and be a Subject. They'd know…"

Steven nodded, then studied the map further. The line cut through halfway the northern region, the map listed it as Sweden and Norway, then curved partway through the landmass to the east - a vast, expansive region… and someone had scraped away the name of this place - then it curved north around a white place, perhaps the coldest area on the planet and then would partway through the northern part of the opposite continent. It then dipped down towards the southern half of this other continent and even covered part of the very tip of the continent opposite it…

"Everything not circled by my line is Zone Zero, and is supposedly unsafe for humans," his father had stated next. "However, you know about the recordings. I'm convinced we got it back to front, and that we're in the dangerous region. Or at least the most dangerous part of it. Nowhere is safe really, son, nowhere and never forget that…"

Steven nodded, and suddenly felt rather glum and a bit stupid too now for the decision he'd made somewhat too hastily.

As he walked slowly, meandering past the broken pieces of the city lying on parts of the path, Steven glanced back towards Utopus, a city he knew by this name, and realised that the bunker was outside and he'd been going there for most of his life so far, and therefore outside Utopus. Zone Zero was real but something was so off about it that it was causing his stomach to churn and he didn't realise he'd been visiting the region outside the city was going to be an extensive journey until his father had showed him this map…

* * *

Now, on the last day, at the last hour, everything was becoming rather real for Steven. His rucksack was packed. He'd said his necessary goodbyes - his father, a few friends, Elizabet, and now he was just Subject 37 as he was walking south. His father had insisted on explaining as much as he could before the finality came.

"Understanding Utopus better will keep you safe," he'd reiterated. Yes, there was the whole mystery of how we might be keeping safe in this city, especially when Steven recalled then the fateful evening when he'd managed to change Elizabet's mind without even needing to make any effort. As Subject 37, suddenly he was looking at the city differently. No longer was it just the city where he'd been living and growing up but instead it took on the trappings of place that was just a by-product of the events from long ago, when the survivors of World War 3 had arrived in this region searching for a place of refuge away from wherever the plague had been taking hold in the south and east, or so the recordings had stated, and it had seemed that the safe region had been much smaller than anyone had hoped for. How then had eighty million people survived inside the region outlined on the map, especially with at least a third of the region in perpetual winter conditions was a puzzle to solve.

"Maybe the aggressive cold held the plague at bay," had been a suggestion from Elizabet when they'd discussed their findings, long before the spell of innocence was broken.

"My father thought the choice of region related to the cause of the war," Steven had said to the girl beside him as they'd been sitting beside the trickle of an old stream further north in Utopus, and they also had decided a long time ago that the stream might have been a bellowing river once. "It might be that all wars begin with a few first victims who might get so ill they cause others to be as ill as themselves…"

"A girl in my building told us all that according to her father, who's an educator in one of the north districts, though I can't recall which one," Elizabet had countered, "that if it was a plague rather than weapons that it must have been a rather serious disease. They had a name for the first person who might get ill with a disease… such a person was patient zero. Even now they'll monitor for people who get ill in such situations. Her father had said it gets done especially when it's an unknown disease…"

"Like, whatever it was that had caused so many people to die so fast so that only eighty million people were left over," he'd replied, and he got a gape from the girl which had made it obvious she either hadn't believed him or was rather shocked over the news.

"You mean the illness of five *years* ago might have been like that one that had happened five hundred years ago?" she'd asked.

Steven had nodded, biting his lip as the idea of a disease, that could kill everyone, had even scared him.

"The people who got sick were all in West District 3," he said, "and it was hundreds of people if I recall precisely. All of them with these tiny itchy red spots all over their bodies. I've tried to find out about what it might have been in some of the books they have in my father's Institute but wasn't able to. Everyone was told to stay away when they got ill, and the people there were told to stay in their housing until all of it was gone. I wasn't allowed to explore even when it was going on… Everyone was told to be inside…"

"I don't really remember it," Elizabet had said.

"It had happened when I was seven," Steven said, "and I know most of the information from my father who decided it was important enough to tell me about it. You would have been four or five at the time. Too young to remember such things…"

"Oh, okay," Elizabet said glumly, glancing down at the street across from where they were sitting for a moment. Steven recalled that she'd asked about the men in their black clothing again after that so he distracted her from thinking about potential other dangers.

"… but let me explain it better. Based on the secret information I've found, the disease of 370 years ago had been spreading fast because people were unaware it was even spreading until it was too late and nothing could be done about it by anyone," he'd explained, "and there was no time for a patient zero for them to find. The whole world became patient zero. Except for the area that would become Utopus."

"Oh right, so how do we know it's safe now, and the disease won't come back?" Elizabet had asked.

"I've found another pencil in another colour than what my father uses for the maps, and I've been making marks on the map he gave me to learn from," Steven had explained. "There are names on the map but they don't meaning anything anymore. What I've realised though by comparing is that the people mostly died first where these cities were so, yes, it may be dangerous for us here but also we may be safe as we don't live like they did. If they spread the disease again though we would need to leave…"

"But *this* is our home…" she'd squealed.

"I know but I'm certain that there's somewhere safe somewhere else that no evil person might know about if they're still around," he'd said reassuring, "but also, maybe… it's better to go to wherever the evil people are living now, and to make certain they're all gone completely. I've looked at the landscape where the University, my father's work place, would be if it had existed back then. When this place was Stockholm. Going by the map, it was south of the old river we've looked at. Also, Stockholm, which was a name I figured out after much searching was half inside Utopus and half outside. It may have been a target back then for spreading this disease in the past…"

6.

EVEN NOW, YEARS LATER, STEVEN was still wondering so often about the people from this place once called Sweden. If they'd ever known what was going to happen to them. That at the end of the century they had lived in the world they knew was all but destroyed…

So because Steven's mindset had recalled a few parts of conversation with Elizabet unexpectedly, it meant that he'd wanted to study the eastern border of Utopus, and for a few minutes he'd contemplated that perhaps he should try go east rather than south. The first three letters of the name of whatever nation had been located in the east, marked by the letters R-U-S still marginally visible in the middle of the landmass, was as intriguing to him as whatever he could potentially find in the south. He'd glanced towards the west border next, and knew immediately this region would be unreachable if the ocean dividing the two continents was still there and hadn't dried out as some people in Utopus were claiming…

"Hmm, too far to travel there," Steven mumbled, "and especially on my own. I'd need a ship to get there and that's if there are even any ships around that haven't rusted to pieces after five hundred years of lying defunct somewhere…"

He frowned and decided to keep this other location in his mind for a future endeavour, and to find a way to get there in the future…

He did have a deep desire, especially after listening to the recordings, to discover what had become of these two other nations. His hand traced over the map following a faded line going from one ocean to the one on the other side of the continent. Two nations that had existed there had occupied most of the available land between them. But why then was the border marking Zone Zero avoiding most of the southern one of those two countries? Steven shrugged. He didn't know. The only way he'd find out was to find old books with possible information about these nations, or to go there…

So over a period of slightly more than a decade he'd been finding out the beginnings of what would end up determining his actions for most of the rest of his life. The first discovery would be: why these borders existed in the way they did around Utopus would be his first effort. He assumed he could find out this information pretty much as soon as he was outside Utopus…

"They're now just forgotten by everyone it seems," Steven whispered. "No one knows their names now. Not just of theses few nations, but all other stuff as well. What was it ever all for?"

Suddenly, he made up his mind. *Going south might be better*, he thought. *I need to find out first why it's called Zone Zero, and it's a place no one here seems to know anything about around here. Did every Subject sent out into the wilderness just go… south…?*

As quickly as he could, Steven had completed the packing up of his rucksack, and then he folded all five maps he had in his possession as small he could fold them and slid them into the deepest part of the bag to keep them safe from the possible environmental conditions he encounter during his long journey. Was he going to find more mysteries while he was walking south through Zone Zero, or was he going to find some answers, and would he find a dusty, desolate region as Elizabet had suggested a few times it would be…?

He was about to begin a journey to find out how and why only one percent of all the population, as had been present on the planet at the end of twenty-first century - apparently over eight billion according to the remnant of recording, was reduced so brutally to eighty million and which had also been the original population of Utopus. This all had happened 380 years ago. However, some people also whispered about a possibility of other people still living out there in other parts of the world in what was called Zone Zero. So, not only Utopus had its secrets but an entire destroyed world had them as well…

"I must find out," Steven grunted as he approached the final outer door of the building that had been his home for all his life.

As he let a cold breeze cool him off for a moment, he glanced up at a balcony on the opposite building. Normally, whenever she needed to stay home, Elizabet had stood there but she wasn't there. *She's at the University right now*, Steven thought, *so I guess she didn't want to see me leave…*

"Yesterday I would have cared much more about her being here," Steven grunted angrily, "but not after how she spoke to me and told me—" Steven cursed under his breath. He'd wanted to say goodbye. He knew full well why she wasn't here. She'd be saying goodbye to Subject 37 and not to Steven Burgard. He wasn't Steven anymore. At least not to any of these people…

* * *

Would he succeed where thirty-six others had failed? Would he ever return to Utopus? Was anyone even caring about the fact he was now Subject 37? What secrets were there for him to discover during his journey? Who was hiding the secrets? Was he one of the good guys who was going to solve the mystery of how the old world had ended?

All these and other questions had whirled through Steven's mind as he'd walked from the building that had been a place to call home to the place from where he'd would depart from this home…

But, I have to remember that I'm still Steven Burgard, just as my father said he would remember it like, Steven thought as he was closing in to a small group of men, among them his father who'd been talking with them until one person tugged at his sleeve to alert him of his son's arrival. Once Steven got close enough to be in hearing range, all the people around his father dispersed rather hastily. As Steven stared after them somewhat annoyed, his father placed a hand over Steven's hand, and he'd just stared at his son with glazed over eyes.

The world, at the start of 'something' of an unknown world was causing a change that his father, Dr Burgard—and others around him, people who should always stay unnamed according to his father—who'd been working towards a solution for the problems we were in the middle of for close to four centuries now. No, they weren't capable of what some 'old books' we possessed said, which they called time travel in the books. However, sometimes it would feel like that because they were living the consequence a past that wasn't of any of our making; nor a future caused by it, not of our making.

Steven begun on a journey that was taking him to an unknown place in the south but which was evidently the repetition of a journey done by three dozen others, both men and women, and almost enforced by someone, as a ploy, to make certain that the society they we occupied had stayed quite ignorant of what had happened so long ago. There was an urgency to the situation Steven wasn't aware of until it was his turn to set out on a similar journey: it would strip him of his name, Steven Burgard, and anything else that was his identity. The journey would come complete with a preposterous new name or title—Subject 37. Until yesterday, he hadn't released that this other 'thing' even existed or was required. Until yesterday, he'd mattered to others living in this place; they'd been friends, work colleagues, family, people he might encounter in the streets… They didn't or wouldn't 'see' him now because this selection had happened. He wasn't certain how or why it had happened, or who was behind the idea, why someone was so brutally in isolating one individual in a cruel, cold, dead world. But, it wasn't going to stop him and his stupid, curious mind from finding out somehow…

Steven Burgard was his name until yesterday until they'd selected him. By who or why was unclear. *Why?* was a repeated thought that would haunt his mind as he travelled to an unknown southern destination.

* * *

The story of Utopus had started in a distant past, when the world was always living on the brink of war. It finally came at the end of the twenty-first century. We, that was his father, several scientists, and Steven, had so diligently been researching in the information they'd discovered—seemingly only by chance. His father had been in charge of the efforts of finding out what the information they'd found and what it all had meant. Among the information they'd discovered, was a message that gave us a dire warning about the future of Utopus. Or so his father would say often enough. As a scientist and researcher, both in relative terms in a society with a definite lack of information, Steven was curious about finding out more information. But this also was putting him at risk in a society that was more dangerous than anyone was realising at times, especially if you'd chosen a path as a scientist. If you became a scientist, you chose the risk of being chosen as a Subject.

They'd chosen him as a subject because he was getting too close to uncovering the truth about the message.

The University was where they would do their 'research.' They listed Steven's father's role there as 'Academist' and the easiest way Steven could explain the role to himself what the role could be was to decide that they were in charge of Utopus. After finding out a few pieces of information, Steven had discovered that they never got chosen to be a Subject. It told him something more about the entire set-up: a scientist was too dangerous to keep around because they knew a lot more than most. We were the curious creatures who would be trying to find out more about things…

Yes, this was also what the society was offering us. So, you could choose to be a Scientist, an Academist, or be a nobody…

* * *

"Have you decided about what to do when you can select a career? When they require you to choose…" Dr Burgard had asked one morning, a few months after Steven's sixteenth birthday; not that the day was any different from any other. He'd glanced at his son with a stern stare that had made the boy flinch, like he was a few years younger, in reality. Steven had stared angrily at his father before answering. "I want to be a Scientist," Steven said bluntly.

"What!"

"I said, I want to be—"

"I heard you the first time. Haven't I been clear enough for the last several years of what the consequences could be of such a decision will cause? It could end up in—"

"I know all that," Steven had interrupted his father's repeated speech about his mother. "I want to do this because she was one too—If you tell me again what the consequences are going to be maybe I'll just stay a nobody."

Dr Burgard had turned away, silently staring from the window.

"Father—"

No reply.

Steven had looked down at the surface of the small table in front of him, trying to contemplate a reason for the silence and the reason his father had suggested there were consequences.

What consequences?

"I must forbid you to make that specific choice."

Steven had glanced up abruptly. His father had spoken rather unexpectedly after only a few minutes of silence. His words, though spoken calmly, had an undertone of fear to them, almost like he'd become a less of a self-assured man than in the previous five minutes.

Why is he scared?

"But I want to—" Steven had blurted out before he'd realised what he'd said then.

Again, the deafening silence was keeping them apart for several more minutes. This time, the feeling it was giving Steven was like what he'd end up experiencing while walking later through Utopus…

* * *

Utopus wasn't so much a city but a collection of buildings. They hadn't given it this name because they saw it as a city, but rather they'd taught us from childhood that it was the name was given to a region that was one of the last places of refuge in existence on the planet—though, we didn't have any knowledge of what had become of the other places of refuge.

That someone else might know, was clear to Steven from the coming and going of the black 'somethings' that to him looked like buildings but quite early on in his visits there he'd overheard the people in the University talk of it as something else, even claiming it could fly off, though personally, he'd never seen it do this.

So, he could have been either a Scientist or an Academist. Out of the two, the Academists had it the easiest. They governed everything. They ran the University, and from certain things that had happened there during Steven's tenure on his father's insistence, there was so much more going on than it seemed.

Steven had guessed that this insistence was being explained somehow by his own suspicious mind, and it fed his curiosity to the level it was now.

"Why do you work at the University?" It was a question that Steven had asked his father ever since he'd been a young child. The father had never told his son any precise reasons, but some of his comments had given the boy a clue: "I'm interested in what will happen to us if we keep everything as it is now. I'm convinced someone is in the background, calling the shots. The things I've seen prove this…"

Steven was more in the spectrum of science than his father ever had realised, and though he'd understood what his father had to do he was sometimes unsure of why. Whenever Steven had stood in the central square listening to the speeches made about the virtues of Utopus, he'd wondered. What virtues? They were claiming they had good housing, clean water, and plenty of food in Utopus. Not even his father, with his daily old can of soup each day, could convince Steven that what was being said was true in any way. Even the thing called 'science' wasn't the same as what might have existed five hundred years earlier. The books he'd so often searched out as he was growing up told him otherwise.

Steven decided not to speak with anyone about what he was thinking as he'd listened to his father, and he vowed not to tell anyone ever what was on his mind. Not even his father. Their knowledge wasn't much but Steven was certain somewhere there was more information to learn, and what they knew of the world was something even fewer were capable to understand. The younger scientists were researching most of the knowledge they were trying to rediscovered, and Steven was one of them.

Also, choices were hard in Utopus. Steven could imagine others - such as Elizabet - having similar conversations with their families as his one with his father. Yes, by now she was a Scientist too, and it could easily have been her going on this journey. As Steven grew up, he was continuously reminding himself that it was the choice he'd wanted to make for himself—even if his father kept reminding him of his objections, uncommonly forcefully too.

"Father, can I come to work with you, so I can see what both of them do?"

The question had taken his father by surprise. Steven didn't tell his father why he'd wanted to go, but he was certain that his time going there would become rather interesting, especially when he'd need to choose his career path on becoming eighteen. The puzzle of what was going on would occupy much of his time and mind for those five years in between…

Until the day came when *he* was a Subject… suddenly.
His mind then turned to the mysteries that surrounded them.
Utopus wasn't a safe haven or somewhere idyllic, as one might have thought.

From the moment that Steven had attended the University with his father, as a boy of fourteen - just after the discussion with his father had happened about his career choice - Steven had noticed that things there had puzzled him. The mystery had increased when he'd noticed it was also puzzling his father in an equal measure. We'd walked to the University on a crisp spring morning, with Steven staring hard at the flakes of ice crystals underfoot to have some time to weigh up the thoughts there were going through his mind. At the same time, his father had been silent too, and occasionally Steven was wondering if now his father was recognising that his son needed to consider the consequences and other such matters in his own young mind without his father putting more ideas in there.

Admittedly, this was true until a day came when Steven had been walking through the city for the reason of going to a job because he'd thought his father had been working at the Academic Institute, and *not* the University.

Both of the buildings were in the Central District of Utopus, and right now he was uncertain which career choice he preferred more. As a child, Steven recalled sitting in a dark building with occasional lights turning on and off, and he was certain his father had identified it as the Academic Institute.

7.

BUT WHEN WE WALKED, IT became clear soon that our destination was the University.

"Why are we going to that place?"

"Be quiet. Just listen. Just observe. Don't speak."

For a man as knowledgeable as his father seemed, and how else might you explain the 'Doctor' part in front of his name, the reply was short and abrupt, and so lacking the substance was unusual, when his usual answers would have startled the boy…

Steven's father was normally a man of great discussions, but that had essentially stopped when his son was still quite young—and this was something the boy had only occasionally been certain of—when they'd witnessed the last Subject departing ten years earlier.

I wonder why they're sent out only every ten years, and not more often…?

With his frequent visits to both the building of learning and government, Steven had noticed something rather profound, and that was that people were going to the University more frequently than they'd do going to the Academic Institute, and this came also with a change of what they'd do in other places. Until the first visit, he'd considered these buildings rather boring. Afterwards, they were like the characters from the few old books that Steven had owned—mysterious, typically out to make life hell for the person about whom the author had written the book, and often stuffy as hell whenever Steven had listened to them. And they had a knack to insult people around them when they wanted to…

Plus, as Steven had realised from his father's career, they were also the people with the excitement for wanting everything at their worst it seemed. It had increased Steven's curiosity, but not in the way that his father had wanted it to happen.

Instead, it had caused him to become even more interested in science. His father's sigh, some months later, had indicated to Steven that his father had given up fighting his son over the situation he'd raised as a point of contention between them. However, the end in their arguments didn't mean Steven had won the arguments with his father…

* * *

Steven had blatantly said he'd be a scientist, at least that he wanted it once he was eighteen, and it had created for the boy the realisation that this choice came with a risk. The risk was going to be a direct consequence of Steven's own damned curiosity. And the cause for the laughter of the others he'd been working with at that time not long afterwards.

Steven wanted to know what had happened to the world he was living in. He needed to know.

This new thought had started soon after Steven had arrived with his father at the University, where they'd gone to a room with a door that seemingly they were keeping locked at all times as was demonstrated in the next few minutes of the visit. In the room, Steven had encountered the first answer to a question that had been going through his mind that had showed him that things weren't as simple or as safe in Utopus as most would assume. When he stood in the room listening to everyone talking they'd introduced him to something from years ago, or maybe even decades ago. This 'something' comprised a metal object capable of transmitting sound.

The sound coming from the device was a message…
The voice was telling the people in the room that Zone Zero was dangerous…
The voice had mentioned that no Subject should go there…

So why not?

They were sending Subjects out every decade, and the next Subject was going to be Subject 37, so Steven's scientific mind had immediately decided that the process of selection had been going on for 380 years, because, obviously, a decade after they'd founded Utopus the first Subject got sent out… or so he was guessing…
So, now there might be the obvious question in one's mind, as Steven realised someone might interpret his past years from this moment in time, and that would be why a scientist by the name Steven Burgard hadn't opted the safer option to be an Academist or a nobody - yes, that was an

option open too and Steven wasn't even sure why people got referred to in that way - and then one might wonder instead this man, called Steven Burgard, though a decade younger and perhaps a decade less stupid and the only son of the most prominent scientist in Utopus, even had considered this as a good choice for a career path. That got you thinking, huh? Steven to himself with all irony he could aim at himself.

The straightforward answer was that he didn't know any answers to the puzzle he'd conjured up in his mind as he walked for the millionth time behind his father to the familiar buildings. It felt like he'd done this so often... The somewhat broader answer was that he was guessing at what he could find as answers out there. The most complex answer to find was she'd left Utopus...

He might have only been a resident of this godforsaken planet for twenty-two years, but he decided that most people who'd lived five centuries earlier, at the start of the 'twenty-first century,' would have shuddered if they'd known what the future would hold.

A future that had commenced at the end of *their* century, and which wouldn't be any kind of future that any of them had envisaged.

Every time he thought back at an explanation his father had given, Steven got a feeling of foreboding thinking back at the explanation of the difference between the Scientists and the Academists, and the explanation gave greater urgency to my plan to become a scientist.
"Why is there so much difference between them?"

His father had stonewalled my question while we had left the University. Literally!

✳ ✳ ✳

Father and son went home, and on the way home both individuals were silent again. Once they were home, the discussion that had happened a few years earlier resumed. "I want you to tell them you're an Academist like me, dammit," Dr Burgard had shouted at his son Steven. "If you're a Scientist you could end up like her. They've never selected an Academist as a Subject. I cannot lose you as I did her..."

Her?

"I want to work on the machine you got over there. You said that Academists only ever work in the Academic Institute," Steven shouted back. "What the hell are you even doing there if you're an Academist. I want to be a scientist to make this world better. They tried to do that too five hundred years ago. She wanted it too."

The accusation had shut his father up. He'd clammed his mouth shut and had repeated the behaviour of four years earlier of just staring from the window without saying a word.

"I'm guessing that you believe that you'd made the wrong choice earlier in your life," Steven mumbled under his breath. "I'm certain of it…"

"I'm not doing my job for the excitement of discovery, son," Dr Burgard said somewhat coldly and abruptly, "though you may look at it as exciting, and I don't blame you."

"But scientists only have knowledge of so little compared to hundreds of years ago, father."

"I'm aware of this information, son."

Dr Burgard turned, and he stared at Steven for a time, almost—to the boy it felt that way at least—like he was trying to put an image into his mind so not to forget his son. Forget him because of what might happen?

"Once, in the past, science was plentiful. All knowledge was. Now, most books that held such knowledge have either turned to dust or soon will—"

Dr Burgard sat down opposite of Steven. The action of sitting down had the air of defeat to it.

"I guess I can't change your mind, is that right?"

Steven shook his head.

"I received a letter," Steven whispered. He reached to a pile of paperwork beside him on the table and handed his father the envelope. His father's expression of defeat went now to that of disappointment, even to another expression that Steven had seen once before. *When she had departed that day he'd looked in the same way.*

Dr Burgard stared long at the letter, and it was obvious to Steven that he was having trouble comprehending its content at first, then his whisper confirmed the contents. "It seems the University in the Central District of Utopus has accepted you."

* * *

And so the folly of the situation had started that day that had resulted in the obvious selection of Steven as a Subject. He still was unsure who the 'they' were in the process related to the selection process. He was actually uncertain who the 'they' were in him being accepted by the University.

What Steven knew with certainty, as he stood watching the world outside their small apartment that they'd shared until now, was that things had changed. There was a marked difference between his past and his present. What the future would bring was something he could only ever guess at. As per the rules, his father had explained to his son on the day, four years earlier, that when selected that the person you were, would seize to exist. "You'd lose the name. You'd lose your identity. You'd lose your place in society. You'd lose your worth. You'd become invisible to everyone." So, because of all this he was Steven Burgard until the previous day until he got the letter, and until yesterday the son of Dr Burgard. Today he was Subject 37…

But he still was that, even in name, to his father. His father risked punishment if they discovered he hadn't denounced his son fully. Like he never fully had denounced her either. Steven was certain there was a further reason for that, and he guessed he might discover why it was if he ever would meet her—if he'd ever met his mother.

The reason, Steven thought, *that he risks punishment is based on what else could be going on. But the reason, though I've seen it for myself, will stay hidden in my mind. No one needs to have knowledge of what goes on between my father and me. They just need to assume I'm accepting this all as the newest Subject, and that is it… and it will be exactly ten years since she left. Will I ever find her? Will I also find other people? Will I discover why they only send out a Subject every ten years. I have no answers except for that it has happened, that there's something going on, and the least favoured answer is that three dozen people who tried it before me had failed. Failed with what?*

Yes, he was certain this question would become very self-evident to him as soon as he'd left…

* * *

The announcement for the new Subject was almost mundane, and not very noticeable. Steven hadn't noticed until a day before she'd left that they'd chosen her. He didn't think anyone had known about him until darkness had settled over Utopus. The information had appeared on the notice boards, people had looked at it, and then they'd just walked away and almost no one had reacted.

He had noticed that everyone had acted differently around him from that day…

Steven wondered what his true task as a Subject was all about? His father wasn't very precise. So, he had guessed that his father had thought that as a Scientist he might have been able to research everything about Zone Zero, and draw conclusions just as he'd while helping with the metal object. He guessed that this thing of a man or woman walking into Zone Zero alone was someone's sadistic idea.

"The purpose for the journey would be for the Subject to determine what the condition is of Zone Zero." His father's explanation, as always, was the same one that everyone else had always told him.

"But what if I find it polluted?" Steven asked again. "Or worse?"

"Then we have to wait."

"Is waiting what we've been doing for over three centuries?"

"You know I can't answer questions about it, son."

"No one ever talks about it, so how would a Subject be able to know what to do?" Steven spat at his father angrily. "None have even come back. Why not?"

No answer came.

Again, as before, my father wouldn't answer certain questions.

∗ ∗ ∗

Steven studied what was passing as the border between Utopus and Zone Zero, and what Steven was seeing in the landscape was leaving him with was leaving him surprised. While located between a few rocks, he was staring at a grassy area, but he noted that some of it was yellow in colour like it wasn't alive in the right way. However, looking further ahead, he noted that the fields and trees looked green and abundant with life.

If it was really in a terrible state over there, the grass there would be as dead as over here.

No one else would ever come to this place, not even Elizabet or his father. Steven threw a stone to be certain he was seeing the field, and to be certain he hadn't imagine his surroundings. No one else was talking about the outside. They don't acknowledge that it exists. Steven could guess why…

Their discussions would make it too real.

It would make it too real that they'd been living in Utopus like fools when they could have walked away from a terrible existence, and they could all have gone one day. Steven guessed he wasn't the odd one out with his fascination for Zone Zero.

"I can't tell you anything," Dr Burgard had hissed, "and if you keep asking there will be consequences."

So I had become an explorer early in my life. Which was what people called themselves five centuries ago? When he explored he felt more connected with the past than he did with his own era. It led to his being a scientist and as he learnt more I had to conclude…

I have to go there.

* * *

"Steven! We need to speak…"

Steven's heart had skipped a beat when his father had addressed him by his name.
"Come, we go somewhere for this discussion."
"I thought you had to address me as a Subject?"

"I'll keep calling you Steven, regardless."

These words changed how other people were treating him in the days since the announcement and made it even more obvious. At the same time, them ignoring Steven, almost side-stepping him with purpose, made it clear to his scientific mind there was even more going on than anyone would tell him.

I might be heading towards danger, Steven thought. *Especially if I'm being sent there because I'm too smart according to someone's opinion.*

Steven's father was looking sadly at his son which confirmed to him that, in part, he was right. Which part? He didn't know. He'd find out later. And then it would confirm whether the attitude being displayed went with the territory. He was guessing every person who'd seen a Subject was looking sad just like his father was doing now. But with my father, there was more…

Steven guessed he was reminding him of her. He was guessing that going had been a risk for her, too.

I don't exist…

This was why it felt that he was departing from Utopus with his soul being left behind even when it felt also like he was doing the opposite…

So why am I Subject 37?

Maybe because he needed to figure out why thirty-six others had failed in their task. No one in Utopus seemed to know what had become of them… not even her. Not even my father knew, and he was by far the oldest here. He was fifty-seven, which meant my father might have seen at least four of them leaving, and perhaps even five. Or six if he could still remember childhood with ease.

Steven was thirteen when she'd left. But he remembered very little of the day—or her. He guessed he could understand his father's unwillingness to speak of her in that respect. Speaking about what you could have anymore made it *more* clear that you didn't have it…

* * *

His soul, he was guessing, had left him on the day that she'd left. His body was just being kept inside Utopus by an invisible boundary that didn't exist, so there was nothing to hold him back—or anyone else. People just didn't want to leave…

"Not even father—" Steven had mumbled as he'd glanced around the room for a moment. "He, too, it seems, is irrationally fearful about leaving. I wonder what I'll find out there." Steven's gaze fixed itself towards the south. That was where he was heading in a matter of hours from now as soon as the sun had risen sufficiently to bathe the bleak landscape in an orange hue.

"I wonder how big the world really is as it seems I'll do a lot of walking."
Walking back to the table, he picked up the map that his father had given him. On it, he'd drawn a shape. "Everything inside this line is Utopus."

Steven knew now that the rest of the map outside it was Zone Zero. He had a name now for the rest of the world. It him with a lot of investigating to do though. Maybe investigating all of it would take him ten years. But no one ever comes back, and that's worrying…

A better future might get started by investigating the past, he needed to guess about what he could do. He could have started with investigating Utopus itself. Even from outside it.

8.

MOST OF HIS KNOWLEDGE OF it, had come from his father, and there was no signs how he'd learnt the history, but Steven could guess that knowledge was passed from his grandfather to his father, and her parents taught his mother. They'd probably learnt it from their parents in turn. Both his parents had taught him as much as possible. He knew his father was an Academist, but for his mother he only had the clues dropped by my father.

I think she was a scientist...

Her location was unknown, though Steven's mind wanted to place her on the road that he would be walking as he left himself...

Steven was twenty-two. He guessed they could consider him intelligent if they assumed him as such from figuring out a few facts such as this. One fact was to figure out how many people would be left over after the disaster that had likely happened a decade before they'd sent the first Subject out. This was a place of survivors, and in his observations, Steven had realised something profound. In the books he found - they were found within the ruins of the city that stood once here - it was described that young people could be rebellious and would gather to raise a voice to get change for themselves. The book had listed a few such occasions with last one happening in the 2030's. However, Steven had noted fast that this sort of behaviour was lacking in Utopus. He'd guessed a full explanation of how people were behaving in Utopus was lengthy, but the basic concept of why it wasn't a done thing was something anyone could likely imagine. Imagine living in a place where they'd condition you not to see what was going on around you. Like, for example, people might have turned a blind eye to the presence of the black metal objects that would arrive, would stay for a time, then would leave. Never had his father explained what they were, but the fear he would see in the eyes of the people coming to tell him they had chosen Steven as a Subject told the boy enough information. They'd feared the black metal objects coming and going more than anything else. They'd glanced over when Steven asked questions of his father about what he was supposed to do in Zone Zero…

Most of Steven's knowledge of the old world of five centuries ago had come from books he'd read; the few that existed here.

The other knowledge had come later. From what Steven had started calling the 'Voice.' It was this female voice recited an account of events that were dating back to five hundred years ago, which all seemed to impact our current situation. The Voice, on a device he would activate occasionally, would become his only form of hearing any person's voice for most of his journey south.

"Father, why do we even send anyone out if people don't seem to care about it?" he'd asked more than once.

"Son, I've told you many times," came as a familiar reply. "The people are afraid. People who are afraid, well, they change. You've changed because of things that have happened—"

The changes his father had spoken of were two-fold. The first change came when Steven went to the University with his father. That was when he came in contact with the Voice, though Steven had to admit that, at first, he'd just been hearing nothing but static, and in part, also Steven's anger towards the others, who were also listening to the recording, had quite possibly played a role in the boy not immediately recognising the Voice. Or, to think that there had even been a human voice audible to any of us…

The second change was his father referring to her departure.

Both these changes had played a factor in him becoming interested in the outside world. Steven was doing what no other person in Utopus seemed to do.

He'd rebelled…

* * *

It was maybe a few months after his thirteenth birthday that Steven had visited the underground building for the first time, though now he'd ventured deeper into the building, now that he was leaving for good perhaps. But even the small part of the building he'd looked at so far had given him valuable clues about a distant past that had differed from a reality that was confronting him every day. Steven had made his decision to be a scientist there inside the strange underground structure. His curiosity had driven him finally to a room deep in the building where a machine stood looking rather menacing, and later when he had gone to the University with his father he saw the same type of object there.

A year earlier, Steven had discussed the virtues of a choice of a career with his father, or more precisely, he'd argued with him about it. Steven's visits to the underground building had been a direct consequence of these disagreements.

It was after being accepted as a Scientist these illicit visits to the underground buildings had increased exponentially. But then something else had happened. His father had taken his son to the structure himself, though in reality we never even left the confines of Utopus, even when Steven had tried to persuade his father to go closer or even inside. Dr Burgard had given his son a device with which Steven could observe the landscape at a great distance. His father had tried to tell him its name, though the boy renamed it to a 'distance viewer,' and while remembering these events later on, Steven had realised that the name had come him, he'd suggested it, and that his father had gone along with the suggestion, but now, deep down, Steven knew that this wasn't its real name, and then he also realised he'd never seen an image of the device in any book so he had no point of reference to determine what the name might have been and whether the name his father had suggested was correct. What he did know was that the object originated from five hundred years in the past…

Steven was guessing he could add these visits to the growing list of choices, good and bad, that he had made in his life because of who he was and what he became.

Yesterday they'd told him he would serve as the latest Subject. As Subject 37. This announcement had replaced the 'perhaps' and 'it might happen' that had been stated before with the 'it has happened' later on. Steven was guided by his experiences to determine what he should do, though at no point did he get a sign of what his task entailed. But they had fulfilled this task in a similar fashion for the last 360 years already. Steven could listen to whatever they were telling him about the task, then he could leave and complete it 'his' way. He still was like a rebel inside…

But no one has ever returned. Will I ever return here, to Utopus, to my home? Will this place be a memory that I'll chase as much as I'm chasing the shadows in Zone Zero?

Steven was guessing that something had happened to all other Subjects if no one had been able to return ever. The sparse information that was passed down by the parents of his father and mother to them, and then to their son, and contained no information showing that any of these people had returned. That meant he couldn't leave part of his soul here, hoping that he'd return one day…

It may be a desolate life in Zone Zero if I survive the journey but if it's so desolate then who is the Voice? Where is she? And… her…? She said she'd left from here long ago and had never been able to come back. Something feels too familiar about the Voice—

The extent of what Steven needed to do once he was in Zone Zero was just guesswork right now, and might be similar during the first several months. Even based on what his father told him…

"I need to find out what has happened to the all other Subjects while I'm over there," Steven had mumbled. "If only to satisfy my curiosity."

During the meeting of the previous day, Steven had noticed they had been staring pretty wide-eyed and unsettled towards the black 'something' which had been descending from the sky at the same time they were speaking with us. They'd refused to answer his questions about what he was doing in Zone Zero, and least of all his questions about the black 'something.'

Steven now realised it could fly around so it wasn't a building, but that made it a possible flying relic from the past. If he could find a few books in Zone Zero, he'd discover what its name might be similarly to the binoculars. But if one of these 'black somethings' flew *in* from somewhere else to here, he was required to be careful… out there. Perhaps, they were an enemy who he didn't even know about.

This new thought gave Steven a certainty that gave him a conclusion of sorts. It meant that if the black 'somethings' were coming from somewhere else that the people of Utopus weren't alone. The sighting also confirmed certain things that the Voice was telling them…

✳ ✳ ✳

The University was situated in the Central District and near it, Steven was now seeing the black 'something' landing with a bellow of dust flying up from the ground around it. Its presence was causing him to alter his behaviour and plans so he'd picked up a book from the shelf that he'd previously planned to leave behind. Only six pages remained of this book, and one page was of something that appeared to resemble the black 'something' though object in the book was light grey and not black…

The blank expressions of the individuals watching it land and them pretending to ignore its ominous nature, and the fact that the black 'something' had even landed specifically on the same day when he was departing, was telling Steven more of what might be going on than even his father was admitting to. Or perhaps his father's silence was demonstrating that he was using another way to alert his son of the danger. And that he also knew…

Steven glared hard at the image in his hands, and then he frowned. The image from the past wasn't explaining him anything about the origins of its counterpart that was now standing in a large open space at the east end of the city.

Steven was now guessing that he'd have to find out the true origin of Utopus and Zone Zero for other parts of his plan, now becoming concrete constructs in his mind, to work. *Father told me enough information to realise that the world might be rather dangerous,* Steven thought, *and the Voice tells there's something out there that had caused all of this. She also says she'd found proof of how this place started—and how to stop it from continuing to be in this way. But then the transmissions had stopped, and father got so worried…*

So now the reason should be quite obvious as to why he needed to depart with his soul. Leaving his soul here might have caused Steven to worry about this place too much, though he already knew he would do that anyway. It was supposedly a home for the descendants of the survivors of the final war, of 'World War 3,' but Steven had seen images from five centuries ago and before that. This wasn't a city like the ones that existed back then. It looks more like one on the first photo he'd discovered in the underground building.

Dammit, Steven, why do you always go so philosophical when trying to sort out your plans, Steven thought angrily. As the only answer to the accusation aimed at himself he was guessing he'd find a semblance of a soul in Zone Zero as he'd always wanted to go there anyway to find out what was so bad about it. But first he would need to do that very rebellious thing one more time, and go to the underground building and find out precisely what was there, and if he could also find out what it was for…

* * *

Before he was leaving Steven had a few minutes to give his father a much-needed embrace. To do this properly he took off his rucksack and dropped it on the group that made some of the dust and sand puff up into the air like he'd seen the flying object do earlier.

The embrace from his father was warm, felt like he was again a small boy, and he found himself copy his father's intensity.

They parted ways.

Then after a minute, Steven picked up his small rucksack and placed it on his back, and as he did this his father spoke, "Wait here, please," he said. "There's something I need to give you still…"

His father might have walked back to their small dwelling or to another place. Steven didn't know. However, when his father returned he was noticing how his father was staring at him with glazed eyes. "Always remember that you must be cautious everywhere," Dr Burgard said softly, his voice breaking from emotion, "Like I had warned you when you came with me to the University."

Steven nodded curtly, silently.

"Have you packed everything you wanted to bring with you?" Dr Burgard asked, "because I won't be returning to the home we lived in after you've left from here… There are—too many memories for me there now."
Steven nodded again.
"You've brought the books with you?"
"Yes, father," Steven answered, "but I've only brought the pages that matter with me, and the paper so I had more space to pack things…"
"I have—I got something you need to bring with you. Please, don't ask me what it is," Dr Burgard said quietly. "Please turn, and I'll put this in your rucksack."
"I have space in the left side pocket."

Steven turned then and felt his father pulling the rucksack open, and his father busied with sorting out whatever he was doing Steven purposely stared blankly towards the south so as not to see what his father was packing. But his ears could hear the rustling of paper. He could therefore guess what the items being packed might be.

They could be the letters that I've seen him write during the last few weeks, Steven thought. *Could they be meant for her?*

"Remember that I must address you… as Subject at the border," Dr Burgard whispered, "but for me you're always Steven Burgard. Remember that every day while you travel."

Steven nodded again. Staying silent.

"We best go now to where you should be departing from…"

Dr Burgard didn't wait for Steven to acknowledge the suggestion. His father simply turned and walked south along the broken road. Steven fastened his rucksack tightly and then after a final glance at the sprawling city north of him he followed his father in his step. Both were silent…

* * *

An hour later, Steven had stopped only for a moment to glance back at his father and beyond him at the city that stood as a shadow on the horizon. His father was standing in the middle of the old road with his head bowed and in a posture that Steven had seen in a few of the books he had in his possession, where rows of men would stand in a similar posture. He could only guess why his father was doing this posture right now. He stared at his father to imprint the imagery as a memory…

Perhaps, this way, I won't forget him in the time it will take me to return here, and hopefully I won't coming back alone… I'll come back, father, and when I do, I'll make certain I come with the necessary knowledge and to bring with me as many of whoever I find who want to come with me to accompany us to find a better, safer place for us to make a home to rebuild our society, Steven thought pensively, *and I'm sure that the people of five hundred years ago will have left information about how to do all this… somewhere. The Voice knew that it exists. I'll find it—*

* * *

The first time that Steven had known that there was somewhere outside Utopus was when, at the age of thirteen, he'd stood beside his father and they'd watched a woman walk away from them, both reacting differently to this departure. Whereas Steven had been angry, at least he thought he was angry, his father was sad. Though it seemed that the memories of who she was were fading too fast, she still had seemed familiar to him, so many years later, as he had reflected on memories…

As he stared with a frown on his face at the clear morning sky of the first morning alone, Steven was acutely aware that he was now embarking on a similar journey to an unknown place, and through a region which they'd been so specifically warned about.

So today it's my turn and I'm glad now that I spent a few days here first, Steven thought. *Will there be others doing this after I never come back…? They can't fault me for wanting to check this building first…?*

9.

THEN CAME THE DREAMS DURING the first night alone…

His dreams wanted to explain things so differently from how things had gone in reality. According to the dream, everything had started for him when he was thirteen, and he lived in a house but specifically he remembered the kitchen. A woman would be sitting there who'd always had seemed to be waiting my father and me to arrive home every day. Or did things happen the other way around?

In Steven's mind, however, she'd sit there waiting for the outer door to open, then he would always see her rush at my father and kiss him passionately…

Not that a young boy such as him would appreciate seeing them doing this, Steven thought. *You should know how boys are about kissing and such stuff…*

There was something so unfathomably sad about realising when suddenly a father was standing alone, after having seen him for most of your life with someone who'd he would hug every day. That was what had made it more certain that Steven's decisions about having a relationship would need to be so different.

There was his friend Elizabet, at the University, and she was the girl who'd lived opposite him, in the other building, but she was only ever a friend. She was in the group that got assigned to me to work with me when we had received the signal. But I'm getting ahead of myself…

* * *

Anyway, the day would come when the woman had walked away from Utopus and that was the day when everything in his life had changed for Steven. It was on that day that he'd realised that a world existed outside Utopus. Steven had wondered about the departure and then he'd asked his father certain questions, which his father would either avoid answering or he'd answer them and every word he'd say would sound like some sort of riddle.

For example, his father would never tell his son who the woman was, and why she had to go on a journey this outside place. It was much later when Steven had found out its name was Zone Zero.

But his father would never tell him ever why she'd gone there, or for what.

However, there was something strange about the departure, and thinking back, Steven was now remembering something specific. She was too familiar for it to be a coincidence for him now. When he'd walked over the road towards the precise spot where he'd seen her last and where she'd faded into the distance, always walking on without glancing back once, there was one specific memory that was now coming back to my mind with increased frequency…

Steven assumed he'd experienced a chaotic childhood in Utopus, and that most of this period had always revolved around visits with his father to where he was working at the time. Steven was hoping now that his father was still working there even now. He was hoping also that his father was still alive because of what he had done as a consequence of Steven's behaviour and actions.

He remembered always being told that his father was one of the most prominent Academists in Utopus, and that he'd wanted me to follow the same path of career, too. Steven was uncertain what sort of role his mother had possessed, but Steven was now certain that the woman at the kitchen table, who'd kissed my father, was in fact his mother. What he never was understanding even now was why she and the woman leaving Utopus seemed to resemble one another…

He recalled a little of her features only, and it seemed his father had never wanted his son to remember her, and if he had asked his father about where she was when he wasn't seeing her at the kitchen table he'd only always say that she had to go somewhere else.

For a long time, 'somewhere else' had apparently meant somewhere else inside the city Utopus. His father might have thought that his son had been too young to understand that his son could interpret for it also to mean outside the city…

* * *

Every time Steven had been walking just a bit further over the old road, that may have been a well-maintained structure in a distant past, and he would instinctively look for 'her' and then he'd wonder if she might be watching him from the roof of one of the many disheveled dwellings still present on either side of that road, though their number was fast diminishing. A young mind wouldn't know to put a missing parent in any other place than what the mind was most familiar which is what Steven was guessing now…

Then there were the last words spoken between his father and himself that might give Steven a clue that something else had happened, and the words came to my mind suddenly. It had started recently. He was uncertain what had triggered the memories but he'd been eating a little the soup he'd brought with him, and he was somehow remembering his mother would also be making a soup, too.

"Mama! Mama!"

Steven was calling after the woman was a memory from a decade ago, and the woman hadn't turned when he'd frantically called after her, and she'd walked on silently, and never looking back at him or his father who'd been there too apparently. Steven recalled bitterly how he'd been thrashing and screaming in his father's arms, even kicking around violently to get his strong hands to let him go, so he could run after the woman.

"She needed to go, son," was all his father had said repeatedly in a monotonous voice, even with him struggling so hard against his father's grip that in the end he'd gone limp and was just a heap of sobs being lifted in his arms. When the day came for that departure he'd vowed to stop it from happening, but his father had been too strong and Steven had really still been a small boy at the time…

In the end, the whole event had such a nightmarish feeling to it that his still young mind couldn't process any of it. Wouldn't process it. He'd really been denying everything ever since…

"Where did she go?" Steven would ask repeatedly.
"She needed to go," was the only answer he would ever get.

And that was all that his father would ever say about any of the topic raised by his son. Then Steven had noticed that his father had wanted to say something else to his son, but he'd always stop short of speaking further, and then he'd look away at the horizon beyond Utopus, where from time to time a mysterious black structure seemed to be visible. So that was when Steven had realised that the structure was there only short periods, and then would seem to disappear from sight by an unknown method. No one that the boy then asked about the structure would give him any answers as to what it was, why it was there, or even how it could be there one moment and gone the next…

Without realising until later, he'd made his decision to be a scientist on the same day that his mother had seemed to stop being around. He'd loved his mother, and losing her presence in his life had caused the rebellious streak in him to assert itself. Steven also became more curious about the world he was living after that day. Up to that day, his days had been too much filled with the endlessly playing in the remnants of what once Stockholm, according to his father, when the boy had asked him.

His father had said that it had seized to be called by this name before they'd finished building Utopus, which also makes him wonder what had really happened five centuries ago which had started a roller-coaster of events leading to the existence of Utopus.

The first time his father had noticed his son had more than your average interest was when Steven sat listening with great interest to a conversation his father was having with someone else at the Academic Institute. Someone who was calling his father by the name of Dr Burgard.

After our conversation, Steven had broached the subject about the choices of career open to him, and he'd stated he'd wanted to be a scientist. His father hadn't been happy at all with his son's decision…

He had said these words to Steven, no demanded of his son, to reconsider his choice and be an Academist like him. When his father had made these demands of his son he had glanced from the window towards the north, like he'd been afraid that someone had somehow overheard his son expressing his choice just then. Steven was as determined as his father. He'd decided what he was going to do, and in the heat of arguing with his father, he had asked again where his mother was, and again was refused an answer, so spat out to let his father know he'd already applied to the University.

But then, unexpectedly, the discussion had taken on a sinister undertone when my father had stated rather plainly, "Going inside this building has consequences."

But strangely, his father had appeared to be like a broken man after he'd uttered these few words, and with that single sentence, all his willpower or ability to fight off Steven's stubbornness about wanting to become a scientist had gone from his body. Steven remembered him slumping back in the old chair that he'd been sitting on before the argument had commenced, and that he'd exhaled, and then just shut his eyes to block out the world—and his son, too.

Steven guessed that his father was able to block seeing the world around him, and could stop himself from seeing his unruly son sitting across the room with folded arms, but his father couldn't block out his son's incessant muttering about what he'd just said the boy. "Consequences, what consequences? So what if there are consequences? It's my decision. It's my life."

Steven knew he had deeply hurt his father with his choices. However, he'd never shown visibly that he'd been hurt Steven's comments or accusatory tone of speaking. The consequence of this singular argument was that our discussions would happen fewer times afterwards, and after a time Steven would accompany his father less to where his workplace. But during the last time visiting him there Steven would finally realise how important his father really was.

His father was secretly using an important governmental position to prepare his son for the possibility of having to go the later journey he was now undertaking. His father's actions were so subtle they went unnoticed even to his son until Steven was leaving.

"Dr Burgard, sir, we may have found something."

A small sentence spoken, and perhaps innocently, and it had changed everything for Steven. He was seventeen by then, and the words set his mind racing…

"What did they find?"

It would be a full year before Steven would get accepted as a scientist. He knew he'd work on the mechanical devices or be involved in the laboratory work, or it would usually be a type of work new scientists would be doing in the early years while also helping with some research, or helping people studying to be another scientist. That was how, a couple years later, he'd ended up teamed up with Elizabet.

After a number of years of this routine of visits, Steven had discovered rather unexpectedly that the Academists were busy with a sort of research of their own, when their normal work generally involved the more mundane governmental realities of running the city Utopus, and up to that moment Steven hadn't realised what sort of work that might be…

10.

IF HE TOOK THE TIME to think things over now, about what those events entailed at the time when he was seventeen, one thing had struck him as odd. Every person who'd addressed his father had always only ever addressed him as Dr Burgard. It got Steven wondering why his father never got called by his first name, and so the boy asked him one day.

"In this place, they can take first names from us. I keep mine from being known for that reason," he'd answered flatly, adding after a short pause, "and perhaps, one day, I can tell you why I did this. But not right now. Not when there's too much uncertainty hanging in the air that's putting everyone on edge."

Steven had been rather certain that his father had wanted to tell me more in that moment, but the twisted scowl on his face demonstrated acutely that he'd felt uncomfortable talking about whatever was on his mind there in that place.

"It's best you discover for yourself what's going on and then be certain who you trust with sharing such knowledge, okay," was all he'd whisper to Steven a few minutes later, and after that the conversation was never brought up again.

Then, a day after the brief conversation with his father, Steven had checked what they had discovered and he was immediately curious why the Academists, and not any scientists, had been dealing with the find. Steven also arrived in the room where a man had led his father to an object on a work bench, with Steven closely following them. Steven glanced around and noticed that in this room there were various pieces of equipment, and most of them had looked old.

I guess they could be remnants from five hundred years ago.

The man, who had guided Dr Burgard to the room, had now walked to a side table on which a large, metallic cube shape was sitting. He flipped a single switch. Steven just watched on and noticed his father listen for a moment, then he looked at the man as if he was going to ask him stuff about the cube. But Steven didn't wait for any explanation, and walked closer to the cube and knelt next to the it to be close to where the sounds were emanating, and then he also listened to the sounds coming from it carefully.

"Where is that sound coming from?" his father asked then.

Steven was more like 'what' rather than a 'where' in regards of the sound. He now wanted to know what the sound might be, and to him it had a rhythmic quality. He could hear that some sounds sounded like long hisses, and others sounded like the sound of water dripping from a tap.

"It's a message," he'd blurted out. His father was immediately interested in the nature of the sound as well but the man beside him had sounded sceptical then.

"A message?" he'd stated flatly, after which he'd said something to my father that had me angry for the remainder of the day. "Dr Burgard, I hope he's not a scientist. You know we don't want their kind here. Not with the risk of—"

Steven's father had responded angrily too, and it made Steven curious why. "Hush your mouth," he hissed at me rather than at the man who'd insulted me just now, then he said something cause the boy to get involved in their discussion. "He gets it from his mother, quite likely…!"

Steven got furious because he still loved his mother, and he was deeply missing her.

"What do you even know of my mother…?" Steven had screamed at them. "She had to go away—She had to go."

Steven remembered the room becoming silent. Because no one had responded to his unexpected question, he ran from the room and rushed home. He recalled his last words before leaving. "They can try to figure out for themselves what the hell *that* pile of junk is."

✳ ✳ ✳

Steven had walked home in a hurry after the outburst and he remembered slamming the outer door of the apartment somewhat harder than he'd meant to. His father had arrived home two hours later, and he'd said nothing about what had happened at the Academy. An hour later, they ate the soup his father had heated silently. They ate silently.

Again, the soup had caused the boy to get vivid memories of a woman walking away from Utopus on an old road leading away from here, towards the south somewhere.

That evening they didn't talk at all, and both stomped to our respective bedrooms for much needed sleep.

Steven woke early the following day, and he was surprised to find that his father hadn't left for the Academy yet, when normally he'd be gone from the house by the time the sun had risen. He sat staring into the space ahead of him with a face that could have been chiseled out of stone. He had his lips tight like he was controlling his emotions hard, as if he was attempting to stop himself from becoming angry.

Steven was still uncertain if the man's anger was directed at his son, or at something or someone else…

Maybe he was angry because his son had told him so abruptly that he wanted to apply to the University, and Steven could tell him he'd already done this. He couldn't tell what emotions were going through his father's mind at that moment when he sat down opposite of his father with disgusting cold porridge. It was tasting more like the paste they might put on the walls to make certain that the cold would stay out.

He looked up at his father, and they stared at one another for a while emotionless. So today of all days he felt forced to lower his gaze first, when usually Steven was who stared the longest defiantly at the other person. His father's next words, and even the tone in which he spoke them, shocked the boy.

"I want you to accompany me today to the Academy Institute, and when you're there, I want you to assist me with research on the object," his father whispered, "and there's something about the object that is puzzling me, and I think I can trust you more than most of them there."

Steven almost dropped the spoon from his hand when he heard these words.

He trusts me, was Steven's first thought, and then he thought, *and I better not mention that I've applied to the University for real…*

Steven knew he could choose whichever career he wanted to follow as soon as he was eighteen, and that his father could protest all he wanted over his son's choice but that he had no right to oppose the choice. He'd be eighteen in seven months from this day, just a week after they'd declare the start of the autumn. He knew that it usually took a year for a letter of acceptance to arrive.

He had thought this delay would give him ample time to help his father with whatever he was enlisting his son to help with, and that it also would give him enough time to persuade his father of the intended career choice. But despite these thoughts whirling through his mind now, Steven couldn't get the comment that had been made by the rude colleague of his father out of his mind, either…

Steven was remembering during his second evening of sleeping in the bunker how he'd laid awake during that day's night thinking about everything had happened before and after going back to the Academic Institute, before he had managed to finally fall asleep.

"We don't want their kind here. Not with the risk."

What had been even more curious was that his father hadn't let the man complete the sentence he was saying. Likely, the man had intended to throw an insult at whatever it meant to be a scientist, and his father wouldn't let him finish whatever he was saying. Steven wondered what the risk might be. Why was it so bad to be a scientist?

He recalled asking a question. "Father," he'd asked hesitantly. "What did he mean about me?"

"I'll explain about it more tonight at home, okay," his father had answered. "Today I need your mind on other matters. I need to you to help me figure out the function of this object so we know what the pattern means. It seems you had an idea about it."

"I thought it sounded like a pattern of some sort," Steven had answered him.

Steven was feeling awkward this day. It seemed he got entrusted by his father to help with a type of important task, yet he'd kept things from me.

They'd normally have lively debates about various topics on the rare mornings that they'd spent together, such as about how life might have been like for the people living four or five hundred years ago, we might have discussed about why Utopus was in existence additionally, although he could say with certainty that these discussions had been rare in the last few years.

We'd rarely discuss my mother.

The only two times that Steven could recall hearing his father speak of her was about seven months after she'd left when his father made a mysterious but short comment: "I hope she, they, are well."

Steven never got an explanation for what his father meant by the words, especially the part when he'd said 'they.'

His mother was often in his mind, and every time Steven had arrived home, he'd expected her to be sitting in the kitchen waiting for us. When she was still around she'd always ask us what we had done on that day, and on most days it would have involved tagging along with his father as he would go to his work. Steven also remembered sitting at his father's work, waiting for him on a narrow bench that was placed at intervals in a corridor there.

* * *

So, we didn't understand all of the message immediately. Not at first. But once we understood it, the impact was profound on every person in the room.

Understanding that the message was speaking of a strange disease that had devastated the entire planet almost came later. In the message, we'd discover that the people of a few hundred years ago had thought it was a disease. According to the recording the disease had happened close to the end of what they were calling the 'twenty-first century.'

The message would never name the culprits and the recording referred to what they had done as a crime. Neither did the disease get named, and Steven was certain immediately that it had happened so fast that no one had time to come up with a name.

However, we had worked out quite quickly that the message was reminding us that soon it would have been 370 years ago that the first Subject had been sent out, and this made it clear to Steven that he had three years left before he'd know who the next one would be.

Elizabet, the others there, and me too, all glanced at one another, all knowing that it could be any of us there who could get selected in a few years from now. Steven caught Elizabet's cautious expression, and she seemed to convey: 'be careful.' He wasn't totally certain why she'd felt he needed to be careful.

He had heard the message when he was almost twenty years old.

Steven was hearing a sound ahead, and he looked towards his father, and some thirty minutes later when they were about to walk to one of the upper floors a third structure appeared to be visible at some distance from us, but when he glanced back again, it was completely gone.

The conversation that his father was having with the man had bored me, because it involved more decision-making stuff.

Steven had guessed from the things he'd observed at the Academic Institute that a lot of decisions had to be made to ensure the safety of the people who'd survived World War 3, especially once many of the survivors got to Utopus. His father had told him that something like eight billion people had lived on the planet before this final war, and that only a percent of them had survived it…

Later, he'd discovered that the message was connected to the war in the most unimaginable ways.

Steven wondered often as to how they might have kept Utopus so clean with eighty million people living there. He was living there in a building of five floors high in District 18-B, and he was living on the fourth floor with his father. Elizabet had lived a floor higher in her building which was somewhat bigger. His building was a slender building with north and south facing apartments, and there were fifty of them on each floor. There were two small bedrooms, each with enough space for a single bed, a small table, a chair, and a narrow cupboard for clothing. There was a living room just as small, with space for two cushioned chairs, a small table with two chairs, and another cupboard…

There was a balcony but his father had never visited it. Steven, by contrast, would sit there, especially during the summer months.

The kitchen was small and had another table and two chairs in it.

We had a shower because he had fixed it, and it was an extra luxury most there didn't possess. We never needed to wash in the stale water in the cellar, which might have been rainwater, although the smell there had sometimes been so awful that it's likely it's also urination—or perhaps excrement…

Let's just say that the area downstairs was so filthy that Steven refused to go there, and the few times he needed to go, he was glad when he would be back home. Then he'd sit on the balcony to get the smell out of his nose. So sitting there had soon become a habit…

So, he'd wonder if the story of everyone having a clean environment, good housing, good health and a decent amount of food available was as true as was claimed. Steven thought that externally the illusion might have held up, but not if you looked around the city carefully. He'd noticed the people who would go hungry more often than should be the situation…

They go hungry, Steven thought angrily.

Steven also thought that the population all around him was in decline as he could see too few children for it to be natural. He would see people sitting on their own balconies who were as old as his father, and sometimes even older than that.

On the day when Steven had followed his father to work, they were met by three men, and then another man had arrived a moment before they began to speak, and he recalled that particular man glowering at me, as if to say with the staring that Steven didn't belong there.

Steven looked as angry at this man as he did at Steven. When they departed and went to the room with the cube again, Steven followed them, saying nothing, and he remembered what his father had whispered before we'd arrived there.

"Remember you're here to study the cube we found. Whatever happens, you need to keep calm and work on that."

They all worked hard to decipher the message. This was work that was going to take us many months to complete, and when they finally figured a way to hear the message clearly out, it even gave Steven the chills, and he wasn't the sort of person to be spooked so easily. There was definitely a correlation between the message, the reason Steven was chosen as Subject later on and what his father had done next.

Steven still remembered how his father stared at him from across the room as we listened to the first part of the message that we'd deciphered only a month later…

Thirty individuals total listened to the message. His father obviously knew or had guessed when he looked at Steven that his son would be a scientist, because their work in the Academic Institute made Steven even more determined to be one. His father had looked in the same way at him on the day when he'd open the letter addressed to him.

Dr Burgard looked at his son, knowing he couldn't alter what was to come next.

Steven would often sit with Elizabet, with them watching the vista of Utopus from Steven's small balcony. She'd often visit him, always bringing with her a basket of food and drink. We never talked a lot, but when we did talk we'd never discussed the choosing of a Subject which was to occur this year…

They'd met once more in adulthood when his father assigned to him further researching the cube, and he'd asked for a team of researchers to assist his son. Steven had ended up with four men and two women in his new team, who'd work tirelessly with him on the project, although he had caught the occasional, "What the hell are we doing this for?" from them all.

Steven knew that both Elizabet and him risked being chosen as a Subject, but he preferred it this way. They could have selected her in an equal measure, but he didn't think she would have coped with Zone Zero so he was glad he got chosen instead. He might cope in Zone Zero, and he was doubting she would have made it far.

11.

As children, they'd always clambered over the small pockets of the old city that had still existed in a few places, and it might have made her more resilient that any other person here might give her credit for, or that he gave her credit for. She was who had decided where we'd go or what we'd do on most days. Unlike other girls, who were growing up at the same time as them, Elizabet had liked to go for hikes, swims, or to explore the old parts of the ancient city that had existed before Utopus had been founded.

"How do you think they lived back then?" Elizabet asked him once.

"I don't know," he had said. "Probably they had jobs, and they did things that we don't even know what they are anymore."

"I wonder what sort of jobs," she had said to him.

"Many more than we have now," Steven had responded. "You cannot call choosing between being a scientist or an academist much of a choice."

She'd leaned her head on his shoulder that day for companionship, though it didn't feel like any type of a romantic gesture or anything of the sort. It had more a sense of finality to it. Like, she had felt she would never meet him again in this way after that evening.

She'd seemed shy, almost withdrawn the following day when Steven had arrived at work, and she refused to look at him even when he tried to encourage it.

Steven was confused and it took him a long while to realise that things were different between us on that day. He was certain she had never expected to display her feelings to him so openly that final night. He had never realised that she had such feelings until he had been travelling for many months already through Zone Zero.

Perhaps, other reasons had existed as well, but he didn't know the reasons until later that day. He never had any time to be alone with her after that evening. She'd hugged him before she left, and he had hugged back, and in hind side he realised now that his effort had seemed a bit too half-hearted compared to hers.

It had been obvious that she'd been trying to tell me more, and he was too foolish to not realise it until it was too late for it.

He was remembering the room where we were doing our research. It was on the fifth floor of Academic Institute, which was in itself highly unusual, but this was arranged by his father so no one was ever speaking of it, or protesting about it. Steven would often look at the two buildings, the University and the Academic Institute, as he was sitting on his little balcony.

Steven remembered when he'd squinted his eyes, and how he'd tried to look at the small windows of the left building, trying to see if he could look through the windows of the fifth floor behind which, on occasion, Elizabet would still be working hard even after I'd gone home with my father. His father refused to let him stay behind without him being there with his son at the same time, which was another of the things that had heightened my curiosity about the things going on even more. Steven did notice that he would go there often on his own, and often many hours before sunrise, and he'd also often come home when it was already at least two or more hours after the evening darkness had set in.

Steven was missing Elizabet, and if things had been much different, he was certain that he might eventually have found out if the feelings between them were mutual or not. These feelings that were overwhelming him had started when he had realised how lonely he was feeling in Zone Zero.

The entire fifth floor got set aside for the research into the message that he'd deciphered in part when I was seventeen. Soon he'd discovered also that it was rather interesting there. We, the people who were doing the research, and perhaps ten others, were the only ones who would use the floor, whereas the rest of the building had three or four hundred people using them.

Before Steven had become a scientist, progress had been slow, and when he became eighteen, and therefore had started working proper at the University, his father had planned for him to continue in this function of researching the cube, even though it was normal for the new people joining the University as a learner to not have a say really in the types of projects or tasks he or she would get assigned to.

✳ ✳ ✳

Something about the message had seemed to keep his father's attention, and his attention and interest for the message grew rather than waned. Something about the message also made Steven wonder whether he was listening to a message originating from the past. It seemed to him like the message sender knew of the existence of Utopus, and more so than it being some sort of future project, but also that there's something more sinister with that place.

All seven of us had been working almost every day on clearing up the message. It was intensive work, but for Steven, it was also and intriguing endeavour. Initially, the six other people who worked on the project with him had their doubts about the work. It had been Elizabet who was the first person to be convinced about the validity of the work.

She had helped him convince the others.

After about a year, a sense of camaraderie had developed between all of us, and the others even had extended it towards Steven's father, who'd come to visit the research room from time to time. We had the transmission cleaned up into several distinct voices after about a year. One voice was interesting…

We became good friends during those years, and the friendship was probably also what helped my father later when he started listening with us to the messages.

The woman's voice in the recording said the most unexpected of messages: "Don't go into Zone Zero. It isn't safe there."

Steven wondered immediately why someone didn't want any of us to go into Zone Zero. If this was a message from a distant past, why did the person know about the zone, when it was a more recent name for the region. According to his father, the name for the area outside Utopus had only existed from the moment when no one was able to see any live animals in the regions directly bordering Utopus anymore…

His father had explained that the stillness made things so menacing for the people within Utopus, and this was the ultimate reason, or price perhaps, for them staying inside Utopus. According to his father, they didn't want to leave Utopus.

Something was very familiar about the voice in the message. Steven was certain it was what the message was saying in that familiar voice, that would become the driving force to keep going forward with everything he was doing. He also saw the reaction of the message on his father, and his father seemed to have to turn away from us all when he'd heard the message. Steven was now wondering if it was because his father had known its significance.

And therefore, his father also knew what the connection was between the warning relayed in the message, and the fate of any person travelling outside Utopus as a Subject now. If there was even anyone doing that anyway. Although, Steven was travelling there so soon…

After Steven had listened to the message, he went home, and he witnessed once again the strangeness of the third structure being there and then not being there. He wondered then about it, and wondered why that structure always felt it was there, and yet not.

Steven was certain the adults in Utopus were blocking out that building from being known by their children to protect them. He couldn't explain how it was done, or even why, but there was something going on with it that made knowing about it dangerous for anyone who acknowledged its presence. Maybe that was the first instance that I'd set in motion things that had happened later in Zone Zero.

Steven always seemed to have seen it first not there, then there, and then again not there. His father had always blocked the building from his son's mind somehow too, but then the day them choosing a Subject was looming, and it seemed to be there more often, and felt more menacing too.

He'd often stopped and stared at the third structure after we had listened to the message, like it would mean he could suddenly decipher its reason for existing within Utopus.

Actually, he had to admit there was a rugged beauty to the structure, and this was first pointed out by Elizabet when she had been sitting beside him on his small balcony. This had happened during one of her rare visits, and he'd assumed she'd come to view the vista, but then she'd mentioned the structure to him, and it was there, and he'd been certain that it hadn't been there just before she arrived. Steven recalled how they'd both commented that it seemed to glint in the sunlight with an uncommon fierceness.

He'd grinned at Elizabet's stubbornness to defy the norm. She did nothing in the same way as anyone else, but she'd changed after my selection, and he still wondered if part of it had something to do with his father warning her to be careful.

Again, she'd placed her head on Steven's shoulder, but it had seemed she did it more from a sense of habit, like perhaps she and her father might have done once, or maybe for once she did it because she actually genuinely enjoyed my company just then.

He was missing our sense of companionship often.

A few days later, the transmission was completely deciphered, and Dr Burgard had called for the people who'd heard the initial part of the transmission, which was just a mess of hisses and dripping sounds but it had been him who'd initially noticed the pattern in the sound.

His father said later, after we got home, that during World War 2, there were people who decoded sounds to warn others about things that an enemy was planning to do. He told him to keep this information in mind while working on the cube.

Steven didn't really understand what his father had meant. He realised it later when he had read something about the process of decoding in the war. But during the research into the cube, we discovered that there was a decoding device within the cube. And now these hisses and dripping sounds transformed into people's voices.

There were four distinct voices in the first part of the transmission, and the first part had sounded like someone was relaying a news bulletin…

—On 13 June 2002, the United States of America, of the old world, of five hundred years ago, withdrew from what they knew as the Anti-Ballistic Missile Treaty. They had ratified this treaty earlier to prevent potential wars with mass-destructive weapons. It was replaced with the Strategic Offensive Reduction Treaty, which was later replaced by the New Strategic Arms Reduction Treaty, which was signed into existence in a city called Prague, and came into force from 5 February 2011, and it was then believed to be a treaty to be renewed every ten years.

Before 2021, a five-year period of uncertainty in most countries kept them at a heightened level of security alertness because of certain statements made by the leaders of several nations. None of the information relating to those statements exists now. When 2021 came, the treaty was renewed, and was last renewed in 2071. It's believed that with each renewal of the treaty, the rogue organisation became more determined to cause a major disruption to the status quo.

It organised certain activities which caused most nations to unify into a strategic force to combat it. A year later, events were happening that caused further measures, which is why Utopus exists. If you were to look at the history of events, there were mistakes made on many levels.

We didn't deal effectively and fully to combat the people who came until between one and two decades later.

There's a name they used in those old days for what their actions were, which won't have any meaning to you, so I won't repeat it, and because we don't know who else can hear this transmission, it's too dangerous to say this information right now.

There was an organisation set up when the people in power had noted a rise in activity.

Its name was the International Criminal Court. They established it to prosecute the individuals who were deemed a threat to the world's security. Its mission was to prosecute the people who were deemed criminals, with the blood on their hands of not just a few, but the blood and freedom of thousands, if not more. That organisation was set up with an idealistic approach, and no one who set it up thought one day all this would happen.

That the crime would be so great that most of the world would be gone. But I'll go through the list of the crimes that the people who did this action were guilty of, and are still guilty of:

First Measure, Article 7.

This document lists the crimes that were done against humanity to cause widespread death and damage, and to be the foundation of a systematic attack directed against any civilian population knowing that this attack would lead to certain outcomes such as extermination, deportation or forcible transfer of population, and imprisonment or other severe deprivation of physical liberty.
We're under the extreme belief that this is still ongoing, with an ongoing threat within Zone Zero of this nature. We urge caution to anyone who might be able to listen to this message to not enter the zone. Danger lies within, which we are still neutralising all these centuries later. We understand a message exists from that time of so long ago, which states: "We shall never surrender." We're of a belief that it's the people who had stated the message five hundred years ago, are the people who causing the events in later years.
As is understood, a chemical or bio-engineered weapon of some sort was used to start the conditions of Zone Zero.
We're therefore also adding the wording of Article 8 to the list of charges against the people who were or are responsible.

Article 8 defines war crimes based on one of two conditions.

The first condition is negligible, as proof exists that the action wasn't committed by any one nation—unless you call the people who gave the warning "We will never surrender" any kind of nation. We therefore determined it to be the action of a rogue group against various nations. We've uncovered historical proof that they meant to deceive the world with their actions.

And many of the people of five hundred years ago, thought that their action would only ever be as attacks against soft targets, but we didn't expect them to utilise their funding for the measures they took to be so thorough with the threat they posed to the world.

In Article 8, it states that the wilful killing of civilians is a criminal act, and as their actions are still present by our last estimation, we are actively pursuing prosecution of the said rogue organisation, or whoever is still alive within it, to be charged with this crime. We furthermore also assume to prosecute them with the biological experiment that they did, which gave them the misplaced confidence to send out agents across this world, and to unleash the means to cause harm to humanity in such numbers across the world. They wilfully had caused an immense pain and suffering, and were the direct cause of the 99 percent mortality rate experienced worldwide.

Under this same Article 8, we're also charging them with unlawful confinement and of taking hostages, although we cannot go further into these charges now. We are of the belief that these charges to be admissible even though no normal administration of government has existed since the events of 2071, and when the horror of this event was unleashed so brutally on the world. We're the people acting in response to the last resolution that the United Nations of five hundred years ago had passed. The resolution was passed in 2086 in response to the increasing death toll the world was experiencing, and this measure is seen as a means to an end to teach humanity this: "Never again."

We hope for others who survive elsewhere have also been told this message: Don't go into Zone Zero. It isn't a safe place. We give you this grave warning.—

And that's where the message had ended rather unexpectedly and in Steven's mind also causing more mysteries to be added to those he was already aware of or had guessed from time to time.

Who is she…?

Utopus was a strange building which no one in Utopus wanted to approach. Steven had looked inside this building a cold evening after receiving the binoculars from his father, which Steven had called affectionately a 'distance viewer' because he'd liked a nickname for the device over its real name. This building was proving what the second message had told us. That this 'World War 3' never had happened with any nuclear weapons.

12.

THEY HADN'T UNDERSTOOD ALL THE messages immediately. Understanding that these messages were speaking of a strange disease that had devastated the planet, that came later, was an important message for us to accept and learn from because the knowledge of this information made it more clear than ever before that they were still living in a dangerous world with the perpetrators unaccounted for. In this message, they had discovered that the people just of a few hundred years ago had assumed it was simply a disease. According to the recording found, the disease had happened close to the end of what they'd earlier had referred to as the 'twenty-first century.'

The message had never named the culprits of the crime, and referred to their actions definitively as a crime. But what the message didn't do is tell where the culprits were from, or what happened to them after 2072, so Steven could only assume they'd perished like almost all the world had done. They hadn't named either the disease or the perpetrators of its spread, and it happened so fast that no one had time to come up with a name for the disease.

They'd worked out that it was as soon as 360 years ago the first Subject got sent out or maybe even earlier than that, and the recording made it clear to Steven he had three years left then before he'd know who the next Subject would be. Elizabet, the others there, and Steven too, all had looked at one another, each knowing that any of us to be selected in a few years from now.

Steven had closely listened another time to the message when he was almost twenty. Hearing such a type of message was a heavy burden for any person, but for a young person like himself, or like Elizabet, or any of the other young people in the room, the burden was exceedingly heavy.

Steven wondered how much he actually really knew of the life there. He grew up in the part of Utopus which had seemed to be the part where all English-speaking people had ended up in. In total, there were sixty densely populated districts in Utopus, and each seemed to have people living in them who would speak a specific language.

Elizabet had been living in the district north-west to his with the 'border' cutting between theirs in the middle of the familiar old dirt path they'd traverse to leave for adventure and which they'd use to arrive home, and they could just about see each other's balcony if they stretched out their necks far enough, though their voices had echoed across with ease in comparison. So, that was how they'd ended up playing together as children a few years later.

He'd assumed their friendship had originally started with each of them just waving at the other individual sitting on the other balcony, with feet dangling from the edge, each daring to defy the warnings of it being dangerous to do such things. Then, a day had come when there was an unexpected loud knock on their outer door. Apparently, the girl had pointed out her friend's balcony to whoever she was living with, and had asked this person if she could go see her friend, to see if the friend wanted to play with her and apparently had promised to be careful if they went out for walks. Steven had immediately realised that he had wanted to play, especially so, because playing with Elizabet, as he discovered rather quickly, was always an adventure of some sort...

Their neighbouring districts were rather neatly ordered into a set of straight streets, lined on either side with ten buildings each side, and each row of building was five floors with dozens of small dwellings on each floor though there were also people who'd sleep in the corridors while this was frowned on. The location of the apartment I had shared with his father had been on the most north-eastern corner of the district. The balcony had overlooked the sparse remnants of what would once have been a massive lake and riverbed bordering what they once had called Stockholm.

He could see easily, when he glanced down from the fourth floor, that the sporadic remnants of the old city still dotted the landscape between the hundreds of buildings now making up the news city Utopus. However, he didn't think that anyone who'd lived in old Stockholm would consider his Utopus a city.

It was more of a place of refuge, and the pretence that there was good housing, plenty of water and food, and that it had clean streets was an illusion that most people might have accepted, but not him, and he was certain not his father either.

He remembered the speeches they would make in the Central District. It was during those speeches when it was most evident of how many people were really living in Utopus. Men. Women. Only relatively few children. In those speeches, they were always telling us that the things going on in the city, in Utopus, were okay, and that everyone was glad, and that everyone had to accept that 'this' was how the world was now and nothing could change it…

The words had sounded so hollow to Steven's sceptical mind.

Steven always saw the opposite of what the people with their long speeches were saying, and although he had never see anyone in the city die from starvation, it was very hard for his practical mind to work out what was so good about the city. He assumed his father had a hard time too with believing anything said, and he was supposed someone in charge.

Utopus didn't look at all like the cities Steven had seen in the few pictures of hundreds of years ago which his father had showed him. In those pictures, the streets looked clean, and there was a sense of variety in them that was missing from Utopus. Everything in Utopus was just grey and white colours, if you were to examine the buildings and some of the buildings of Sweden, as his father had stated they were of the old city, were red. No buildings here were ever red…

The buildings in other photos that my father had showed him, the buildings could have a multitude of colour, and they'd have occasional lights on them too in many colours. His father had told him that the buildings with lights were showing public buildings where people had collected food, clothing or other things.

In Utopus, only two buildings were considered the important, and three if you included a structure with the capability to appear and disappear. The University was where scientists worked or studied. It was a massive building with brown beams, many glass windows, and six floors.

It was the closest building to where my father and him were living, and Steven had often walked over the dried-out riverbed near his house to get there in an easier, quicker method. He'd walk west to the nearest bridge and he he'd cross the bridge to get to the Academic Institute. Whenever the boy had been walking to this location with his father, they usually would take this route. If Steven was walking there alone, his route would be directly north over the riverbed. And this route most often would cause him to walk past the third structure.

One thing that Steven had quickly realised about Utopus was how sparse the information about everything and how limited the knowledge seemed to be. By the time they'd uncovered the second part of the transmission, it was only two years left until they'd select a next Subject, and Steven recalled there was an increase in the sense of urgency that his father had showed in uncovering the full transmission. His father had seemed as much urgency to uncover the message as Steven did himself.

For Steven, the urgency was different by then. It would be two years before they were selecting a Subject, and if he was selected he wouldn't be around anymore to work on this project. It seemed that by the time he was thinking such thoughts even Steven himself was enjoying the work.

His father and had often looked up at the night sky to see if between us might have been able to locate whatever had been capable, still, to relay the signal even if we'd both been convinced that nothing of the old equipment of five centuries was capable of surviving the passage of time. This reasoning never had explained how the cube had survived. If it was capable of functioning after this long there could be other equipment from the past capable of the same. The message had been uncovered, but we saw nothing up there. Steven, however, was convinced, although privately, there was a link between the streaks of fire visible in the sky occasionally, and the reduction of repeats of the signal being picked up by them as work went on.

That must also be the direct cause for my father's urgency, too.

Whatever it was, up there, that was sending out the signals was losing its power, and was now crashing back to the planet, or Earth, as people of the past who had sent out the machines to send the signals had been calling this world.

They were already aware that World War 3 had been started by something that a rogue organisation had done to the world. What it was exactly wasn't yet clear until much later. They knew the signal was repeating all the time, but that every day it was now diminishing in strength. There were people at the Academic Institute who'd immediately been convinced that the signal had been sent out four centuries ago, but neither Steven's father nor Steven himself thought this was correct.

Something about the message was indicating to us that there was more, but unknown urgency to find out what really was going on, and that was why his father was always making certain that his son was among the people working on the signal. But then, the dreaded year 2522 had arrived, and therefore the year in which a Subject was chosen, and it had happened despite the urgency of the warning against sending anyone out there… or, perhaps, in spite of the warning.

* * *

But, right now, Steven still had two years to go until the selection was happening and his mind was always contemplating what would happen when they, unexpectedly, had uncovered the second part of the message.

The second part of the message had gone into greater detail of what threat the people had been facing all those centuries in the unknown past. Apparently, the message would therefore confirm that the method wasn't by any weapons that the people of five centuries ago possessed known by the rather ominous name of 'nuclear weapons.' The first part of the message had been correct when it had mentioned in this portion that a 'chemical or bio-engineered weapon of some sort' was used for the attack...

From what we could understand of the plan, they'd believed that attacking a few soft targets would never give them the means to win whatever war they were waging, so they'd stepped up their actions by a few notches, and had used the wealth they had amassed over the next few decades to engineer a more lethal weapon which no one had expected and had suspected would be used until it was too late...

The decimation of humanity, and of almost all the animals that had existed at the time, hadn't come from a nuclear weapon but from a type of bio-engineered weapon, and it had caused a 99 percent mortality rate, and the effects its devastation were still visible if a person was looking closely enough at Zone Zero.

The initial selected Subject had left in the year 2152, so the events described in the message had happened by the year 2142. But personally, Steven was of the belief that the events had really started in the year 2072, when the rogue organisation had emerged. Whatever they'd done had taken around seventy years to take hold fully everywhere over following decades, and not a matter of days as some people around Steven were assuming. If they'd unleashed the war with a bio-engineered weapon of some sort, it took long for its effects to be noticed or felt...

Steven was uncertain if the people living on the planet at the time had known at all what was happening to their world, but the people who'd sent the message to us had knowledge of the facts it seemed. The second message was going to clarify much more of what was going on back then as we would discover in the following weeks. Then we'd ended up with decoding the rest of the messages sufficiently to get an increasingly disturbing message of facts and news, but then, as time went on, and as it got closer to choosing the next Subject, Steven had noted a disturbing change in the people working with his father, as well in the people who were on my team. For the most part...

During the following summer we'd uncover the most important segment of the second part of the message. Proving that the second part of the message was the most crucial part that we'd need to pay the most attention to. The message gave us many clues about the past, and again such list of clues would end with warning us. This part of the message seemingly had wanted to relay information dating from around the year 2056 and onward, and from the message, we'd realised that the world had already been altered by the time the later events would happen, as relayed within this message.

—In 2051, a failed coup that apparently took place at the same time in several nations had taken place in what had been the European Union.

It became a certainty from the finding resulting from our investigations that the actions of unknown outside forces had caused these events, and that the people who were behind the events were the same people who'd stated, "We will never surrender."

As was stated in the earlier part of the recording, there had been no normal governmental administration in any part of the world since around 2071, and then about a year later, war had been declared on the world by this same rogue group. Everyone listening in the room was immediately assuming that this indicated that it meant an all-out attack with weapons, such as their stock-piled nuclear bombs and other destructive weapons at their disposal, got utilised for their attack. When no such attack came, they had assumed that they'd avoided war, but then the illness had taken hold in many countries at the same time.

One of the final few functioning governmental organisations that was still active in 2071 was apparently the World Health Organisation, and every person in the room agreed that they could have been the intended target of the rogue organisation in the first place, which had determined that the new disease would be more serious than "SARS" had been previously which had previously been identified to be among one of the worst diseases to still be present within the general population, apparently since the eradication of AIDS and related diseases in 2057, and the creation of a vaccine for both diseases in the years 2053 and 2058…

We all therefore assumed that they had assumed they would have been able to eradicate SARS in a similar fashion, and it seemed that they were partially successful with this by 2065.

However, then came the year 2072 when the aforementioned rogue organisation had started spreading the lethal bio-engineered weapon across the world, which had ultimately caused the 99 percent mortality rate by 2142.—

Steven and everyone else were still uncertain in what way they had spread the 'disease' so fast across the planet, but further investigations determined a probable cause though such investigations were going to take a long time to complete. Steven didn't realise back then that he'd be three times older by the time the world had a semblance of peace restored to it.

—Their belief now was that the rogue organisation had used certain insects - which were also dead because of their actions - with bio-engineered alterations to their cell structure to spread their engineered disease. We figured out from our evidence that had somehow already been in our possession, though uncertain how or from where, that one lone person could have easily carried one of these insects with them in luggage. For the rogue organisation, it seemingly had soon become so much more lucrative and maybe even easier to send people out with these insects than to smuggle drugs or weapons into other countries. Though we never found out if the people in the rogue organisation even survived what they unleashed.—

"It's like they had opened Pandora's box," Dr Burgard said. No one asked for a meaning and we all somewhat instinctively know what he might have meant though we neither knew the origin of the words or how he knew them. We were still determining the connection between this event and the failed coup within several of the nations within the old European Union, however we did understand that certain undetermined events of 2016 had also triggered those later events.

The rogue organisation had sent out individuals to every country when the coup didn't happen, but they did end up sending most of the men and women within their ranks into Europe, where they knew they could do the greatest damage.

13.

THE BIO-ENGINEERED AGENT WITHIN THE particle that was inside the insects got delivered via the insects used for the effort into plants, animals, humans and the food consumed by all. Steven recalled then that no one had bothered eating from the platters with bread that had been present in the room next to where they'd been doing their research.

—For the plant life of every location, where the group had unleashed these infected insects, the effect on the plants had an added symptom that they'd affect other plants, and rather than killing the plants outright, and this had caused the events of disease and death to spiral out of control without people realising what was going… until it was too late. People just couldn't keep checking everywhere sufficiently. The natural biological hierarchy of plants being eaten by animals, and then some being eaten either by other animals, or in the stock of cattle which had existed in Europe being eaten by humans, was inevitably happening next…

The illness didn't happen immediately, and we were certain now that the goal of the bio-engineered toxin had been to be of a type that would build up as people were eating food, and that a day would come when the toxin would have reached a level at which it would become intolerable for humans, and this was when the 'disease' would strike the person down. The disease, in most cases, lasted a relatively short period of time from indigestion of the toxin to when the patient was close to mortality. Some of our group had then noted a comparison between the stages of this disease, and a disease that had existed in the early part of the twenty-first century, known then by the name of Parkinson's disease.

It was displaying the stages of its illness in the following way.

During stage one of the disease, a person would typically get mild symptoms, such as tremors or shaking of limbs. A person in this stage of the disease usually would have a loss of balance or abnormal facial expressions.

We'd believe, for a while, that the disease that began in 2072, was a variation of this illness, because of the similarities that were occurring to the people who'd reached the toxin level, at which the disease of 2072 would manifest itself.

The second stage of Parkinson's disease had often involved the inability of a person to walk or to maintain their balance, and we would see this as well in the illness that the rogue organisation had caused. However, after this, the differences between Parkinson's disease and the illness the rogue organisation would become more apparent. The patient would then suffer a complete shut-down of their organs and would complain of a severe pain in their digestive organs. They would take the patients to a hospital at this moment, and many doctors would have tried to save their lives, but too often when they had tried to operate on the patient, they would find something strange had happened with the person's organs. Whatever had been contained within the bio-engineered chemical that the rogue organisation spread, would literally have melted away the organs in such a way that you couldn't determine what had been someone's stomach, lungs, liver, heart, or kidneys.

Usually, the moment that a patient had got to this stage of this illness, progress had usually been so fast that in many nations around the world, no 'patient zero' could have been able to be determined.

Therefore, entire nations had declared themselves 'Zone Zero.'

It was why the regions outside Utopus were still carrying such a name, but as previously warned… it isn't safe in the zone.

Don't go there.

Zone Zero had become a code word to show that a nation was unsafe for others from outside it.

We'd determined that the general welfare and ability of a nation to look after its own needs, also had dictated whether it could withstand the illness the longest, and the most interesting finding according to the few scientists, who'd worked on dealing with the emergence and aftermath of the disease, was that the more isolated nations were the nations who'd ended up as its first victims.

Therefore, the year 2016 was so important to remember

according to the later scientists still trying to work on this disease. This was when we'd become isolated. And yet, it didn't matter, because the people within the rogue organisation had their own agenda. An agenda of actions that had resulted in the creation of Utopus, Zone Zero, and all the clear and present dangers which still exist now.—

And this was where the second message had ended.

Near Utopus there was a strange building which no one in Utopus seemed to want to approach. Steven had looked inside it one evening after receiving a device from my father, which he'd called 'distance viewer' because that sounded so much better than its real name. Steven was certain that the building was proving what the second message had told us. That this 'World War 3' had never happened with any nuclear weapons.

Steven had gone back to the building outside Utopus during an night after hearing the second part of the message. There was an reason that I knew was adding to the danger of our current situation was causing his curiosity to assert itself even more. He'd gone there again, maybe even for a final time before he would leave for good, to convince himself that he could go there, and that Zone Zero wasn't as dangerous as the woman, relaying most of the message, had tried to imply several times during the recording. The urgency was so apparent that it had almost become comical for all the wrong reasons…

He had waited until his father had gone asleep, then he'd put on some dark clothing and walked downstairs to bottom floor of the apartment building where I'd been living. A little girl, walking upstairs from the cellar had met me partway down, and Steven remembered putting his finger over his lips to make sure she'd keep quiet. He didn't even find out what her name was.

To his amusement, she'd copied his gesture, and he was uncertain for a moment if she'd ever told anyone about seeing me that night. She too was doing some exploration of her own kind when he'd met her, and possibly we did some trade-off. Steven wouldn't tell her parents she was out of her bed, and in return, she wouldn't tell anyone that she saw him.

He'd ran most of the way to get to what he'd perceived to be the 'border' of Utopus and looked around for likely people who might discover him that night. To him, it felt very much like one of his adventures from his childhood, only this time it wasn't through the rubble of the old city, Stockholm, that he was clambering, but instead it was his first taste of what Zone Zero might be like…

It took him almost an hour to reach the building he'd looked at with his father through the device his father had found and might want him to have for any journey his son might undertake. He was rather uncertain about what he'd find inside the building, and during the first visit I hadn't gone that far inside. It was just far enough to see the photo of a woman hanging in the first corridor after the first stairway inside the building.

Steven had learnt during the later journey that his father had got the name wrong of the device first as he'd first called it a telescope.

One thing that had intrigued Steven immediately about the strange underground building was that it had seemed to have been some sort of defensive structure. It was entirely underground, and there was a hatch of metal at the top. It might have been well-guarded, and it might have been enclosed by a metal fence of some sort when still in use, but nothing about the building had given him any clues about what its intended use had been…

Steven knew he didn't have long to check the building over, so he decided he needed to go check it once more later on, either many months before leaving or visit the place for several as he was leaving as Subject 37, and shortly after they'd found the third message, which was shorter in nature compared to the others, he took my chance to go check it again.

So, I've decided already I'm Subject 37, Steven thought as he stood in front of an old door, investigating it for a way to open it…

Steven had been walking through the dark building for an hour and had been trying to open a few of the doors in the first tunnel. Initially he'd almost given up and had sat beside the outer door on a cold stone for a while, thinking pensively at what to do. Would he just go home? Then he glanced at the door and give one more try. Then after he'd finally wedged open the outer door open, and then had squeezed through the narrow opening, and he'd walked through long empty tunnel. After fifteen minutes he'd found the first door…

He'd glanced for the longest time at the photo of the woman hanging in the first corridor, almost staring in a trance at her, and although he couldn't make out her features because he didn't have a light source with me, the one which my father would give me shortly before I'd leave for a final time, what I could see of her photo was breathtaking…

✳ ✳ ✳

Steven had arrived home long before his father had woken up. Steven now knew what was at stake for the remains of humanity, for both for himself, and for the world. Once he was inside the building, or at least the portion he could visit in the time that he had available, had been much more mysterious and larger than he'd ever imagined. He'd only dared to go to the end of the first tunnel. At the end of the tunnel, which had taken him an hour to traverse, split into two side tunnels. The left tunnel had the flicker of a light at the end of it.

"Too far away," Steven grunted under his breath. "I'll have to go there whenever I come back."

Steven stared for a moment in the other direction, and he was certain that the pitch black there could hide someone waiting to ambush him. He was certain that there was movement in the darkness. He was letting his imagination get the better of him. He frowned angrily.

"I need to check there but only when I have a lamp or something," Steven said, "and if you're there I'm NOT afraid of you, you know…"

His voice echoed, startling him into the realisation that he was throwing caution in the wind right now. There was an enemy somewhere. They could have a means of discovering him here through a method unknown to him. He needed to be careful, now even more than before. There was limited time left until the selection. He needed a plan to get him to be the choice…

* * *

After tiptoeing through the silent dwelling and glancing towards the bundle on the bed, which was his snoring father, Steven walked to his familiar almost defunct bedroom and dropped down on the bed. He was now going to travel to the Academic Institute without ever showing an ounce of protest of contention. Not even towards the Academists who were so against him being there…

If that place wasn't so destroyed and cleaner, Steven thought, *then many of us could be living there instead of this hell hole of a city. I'm certain that the place she's describing in the recording is also underground. Another bunker.*

Steven glanced towards the curtain when he could hear the first signs of his father possibly waking up. So he turned towards the wall and decided to pretend to sleep until his father called out for him for their breakfast. Not even his father could know what Steven was attempting to achieve in the few months before the selection was coming. In the end he'd cause the people who did the selecting process to have no other choice other than to choose a man called Steven Burgard…

***

So, today a new routine of Steven being a rule-abiding son and occupant of Utopus began, and if his father noticed the difference, he never showed any signs of knowing about his illicit visits to… somewhere. Steven hoped that his father would assume that the visits were to explore more of Utopus before any possible departure and not any visit outside, to an old bunker in Zone Zero, to a place possibly as old as the city itself, or older than that…

Steven now had a daring plan. A plan he wouldn't inform a soul about until the world was safe, or maybe not even then. He was prepared to take the plan as a secret to a grave…

***

The message Steven had been listening to was as follows:

—I'm uncertain of my surroundings here.

There's so much chaos here that it frightens me. One thing that's certain is that I miss them both. I had to leave them behind, and I'm not even certain if he remembers me. I cannot give any names here, as there's a risk of this message being heard by those who aren't benevolent. Danger still exists and it can harm them. Both of them.

I'm uncertain my message will ever reach them, but if he's like me, then he can uncover what's hidden within my messages, and therefore warn the others. He can send us information, which will help us make sure we can reverse what's going on. There are people around here that we cannot trust. If they discovered I'm sending these messages, I'd be at risk, and so would be all the people that I love… especially her. In particularly her.—

Steven was certain that this part of the message was more personal, almost like someone is dictating something to go into a journal they are writing about what goes on around them…

Steven was uncertain who the 'her' was who had spoken in the latest part of the messages to be deciphered. However, the woman who'd spoken was the same person who'd given the first two accounts of the disturbing events that had happened in the last five hundred years. She was a key to everything…

Steven had often wondered, after hearing the latest message and re-listening to all others when no one was around, whether the true purpose of a Subject was different from what we were being told about its purpose. The only way to know, was to wait for the day to come and for him to see who got selected -finally - and then see if this person would go into Zone Zero for real to do what they had wanted from them, or that the person would go into Zone Zero to do things with the message in mind. He was still hoping that the choice would be him.

There were so few who'd heard the message really, and Steven's father didn't want the knowledge of what it said to get known too widely.

When Steven had asked his father about the messages, he was quick to tell his son to keep quiet and did it rather abruptly, and only to discuss it when they were home, and therefore alone. He now knew there was a correlation between how his father had acted, and why his father had acted in a certain way in one of the last conversations between them of any length. The nature of his father's had been rather cryptic, and Steven had already been chosen as a Subject when it had happened…

"Be careful during your long travel. Always remember what was said in the message… about Zone Zero…"

"I will be careful, father," Steven had told him as a reply.

"I told you that there would be consequences if you chose a career as a scientist," his father said plainly to me in response.

"But it was my choice to make," Steven said to him flatly. He remembered scowling angrily at his father because he seemed to be talking to him like he was a thirteen-year-old boy rather than the almost twenty-two he was by then.

Steven felt anger well up in him, and he was ready to have a go at his father, but then his father looked at him with sad eyes, and when Steven looked even closer, he saw his father was crying openly, and he'd never known him to cry until then. What his father said next gave him the same chills down the spine as he'd felt a decade earlier…

"I was so certain that she'd succeed, but I'm uncertain that was the case really. Then—you became a Scientist just like her. And now they've selected you as a Subject, and because of this I cannot openly acknowledge you as a son anymore. Not really…"

His father had immediately and rather abruptly walked out of the living room to his own bedroom after the comment, and the only time after that Steven got the chance to speak to him afterwards was when the time came to say goodbye, and even the way this had happened odd. His comment had left me sitting there on a boulder just a few meters outside the border, staring after his hastily retreating figure with a puzzled expression, and me asking constantly, "Why?"

14.

BUT HE KNEW HE WAS getting ahead of himself now and he was realising why, so often, he'd been repeating historic information and various events in a monotone. So, he'd stared ahead and then repeated a process he'd been acting out many times before, knowing if anyone was watching him now, he'd appear like he'd gone quite mad…

* * *

So, Steven, you need to still tell yourself about what had happened in this last year before the selection was about to happen, Steven thought, *and I was very nervous during the following year. I kept remembering what my father had said. He'd told me that choosing the career as a scientist carried risks. I was concentrating on my work to decode more of the signal before the time literally ran out for me. I became more certain that of all the people who could be chosen that it should be me who was chosen. You now ask yourself why I'd want to be chosen for something that could be one of the most dangerous things possible to do. To be honest, I'm uncertain of why I had wanted to be a Subject, but something about everything I found out had compelled me to wanting to do it.*

He remembered only one departing Subject, and it was a rather strange event. He remembered only that from that day that his mother had departed and, according to his father, she had to go somewhere else. He wondered often if he told his son the truth about that day. However, seeing how he had reacted to the recordings was telling him that a lot more is going on around here. The warning in the messages was telling him that things are extremely dangerous. He was, until that last day in Utopus, uncertain of how dangerous it could be.

Steven thought that after the third message, the people at the Academic Institute stopped being interested in what was being said in the messages. Only his father, Elizabet, and Steven were there in the end to listen to the fourth message, which had elaborated further on the information that was given in the second message. But each message had a warning attached to it that became more and more desperate as more of it was relayed. He caught his father re-listen to some the recordings like they seemed to matter to him in some unknown way.

When his father noticed his son was looking at him, he didn't even hide his tears. Steven decided not to ask his father about his emotions. Steven thought it would get too awkward when a child needed to ask a parent why they were so upset.

Then a week later, his father walked past him at home, and just placed a hand on Steven's shoulder gently, and when he looked up at his father, he got a nod, but my father's face had a grim expression on it which made little sense to me. He tried to communicate something to me then, which he was too afraid to say…

* * *

A few days afterwards, Elizabet came to visit me again, and she was in a rather chatty mood. She tried to cheer me up. She saw that Steven's father was upset and thought that she could convey her sympathy for how he was feeling by making his son happier. Steven was rather uncertain how he could get to be happier when he knew full well that they both were at risk of being a Subject. The conversation that day was odd.

"Do you ever wonder about why people had an animal as a companion?" she'd asked me. "They had a name for it according to a book I found. It's a pet."

"I don't know," he had said, and to be honest, he didn't know, as it wasn't something he'd considered or thought about until then.

"If I had lived five hundred years ago, I would have owned a dog," she had said.

"A dog?" he had asked her.

"Yes, they had many types. Small ones and big ones, ones with short hair and long hair," she had said, grinning broadly. "I saw one type I liked a lot. It's a white and brown version of a dog, and in the book, I found they called the one of them—Maggie."

"Maggie?" he had asked her, "Is that actually a name for a dog?"

"Yes, this one was called by that name. It seems a woman wrote the book at around 2024, and it lists her dog on the back cover as her dog."

She had showed me the photo she had taken from that book. When I asked where the rest of the book was, she shook her head.

"Most of the book got rotten away by damp, but the page with the dog on it was still visible, so I took it with me," she had said.

She had then showed him the picture of the dog, and to be honest, the creature looked like a pet he could own if dogs had still existed. But he'd seen no dogs of any kind ever in Utopus, so he knew it was just some wistful thinking about something that neither she nor I would ever have or experience.

After the conversation, the almost obligatory leaning of her head had on my shoulder come, and the rest of the afternoon they had sat silently watching the landscape. That day, they didn't see the strange third structure appear, and now Steven thought it over, it had been missing from the landscape for the next couple of months.

His father arrived home earlier than usual that day, and he'd raised an eyebrow when he'd walked onto the balcony to find them sitting side by side. He made them all soup, and during the meal had entertained them, well actually Elizabet more than him, with stories. It was then that Steven realised how much his father really enjoyed telling a story with something scary about them. He'd tell a story, and then get to what *he* called 'the good point' and say something that scared Elizabet enough to cause her to grab Steven's arm and bury her face against his shoulder, while also giggling nervously.

During the evening both his father and him were a lot more positive, and when Elizabet had left to go home and Steven shut the door, his father had prodded me. "You should do more than just let her be a friend," he had said, winking at him teasingly.

"Do more in what way?" Steven had asked him, realising that he'd asked a somewhat stupid question as he still didn't quite understand back then she would have had feelings for him.

And yes, I guess that's too late now. Like everything else is too late now.

That evening, they had talked extensively, like the intervening ten years had never happened.

However, things had changed the following day, and his father had tried to warn him of things to come. They were walking on the road leading from the western bridge which they'd always walked along before getting to the Academic Institute. But, that day, my father had discretely pointed at a man and a woman who were walking over the road in the same direction as they were, but on the opposite side of the road. Those two individuals walked in silent, never seeming to acknowledge each other, and to Steven their posture appeared to be someone carrying a heavy burden.

"They live every day with that consequence. They said goodbye to a daughter ten years ago," his father had stated plainly.

Steven watched them until they had turned a corner and were out of sight. But seeing the individuals made him understand what the word 'consequence' meant. His father had pointed out two people who had apparently lost a daughter. Steven guessed it was his father's way to prepare himself, and Steven too, for the possibility arriving in the future for them. They were fully prepared for the emotions it was causing...

The last week had felt like he had slowed down time somehow. Every day dragged on, and even all the science and research were making Steven bored in the week which followed so he kept his attention on the work by remembering what his father had said years earlier.

"I hope she, they, are well..."

Steven had wondered for all these years what his father had meant with those words, and some part of him had also ended up making another decision because of the comment. Which had been a promise of sorts...

"If I get selected as a Subject, I *will* find them."

Up to that moment, Steven hadn't known who these 'them' were. He knew this would get answered if he could find whoever it was that his father had been talking about so rarely. And then the selection had come. His father had pulled his son into an embrace on the evening prior of the announcement.

"Whatever happens, you'll always be Steven to me. But outside this house, I can only acknowledge you as a Subject afterwards, understood? Because if I don't this all can have more consequences than you could ever imagine."

Steven remembered listening to the comment with a dry knot in his throat, and just nodding at his father when this was said...

* * *

Steven didn't sleep much when nightfall had come that day and he'd tossed a lot, and he'd dreamt of turbulent imagery. One dream was of this woman who had stood somewhere unfamiliar, staring at him for a while. Then, in the dream, she would turn and walk away. He'd call out to her in his slumber, but he was uncertain of what he called out in the dream or whether she ever was able to hear him. What he did remember from the dream on waking up was her odd appearance.

There had been one thing that had always eluded him, as a thirteen-year-old boy, was why the woman he saw had this odd bulge in her stomach…

✳ ✳ ✳

Steven had left behind a lot of memories of when he'd departed from Utopus. He had also left Elizabet behind, and therefore also all the missed chances. He was certain she'd loved him, but he never had any courage to acknowledge the feelings. It was during the morning when the announcement would happen that he'd realised that he loved her too. But by that moment, it was too late to do anything about it. Now he hoped Elizabet would wait for him to return, but he was uncertain this really could happen, so he guessed that she was lost to him. Also lost. Just like his father and mother were both lost to him, too. And just as he'd lost the many friends that he'd had there.

He was guessing that Elizabet was watching him walk away over the road from behind one of the windows of the building that she was living in. He'd considered visiting her there before leaving but had decided against it as she too wouldn't acknowledge him as anything other than a Subject. She had to do this, like his father, to be safe from the consequences that could come from ignoring the unwritten rules about Subjects. He realised there was something psychological about someone enforcing such a rule, and that this rule had both an impact on the person leaving and everyone who was staying behind. Steven was certain she would be deeply upset for not being able to say goodbye to him…

And then, also, his father hadn't said farewell to him.

Not in the normal sense of what might have passed as a proper, normal farewell. It didn't include the word 'goodbye' in the sentence spoken to him. But what Steven *did* remember was how ominous his father's words had sounded. His father had behaved like he knew something that his son did not. His father had whispered a few words into Steven's ears, and he'd forced Steven to lean closer while he spoke. It was the strangest words a father could have said to a son as a farewell.

"Always remember—and don't lose your rucksack, whatever happens."

"Remember? Who? Or—what?" Steven was wondering as soon as he'd heard his father's words of warning. "And what about my rucksack?"

His father didn't tell him. He held him close for a few more minutes. Then he pushed Steven away abruptly. "Go—now—" he said as the last words. So Steven had turned and had done what he had seen happen exactly ten years earlier. He did what a woman had done before him. She too was a Subject. *So, where is she now...?*

He might be able to understand why his father, and even Elizabet, had behaved in the way they had done. No one in Utopus wanted to acknowledge the idea that they'd have to say goodbye to a selected Subject. And frankly, Steven realised that he'd ended up contemplating a lot about the situation, and that it had unsettled him in that someone *could* exert so much control over other people and thus compel them to behave in this way, even when they were receiving a warning about the danger that Zone Zero was posing increasingly.

It had something to do with the black structure there at times...

It was too much of a coincidence that it kept appearing and disappearing in such mysterious circumstances. Steven had seen the impact of it suddenly arriving on the people who'd come to speak to him after his selection and had looked towards where it had appeared out of nowhere, and although Steven had been certain that, hours or even minutes before his selection, the structure hadn't been there, and then when we'd glanced there suddenly it had been...

The structure was making everyone nervous.

This was possibly why they ignored the message that had been received and therefore had still foolishly selected a Subject. Their decision that day had influenced every subsequent decision being made there, even the decisions of his father, and he'd risked a lot to allow his son, especially after all the misgivings about him, to keep working after that day on the cube.

Steven was constantly the most worried about what might happen with Elizabet now. He was certain his father would do everything he could to keep her safe. The people connected to the mysterious structure were trying to keep everyone from discovering what it was for and what function it was serving, or perhaps they themselves didn't know what it was, and the way they'd behaved around him when he'd questioned them about it when, one day as a boy, he'd felt emboldened enough to confront them with questions, made Steven think that they, too, were fearful... somehow... of something... of someone...

He'd discovered from their behaviour that they had *known* that the decision to make a person into the next Subject was somehow connected with what went on inside the black structure standing ominously in the desolate field behind them...

Steven was uncertain who exactly was making such decisions; however it had seemed his father had suspected something, but that he was unable or unwilling to tell his son.

However, something was certainly different this time when it came to the selection, and it had seemed that his father *had* also intended him to be chosen, and then there was that something he'd given him to take with him, which he had to make sure that he wouldn't lose under any circumstance. This was likely the reason for his father's last words whispered at him. But later, Steven would know that 'others' might know the information as well, and because of that chance his father's life was now at risk, and perhaps the lives of all the people who had worked with his father—and with him. *This meant that Elizabet might also be in danger...*

Steven had been told that his *only* task during his journey would require for him to investigate Zone Zero. The people who'd come to speak with us about Steven being the new Subject were trying the damnedest to make sure he was going to do only that. He now knew he might have been sitting on the balcony just behind them, sitting next to Elizabet if he'd chosen a path as an Academist, but he realised then that perhaps then they might never have grown so close...

✳ ✳ ✳

Steven had stood staring into Utopus, at its expansive vista, for a long time after initially walking away from the city before he'd stopped and had been contemplating over past events. He needed to look one more time before he would visit the bunker. He then would search through the bunker for as long as it would take him to get more answers from this place. And then he would leave to go south...

Steven was fully aware that the old road wasn't empty.

Not yet at least.

After taking in the vista, Steven had looked for the first time at his father, who was still standing *alone* on the road, with his head bowed like he couldn't watch me leave or that he didn't want to acknowledge he'd lost his son now, and then at the distant building which he knew to be the University, which had changed my destiny, and then at the Academic Institute, and imagining that Elizabet was staring from a window on the fifth floor towards the south, perhaps thinking about him right now…

Please, remember me, Steven thought, *please, both of you remember until I come back if I can do that…*

But he'd turned and continued on towards the bunker that his father and him had been looking at through the distance viewer, as I had called the device as a small boy, or as the binoculars as the proper name was, and which was the precise moment he saw the strange black structure decided to become visible again…

15.

I'M CERTAIN THAT SOMETHING MECHANICAL is causing it to do this, Steven thought, frowning with some worry. *Magic doesn't exist. There is some sort of technology that I'm not aware of, something maybe from the past, from the time when the cube was built, that can do this. I need to find a place with old books from the past that haven't crumbled to dust and find answers about this phenomenon…*

The mysterious structure, which had always seemingly appeared in the middle of the city, and always in between the University and the Academic Institute, had arrived back in the city only moment after he'd departed, and that made its movement too rhythmic to be normal. There was something so unsettling about its appearance. Steven had felt this way about the structure ever since he'd seen it for the first time. Or, more precisely, when he'd noticed it for the first time. He had stood there staring at it through the distance viewer, and its presence had unsettled him.

Then Steven had got a dull, discomforting but familiar ache in his stomach.

The pain had stopped abruptly in the moment when he'd glanced away. It was then he had checked if his father was still standing on the road, and he was there. It was almost like his father had turned into a statue of some sort. Steven glanced once more towards where that third structure had been a few moments earlier, and again he had this impression of it becoming smaller, less visible or something along those lines, and then disappearing.

Steven still wasn't certain if the feeling he was getting in his stomach was being caused by the structure, or if it might be a type of nervousness caused by the impending journey that was about to commences.

He glanced over the panorama for several minutes more before he turned in the direction of the bunker, and this time he would thoroughly investigate everything he could access, and from his findings work out what it had been and also find paper and pencils to make notes about what he'd found, and then to ascertain whether there was any connection between it and Utopus, or even between it and the mysterious third structure. Like, for example, to find out if something inside the bunker was controlling its arrival and departure.

* * *

Utopus had been Steven's home for all his life, and at this moment he was still uncertain how he felt about the fact he was no longer in Utopus and had been told to travel away from everything he'd ever known all his life. What he was certain of is that he would have wanted to bring his father and Elizabet with him, but their reactions showed him they weren't much inclined to leave. Not until he could break the spell of the dark structure's menacing influence over the people of the city.

His father had reacted angrily when Steven had told him to come with him to check the bunker or whatever the building, we saw through the binoculars was precisely. And he'd whispered to Elizabet, while we'd sat on my balcony one of the last times, about coming with him there, and she'd shook her head, and soon after that she'd left.

It was on a particular day, in those last weeks, when Elizabet had arrived with a basket full of food, and we'd watched the sunset together. There may have been a few fruit-flavoured beverages in the basket as well.

Steven had almost reconsidered looking inside that bunker because he'd become so nauseated after staring at the third structure. So, he distracted himself with memories of his friend…

When Elizabet had arrived that day, he was ready to settle down on the seating in the living room rather than on the balcony, and to read a new book he'd found a few days earlier. He'd found it in a ditch, and he'd gone looking for books around there because Elizabet had told me that had been where she'd found the part-rotted book with the picture of the dog.

The ditch had been visible from his balcony, and when he was standing on his balcony, and he'd been leaning on the portion of the banister that was still attached to the building and whilst also drinking a hot drink, although he couldn't remember now what the drink it was, and I'd glanced down by chance, and he'd seen the book just lying down there. It was a book about the future, and the person who had written it had a different view of what the future would be like then what it obviously was like now. He'd gone downstairs hastily to get the book. He'd been uncertain how the book got there, but it had immediately fascinated him. From what he'd understood of the story, the book was about a man who'd made a machine to get up to the nearby planet, which the book was calling the Moon, and some ideas the author gave in the book make Steven think the book had also been intended as a form of entertainment in the past for the people who'd lived in the original city Stockholm. He'd thought for a time about the sort of person who might have owned this book…

Funny enough, he knew that there were people also in Utopus who had a rather odd name for this same planet. They would refer to it always as "The White Lady," and one of the people who'd told him about the name had then claimed that the idea for this name had come from a book about a game they found.

"The book said it was a game they'd played for few decades at the time," the man had said. "We don't know how the game was played, but it was with pictures like in a movie. The moon in the game was apparently special, shown sometimes as a beautiful woman…"

There had been a date in the book, just like with the photo he'd found inside the bunker, and this book had references that stated that someone had caused a war. The book dated back to over six hundred years ago, but according to something written in the front of the book, the story inside it was based on a book that was even older and written in French of the past. Steven considered himself a practical man, and he could see the virtue of someone dreaming up an idea of going from this planet to the other planet visible in the sky. The book also taught him something which he'd told his father, who had been quite surprised about him finding the book.

It contained a word he still was keen about…

Apparently, the people who'd lived five hundred years ago, and before that too, had a word for when the Moon would disappear from the sky. They'd called the process by the word of 'waxing.' He couldn't explain fully to father why this word had matters, and thought it related to us lacking in the knowledge of scientific information, but then Steven had suggested to his father about hoping that one day us being able to go to the other planet, and his father then had suggested that it had happened six times. His father then told Steven that the visits had happened a hundred years after the book was written. That those people walked on the Moon… on the planet we see at night in the sky…

* * *

Later, Steven had thought about the conversation over the bowl of his father's soup, but then as he'd sat outside the bunker considering about going inside it tonight or the next morning, he'd glanced up to see the Moon as a large, orange-shaded shape in the sky which had caused the moments to flood back.

We ate a lot of soup in these last few weeks it seems, Steven thought, as he glanced down at the small container of soup he'd been heating, and which might have been the reason why he'd turned his thoughts inward. *To me it had felt like the final weeks before I was going to depart…*

Steven was contemplating about why there had only been thirty-six other Subjects before he'd set out on their journeys, each with an individual story he might never know about and who'd gone on their journeys to do something he was doing now as well, and then he wondered why no person had ever returned. The warning had mentioned several times that the region outside Utopus, which we were calling Zone Zero, was a dangerous place, and based on Steven's own assessments it had also mysteries to discover.

There were a few things that his scientific mind regarded as contradictions, or as things that couldn't happen…

One thing that had kept occupying his mind was how short a life span of the average person seemed to be in current times compared to what it might have been around five hundred years ago or earlier. If the other Subjects had similar short life spans, then most of them would have perished either during their outward journey, or they could have done so on their way back to Utopus.

Some of them might not have wanted to return because of what they had perceived Utopus to be as a place with a threat. The shorter life span was likely contributing to the idea that no one would ever return from their journey through Zone Zero, and it might have been one reason they would send someone as young as him out in there.

His father had told him that the people of five hundred years ago would easily enjoy a life of well over a hundred years if they were leading healthy lives, ate healthy food, and did a good deal of healthy stuff,

113

although when he'd asked his father what 'doing healthy stuff' had meant, his father had been at a loss of how to explain the concept to him. So, Steven had figured out what it might have meant…

"Yes, so yes, running or walking or whatever seems healthy," Steven muttered as he recalled the conversation, "and I do it a lot, but I don't feel any healthier because I do it."

In the past five centuries, we seemingly had forgotten most of information of what life would have been like back then, and because Steven could easily see how worthless life could be for some of the people living in Utopus, and it made him really wonder why this was.

According to the author of the book that he was now paging through again out of boredom, the people of the past owned machines on which a person could play a game though the text didn't mention a name for the machine for unknown reasons but Steven figured out that the author might have assumed that the person reading the book knew the name of the device, and he found out from the story that the name he'd been told about was a moon in the game. And he hadn't believed the person who had told him…

I never believed him, Steven thought, *because everything that person had ever said was always too fantastical… However, I'm now uncertain if the person was just telling me a story he'd made up, or that such machines and games had existed. I wonder if I'll ever see such a machine. But honestly, the name sounds a lot more interesting than calling it the Moon…*

However, that people would even refer to the Moon by another strange name made Steven realise that there were people in Utopus who might see it as a requirement to be more spiritual, and most of these people were also Academists, so perhaps there was a correlation between the situations.

From the perspective of a life as a scientist the images in the book were interesting. The book showed the man in the book as he was building the machine, then later images showed him flying up with the machine towards the moon. However, as he'd seen objects burning as they came down to the ground, he realised therefore that they'd need a lot of power to get up to the other planet, so the method in the book was rather simplistic to me and the book also never showed how the man got back down to this world…

∗ ∗ ∗

A few hours had passed, and Steven was now contemplating over what his father had been talking about many years earlier, which was about something else, but now felt connected to what the book was telling in the story. During their conversation, a few days after they'd talked about him finding the book, his father had used a word - utopia - and he had said the name of the city, Utopus, had come from this word. He'd claimed the word meant: an 'imagined place' or similarly, and it seemed to be a contradiction in Steven's mind to this day…

Utopus was hardly an imagined place unless you were to include the third structure with its ability to appear and disappear. Steven was still uncertain what the true purpose of the structure might be, and was even less certain whether it might have originated from four or five centuries ago, like Zone Zero, and like everything else around him here.

Because of this new thought, Steven now began assuming that the places and buildings he was encountering could hold the memories of the people who might have used them in earlier times, and Elizabet had suggested an interesting theory about the buildings when she was discussing the concept with him…

"Buildings might remember the people who'd lived in them before," she'd stated to him one time, a few days after his conversation with his father.

They were both looking at the vista from an open window of the Academic Institute towards the northern region of the city, and they were staring at the old forgotten landscape of old buildings present there, which, his father had explained to us as he passed us by had been Stockholm in the past.

"Buildings are just buildings," Steven had scolded her.

"No, they all have a soul," she'd snapped back at him. "When a person lives in one, they leave behind something that the gives it a soul…"

Steven had shaken his head when she'd said these words, but right now, as he was staring at the entrance of the bunker, he could believe her, though he couldn't claim to believe in souls, and even less in the case of buildings. *Or, at least, I don't think I do,* Steven thought, frowning for a moment. *Or at least I didn't believe it back then…*

"If you think buildings have a soul," he'd said, "then the structure that keeps on appearing and disappearing must be haunting us…"

Apparently, the idea had made Elizabet laugh—a lot!

"I didn't say these buildings have souls… I said those ones over there have souls," she'd said, as she'd pointed then towards the buildings north of us.

"Why only those?" he'd asked her.

"Because, back then, the people cared about how they were living," she'd answered, "and cared about what they did with their houses…"

"And we don't?" he'd asked her.

"Look at your house, for example," she'd explained. "You possess just a few pieces of furniture. There's no colour on the walls. A nice colour on the wall would give it a soul."

"So, if I made the walls green, or blue, or purple, according to you, that would give it a soul?" Steven had asked her.

"It may, but there are all the other houses in here also with no soul," she'd said coldly. "There's this whole place with no soul."

After that they'd run out of things to say but he'd understood what she had meant with what she had told him, and now more than back then. He would be able to get to find examples of what she'd suggested much later as he was travelling in Zone Zero. Suddenly, those words of hers mattered to him, and a part of him wished he could have shown her his findings whenever he came across them later.

Remembering the past was suddenly important to make sure we learned from it, and it was what we needed to do right now to make certain that the mistakes, described in the recordings, wouldn't get repeated. Many of the things he would subsequently discover during his travel would demonstrate that this was the correct assertion.

One of the first things he did during his journey was to visit the bunker. When the morning light was still low he used the half-dark to gain entry into the building, and did this at the time so not to be seen by anyone at all.

The building would cause its own range of memories for him to deal with later on. He had entered the building with two distinct questions in his mind: What was it for? Why was it there of all places?

Days later, Steven would walk from the building with ten times more questions than when he'd entered it. He was certain his visit into the building would answer the 'what was it for?' question, and during his exploration of the building, he kept contemplating over what Elizabet had told him about buildings having souls…

The 'why was it there?' question was a lot tougher to answer because of certain things he was finding in the building. He wasn't entirely sure why the building was even there, and the discoveries inside made answering the question even harder.

16.

THE DISTINCT NOTION THAT HE'D walked into a building filled with secrets became apparent very fast, and he was certain also the secrets got buried together with the people who may have last worked inside it. There was evidence that some of the people who used it also either lived or worked there or had done both, but Steven rather wished momentarily that he hadn't gone further inside it, so he'd only have the memory, the nicest memory perhaps, which was that of seeing the photo of the woman in the first corridor. He still wondered who she might have been…

*****

Steven had stayed in the bunker for several days, and contemplated a few times to secretly return to Utopus for visits with Elizabet, but he'd remembered something that his father had tried to whisper to me: "Once a person is selected as Subject, it's Utopus that—"

These words made it certain that Steven couldn't return to inside Utopus even if he'd wanted to, and this was why he needed to make Elizabet a memory. He wanted to return to see her again, but he could only come back there if there was a certainty that she wasn't in any kind of danger.

It was a few days after leaving that Steven had made a small mark in a small notebook he'd found in the bunker, so he could keep track of how long he'd been away from Utopus. He'd assign a memory to each of the marks, most of them to do with Elizabet.

His father had always told to him to remember. Though, he was uncertain really what he should be remembering. But it was a sentence, which his father couldn't finish, and that explained most of what Steven had needed to know. He was certain his father was about to tell him something about Utopus, about its secrets, but something had stopped him continuing to speak. So now Steven would use his memories to determine what the secrets might have been.

Because Steven was able to remember most of what had happened in his childhood whenever he was eating soup, he tried to always find something of this nature during his journey to use to trigger more memories. He'd make soup from plants and the flesh of animals he'd killed and then eat the soup. The taste wasn't as good as his father's soup, and initially he didn't get any memories come to his mind from these actions, but over time he got better at making the soup, and later he'd even find other means to get information dating back to the time of five hundred years ago that would also help him. Slowly also he'd remember more.

The information became more important as time went by because Steven realised they'd lost so much when the disaster of 2072 had happened…

His father had stated that too much got lost, and that society would never again be like it was previously.

However, Steven later would read some interesting information he would find inside a building filled with old books that he would come across during his journey. It would be book written by a man who'd lived six hundred years ago, and his book was saying: 'History has thrust something upon me from which I cannot turn away' and the words would puzzle Steven for a long time as to what they meant, but he'd learn to understand them. He never found a name for who had said the words, but Steven decided that the man may have been among the most important people at the time that he'd written them down. Steven realised that the same applied to the woman whose voice he'd heard in the message, and that the words also applied to her. And to himself, too. And to anyone working to make the world safe again…

Something about how she'd sounded in the recordings indicated to Steven that she might have known that the things she'd said and done were things she couldn't turn away from. His father had done things, as the years went by, that he couldn't turn away from. Even the woman Steven had seen walking over the road away from Utopus, just like he was doing now, had been doing something she couldn't turn away from. That was the fate of all the people who cared about this world.

Such people would go down a path they couldn't turn away from, and they would work to make the world a better place for everyone. Steven thought this was also true for the people of five or six hundred years ago.

It was still true now. But he also thought the view had its downside.

The people, who might be against the way the world should be functioning, also ironically couldn't turn away from whatever it was or is that they were believing in, which was what the message had been telling us as well. The messages had referred to them as a rogue organisation, however, they probably had believed that they were doing something they couldn't turn away from. But then, Steven had wondered what the man, who he'd found on the second day there in the bunker, might have been thinking, before he'd ended up with the hole in his head. What did he believe, what sort of memories was he thinking about, and why did he need to that action…?

Steven had stood for several minutes staring at the building before he'd gone been inside…

Up to that moment he'd only seen this building from a distance, using the binoculars. He'd visited the bunker five times before the selection process had happened. But always he'd ended up only just a few meters inside the building, only a few meters from the outer door, but he'd never had gone any further inside than that. But because he was now outside Utopus, his view of the bunker had changed. This time he'd wanted to go in and explore all the parts of the structure, and to see if he was able to figure out what the place had been intended for in the past.

*** * ***

When Steven had got to the door, he discovered that the storm which his father and he both had observed through the binoculars, had torn the door off clean, however the angle at which it got lodged in the door frame made it almost impossible to get inside the building.

This caused Steven to realise that so many dust storms had been happening south of Utopus that he wondered how the city could even stay safe. The storm he'd watched was so strong, and this had been why the door was pulled off the rusted hinges, and a chair he'd seen leaning inside the building was now somewhat further inside, leaning against the left wall before the storm, was knocked over by the wind, and it had settled itself several meters outside the building.

An urge happened for the man to pick up the chair and to place it back against the wall, but Steven decided against this because the chair would just get blown out when the next storm would come along. The chair lying on the ground reminded him he'd been coming to the building in the middle of the night several times before day when he shouldn't have done that. He was uncertain, but the memory caused him to blush. He stood staring at the chair which had become a toy for the wind of the storm he'd witnessed and realised that it would get further out there in the landscape in the next storm? He then realised that it didn't matter about the chair. So, he just left it there, turned and entered the building.

The first corridor had become darker as he walked further into the building. It was an overwhelming darkness, although there was an unknown light source next to the first stairway which alleviated some of his anxiety. The darkness seemed to be hiding the secrets of the building, and however much he tried, he would uncover none of it.

He had stopped at the photo of the woman on his previous visits because she had this compelling appearance. He rather wanted say that she was the reason for stopping rather the irrational fear each visit to the building would cause…

The faded colours of the paper, on which photo was being displayed, was showing both the age of the photo and of the building itself. Her hair was perhaps a light-yellow colour, and she'd cropped it to just above her shoulders. Most women in Utopus would wear their hair quite short, which was done for the convenience of caring for it, and which seemed not what the woman in the photo was doing.

Elizabet had always differed from everyone else. She had black hair and wore it to a length that reached just below her shoulders. She seemed to always pull the two parts of her hair to either side of her head, and then back and she'd fasten it at the back of her head in the nape of her neck with a string he'd found for her. But compared to what Elizabet did with her hair, the woman in the photo in the corridor had her hair all loose. The second feature Steven noted about her was that her clothing might have been dark yellow or even a light orange colour, which was so different from the clothing people would wear in Utopus, which usually was a shade of brown or green, either light or dark. Steven glanced down at his own clothing, realising now it was neither brown nor green. It was grey and black.

Although his father had always seemed to have been wearing an even-shaded dark grey type of clothing, which was a kind of odd too. The woman in the photo had distinct bright red-coloured lips, and Steven now realised he'd seen no woman in Utopus with their lips coloured in that way.

Steven was uncertain why the photo was there, or who might have placed it there, or even why someone would have forgotten to take it with them as the last occupants had abandoned the building. He knew then that someday he'd want to meet a woman such as this person. Not that he'd want to meet such a woman instead of Elizabet, but there was something about the way the woman was looking in the picture which allowed him to feel connected to her, and he was uncertain why. She possessed the same sadness in her eyes which he'd seen in Elizabet's eyes when she'd looked at him in the moments after the announcement had come, when they were telling everyone in Utopus he'd been selected as the Subject. But this woman had a quality to her that not even Elizabet possessed, and he wondered why the women there had lost that aspect of their appearance. The sadness in this woman's eyes made her rather beautiful, and he was certain that she was telling a story with her eyes to the person who was looking at the picture of her. Steven would recall what was on his mind afterwards for a long time… *Maybe she was longing for something she could never have. He wondered if she ever had any children. Or whether someone had ever married her?* He looked at the photo a few more minutes before thinking pensively, *did she have a long and happy life?*

There wasn't really any clue of this being the case from the photo. It was just a photo of her. He saw something on the bottom on of the paper and he could only assume it to be a date. The paper had somewhat curled up, so he had to move his hand over the photo to straighten it to see it.

The date listed was 1962. At least, he assumed it was a date.

He was fantasising for a time about who she might have been. He sensed a connection to her, so he concluded the obvious assessment about her. "Perhaps she was secretly a famous scientist, and this photo was to celebrate something she had done."

Even though he was hoping for his assessment to be true, somehow Steven knew nothing his thoughts might be true. There was too much sadness in the woman's eye for her smile to be real, and even though she was smiling, the smile did appear to be fake to him, like she was putting it on her face to please others rather than herself.

Steven could imagine that she'd gone through a pain in her life that he'd never know about, and the sadness in her eyes told him such information. But whatever her life had been like, he felt connected to her and that, to him, was what mattered most.

Steven looked at the photo for a few more moments before he'd walked on, deeper inside the silent abandoned bunker, to begin the effort of making my first Zone Zero discoveries. As he did this, Steven was thinking more about how long ago the woman had lived. If the number listed under the photo was a date, then the image had been created before the later events that began the process of change that would lead to Utopus had been happening…

Steven remembered he'd been reading a book in which the words 'cold war' had been listed, and some of the dates listed in the book were from around the same period as the date on the photo.

So, he wondered if the woman with her alluring red smile had lived during this cold war, and what her life might have been like because of it.

Maybe something had happened during those times that had caused her to feel so sad.

Steven dawdled through the first corridor and then the second left corridor with the flickering light at the end of it and was in deep thoughts about the woman while he walked. However, as he neared the end of the corridor he'd increased his pace, and after a time, he was walking rather briskly. He arrived at the first stairway probably an hour later, although he was uncertain of the time that might have passed him by until later, because it was so dark in there.

The first stairs gave him the first moment of hesitation. He considered momentarily if he was doing the right thing with going into the building and checking what he would find inside it. He walked down the first stairway slowly, considering every step…

* * *

As Steven got closer to the next door, he could understand why the man, he'd seen propped up against the wall in the first small room that he'd examined, had wanted to kill himself. He felt now like he was walking into a place of death. The brightness, however minor it was, felt like a welcome relief. He couldn't recall from the second hesitant visit that this corridor had been this long.

The earlier set of stairs suddenly had felt too long, and although finding the dead guy in the small room after that, Steven was glad to be somewhere small and bright instead, although he was rather uncertain where the light was coming from that gave the room its bright appearance.

In the room, was where he'd found the dead guy. He was lying to the right of the door he'd walked in through, and at first Steven hadn't seen him, because he was paying too much attention to looking up at the ceiling and trying to figure out where the light was coming in from as it wasn't from the rows of tubes he could see hanging at regular intervals. He never found out any source for the light source, so he'd looked around him. Steven had first seen the other door, which had this dent in it, and he was certain that only something heavy could have caused it. It was then that he saw the dead guy.

Steven could immediately see that the dead body was that of a man, but his body was so old that he'd turned into a skeleton with rags of clothing hanging off it. He had knelt then next to the skeleton to examine it better and then had seen the cause of his death. The skeleton showed a gaping hole in the left side of the skull, and his hand was still grasping the gun which seemingly had been the reason for the hole in his head.

The clothing was disturbing Steven more than how the man had killed himself as it possessed a similarity between itself and what he was currently wearing. Steven determined that he'd found a man based on the last remaining features of what once had been a face. The man might have had yellow hair, just like the woman in the photo. After a gingerly executed examination, Steven determined that the clothes the man was wearing were in fact like what he was wearing. It was disconcerting to a degree for the dead guy's clothing to be in such rags. Steven wondered who the man might have been during his life, and even more wondered if he'd been a Subject. He seemed young…

When the thought of the dead man having been a Subject had entered his mind, Steven wondered then if no person returned because they'd perished during their journeys, and this thought had again made him wonder about the Subject of a decade earlier, whom he knew had been a woman… immediately, he thought that she might be dead too somewhere.

17.

THIS SECOND THOUGHT CAUSED ME to get up abruptly and to press on with my exploration of the building. After he'd got up and had looked some more around the room first, he'd decided on investigating everything he was a scientist first and therefore inclined to investigate anything that was an unknown to him. Several things in the room had been disturbed, messed up, made into a disorganised heap.

By someone...

Looking closer at the features of the room he was in, Steven realised that he should make haste.

When he first had looked up, Steven had been uncertain about the unnatural brightness of the room, but then he'd noticed some rubble near the second door, and when he'd looked up again, he noticed that there was evidence of damage in the structure of the ceiling, and that this was where the light was coming from.

Steven was certain then that the next Subject who'd arrived after the dead man had arrived here, if he was a Subject, couldn't have gone further into the building into the deeper bowels, and might have found himself or herself at the end of a corridor, like Steven himself, at a door that was so obviously blocked by a lot of rubble, leading to nowhere. A part of him also then had realised that the small room would have become a place of burial for the dead man lying there, eventually. Steven felt a need for more haste was now a very necessary endeavour suddenly, although he'd still wanted to be as thorough as he could be with investigating the building. He'd squeezed through the opened-up section of the second door, which he'd pried open somewhat more in the past couple of hours. The rope that he was carrying with him, which he'd grabbed from a storeroom in the cellar of the building where his father and he had lived, was making this task somewhat more difficult.

His father might have seriously been wondering why his son had brought the rope with him, and a smile that had flashed over his face perhaps had betrayed he could guess his son was going the bunker first...

Uncertainty had overwhelmed him in that moment, and he'd wondered why he'd even had brought the rope with him, but something told him that the metal disk-shape at the top of the building might be an exit of some sort, and he was now guessing that the building was deceptively small. And deep too. It took him ten or twenty minutes to squeeze through the opening, and when he finally got through and had turned, he realised that finding yet another corridor instantly had made him somewhat despondent. And for several moments, Steven had considered squeezing back through the open door and leaving. But he'd remembered looking through a small opening in the disk-shaped opening and seeing some metallic object below him. He needed to find out what this object looked like from the ground looking up. He ascertained he'd get to this location, where the metal object stood looking all menacing, at some point, and Steven seriously hoped the whole effort of exploring the building wasn't going to be for nothing.

So, he walked through the second corridor with haste, partly also because he knew now that the small room could collapse at any time, and therefore trap him inside the building for good.

* * *

Steven realised that his nose informed him of everything he needed to know about this place. The odour came from his surroundings, and the building was exhaling it. The building had an oldness to it, and Steven realised it reeked of 'old.' He couldn't recall he'd smelled the odour when he was there last time.

He had to cover his face with a sleeve because the smell was assaulting his nose, and caused him to feel dizzy for several minutes, and he hesitated about being there or about doing the impossible task of discovering the building's purpose.

But Steven knew he needed to go further inside, so he walked on a hesitant step after another, and was glad when he found the earlier glimpsed circular room after having walked through a long corridor, which was divided up into sections with additional doors. Someone had pried each open after exerting some force in the past. Each was showing evidence that the violence inflicted on them had come from both sides. Someone had used excessive force to open the door to gain entry beyond, and someone had in equal measure used force to get out. Steven was rather disturbed by seeing the door in this state, and it made him think about the movies his father had often played on a machine he'd fixed for this purpose.

There had been several movies that would come to Steven's mind at that moment, but there was one that made him stop and listen every time he would walk through the next door he'd found inside the building. It was a movie in which a girl got trapped in a car with a guy, and after a time each of them would see strange people walking by, who would never stop to help either of them.

And in the movie, there was also this person, whom Steven could only assume to be someone in charge of the others, and he had appeared to be rather menacing. It was this person who he could imagine walking in the corridors of the bunker, and he imagined it every time a door made a loud groaning sound as he had opened one. He was almost imagining that he'd find someone like that standing there on the other side of the door. And then he began imagining that even the dead guy would get up and chase after him…

It had been something from those movies that he wished he'd never seen.

However, after about an hour of walking and having my mind play tricks on him in this fashion, Steven finally had arrived at a particular door he was most interested in. Behind the door he finally had found the circular room. It was there where the tall metallic object was standing. He walked over to the balcony and realised soon that the balcony had no stairs to go up or down on. There were several doors, which he tried to pull open, but they were all locked.

Several metal pipes were beside a door, and two of the pipes passed through the door to whatever was behind it. From the square image on the door, Steven assumed this door went to a location that was powering the building right now, even if this was happening somewhat haphazardly. He glanced up and noticed that a pipe rose all the way to what he assumed was the underside of the disk-shaped exit he had found at the top.

He'd spotted something metallic towards the bottom of the shaft when he'd been peering down a few days earlier…

Has it already been three days since I left Utopus, Steven thought.

He also wondered then about the entire structure, and realised he might be in the exit area of a larger structure, and that the part with the metallic structure standing within it, had been kept away from the main building for specific reasons, and that the distance between it and what he'd found before had been for specific reasons. It then made him wonder where the primary structure was located, and if there was anyone there who could know what the metal structure might have been used for. He spent some time trying to figure out how deep the shaft might really be. A few shards of rubble, which he pushed off the side of the balcony with his boot, made him flinch somewhat when they'd echoed far below him before making a reverberated sound through the entire shaft. He pulled the rope loop from across his chest, and then looked around for a way to fasten it securely.

The pipes had appeared to be promising initially, but he realised they were also too slippery. Steven saw something that looked like a hoop embedded in the floor of the balcony. It felt rough to the touch so Steven knew he could use it for what he'd intended to use it for. His father had taught him to knot ropes together, which was supposed to keep the knots from going lose. Steven had to guess that was why his father had smiled on seeing me hauling the rope. His father knew he'd remembered about doing the knots in a rope…

After Steven had made additional knots in the rope to allow him to climb up again after he was done with exploring the bottom of the shaft. He was uncertain if the rope was long enough for what he'd wanted to do, but at least he knew he needed try to reach the bottom of the shaft.

Steven sighed with relief when he noticed that the rope was hanging only about a meter above the metallic floor. The floor was strange, and it almost touched the metal structure, and he couldn't see any space anywhere around the structure to go to any lower floors if he wanted to.

He noticed the rubble he had knocked off from the balcony was lying around him in a wide splatter, and Steven felt a need to grin as he then knocked the rubble down through the small opening around the metal structure with his boot, however no sound ever echoed back, so Steven wondered how deep it might be below this floor. He tried all four doors in the corridor beside the floor, and one door led to a cupboard, and it was empty, and two doors were covered over with the same indents present as he'd seen before. The final door was open and had the indents, and the door was ajar, and he assumed that the door handle got broken off whenever the last person here had attempted to open it.

Steven had listened for a while to determine if anyone else might be in this part of the building, and that was then when he'd noticed the sounds… He needed to assume they belonged to an animal scurrying off.

He wondered if the animal he could hear had somehow got into the bunker after climbing in through the opening in the roof of the shaft, or through passageways somewhere else in the building which small animals might love to use.

He had noticed the same kind of sounds from animals, who might have been living in the building that was his home, and the animals there had been likely there because of the filth that was present. He could imagine the animals in the bunker somehow becoming as large as him, and for several minutes he thought there was one such animal was sitting behind the open door, just waiting to attack him.

His father had claimed that people would show movies all the time with many different made-up stories in them when it was five hundred years or longer in the past, which would have many strange monsters and creatures in them to make the people, who'd watch them, to feel scared. He thought it had been a movie with the girl, although it hadn't look scary. But he'd been scared for several minutes just now, and he reckoned it was his mind playing tricks on him again…

That might have been the purpose of the third structure it seemed if he thought about everything more closely. Steven was wondering what had allowed the structure to appear and disappear as it had done, and why everyone in Utopus had always behaved like it was evil. But also, standing beside the tall metallic object, and now knowing that their floor below my feet had no bottom underneath I wanted to off it as fast as I could as the floor could somehow disappear if the roof collapsed, and a large stone dropped.

So, he'd opened the door. Elizabet would have laughed a lot if she'd been there with him, because he'd sighed out so dramatically and over the top. He saw another corridor behind this door, and for several moments, he was rocking back and forth and bumping his head against the door in frustration. Then a light turned on just above him. The light turning on had surprised him somewhat. Although a moment after, he felt disappointed when the light turned off again. But he didn't need to wait long before the light came on again, and Steven had reacted to it by moaning, "Come on, stay on, please stay on."

The lights turning on became a bit of a game. Steven would see the first few turn on, and he presumed it may be equated how insects would behave around a light source, how they'd hesitantly fly towards it, would back off, and would want to hover around it for a while. It seemed these lights were having the same effect on him in the corridor.

A few lights had turned on, some fully but most attempting a half-hearted effort and only staying on with an orange glow as seen when the sun rises in the morning or sets at night, but with an unnatural darkness to it that only comes from it being an artificial light source. Some lights would flicker on and off in an irregular pattern, and there were a few that would never turn on, and those were the ones that worried him somewhat. Long pipes, either thick or slender, located above him that were running just below the ceiling. He saw some of the narrowest pipes stop at each of the light sources, so he had to guess that they were some sort of mechanism to allow the light to turn on—or off. There seemed to be some damage to the narrow pipes, so he guessed that the animals, that at this moment he could still hear, were the culprits for the lights not working in places.

Steven constantly had to remind himself that the sounds in another part of the building were small animals, and hope that the lights would stay on, and before he was at the other end of the corridor. He turned to look to check if this was the case, and the lights had stayed on. He then stood there for a comparison of this corridor with the long corridors of the Academic Institute.

They seemed to have a similar set-up with lights there, because when I sat there waiting for my father, the lights were on where I sat and when my father was speaking to someone, Steven thought, *but either end they seemed to be off and that caused the corridor ends to be in darkness.*

Before Steven had walked further into the building, he'd pried the gun from the skeletal hand of the dead man and had placed the weapon in his right pocket of the jacket he was wearing, that had been given to him by his father. His father had given the jacket to his son a few days before the journey had started. The gun would be able to serve him better than a dead man with a hole in the side of his head which was likely self-inflicted…

Now with the gun in his pocket, Steven was in readiness for whatever he'd find at the bottom of the shaft. His hand had positioned itself instinctively over the bulge in the right pocket, and each time the animals had scurried around he'd grasp his hand around the bulge in the side pocket. He didn't even know if the gun worked, or if there were any bullets in it.

He had talked to himself, saying stuff such as: "Common, Steven, you're gonna let some small animal or empty building scare you like this." And then he was getting rather annoyed about how he was behaving, and reconsidered about being there, and was about to turn to leave, when he just decided to himself about looking around for a few more minutes. Steven saw a door ahead of him, and he decided that he'd just open it, glance in, then turn and leave.

Steven stood for several minutes with his face leaning against the cold door…

Fuck it, Steven was thinking angrily as he stood there, and so now *I know how damned cold it is down there as well.*

He listened to check if sounds were coming from behind the door, but he frowned when he realised that a thick metal door such this one would stop him from hearing any noises from the other side, and besides, his ear and the side of his face were getting too cold from leaning against its surface.

Many times, he had one specific thought as he'd walked through the metal building: "The gun will help me."

Steven had opened the door and had to try in this action because of the sheer weight of the door. The process went slowly, and each time he pulled it somewhat, it had made this groaning sound, which made him wince, and because it had sounded like the sound made when had a bloated stomach, and lets the inflation go… down the other exit, down there. And the sound that the door made was like that sound but at least a hundred times amplified.

He got annoyed when, behind the heavy door, he found yet another passage, but then he saw that the door at the end of the corridor was wooden. He might be able to kick it in with his boot if he found out it was locked.

18.

AND NOW HE WAS UNCERTAIN why this door would be unlocked but he'd felt some relief it wasn't locked. But he'd still opened it cautiously though, with his hand inside his right pocket and holding the gun this time. He felt a need to use it if he saw something behind the door that could do me harm.

His father had claimed that five hundred years ago there had been people on the planet who had felt the need to always use a weapon such as what he now possessed to defend themselves even if, according to what his father assumed, such a threat hadn't really existed.

Steven had found the idea strange when his father had told him about the behaviour towards such weapons, but now that he was in this strange building, devoid of life except for the animals he could hear constantly, he understood somewhat why perhaps they had needed their guns. The world probably had scared them. Because Steven had read in the books, he'd discovered about this thing called a 'cold war,' and that around six hundred years earlier there were two big wars, he could understand why they might have been afraid.

To be honest, at that moment he'd been fearing what Utopus might really embody, especially later when he'd found more information about the city's origins.

The room behind this latest door was a sizeable, excessively dusty, and the last individuals might have left from this room in a hasty retreat, because everywhere there were sheets of paper and personal items lying on the floor. All untouched by the passage of time, all in a condition like the people might have departed only a day before...

Looking closer at the floor, Steven saw the evidence of two of the animals. It was evident that a few animals made this room their home from particles that looked like excrement. He pulled up his nose at seeing the small objects. Their presence had always disgusted him…

The dust, cobwebs, and the rust on every metallic object in the room betrayed the age of the location, and Steven was certain they'd been abandoned it for a long time. And the silence in here was getting to him. He listened for any sounds, but he couldn't even hear the animals scurrying about here. He guessed that this deep inside the building none of the sounds from outside it would be able to penetrate it.

The air inside the room felt perpetually chilly, and even though it was close to the middle of the hottest part of the year, and it was clear that the chill of winter would probably never leave the insides of this building. It easy to mistake this location for the cellars of the building he'd been living in whenever the coldest part of the year was causing the landscape to get covered over with snow, and for all the surfaces to covered in a crisp layer of ice crystals which had always been a cause for a highly dangerous activity that the youngest of the city engaged in; to challenge one another to hold their tongues against the ice for as long as each would dare…

He'd noticed a chill in the metal here in many places, and though such cold was only present during the winter outside, in the building as he'd investigated it was all year round it seemed and might possibly be even colder when it was the icy part of the year.

Utopus seemed to have been placed in an odd place by whoever had wanted it built, Steven thought, *because during part of the year there would be a snow-covered landscape, and the wind can be so cold it really causes you to dislike it. During the icy part of the year, I'd just stay in the apartment, and not even bother with going to the University or Academic Institute…*

Most people didn't ever go, but his father and he would go, and they did it mostly because they knew both buildings would be empty of people during this part of the year. Especially in the years when it was even colder than normal…

He'd gone to both places, on his own accord, to discover what secrets they could uncover and solve beyond the normal discoveries. Additionally, it also struck him as odd, to a degree, that during the coldest part of the year the third structure was never seen in Utopus…

Steven finally walked into the room behind the door after he'd first stared at it from the doorway for several minutes. He had been curious immediately about its function. *Why is it here?* he thought.

The room was sizeable in its dimensions.

Not just in the width or length but also in height. There were two stairways leading to two different balconies. There were more doors, but he decided not to check any of them. The middle of the room contained the tables. *Three of them.* He was certain around eighty to a hundred people could be seated around those tables. There were three more tables beside the wall. He hadn't noticed them immediately because of the lack of lighting in that part of the room…

The only two illuminated lights hung above the door through which he'd entered the room, and one further light fixture above a door opposite of him. He checked over the first door before looking around the room at what it might contain. Now he wanted to check at least the nearest doors. The next door he was checking had been left locked by the last occupants of the structure, so he guessed he had found the purpose for the exploration inside the metal building. Anything he would want to know or learn; he would need to find inside this room.

Steven walked to the other door and tried to open it. Someone in the past had locked it. *Why do mysterious doors always have to be locked? Can you explain that to me, huh, Steven?* he was thinking as he stared at his reflection in the small window in the door. The man staring back at him was showing a scowl on his face. He glanced through the window somewhat hesitantly. Behind the door was darkness. Steven shook the door to see if he was able to trigger the lights beyond the door to turn on, but his shoulders sunk when they didn't. For a long time, he stood there peering through the window, wondering what could be behind the door.

Maybe, in the future if there's a chance for that, Steven thought.

The room he was checking out wasn't the most extraordinary room he'd ever come across. The credit for such a room might go to a room inside the Academic Institute with its strange objects, which his father had claimed were all hundreds of years old. His father had said that many of them were even thousands of years old. Steven was uncertain how they'd got hold of all those items, but it was clear from all the dust present that the stuff there had been there for a long time.

Steven was uncertain what to look at first in the room, but then I remembered how my father had determined the importance of things. His father had always looked at when an item was made, and then had looked for related things. But as he looked around, somewhat desperately, he'd spotted something lying on a table, and the item seemed familiar. He walked to the table and stood staring at something his eyes first only registered as a drawing of some sort.

But after just minutes, Steven realised it was a larger version of something in the side pocket of my rucksack. It was a map that someone had left behind. He walked back to where he'd dropped his rucksack on the floor, close to the pillar on which he'd seen some else intriguing, although he'd ignored it at first.

As he walked back to the table, he unfolded his copy of the map and he stared at the line his father drew on it so long ago. It felt long ago, although it was only something like five or six years ago in reality. He placed his map on top of the larger version of it and realised immediately there were noted differences between the two maps. For a start, the bigger map had a lot more detail, and most names on this map were fully visible. The first name which immediately piqued his curiosity was the name which had started with R-U-S on his map, and he found it listed as Russia after searching for a while. He noticed an area that looked like the same shape as where his father had marked the map with an X shape, and explained then Utopus was there compared to the rest of Europe, or to Zone Zero...

The large map was confirming the name of the previous city had been Stockholm and that it had existed in the place of Utopus until a few hundred years ago. Then, Steven noticed how many roads had existed, or at least he assumed the many fine lines were roads...

Steven copied as many names as possible from the larger map onto his own smaller map, then he studied all the roads. It surprised him to find an X shape shown on the large map, and then spotted the black line drawn from the X to an area circled on the map at the northern side of what the map listed as Spain.

A line ran through all of Europe, or Europa as the map was naming it, drawn to an region just inside Spain. Steven straightened up and stared ahead of him, contemplating about what he'd just found out in the past twenty minutes. Someone had tried to draw a route as a hint for whoever would find this map from Utopus to an unknown destination in the southern part of Europe. He was uncertain how old the map might be, nor did he know how long ago someone had been here for a last visit. He wasn't certain if this was a message about what had happened in this building at the time when it was being abandoned, or if the cryptic nature of the line drawing was created by another of my kind, a Subject from the past, without any indication which one; that another Subject had been here before me and had drawn the route.

Perhaps the last one? Steven thought. *Is this a route?*

Steven glanced towards the other table to check whether there might have more clues over there which could prove to be useful. He saw an old book there. Then he walked to the table and picked it up, then after examining the book he opened it. There was a four-digit number, which was reminding him of the number listed in the first corridor, but the other two parts of the writing were a bit puzzling to him as we numbered what his father said were months...

He saw three letters listed and wondered what A-U-G might mean.

He quickly figured out that the two digits in the front of the book would represent a day, but he was uncertain of the letters. *In Utopus we don't really use any measurement of years except for the chart that someone created, and on this chart 3,600 days are crossed off and afterwards they select a Subject a few days later,* Steven thought, *and a day after goes away after which a new chart get hung up...*

Every ten years, they've been sending a Subject to discover the state of safety in Zone Zero, and Steven could remember the Subject of a decade ago, his mother, and he was certain he could vaguely remember the woman who got sent out a decade earlier. However, Steven had only two been when the previous departure had happened, so he was certain to be confusing his mother leaving with someone else. *If I remember this other person even correctly,* Steven thought pensively and frowning for a moment. *There's so much we don't know yet the information is right under our noses if we just looked for it...*

He had looked around the room for other reasons why someone could have deserted it in such a haste, and then he saw the display. He hadn't noticed it until he stood in the centre of the room as it was dark there, but as he'd walked around more of the lights had turned on, and he'd only noticed this display in that moment. In the half-dark stood a display like another he'd only seen once before. In a room beside where they'd listened to the messages on the cube for the first time after deciphering the code to get it activated in an audible fashion rather than the clicks and hisses, they'd heard until then. But when an Academist had noticed that Steven saw the device in the next room over they'd quickly closed the door.

I still remember how people had reacted to the message, Steven thought bitterly. *I still remember how people reacted after they'd selected me as Subject, and up to a certain moment I'd considered doing they'd expected me to do things their way to succeed.* But his father's warning had altered Steven's perception. Now he was travelling to solve a mystery. A potential deadly mystery without any outcome with a certainty for him. He was uncertain what the mystery had been, until this moment, when he'd spotted the display in this long-abandoned room. *—and laughably they'd given me a haphazard sort of explanation about who I am supposedly, and what I'm going to do while I'm travelling a Subject, and which was—what—exactly?* Steven was thinking as he stared at the familiar display in the room.

Steven recalled the conversation during his father had angrily observed with a scowl on his face. His father had shown anger towards the two visitors and not a wayward son who'd made such a foolish, hasty decision about his career choice. Steven had smirked as he recalled now how much both men visiting their dwelling, had stammered. A lot. While they'd faced him, Steven had refrained from laughing or grinning because his father had been rather stern at that moment...

The general explanation was that he needed to check the conditions within Zone Zero, which, apparently, was still polluted from the effects of the World War 3, which had happened 370—no it was 380 years ago, and he needed to go into the zone, apparently alone as they'd stated though they couldn't explain why alone or anything else, and he needed to discover what the conditions there were. All he could do when he heard them say this nonsense was to ask with his mind: *Alone...? How can I do all it alone...? Who was the stupid bastard who came up with the stupid rule...?*

It was the preposterous nature of the task that really made me wonder then. How could they send someone alone? He'd been aware by then that thirty-six other individuals had been sent out to fulfil this same task, and none of them had ever returned from their journeys. Steven also wondered why someone would get sent out only every ten years, and not three, or five, or even every year...

Steven had asked them, even had asked his father, but had only got glances towards toward where the third, obviously temporary structure was standing as an ominous feature against the empty skyline as an answer. When they'd glanced again where it had been standing minutes later it was there, and then about ten minutes later when Steven had looked in that direction again to look at 'them' angrily, it seemed to be gone from view again. Almost like someone was playing a game with him that day.

So convenient for the structure to come and go, Steven thought, frowning momentarily, that at that very moment he was the angriest at the decision to be selected as a Subject....

He'd wondered in the days that would come, until it had been time for him to leave, about what he'd known of what had happened, both from the message and his own assumptions, of what exactly had happened. They had told him Zone Zero was polluted by them. *Whoever the 'they' was...*

Was the pollution somehow as dangerous as the messages had mentioned some danger in Zone Zero? In the message they'd mentioned about someone who wouldn't surrender. It hadn't sounded like something to do with pollution, but Steven felt uncertain what else it could be. He'd been told to find out the condition of Zone Zero and then also told to come back with this information to tell the others in Utopus.

But if they sent other subjects, Steven thought, *wouldn't they already have that information...?* So, it had left him questioning the most puzzling thought one more time: "Why didn't any of them come back?"

The disease, as mentioned in the recordings, had spread around the world fast, and was apparently devastating, according to the message. It hadn't only affected humans, but had also caused much of the plant life, and after that animals to perish as well. Steven guessed it had something to do with everything being a part of the food chain.

It had caused a 99 percent mortality rate according to the message, and Steven had often wondered if the disease had affected the plants and animals on this planet with similar effects as it had affected humans. He was already long enough in Zone Zero to believe that this was a correct assessment.

Steven found himself admitting to himself that Zone Zero was a mystery to him, and that he didn't really know if a singular Subject travelling there could ever solve such mysteries.

19.

HOWEVER, THE BUILDING HERE WAS an even bigger mystery when he stared at a screen on one of the walls, and his mind was already comparing this display to one at the Academic Institute; the one that an Academist hadn't wanted me to be able to study. Steven recalled how much disdain had been present in the man's voice who'd asked why I was there and had already assumed that I was a 'scientist.'

There was a link between what he'd found in this building, and what he'd observed back then.

This building was obviously a relic from a long-forgotten war, and whoever had abandoned it did this perhaps because the effects of the war, which wasn't with the weapons they called 'nuclear weapons' but through almost a mundane, laughable nature. The people of five hundred years ago had never expected these events, and when it was too late, they had no way of stopping what was happening around them.

Steven surmised that the people who were saying they would never surrender were ridiculing the world at large. A part of the rogue organisation was playing bee-keeper or butterfly catcher or something of the sort. However, the proper method of their 'conquest' of the world had taken on the form of several revolutions.

To Steven, at least, there seemed to be a warning in all this, especially in the warning in the transmission, saying that humans might end up seizing to exist if we didn't listen to the warnings listed in the recordings. Steven crossed his arms over and considered extensively as to what this building could represent.

His father had told him he thought the building was part of an organised effort of defence that the people of five hundred years ago had felt necessary to exercise. Steven had realised fast what the impact would be if the reality had become true one day. In the warning, they had stated there was a 99 percent mortality rate and that the population had been about eight billion back then…

It had meant that Utopus had started with only eighty million humans *alive*. There were very few children, so he assumed that the population hadn't have the time to grow much since the war. If a similar thing was to happen now, it would leave the population at less than a million, and that number wasn't likely 'enough' to allow the population to sustain itself in sufficient quantities for it to survive…

It's possible that humanity is slowly recovering, Steven thought.

But if the people who'd caused the events of five hundred years ago were still around, they could easily cause it all to repeat. Steven assumed that this was what his father was afraid of, and that this was what the true nature of his mission might be as a Subject. Not to just check for evidence to find out if the world had healed, but to prevent the same mistake from happening one more…

So, we were once this 'human race,' Steven thought sarcastically, *and some among this race had the idea, the audacity to think that others weren't worth enough to be alive…*

As he understood it there was a reason for the display he was looking at. Something about it was showing him the locations of the places, such as this current building. Better that the entrance collapsed and buried everything. It was maybe better if the building with the tall, metal object was buried and gone from existence, if that alone would safeguard the future of whatever was leftover of the old world.

He compared in his mind what a desolate place such as Zone Zero could reveal, compared to their research inside Utopus, and he realised something rather profound. Steven knew that the language he was familiar with most, was spoken hundreds of years ago by many people but not in this region really. Elizabet spoke English too, but she'd told him her parents would speak in the original local language that the people living in old city, Stockholm, would have spoken. There were people in Utopus who could only speak one language…

Sometimes, meals were shared in larger groups, and at those events it would be almost a game to say certain things, and then have it translated in various languages, then have the answer be translated too in various languages. It proves that cooperation was emerging among the people who'd survived. A sense of cooperation might have restarted when the survivors had banded together in 2142. That was the biggest lesson we could learn from World War 3. There were two other wars before this last war, and Steven had read about them in a few books he'd been able to find, but he couldn't believe that humanity had learnt the lesson until after it was too late for them, which had been the case after this last war, and Steven was certain he wouldn't really want to have another one to happen.

Steven had hurried to pack his belongings, and while he'd been showering hastily, he'd heard his father return home. He guessed his father had wanted a final moment with his only son before he, Steven, had stepped from the house as Subject 37 and Steven remembered that they stood staring at one another for a while, then his father had sat down and motioned for his son to sit down too. Steven had guessed his father didn't want to rush this last moment, and he couldn't blame his father for it. Steven immediately wondered what his father had wanted to talk about when he'd pulled a book from under his coat.

"I found this earlier—" his father had said, and he'd pushed the book in front of me.

Steven had stared at the book, and he'd felt somewhat puzzled.

"Read it—" his father had said.

Hesitantly, Steven had opened the book. He'd looked at the almost faded title of the book. It had a strange title. He couldn't find a name for the writer of the book. There was a date. Listed as from 2044.

"But—" Steven protested at first.

"This book proves, more than anything else can, that 478 years ago things were normal enough still in this world for someone to have written this book," he'd said. "I don't know who has written it or why. The name is too faded to figure out. But make sure you remember this story while you travel and remember that someone long ago wrote a book in which she'd warned about the consequences of being too impassive about what is happening to the world. The person was born before the events in the recording happened. It says so on a page at the back. She never expected the events that would come less than a decade later after this book was created..."

"Why did you show me this?" Steven had asked.

"For you to learn a lesson from it," my father had said, "Read it before you go. I'll have to call you Subject 37 once we leave this house, but to me, you'll always be Steven."

Steven had sat back, then he'd picked up the book, and had read the book thoroughly. In the part-torn introduction, the book stated it was the last ever book to be written by this unknown author of a book with a half-faded title. He'd read the book and by the time he'd finished reading Steven realised what he needed to do once he was in Zone Zero.

Afterwards, Steven got up and walked from the house carrying his rucksack, and he didn't even bother closing the door.

Neither his father, nor he, would ever return to it, anyway.

His journey had started in such a simple way. Just with him walking from his house for a while. Walking over the road south until he noticed that his father was waiting for him. To Steven, the walk made him realise what he'd miss in Utopus. He would miss going to the Academic Institute, and that even though people there had looked at him with disdain even after he was selected, and suddenly he didn't mind it. Except for Elizabet or his father, nothing else here mattered anymore…

Besides all that, there was one other thing that mattered to him, but he'd run out of time to work on it. He'd cared about finding out more about the message discovered. Steven had his own views of what the message might mean for everyone. It told them of a war, of people who didn't want to surrender to something, and of something that had happened to the world he was living in.

He realised that going into Zone Zero would allow me to find an answer to the question, 'Why?'

The world of five hundred years ago was both fascinating and strange at the same time. He wasn't certain how they spent their everyday lives, but the books told him much about that world…

Steven had found information about the lives of the people of many centuries earlier in a few of the books that he was able to find among the ruins near his dwellings, and some of these same books would have dates listed in them. Steven had tried to work out how every day might have been like if he'd lived during that time. He would find other books which all contained stories in them of some sort, and the most fascinating of them all was a story of a man who was building a machine to go to a distant future.

He could imagine walking along the road, and then suddenly seeing a machine appearing with such a man in it, and if the man asked if he, Steven, wanted to come with him to the past, he was certain he'd say 'yes.' Steven would fantasize that all previous thirty-six Subjects had all somehow met such a man with a machine and had gone to a time of five hundred or more years ago to live the rest of their lives safely away from horrors of this world.

But he knew it was just a fantasy, and that such a man would never come.

Steven concluded from the rather pessimistic view that people had established Utopus to survive a war, and like everyone else, he'd walked foolishly around a place that was apparently dangerous if he trusted the words of the message word for word. He wondered if the people in the past had enjoyed every day, had proper type of work or were able to have fun with friends, but that it was all lost on the day that Utopus became necessary.

What he concluded from his pondering as he had walked along the road was that the structure, inside Utopus, that keeps appearing and disappearing, had been doing this since Utopus had existed. He contemplated again over the story of the machine capable of travelling to distant futures, and he wondered if the building was something similar, but as soon as the thought entered his mind, his rational, scientific mind had dismissed it as a ridiculous idea.

He reviewed what he knew of the war once more as mentioned in the message. It had suggested that the war had come with terrifying consequences, and that Utopus was established because of those consequences. He recalled reading about two other wars. It had stated that well over a million individuals had died during these earlier wars, and many more likely in others. But compared to the mortality rate suggested for World War 3 in the year 2142, the number had been minimal by comparison.

However, Steven was certain that, for the time in which it had happened, the number had been as terrifying them as the events of the past 370 years were for his own fragile society. And yet, his society had come away from it with good housing, good health, and the best of everything... *at least that was what they had wanted to convince us with.*

The cold war, which got mentioned in yet another book, seemed to be like what was happening now in Utopus. During this time, at least according to the few books I found subsequently read, people were trying to convince themselves that they were at war with each other, and it was claimed in a small picture with this weird cloud, which seemed to resemble a few of the mushrooms growing in the ditch near my old apartment, was how this cold war could be won.

I've got no idea what this cloud might have represented, Steven thought, *but a cloud of smoke surely can't just get rid of two groups of people who are hating each other, can it now?*

Perhaps the woman whose picture he'd found inside the metal building, and which he'd taken with him was perhaps sad because she had known that such a destructive cloud could happen. She'd been perhaps sad because she'd been so scared of it happening.

It might be that the people who'd lived during this earlier time had lived in fear. When he'd stared at the faces of people in those books their faces were showing him that they'd feared their version of the world. Steven was guessing that the hundreds of years that had lead towards what had caused Utopus to be established were fearful, violent times, and if that was the case, no wonder there were people who would tell others they wouldn't surrender...

This violence wasn't just present whenever there was any war, but that it had also been happening in the cities themselves. Some books would tell of people being shot dead for what they'd believed.

But Steven wondered what the difference might have been between their sort of believing and the apparent belief of the people who'd said they wouldn't surrender ever. Later he'd know that there was even a word for the behaviour, and it had apparently meant that someone had a belief in something specific. It was the word 'religion.' Some people in Utopus still would say that they 'believed in a higher being,' and would go on to say they have a 'religion,' but no one he knew was this way.

Steven decided then that he was too much a scientist, too practical for him to divulge in this way of a belief in something as described in the books. Besides, what do we have as anything to believe in any way? The world is broken beyond the ability for humans to repair it unless they found a way to coexist without any war, and no amount of believing in something invisible could ever fix the damage done by the people of the past or the damage done by nature...They could only fix the world if they worked at it and worked hard.

That had been why people had arrived in Utopus. Humans needed *safe* communities. They would fear communities because they'd assume violence or war would come to it, but they also needed it because it would also make them feel like they were safe.

Like what had happened when Steven had spotted the little girl as he'd walked at night through the darkness of the building, he'd been living in. She'd looked scared when she saw me, because she hadn't known who he was, yet she'd stared at him like she felt brave for wandering around in the building all alone at night in the darkness. All humans were like this now, and now more so since World War 3.

As Steven had walked towards the border of Utopus, he'd seen the same fear appear on the faces of the people whom he'd pass on the way there. They feared what he represented, but they also felt safer because of what he was. They had looked at one another with the fear on their faces. Steven had seen it, and they knew he had seen it...

Steven saw fear too on the faces of the people who'd been present in the room when all of us were listening to the message.

We, they, all knew the threat posed in the message was real. There were fearful warnings within it, and when everyone had glanced at others for reassurance, we all saw the same fear on each other's faces. We had all wanted to ask one another one specific crucial question: "What had caused 99 percent mortality? Is the cause still around? Could it harm us?"

We'd all been too afraid to speak...

The message had also mentioned a connection between people who'd believed in something and were trying to establish something for 'the people who were pure in their believing,' the unnamed people who didn't want to surrender, and the disease that had caused for almost all humans to die in a relatively narrow window of time. The books and the messages had told us people had started with such behaviour at the beginning of what the message had called the '21st century.'

By his calculations that was well over five hundred years ago rather than anything directly connected with the origins of Utopus. Steven couldn't believe that a war could have gone on already for over five hundred years. I won't accept it, Steven thought brittlely.

Earth, which until relatively recently had been the name for the planet, had endured so much war that it made Steven honestly wonder how it could still exist with everything that went on and afterwards. The rogue organisation mentioned in the message did more damage to this planet than all the previous wars combined. And from the message, something was happening, which could mean it could happen again.

The message warned not to send any other Subjects out, because it was too dangerous, and yet they had still sent him.

20.

... I GUESS I'M TASKED TO find out what happened in that hell hole then, and yes, I'm getting angry now because I must keep repeating the same things to the questions you want to know. I guess you don't want to about my journey and what I found then, right? Oh, so you want to know... Right, let me keep figuring this out, and okay Steven, he thought angrily when for a moment his mind had gone blank. He would let his mind again but finally had to accept defeat and know he needed to write things down thoroughly.

Is having to repeat the same information or events over and over a sign I'm already going mad because of this journey done alone? Steven thought.

He had been walking from his old dwelling over the road towards the south border, and his father had stood there, waiting for him to arrive... and to leave not long after. As he was quite aware of what he'd written earlier already, Steven suddenly felt a need to stop his behaviour and just leave immediately. *I guess I'll just skip forward then*, Steven thought, *to when I had walked away from this old metal building with its secrets.*

* * *

So, Steven had grabbed the rucksack, now lighter from him having consumed several containers of the soup brought from his former home. He'd planned to find food inside the bunker, but weapon would possibly render that unnecessary. He'd hunt instead. As he'd done with his slingshot device since he was close to two decades younger. He repacked everything in such a way to have additional space for a few of the items he'd found in this room. He wafted over the surface wherever he grabbed something to bring with him. So not to leave a visible mark that something was now missing. After a little over an hour, he stood ready for his real departure. Now much better equipped and prepared than before...

It did take him some effort to leave the building, and he'd almost forgot to bring the mask he had found with him too, which he'd planned to wear as often as he could to protect himself against any possible poisonous gasses or fumes which could exist in Zone Zero. He wasn't prepared to take any stupid risks that where avoidable with simple preparations. He didn't yet realise then, that far more dangerous things were awaiting him during his journey through this old desolate Europe, which was only recognized now as Zone Zero. That the story of his discoveries, meeting his mother and sister if he could, and then if he'd succeeded in that for us to reunite with his father was only the beginning of a long story that would occupy the rest of his natural lifespan, that Steven would only discover at the end of it all…

Steven could only vaguely imagine what the other parts of the world might look like, and if the message they'd received was anything to go by it wasn't any prettier than anywhere else.

Most people in Utopus feared what was out there, which was obvious as the current version of the rogue organisation wanted to terrorize them. That was likely why they did no kind of attack with these called nuclear weapons as stated in a later section of the message. So, when he though closer about everything, Steven realised that the rogue organisation wasn't benevolent to anyone on this planet when they did their version of being peaceful, and then Steven had also been wondering as well as to how many of their own so-called 'true believers' might have died from the very disease they had spread to remake the world into their own warped image…

My father had been correct, Steven thought. *The disease has left the world to the people who may truly be entitled to it and that is the people who ended up immune to its effects, and that is all the offspring from those survivors back then. I can only imagine what the effect the disease was on the people affected by it. In the message, it was suggested its effect was like a disease that they had back then, but that this disease was so much faster. The more worrying thing is the people of the rogue organisation who survived… Until they're all gone the threat, they pose remains…*

That had been the secret of their success, if he, Steven, could call 'killing off' all of lifeforms on a planet any type of success. Steven had then smiled wryly when he realised that everyone in Utopus had thought that they were the *only* ones left on the planet, and as Steven noticed fast that he wouldn't discover any people or animals during his journey, he was almost certain he was correct with the assessment. But then, during the first trek away from the bunker was when he saw a bird. A bird, of all things. Like in the story that he and Elizabet had read on the singular sheet of paper they'd found inside a derelict wooden building with a tower beside it with something hanging from it that had made an echoing sound when they each had moved the cord hanging from it. This building had looked even older than the buildings that had belonged to Stockholm…

Steven always sarcastically went like: "Hurray, I've succeeded with my task, now someone tells me I can go back and tell them stuff is living over in Zone Zero…" —*and yes, I need to say it all rather sarcastically too,* Steven thought, *every time I found a contradiction so far, I've had that thought pass through my mind.*

But rather than turning back, Steven kept walking. He'd given himself two new purposes to keep going forward and attempt to succeed. The first reason was to make sure his father hadn't misplaced his trust in his only son by giving up now, and the second reason was to find out where the hell the outlined route would lead to.

I guess to this place in a mountainous place where there could be people, Steven thought. *So, in the north of Spain… Or wherever the place really is.*

As Steven walked along a particular road that might have been picturesque for the people who travelled there in better times, Steven noticed he was seeing very few leaves on the very few trees that were present there, and those that were there were showing the first few browns and reds of the autumn. When he'd decided on being a Subject, these leaves would have just started to grow. This showed Steven how long it had been since he'd handed a letter to his father…

✷ ✷ ✷

Steven had so often been told that everything outside Utopus was dead that message and repetition of it became ridiculous as he'd walked on during this early part of the journey. *So how then can I see these plants grow leaves,* Steven thought, *and then get ready for winter? It's what my father had said as well, or more precisely whispered to me. Zone Zero isn't as dead they've always claimed it to be…*

Later, Steven would discover an unnatural obsession from certain people towards his father, and discover that an awful lot of questions about him were being asked. *Well, I can you say something interesting about him?* Steven had often asserted for his own benefit in his next thought, *and so after we had said this goodbye, and never even gesticulated the word, because it wasn't so much a goodbye, more like a sarcastic attempt of two people who'd so obviously cared for one another* to have to behave like they were complete strangers to one another…

He said goodbye to me, and I kept looking back towards him when I walked away, Steven thought sadly, *and he just stood there, and the way he stood there was weird.* Steven stopped walking abruptly. He stood in the same pose that his father had stood in. In this moment, as he realised how alone he was, Steven wanted to scream at the top of his lungs: "I'm Steven Burgard" so to let the whole damned world realise that he still existed, and how alone he was now…

But my father had said that to him I'd always be Steven, he thought, *and he had told me so…*

This would mean that all the rest of what his father had said or done afterwards was all just a show to give the pretence of compliance with whatever rules the people in charge were enforcing, and who I now fervently believed to be the occupiers in the third structure who might also still be believing themselves, like the people of Utopus did, that everything was still status quo…

That they were still controlling everyone in Utopus, and even everything outside it.

They had wanted to maintain an idea of mystery or deception, even with what they were doing over there in Utopus, and his father hit back at them in an equal measure of the same.

Or much more, Steven thought. He had slowly turned around as he'd contemplated over his status. *If they're using the deception to intimidate us all,* he was thinking as he glared north, *and is that why the people were walking past me without looking at me when I was selected as a Subject. No one, not even any of the few children, would look at me, or acknowledge after that day.* He tried to glance at the now exceedingly distant vista of Utopus which triggered a memory…

* * *

Steven could just about see the island in the distance with my distance viewer as I'd told Elizabet that my object was called. She knew perfectly well it was called 'binoculars' but she'd played along with the fun of giving an inanimate object a name. That had got me thinking about the island as I had studied it with the binoculars. The island had probably been surrounded by an expansive ocean that could have gone to the opposite landmass, but now the island sat lost in the middle of a dusty landscape with the water far away from it…

The sun was shining brightly on everything, and the shininess of the dust made it appear that any water there still had existed in this landscape was so much closer. When Steven sat with Elizabet on this coast one day, on one of our few days that they'd go for a walk to the east, she'd noticed the phenomenon, and had told him about it.

"Is it dust or waves?" she'd asked.

"It's dust," Steven had said.

"No, there's water out there," she'd countered.

The conversation had locked them in a "yes and no game" for perhaps an hour before the weather conditions had proved to her that he'd been right all along…

* * *

As Steven travelled more and more south, he saw the same phenomenon every time where the landscape had wanted to play tricks on him. But then a lot of things during the journey started doing the same sort of things. Mystery was all good and fine when it was only a story.

Like, the stories his father had kept telling him. His father would say that it wasn't not good to have mysteries when the world had been broken to how it appears to be now. Steven had an example of such a situation. He knew that the third structure exists—somehow. That a Subject exists too for the people around me to fear—somehow. In that situation the faces of the children were the worse. Those children had gone from waving at me on one day to ignoring me the next day. Steven had no answers for this behaviour other than that fear was doing it.

Another example crawled itself into his mind. This one so vividly that Steven had bent over and was brushing over his head with clawed fingers for a minute to dispel the fear from his mind. The fear didn't come from memories of other people in Utopus but more of seeing in his mind what his father had demonstrated one day with creepy accuracy. His father had fixed an old device to show one of the old 'movies' we possess, well mostly fragments of them. In one such old movie that he'd watch with his father, Steven had discovered that the people in the past 'could' be the masters of suspense, and that they were good at scaring people who would watch these movies… and when some birds near him flew up a moment later, with them breaking the pressing silence of Zone Zero, that was when such a movie came to his mind.

Birds can be scary when you expect the world to be empty and lifeless, Steven thought as he glared angrily after the flock.

Steven had stopped to eat something, and had eaten a few of food stuffs, made of grains, that he'd found in his bag. Steven didn't recall packing them, and he assumed his father had obviously packed into his son's rucksack. He was sitting there looking at his little map, at the line drawn on it which he'd copied from the larger map. By that time, he'd managed to travel as far as the sharp bend in the route that was visible. *My next move needs to that I go across to this other coast*, Steven thought, *and follow the route down to this place where, apparently, I can go over the water on a bridge of some sort…*

That was when he'd spotted the unknown package in his rucksack. Something which Steven was certain that he hadn't packed it in there. He lifted the package, opening it. What he found inside it would become an obsessive pastime for him whenever he was sitting down for a rest somewhere. Steven knew he'd only heard part of the transmission, but his father, and yes, it was his father's handwriting written down, had likely spent dozens or even hundreds of hours transcribing all the messages word for word it seems…

Reading these texts would distract him, at least for a while, from seeing the genuine horrors of Zone Zero, but the text on the papers would also amplify what he saw around him. Steven was reading the first page. It seemed to contain a continuation to the last message he'd heard, and the words took on this somewhat personal approach, like someone was telling him something from a book or something:

> —Most think that the failed coup only happened in the nations inside the European Union, but we also have evidence that a similar incident happened on the other side of the world in a nation once named the United States.
>
> The details of what happened are vague, but this outlines what we have discovered.
>
> In Europe, a coup attempt happened in various of its nations in 2051. I think this influenced this other nation to close its borders to the outside world, but we have a sign that it too was subjected to an attempt to do a coup. Closing its borders didn't stop the disease spreading there, and because it had its borders closed, the devastation there was faster and more thorough than in most other countries. The citizens of this nation had tried to go north towards a second nation that had occupied the continent at that time, but mostly it wouldn't let people cross into its territory. The information we uncovered claim to show that this nation thought

they could do things by themselves with no need outside help or outside intervention, saying that 'God will protect us.'

They might have directed the message stating 'We will never surrender' as much towards the European nations as they had directed the message towards themselves.

United States would become a victim of its own attempt to keep the disease out. Not only did it have the fastest mortality rate, but it also seemed to suffer a total collapse of its economy and society. As food became scarce, they would stockpile any available medicine which a few people would sell at ridiculously high prices, and most people didn't want to face the waiting for the inevitable.—

The message had puzzled him after he'd read it several times…

To him, it seemed even more now that the person behind the messages wasn't conveying information from a distant past, but that everything was something they were witnessing right now. Steven glanced around to make sure he was alone. And that had been when those damned birds had to fly up again. He saw it wasn't a few of them... it was perhaps a hundred or more. They would swirl in the air, and for a few moments Steven convinced himself that they were a secret weapon of the rogue organisation and they were going to attack him. It caused him to fall backwards in a rather undignified way.

After getting back upright, Steven looked at the stack of papers, and he noticed that each page had a lot of writing on it. He guessed that every day he would need to try to read some more of its contents.

A perfect distraction for an otherwise boring walk, Steven thought.

He repacked the papers carefully, but he was uncertain if his father had intended for them to be discovered by his son. I guess that my damned curiosity is getting in the way again, Steven thought, grinning, and again, this is proof that secrets exist which will make my task as a Subject harder, but also at the same time more fun. I know books must still exist somewhere within Zone Zero in a long-forgotten building of some sort, so I could try to find information to compare to what's written on these papers with books from hundreds of years ago…

21.

STEVEN WASN'T TRYING CAST TO doubt on the narrator of the message, but Steven needed to know how genuine this information was. He doubted some information that he'd found out, and this doubt wasn't dispelled easily. The means to getting it dispelled would come much later.

So, he got up and walked on. Steven was now looking for a T-shape in the road. At the T-shape, the road either led south or west, and he intended to go west. The old road he'd chosen would take him past the south end of a large lake, after which he'd keep going south until he'd get to a place marked on the map as second city dating from the past which was only evident by the similarity in the mark for Stockholm and this one, although neither map had any information on it for the name for the second city…

A few weeks later, Steven was staring at the vastness of a lake, which had seemed oddly out of place in the dry, sparse landscape. He saw the places where buildings would have been standing near to the lake, which were now standing in the lake instead. It did look so comical to Steven. He saw a sign, which he assumed had something to do with the roads he was walking over, was standing some ten meters from him in the water.

It looks like someone has come along, Steven thought, *and that they've pushed it there as a joke.*

Steven turned away from the lake and walked on, thinking mostly about the page he'd been reading a few weeks earlier, and he wondered for a moment if there might be someone over in the United States, right now, who'd been told a similar story about Europe and who was on a similar journey as him. Steven guessed he'd never know—neither would such a person know about him, ever. Not unless he could get over there somehow, and so another facet of his plan from later settled in his mind…

Steven had been resting when he heard a sound that was alien, and after checking everywhere it was then that he'd discovered the first of the many black flying objects that would haunt him throughout the entirety of the rest of the journey. He hid away in the undergrowth until the noise had faded…

* * *

Now cautious with his journey, it was in the first few days after arriving in the other ruined city, most of his days were now spent following an old road south, beside what was a coast beside an ocean in the past. The road once would have run alongside a sea and not beside a sandy wasteland, which had supposedly dried out many decades or even centuries ago.

However, also now, a month later, he was seeing a notable difference in the landscape. Steven stopped and wrote down a few quick scribbles with the stomp of pencil he'd found beside the road a few days earlier. There was a definite increase in greenery and vegetation in the landscape, and it seemed the more to the south end of the country he got, the more the landscape was giving him the appearance like it was recovering from the assault from humans on it in the past. Although the recovery was sporadic in places, and in some places, it had even seemingly erased all traces of human mastery over the land that had been there before, there was still enough 'brown' in the landscape to cause Steven to feel deep concern.

It needs help from humans to recover fully, Steven thought. *It needs to be cared for so the damage done to it from the effects of the disease can be removed from it— eventually.*

Steven walked past a sign, for something unfamiliar that he couldn't figure out what it was for however long he stood there staring at it. "What the fuck," Steven muttered as he stared at another of the 'signs' he'd been spotting with more regularity but this one was showing something that resembled the old car up ahead of him. He tilted his head sideways and smirked. "Now why would they want one of those things on its side," Steven quipped, "or is a secret sign to create a barrier to stop someone from using this road?" Steven glanced at another nearby sign and that one had been the target of an assault of a certain kind. Steven pulled his gun from his pocket, and aimed it at the sign too…

Steven guessed that he needed to get some practice of his own. He was uncertain how the weapon worked, and he traced over the surface with his left hand, noted an opening, and realised this was where the projectile would come from. He pointed the gun away. He didn't want to be so stupid, and then accidentally be shooting his face off in the effort of discovering the workings of the device, and he aimed the gun toward the damaged sign and glanced down to determine as to what to do next.

He glanced back at the gun, suddenly feeling hesitant. The device possessed several components which he was guessing had a part to play in getting it to work. He aimed the gun and decided that the loop of metal he'd noticed then had something to do with getting it to work, but when he tried to push it, nothing happened. He frowned…

He saw something written on the side of the gun. He squinted then read the letter first, a letter 'S' and then in an angle beside it was a plus and a minus sign.

A small knob was pressing against the plus sign. Steven tried to move the knob towards the minus sign, but nothing happened. He realised there could be bullets inside the handle of the gun, because somehow, he found a way to check the back when he was still at the bunker, and then had tried to get them back inside the gun, which was rather annoying.

The funny story that his father had once told was distracting Steven from getting overly frustrated with his efforts…

His father had said that the people of hundreds of years ago had a thing they'd say. It had something to do with a bird they called a chicken. His father wasn't sure what sort of animal it had been, but according to his father, the favourite thing to ask a person would be: "What came first, the chicken or the egg?"

Steven's scientific brain would say, "an egg." His father would always laugh at that point and ask him then, "So, where did the first chicken come from then, wise guy?"

That was how he was feeling about the gun right then. He was wondering what came first with the gun. Was it the loop to pull first, or did he need to pull something away to get the loop to work? He was about to just throw the gun in the bushes and move on without it, when suddenly he'd noticed a movement in the upper part of the gun. He pulled it with his hand, heard a popping sound, well, not really a popping sound, but it was close to one.

He saw that the motion had also pushed the metal loop on the top of the gun into another position and he held the gun up again and pushed the metal loop again, and still nothing happened. He was certain that he was close to an answer.

Steven repeated the actions from moments before, and he tried the gun a few more times, and still nothing happened, and he looked at the gun and he was so certain now that he was missing something. He saw the 'S' with the plus and minus next to it once more, and he frowned then when he realised the attachment could be the answer.

Okay, stupid scientist, Steven thought, *you need to learn to use your brains better.*

He pushed against the knob with his thumb. It moved. He lifted his arm and aimed the gun at the broken, bullet-ridden sign and he pushed his forefinger against the loop, and next his ears were ringing from the sound the device had made. He also ducked instinctively at that moment, when he heard a sharp clattering sound when he'd hit the sign, but not anywhere where it could have gone through the sign.

Steven straightened somewhat hesitantly. He had to try again. He went through the same motions as before, and this time he held my arm with the other hand. But moments later, he got almost the same effect. He caused his arm to fly up, and he jumped when dozens of birds flew up near him, making their own loud noise.

Steven almost felt like a young boy again. He stamped his feet frustrated, both over his ability to be so clumsy at learning this skill and because the birds had given him a bit of fright for the one, he gave them. He tried again, and again held his hand with the gun with the other hand…

After a moment of him checking his surroundings, mostly for the possibility other people being nearby, then he glanced back at the partly destroyed sign and then at the second sign and he shot, and this time the shot was true and he stopped then, because he didn't want to waste the few bullets he possessed, and he was uncertain where to get more. He knew he might as well pick up a thick chunk of wood to defend himself against whatever he would or could find in Zone Zero.

Steven made sure that on the device the knob was back to the minus position before he'd put it back in his pocket. Now, finding bullets was more urgent. He cursed under my breath as he had just left a city, but then he thought the sign he'd been shooting at was used to tell of another city further south. If he could reach that city before nightfall, he could search there for the bullets. He was certain of it...

* * *

There was a soft breeze in the air, and the sunset bathed the landscape in an orange hue, when Steven got to a small building to the side of the road. He figured out from the sign showing next to the sign that the so-called 'quick distance' in the numbers from twenty-three on the last sign was a lot longer to travel than he'd expected. To add insult to the matter, this sign said twenty on it...

He was uncertain what the letter 'M' might have meant in the past when this road was in use.

Steven entered the building. It was a simple wooden building, which was rare to see in Utopus where all the buildings were made of a grey, cold stone, which had seemed like what they'd made the bunker of as well. Inside the house, he discovered evidence that the people who'd lived in it once had just abandoned it, taking nothing with them.

I guess they had no time to do that, Steven thought.

He climbed the stairs to the upper floor, where animals obviously had caused mayhem with the bed and other furniture. He went downstairs again, and looked for a moment into the tiny kitchen, almost as small as the one they'd in Utopus, and then he saw a seat that was large enough for him to lie on. He rested a while on the chair. Then the urge to keep moving on set in and he got up and left the small house hastily behind him...

It took him the rest of the day to get to the next city, and when the sun was close to setting, he found a building that might have been a trading place where people bought things, like Elizabet had once suggested of another such place.

The other trading place was found because they, Steven, and Elizabet, had gone exploring in an area east of where we'd lived to explore the group of houses she'd discovered, which may have been a town once. It had the remnants of a long street that had stretched through the town, and several meters from the street were metal tracks that he'd seen in other places. Elizabet had thought it had been a road for a vehicle that must have been able to slide over it...

Damned memories, he thought, *dispelling the rest of this memory for now.*

*** * ***

Hours later, in yet another town Steven found a somewhat better temporary dwelling where he could stay overnight…

How many towns has this region have? Steven thought.

Steven lay down and looked at the ceiling above him and thought about his journey so far and he'd not got that far yet and he hadn't even got to the massive continent south of him yet. He was tired from the journey, but not ready to sleep and he glanced over to his rucksack, got up and grabbed it, then sat back down on the makeshift bed he'd made, then he opened rucksack after listening for sounds outside, and took out the package with all the papers in it.

Steven undid the bindings, lifted the outer covering away, and placed the first page, which he'd already read, to one side and picked up the second page. He leaned back and glanced at the page for a while without really seeing its content. He noticed how tired he was moments later, but then he perked up a bit when he had looked at the top of the page and saw his father's familiar, elegant handwriting there. *I didn't know that any person could write in such a beautiful way*, Steven thought, then he had smiled wistfully at the memories flooding back. *He had his head bowed, and he gazed intently at the road below him, and never even looked to see where I was walking. It was like he was trying to send this message: "My son has departed, so now I take on my shoulders the weight of the burden." Steven knew he himself wasn't a philosophical man, but his father's posture had showed him that the actions of having to let his son go were weighing heavily on him. The last thing I saw was that he'd shut his eyes, like he was blocking the world out by doing this action and therefore I don't know whether he'd seen me going into the bunker, either… I guess very few can write in this way—now.*

The page he was reading was rather gloomy. This part of message was showing me that the situation with the Subjects had another more sinister reason perhaps, and that it was because of what the rogue organisation had done, that they started doing investigations to discover the truth about everything…

Am I a spy…? Steven thought as he recalled one of the movies his father had shown him.

—There's clear evidence that shows that causing mayhem through a coup had started a century earlier than this, and it had affected different countries in different ways, for either the right or wrong reasons. Sometimes, such a coup was an attempt to rectify the damage being caused to the nation by a leader who'd been in power there for several years or even decades.

The old continent of Africa, south of Europe, was prone to such behaviour from as early as the era between 1900 and 1945, when many wars were happening, and several countries saw the wars as an opportunity to break away from the nation to whom they'd previously sworn allegiance.

After the war that had ended in 1945, the 'coup' took on a more sinister approach and aim most times, and by the end of the century, it wasn't the coup that would matter, but often the outcome. Some people have said that the events that had commenced in 2002, had directly resulted from these coups. There's evidence this isn't the case. Far from it. The people who had started the events from 2002, and beyond this date, had done such actions so to further their own agenda, regardless of what nations might suffer.

I've stated before that they're who had spread the disease around the world. They did much more damage than with their coups. They'd say that the coups failed, but only at first. Later, much later, they didn't fail, when the nations of this world had lost their ability to withstand the impact of their action. The process was slow. No one had recognised it for what it was in 2051, and then when the rogue organisation took hold in 2071, there was no one left to fight them.

It's them who are causing the harm now that is related to the actions of the earlier rogue nation. I've found the proof of it, but I need to care about getting it out. It's dangerous here, but not as dangerous as it's in Zone Zero. Do not send anyone else. It will cause them to discover what I did, and then she's also not safe anymore.—

The 'she' in the last sentence still was puzzling to Steven…

He guessed it was perhaps someone else who was helping the sender of the message who was referenced here. It was obvious from the text that it had been a part of the message he'd been working on but personally, he'd never seen this text before. It was transcribed in his father's handwriting, and Steven wondered how and when his father had got hold of this text.

22.

HE RECALLED HOW HIS FATHER had gone into work early, often leaving the house several hours before the sun would rise. Had his father worked quietly for years on the message too, without letting others know what he was doing? It presented a puzzle to him. It made him wonder now who exactly my father might have been besides a stern father, and why he'd risk his important position at work and in the community to get a message written.

On the morning of his departure, Steven had heard his father arrive home while he was hastily showering. He had thought he'd come home like that to spend the last few hours with a son he might never see again. Now Steven was certain he put the package of papers into his rucksack. He remembered cursing at the time because his rucksack had seemed heavier. He now realised why…

The papers he had then found gave him a message about events from the past. He had only read the first two pages, but every page had the same tightly-written content on it as he ran his finger over the side of the pile, and he wondered for whom the message was meant. He doubted now it was for him as some twisted bedtime story, or anything of the sort. It was likely he needed to take this information somewhere.

Was that 'somewhere' in Zone Zero? Steven thought.

How could he take papers to anywhere else if everyone and everything was dead? He thought for a while, staring at the other wall without seeing it.

"The map," Steven mumbled.

He opened his rucksack again and lifted the map from the pocket where he'd placed it in. He moved the pile of papers and the loose sheets beside him on the bed and spread the map out on the table that he then pulled closer with one hand. He studied the line that someone had drawn. He was sure now that it was a route someone had purposefully placed on the map, and the line looked too fresh to have been created when the map was last in use, and he traced his hand over the map, following the line.

By his calculations, he was close to where the map seemed to move over the blue colour, which he figured out to be the sea. He realised also then that he'd been on this journey for a totality of ten days, or fifteen if he included the time in the bunker. He leaned forward and looked carefully at the map for a moment. He was certain the other map user didn't mean for him to swim through the ocean, because then the papers would get wet. It was this moment when he noticed another line next to the drawn line that was obviously placed on the map when the map was created.

Steven hoped now this other line represented what he was hoping for, and that there was a bridge at that location for him to use to pass to the small peninsula sticking up from Europe.

Steven sat back up and contemplated over his other predicament. He needed bullets for the gun. *In the old city next to the bridge, there should be a place where I would be able to find bullets*, he thought as he stared again at the wall opposite of him. He didn't realise what he'd been staring at until he was packing everything for his journey the next morning.

Steven lay down on the makeshift bed again, after moving the papers into the rucksack. Somehow, it felt dangerous to just leave them lying on the table, even though he knew no one else would come here. There were no sounds other than the gentle creaking of the nearby old wooden building, although he was certain that he didn't want to be inside it if one of the dust storms came. He stared at the ceiling, and the large brown circle of damage there caused him to have strange ideas come to his mind.

Steven imagined seeing faces or shapes of things on the ceiling. Even Elizabet's sad, smiling face was there, too.

As the darkness of night filled the room, his mind drifted off, thinking about the stories his father used to tell to entertain a boy. Steven frowned when he realised suddenly that he possessed very few actual memories of his childhood, and just a few of him growing up. *I guess that was one reason my father never talked to me about that*, Steven thought, *so I had no memories to impede what would be my task…*

For a time, the memories focused on Elizabet, and he realised that those memories were just as few and he was remembering always playing with her as a child, but never was he remember where or when. He remembered being friends with her as he was growing up, but it always seemed to be something vague in the background. Even the memories of her visits, when he was an adult already, were few.

Steven now tried to remember his mother, and the only image he'd ever had of *her* was of her walking away and him calling after her: "Mama, Mama." His mother was the genuine mystery in all these events.

His father had claimed he'd loved her, yet he would never speak about her. He'd claimed that he couldn't speak about her, and Steven now wondered why. Something had happened to her when he was thirteen, and it was obvious to the rational part of his mind that he was shielding him from the event for various reasons, including the trauma of losing a parent. He'd only ever said that she needed to go. Steven frowned when he realised, for the first time with some clarity, that his father never had said where his mother had to go, nor that he had said why.

He remembered his mother vaguely. He remembered her having coppery brown hair, grey eyes, and in his mind, she always seemed to smile, especially at her son. His father had his black hair, and Steven's hair almost took on the same colour as his father's. But then Steven had stared a few times at a reflective surface, and he'd studied his eyes, visible in the smudgy mirror and they were a darker copper brown but mostly like his mother's eyes, or so his memories were telling him.

Steven smiled when this memory came to my mind, and he realised suddenly that he liked the sort of memories where he could see the three of us together were among the best of them…

* * *

Steven was uncertain when he'd fallen asleep finally, but he got woken up by the most peculiar sound he'd heard his entire life. It was a sound he'd never heard before. It took a while for his mind to figure out where he currently was and what he was doing there, and he stared around with glazed eyes.

A few moments later, he heard the odd sound again. He chuckled softly then because the sound had a comical feeling about it. When he laughed louder, the creature which was making the sound wanted to repeat the sound, almost as in answer to his laughter. Steven got upright and he packed all his belongings that were still spread on the bed into the rucksack, and then put it on his back, and then he exited the building where he'd been resting and sleeping.

He saw a bird sitting near the doorway of the house. It was white, with a thick long neck, and it was rather fat. He wondered how a bird of that size could fly. He laughed again. It made its sound again, which Steven could only interpret as it also laughing. He was uncertain as to what sort of bird this might be. But then, as it kept making the annoying, repetitive sound, he started to feel annoyed. He walked back inside the house and looked around for something useful as food.

He checked the cupboards in what had been the kitchen. All empty…

When Steven walked back into the living room, he stared again at a specific place in the room. Suddenly, he realised what his tired eyes didn't register the evening or night before. There were things lying on the floor that resembled the bullets in his gun. He walked over and knelt and studied the small objects for a while. Then he took his gun out of his pocket and remembered how the handle storing bullets was supposed to open. He compared every bullet lying on the floor with those in his gun.

After perhaps an hour, he possessed over two hundred bullets, which he was certain would work in the gun.

He saw a box lie on the floor near him and emptied it to put the bullets in it and then saw a small duffel bag near where he was kneeling and pulled it towards him. Steven placed the selection of bullets, collected as suitable, into the box, then he lifted a few handfuls of the other bullets into the bag loosely. If he couldn't use them for guns, at least he could get the powder from them as I suddenly was remembering how his father had said something about the powder being useful for many other things…

Easier to make a campfire now, Steven thought.

Steven straightened up and balanced the duffel bag in his left hand. It was heavy, but he was certain he'd be able to carry it too. He now had his rucksack, the rope, a gun, and an extra bag and he placed them all on the table and was about to sort them out when the damned bird started its cackling laughter at him, and it made him curse loudly and pull his gun from his pocket and to only turn around to see the bird standing in the doorway. Steven smiled then…

Okay, my morning meal came walking my way here, I guess, Steven thought, grinning somewhat.

He grabbed the gun's upper part so as not to startle the animal, pushed the knob on its side, and pulled the loop back, while aiming at the fattest part of the bird. A shot rang out. He heard other similar birds flying off at the same time. They would go to wherever had been their destination without this one. The laughing bird would become a welcome morning meal for him…

He lifted the bird up from the floor and realised then it was much heavier than he'd imagined a bird could be. He placed the carcass on the porch, and then set about figuring out how he could build a cooking fire on which to put the bird. He walked around the building and saw that once long ago someone must have had a fireplace in the building, because he found a stack of cut pieces of wood underneath a roof.

The pieces closer to the ground looked rotten, and on touching them, it was obvious they were too far gone to be of any use, but few at the top were still useful. He spent an hour moving the wood from under the roof to a place two or three meters away from the front of the house. He had trouble starting a fire, even with the methods his father had showed him, but maybe two hours later he had a decent campfire going…

Steven threw the bird on top of the fire without even trying to take the feathers off.

He wondered what the bird would taste like after he cooked it. He added more wood on the fire, then went back into the house, and grabbed the bags and rope from the table, and carried them all outside, where he put them on the ground several meters from the fire, making sure they were on the side of the campfire where the wind was coming from. He figured that with the house being so old, that a spark from the fire easily could set it to fire and he didn't want to lose his rucksack or anything in it and losing them would probably defeat the purpose of everything that his father had been doing. Steven imagined that he'd be angry if his father realised that all his work was gone. He checked the bird when he saw the skin of it turning a nasty black colour, and used a stick to pull it off the fire and then used his boot to stomp out the few live embers that had fallen with the bird.

He went back into the house because he remembered seeing a small knife in a drawer when he'd rummaged through them.

He decided to bring along the knife as well on the remainder of his journey and realised he was better equipped for the journey than at the time of his departure from Utopus. By the time he'd eaten the bird, which tasted rather strange, he'd formulated most of the broad plan he wanted to go with on his journey.

Steven eyed the bird and decided that it being here would mean that elsewhere on his journey there would be similar animals, and so he should be on the lookout for them. That was also what would make him much more aware of his surroundings he was guessing, and why he might be able to avoid later troubles easier if they came his way…

* * *

After another twenty minutes he was ready to depart and get to the bridge as fast as his feet could carry him there. Then, just a minute before he would depart, his instinct telling him that someone could come along and discover, somehow, he'd been here.

So, Steven threw one of the few pieces of the burning wood on the porch before he walked away. If it caused the house to burn down, whoever came past it in the future would think a flash of light from the sky had done it during a storm.

* * *

Steven had been walking for several days before he saw another sign for what he assumed was the city he was hoping to reach.

This time, he was happier as the number next to the name showed a lower number. It said '3' and although he still didn't know what the number meant he'd calculated in his mind how many days he'd been walking. It was easy to do this afterwards, because on the morning after he'd departed from the house, he carved a tiny indent in the gun's side handle.

Big enough for him to know it was there, but too small for anyone else to make sense of it if they somehow got hold of it and wondered what it meant.

Steven was staring in some awe at his surroundings as he finally arrived in this next nameless town many hours later. There was a mixture of houses here, some were made of wood and the house he'd found a few days earlier had resembled them, but others were made of stone, and were like how the buildings of Utopus had been constructed, except these buildings had varying colours to them.

We'd walked into several buildings where we saw shriveled foods, tins of food, and in one of these sort of buildings it appeared that people had left in a hurry, leaving little bits of paper and round metal disks on the cupboard, Steven thought, smiling wryly, *and I got curious and use a metal pipe to knock a machine near it open, and*

Elizabet and I had looked in wonder at the many pristine papers and metal disks inside. The papers on the cupboard had lost all the colour or markings on them, but the ones in the drawer had numbers on them - 100, 50, 20, 10. The coins had the same, with several with the number 5 on them...

Steven remembered their conversation so clearly. They'd arrived at a sign listing I-N-D then there was a missing part at the beginning and in the middle, and there was the letters B and G partly visible under the rust. Listed with a 1 beside it. Someone had purposefully made a hole in the sign to remove the ability to see the town's full name.

"I read something in a book about a 'shop' and I think this building was one of them," Elizabet had said resolutely, "and these were used to pay for the things here."

"People were buying their food back then?" Steven had asked and he'd immediately felt so stupid as his friend had seemed to know this information, and he did not...

"Yes, and there are several of these buildings here—" she had said. "People didn't just live here, they also bought food, and I think it was one work people did then."

We'd walked on and arrived at a building that had made both of us curious. It was a building where people might have worked, but the tower at the top made it seem rather special. It stood alone, away from all the rest of the houses, and we both wondered why it stood so near to the lake.

"People came here to meet each other," she had suggested. "Like when we all get together for the speeches in Central District."

Somehow, I think the purpose of that building was more fun, Steven thought, than any of the times when we had been standing there and were forced to listen to three hours of speeches. My father was fuming when we arrived home days later... we'd been at that mysterious town with its two lakes and the place for building machines for many days...

23.

STEVEN SPOTTED A BUILDING THAT resembled a place for buying things from his most recent memory, which resembled the building that he'd visited with Elizabet, and he walked inside it, and he looked around as this place somehow seemed different. He looked for the cupboard where they would have kept the papers and metal disks, but he found most of them had been emptied out.

The rust as showing on the machines that stood there in shambles, and Steven assumed they were some sort of machine for a purpose that was an unknown to him, and it told him that the damage to them was likely hundreds of years old.

It was even worse in that building with the huge machines near the town with those two massive lakes beside it, Steven thought.

He walked around and minutes later had found several metal containers which he remembered his father coming home with when he still lived in Utopus. His lips curled into a broad smile when he spotted a container with a familiar picture on it. It was his father's soup. Steven wondered for a moment how to open the package, then he remembered the knife that he'd brought with him. He retrieved it from the pocket in the rucksack.

Steven placed the container in front of him, and plunged the knife downward hard, hoping he would hit the top of the container and not the cold, hard floor he was kneeling on. If he did the latter, he knew he'd break the knife.

He stared at the knife sticking out of the container for a moment. He figured that he would need to eat the soup cold as he felt hungry, so it didn't really matter to him at that moment then as he opened three more of the containers in the same fashion to look for an easier method to do this, and as he lowered the fourth container away from his lips, he spotted something hanging near him.

Steven looked at the picture on the container and noticed a tool shown to use to open a container such as the one in my hand. He felt his face burn from blushing without there being any reason for it because he realised how stupid he must have looked to a person using the shop five centuries ago because of his knife plunging technique. Steven grabbed the tool from where it hung, and grabbed another soup container, and tried to use the tool as demonstrated in the picture. He was about to give up with this method after a few tries when he noticed a drawing on the other side of the device. He tried again and heard a soft clicking echoing as the tool punctured into the container and he wondered what to do next and decided that rotating appendix on the side was connected to how it should work. He took hold of appendix and turned it. The opening became larger, so he turned the tool again.

So that's how father always opened the containers he brought home, Steven thought, and he smiled for a moment, a*nd I guess father cannot ever try to claim to me again that he did with his nails when I had asked him how he opened it....*

Steven spent the next few hours opening more of the containers with his new tool. Some of the foodstuff in the containers had got spoilt in the intervening hundreds of years, and sampling it caused him to make faces as it was either too sour or too bitter. He skipped any containers that were showing signs of rust on them. He doubted that the food in such containers stayed good for five hundred years, but he guessed that either way, he'd have food.

He sat staring up at the sky for a while, aimlessly and without focusing on anything that might be visible up there, and wondering about the whole idea of how and where he might be able to get food from and he remembered a book he'd read, in which it had suggested that fifty thousand years ago humans had hunted animals. Steven had never wanted to believe it was something real...

But then he had remembered the laughing bird that he'd shot dead and realised that the only way for him to feed safely enough would be with fresh food that were well cooked, and not the foods found in old containers from hundreds of years ago. So, he made the 'feast of soup' the last of a kind....

He didn't want to leave just yet, so he sat there resting against one of the cupboards which, if he had understood the words listed on the side correctly, would once have been used for keeping food frozen. He wondered for a moment, if he could fix the cupboards with the skills he possessed, then he decided there was no point in trying. He closed his eyes for a while then…

Not a long period of time had gone by when Steven opened his eyes again and eyed his rucksack, and he thought about the papers he was carrying with him, so he grabbed the package for the purpose of reading another page.

Carefully, Steven opened the package from his father again. He hadn't looked at it for several days, but today he decided that he needed to read one page every day, and then count the notches on the gun and in that way could work out how many pages there were in total. He figured already from the text that whoever had said the things in the recording was telling the information from memory, much as he himself was memorizing past events whenever he could, and he knew from this that it could cause for events to get all jumbled up.

If the woman in the recording had been located somewhere dangerous when she was doing all this stuff, it would mean that by sending a recording instead of writing it there was nothing for an enemy of the person to implicate such a person. He had to assume that the information got told in this way because such an enemy had already existed in the past…

The person mentioned in the messages that had warned them, of the dangers in Zone Zero. He would therefore assume that the same person was telling all this information, and that therefore they were telling about why the zone was so dangerous, perhaps even how. Steven became suspicious of the idea that they, the Subjects, were only ever going to Zone Zero to check if the pollution had reduced enough to begin making Europe safe. Or at least safer…

The task sounded just too simplistic at this point, and the information that had been provided didn't explain at any time there were thirty-six people who'd never come back to report on whether it was in fact safe or not. With this thought in his mind, he had stared at the third page…

—The last time that the United Nations had existed, amazingly, might have only been a short four years before these following events had happened. As one of their last actions they'd sent a sniper to the place where the rogue organisation base might have been situated, apparently.

Television and radio had seized to exist ten years earlier, so the rogue organisation didn't have any means to transmit their message across the world, as the earlier groups of terror would have done. They found other means to make it known that they, and only they, were in control. However, evidence exists that they themselves weren't immune to the disease.

In 2089, they told the world, in other ways, that the disease spreading in the world had been a way to get a place by the side of the god of their belief, whoever or whatever this god was to them. They said that all the people getting ill, and not in their organisation, would get punished for eternity for 'sins.' In the information that I'd found, it became apparent that over the 150 years before this, others had lived in this period of history with a similar view… that, apparently, salvation might only come from an extreme form of believing in something otherworldly.

I'm uncertain from what I have found if there's any connection between how the people of a 150 years ago assumed as fact, and how or what the individuals within this rogue organisation might have considered as their belief instead. I'm worried, though, that this way of believing still exists now.

In 2090, the rogue organisation had succeeded in assassinating the last leader of what had been this United Nations in a revenge attack. This had led to the arrests in which several of the people were heard shouting: "We will never surrender."

The following year, there was no one left to call themselves this United Nations. Most of the last people who were part of the organisation had died from the disease. The people who were arrested had escaped after the rogue organisation had assisted them, and no one heard from them again until fifty years later.

In 2142, they sent a transmission out. We don't know how it could be sent or how the survivors in various places could receive it.

The message had only a few words: "There's a place of safety in the north. If you're alive, you can go there." We don't know who had sent that message.—

Steven glanced around for a few moments, expecting angry people to come running at him at any moment. A shiver went down my spine and the hairs on my neck stood up…

He was certain that what he'd just read was about his home, about Utopus, and the way the message was written, made out that someone didn't want the true nature of its existence to be known as far back as 370 years ago. *Or longer…*

The sense of urgency was sudden. He'd made progress much faster than even he'd thought possible, but he was still at the northern end of this latest city he was passing through, and he was uncertain where exactly the bridge that was marked on the map might be. Now he also had the feeling that the people being warned about in the messages shouldn't ever see him…

He put away the papers away hastily and looked around again. He was imagining that hundreds of men, all wanting to kill him, had now surrounded me. He felt like they were standing around him, hiding behind all the cupboards and shelves here.

He got up and stared over the top of the shelves to see if he could see anyone in the building.

It was empty everywhere he looked. *Dammit, Steven, you and your paranoia…*

Steven picked up all his belongings, after putting the new tool inside the duffel bag first, and he sauntered to the window of the building. It was part broken from something that struck it from the outside in the past, and for several minutes he stood there craning his neck to look in all directions of the street. No one was outside either.

He smirked when he realised he was letting his imagination get to him, but he still exercised caution.

He was now certain that there could be someone out there who could mean to do him harm… perhaps the people of this rogue organisation that had been mentioned who'd somehow survived since 2142 and could be the ones that the message was warning about.

Steven walked to the door and stepped onto the broken pavement with caution. Something made him look up, like he was expecting something to come chasing after him from the air. He listened, but all he could hear was the sound of the wind, a few sounds he could only assume were a few birds, and the stillness of the air. It was that stillness which really got him worried.

Although the part of the city he was in seemed to have been designed that it had more people working there than living in it, the surroundings felt like there had to be people walking around and doing things.

Looking once more in both directions, Steven turned left. The sun was directly ahead of him, and from this he figured that going left meant a southern direction.

He also wondered how far he was from the ocean, as the occasional waft of wind was smelling salty and then he had two conflicting thoughts. The first thought was that he wanted to reach the bridge as soon as he could. Beyond the bridge lay a region, which, according to the message, was too dangerous to visit. He wondered also for a while whether he should just give up and make this city his permanent home.

But as he trekked south, he realised that something dastardly had happened here in the past, and that this place wasn't safe, like anywhere else, as it seemed.

The words of the message kept gnawing at his mind: "There's a place of safety in the north. If you're alive, you can go there." He wondered how his father had reacted on hearing this message. *He'd always told me that Utopus existed because it was the only place people could go to after the disease spread throughout the world, Steven thought, and it started soon after leaving, that it didn't exist for the posterity of people, more than a sore reminder of the failings of the generations who'd come before. I think that's one reason so much of that 'old world' was still lying around in a destroyed state…*

He knew he needed to get to the bridge, because it would give him the best clues to what he was now considering might be the current state of the world.

As Steven walked, he contemplated over everything he knew about Utopus. He knew it was a large area, and that the place where he'd once lived lay on the most southern side of it. He wondered for a moment why he had to go south, and why not north or east instead…

In each building lived two to three hundred people. He knew there were many houses near where he had lived. One time he had stood on his balcony and tried to count all houses he could see.

When he could only count eight buildings, he'd grabbed the

binoculars, and walked to the roof and looked in all directions through them. *There were forty.* He'd decided that the number 18-B had something to do with the houses, too. And if there was a 'B' then there was also an 'A,' so I decided that day on there were at least thirty-six districts with at least forty buildings in them with each two hundred dwellings. He knew they'd divided Utopus up into twenty-seven areas. That allowed for a tenth of all people who'd survived the disease…

Where are the other nine places? Steven thought, frowning. *Maybe we need to find them. And warn them as well. Whoever this 'we' really is… and warn about what exactly?*

* * *

As he looked at the deserted buildings of the city he was passing by, almost darting from one bit of shadow to the next, Steven thought about what he'd learnt so far…

In the old country, which had existed five centuries ago, there was Stockholm. Now he was walking to another city, but its name was eluding him, and he knew he'd passed through at least another city before reaching the most southern city…

Steven started considering that Utopus wasn't as big as everyone had ever thought, and instead that there were other places like Utopus somewhere else. *If these other paces existed, then where were they? Were they also places of which had been suggested that they would be safe? And who had told the message, anyway?*

As he walked, the breeze coming from the direction of the sea was becoming stronger. But Steven knew that he, as a scientist, was often too curious about his own good. So, without noticing it, the city became a distraction to him as he got closer to what he assumed to be the central part of it. He saw a sign showing somewhere that could have been a place of study, and because it was late in the afternoon and because he was tired too, he headed to this building as his next stop.

It took him another two hours before he found this building, and he cursed several times about the fact he'd never cared to learn more of the language that some people in Utopus had said was the old language of this land…

In the building, he saw immediate similarities between it and the Academic Institute, even down to the long seats standing against the walls in places. The middle of the entrance area could have been a place to eat. He saw a metal rectangle on a pillar and went to look at it first. It seemed to be another of those markings that shows a date.

This marking stated 17 Nov 2038, which had meant that the building was still in use about forty years before the spread of the disease in the world. Steven smiled because this building seemed to him like how it should be, how 'normal' should have been if the world was different. He was certain that Elizabet would have enjoyed walking through this building.

He had walked over to the eating area and past two strange cabinets, then back tracked and stared at them for a moment. Each one was covered over with glass, and inside them were a lot of small packets lying. A cloudy dent in one of the cabinets indicated that someone had tried to get inside at least one of them. Steven wondered about the purpose of having a glass over them and reached up for his gun.

24.

BY THE APPEARANCE OF SOME of the packages with evidence of having been partly eaten by something, he figured it contained food. He pointed his gun at the cabinet with the dent, and shot at it…

The shot echoed through the building, and he instinctively ducked when he heard three similar sounds, then cursed when he realised he was getting scared from an echo. He shot once more, and although he still flinched, he stayed standing up. Both the glass covers had shattered into thousands of small pieces.

Steven ignored the lower racks where the glass had covered the packages, and opened his duffel bag, and started grabbing all the packages which hadn't been chewed on. Occasionally, he looked at the strange names on the packages.

He had wondered what one of them tasted like and opened a package saying 'chocolate' on it. He had wondered if anyone in Utopus, who knew me, would have laughed on seeing me then, and Steven almost laughed seeing his reflection in the back of the cabinet and he had an expression of wonder on his face, and he easily could mistake his face for the face of him of ten or more years ago. He'd never had nothing like this chocolate, and for a moment, he felt sad that Elizabet wasn't there with him, sharing in this newfound joy.

After eating a few of these chocolate pieces, he picked up his rucksack, placed it back on his back, then picked up the now much heavier duffel bag, and just tied the mask onto my rope, and walked through the building to explore it. The doors were locked, but then he got to a stairway which he ascended.

When he got to the upper floor, and the building only had two floors, he saw a door at the end of a corridor, and he squinted his eyes to see what was beyond the door. Steven was certain it was a place he would want to check. He walked to the door, and cursed rather loudly when it was locked, and again when he realised what was beyond the second door, shelves upon shelves with books, so many books. He was about to give up and walk away when he remembered his actions downstairs and he moved backwards several steps because these glass panels were so much larger, and he didn't want the glass from hitting him, so he aimed his gun carefully, and he realised he was getting good now at operating the gun, and shot at the door.

With a sound almost matching an explosion the glass in the door shattered.

Steven almost walked forward, towards the door, when the glass in the second door shattered as well with a second loud bang. He stood there staring at the carnage with his mouth open for several minutes and tried to work out what had happened. Did the sound or force from the first door shattering cause the second piece of glass to shatter too? He glanced down at his gun.

He realised that his gun was way more powerful than he'd imagined until then, and it made him understand suddenly how the man, who'd shot at his own head, might have ended up with such a large hole in his head.

Steven walked to the door and used his duffel bag to push away the bits of glass that still clung to the door then he bent over to pass under the wooden beam in the centre of the door and was about to do the same with the second door when he saw it move. He tried the handle and smiled as he was just able to pull it open and walk through it. He looked around the room. Most books looked too old to be of any use to him, and he touched the few lying on a table, and the book crumbled to dust. He felt like he was here for nothing, when he noticed some of the books were sandwiched between others. Perhaps having other books beside them had protected them from damage.

Fifteen minutes later, he'd found an interesting book. Steven saw its name, and looking inside, noted that he was correct in his assessment; it was the *same* book from 2044 that his father had shown him once...

The name of the book puzzled him, and he assumed that the name below these words belonged to the writer of the book, but like before, the page had faded too much for me to figure out the name. He'd always been told that Andromeda was a goddess and people had believed in her existence many thousands of years ago. So, he wondered what a make-belief woman might have done to create this story, but as he read the book, he noticed similarities to his own situation…

There was a story that his father told him once. It took place something like two hundred years before his father's birth, and as he was in his fifties, it put the story slightly more than a hundred years after the disease had spread across the world. Apparently, two brothers had lived in a building with their younger sister. When they were living there one after another of their siblings got chosen as a Subject.

Steven had guessed from the story that was the reason why he didn't bring his father or Elizabet, and the story had shown how futile such an idea would be….

Those three individuals went after their sibling. According to what his father told him, it caused many issues when they did this, and it caused some of how people behaved now. The book of the previous night had a similar idea to it, for sending out just a few to deal with a disease. In this book, the disease had come from somewhere beyond this planet's atmosphere, or Earth, as this book called this planet.

Steven wondered if the person who wrote the book somehow understood the behaviour of people when it was written, and from what she wrote in the front of this book it was created only a few years after the date underneath the photo found in the bunker. He pulled the photo from the pocket in his jacket where I kept it and looked again at the woman like he'd done so many times before since starting his journey. He wondered if the person who wrote the book knew the woman in the photo somehow, or if she might have heard about her.

Steven ate a few chunks of the chocolate food, then he checked the room with books more before leaving. His reasoning at that moment was that he could probably learn new knowledge about the world of five hundred years ago. He started with the books with pictures in them. Most of them were of strange places he knew nothing about, or of people whose names were below the photos but who were now not relevant anymore. He contemplated over all the stories his father had told him about the past, and he wanted to try to match the stories with the names or descriptions of events he'd described or that he'd heard in the recordings.

Steven sat staring for a long time at the next book he opened. Elizabet had told him stories about her life, and he knew she was two years older than I was or maybe younger because right he couldn't remember, and although she'd never used her last name, Langberg, it was the same as the name of the woman in the book I was holding. It stated her name as Miriam Langberg. He recalled the story that Elizabet had told him in which she'd said that her grandmother, who was possibly the oldest person that Steven had known beside his father, remembered a story she'd been told by her grandmother when she was only eight or nine.

As Elizabet's grandmother had been twenty years older than his father, it meant she was told the story more than seventy years ago. Apparently, Elizabet's grandmother's grandmother had heard it from her grandfather before that, who was told about it as a child, but there was no certainty anymore by whom he was told, or whether he'd created the story. He had told a story which he'd claimed was around 250 years old, and when Steven had heard the dates, he'd realised that placed the story at around the same time as the timing of the start of the disease spreading over the planet.

Which was why I had dismissed it so readily? Steven thought.

The story of this man was of an ancestor who'd lived until the same year as the disease, and she'd apparently died a few months before they'd discovered the first cases. She was over eighty years old, and about thirty years before she had died, she'd discovered how to cure another disease that had existed…

When he had read this book, he'd felt shock… genuine overwhelming shock. Steven had wanted to grab the book, rush back to Utopus with it, and show it to Elizabet. Every detail, as it was stated in the story that Elizabet had told him so often, was true according to this book. He decided only to bring the three pages about the woman with him, among them the page with the text below a photo listing a woman called Dr Miriam Langberg, apparently the founder of the Institute for Disease Control, and the discoverer of the cure for cancer, who'd died on 16 Mar 2072, and who'd also worked tirelessly and extensively on finding the cures for other prevalent diseases…

'When she died, she'd just started her work on—'
"Dammit!" Steven cursed loudly.

Steven had cursed several times as he stood there and carefully tore away the relevant pages. He wished the book had been more intact, but the rest of the text had gone missing. The one time when he wanted something to go his way was right now…

He got so angry that he threw the book across the room, and then, for good measure, three more books that had been near him. It took a while before he'd calmed enough and crawled on hands and knees to the book. He picked up the book again and tore out three other pages that seemed to be about her.

Steven decided that he could at least show Elizabet a part of the story at a minimum. It was then that he'd noticed one of the other books he threw, and then recognised a woman staring back at him from its pages. The woman with her yellow hair was the one thing that always intrigued him this entire journey, more than anything else could. When he looked through the book, he realised how many photos had existed of her, and she became even more fascinating.

Steven looked through the book slowly, staring at each page. The book seemed to tell a story with this woman in it. An overwhelming sadness washed over him when he finally understood the reason why this woman had been so sad. He closed his eyes and shut the book hard. He'd hoped for so long that she was someone who'd been leading a long and happy life.

To find out that the photo in 1962 was the last one ever created caused Steven to realise suddenly how little meaning a life could have. He picked up her photo again and looked at her face, at her alluring smile.

"I'll give your life meaning," Steven said. "I'll do everything to honour your memory."

Steven knew he meant it when he said the words. He suddenly felt very determined not only to succeed but also to return to Utopus victoriously, and to show them there that the world outside was one for them to use again.

He got up and explored more of the room with the books and tried to learn as much as he could from it and he figured out that there was one way he could succeed, and that was by knowing all the things that the last users might learnt in this room hundreds of years ago. He walked past the shelves, grabbed every book that didn't immediately become a pile of dust, and placed them all on the tables.

Steven was certain that the next person to come this way as a Subject, and possibly to go inside this building, would wonder why all the books were on the tables—or they'd wonder why there was a large dust pile on the floor. Either way, Steven felt he was creating his bit of mystery for others to solve. It felt somewhat hilarious to him to be the orchestrator of mystery when he was tasked with solving them…

He sat down on the only chair and almost fell on the floor when it collapsed.

He sat down on the next chair in a somewhat more cautious manner and pulled a pile of books towards him. He wanted to learn specifically about the period of twenty to forty years before the disease came, so for each book he grabbed he checked for the date as specified by his father when he was still on Utopus when they'd look at books.

My father did it with this purpose in mind, Steven thought.

The first book was about different countries. Steven wanted to know more about what the names on the map had meant. He checked through the pages somewhat randomly and noticed a few interesting bits of information. A portion of the text said something about an ocean that had been made dry, another about a discovery made.

He noticed that none of them spoke of any form of conflict, yet the message had mentioned 2051 as the date when things changed. He figured out that life went on as normal for most people while the people who governed the world had worked on solving the problems as they came.

I guess that in five hundred years nothing has changed, Steven thought as he smirked a bit, and now they're called Academists instead.

Another book was about the work that the people would be doing. He selected this book because he'd remembered the comment from Elizabet, when she'd said that people did a lot more different work hundreds of years ago. As he looked through the book he saw it listed names of unfamiliar types of work, and he realised Elizabet was more correct about stuff than he'd ever gave her credit for. He looked at some of the words with interest, and his mind tried to categorise them either as a scientist or academist, but there were some names that left him feeling confused.

The one name that fascinated him the most was the biologist. According to the description, it was someone who would work with living organisms, and for a few minutes he was wondering what this might mean.

I'm alive, so I guess it's a person who knows about things alive, Steven thought, *so, I guess the dead laughing bird that became my morning meal won't be interesting to them then...*

Suddenly he had the idea in his mind that he wanted to know better what the things from five hundred years ago were called. He grabbed a thick book and looked in it. It had so many unfamiliar words listed in with an explanation and sometimes a photo below it. He glanced towards his rucksack and noticed the 'distance viewer' sticking out on one side. *I think I'd rather check its proper name so I can tell it to my father*, Steven thought.

He paged through the book. He was uncertain of the name he'd been told, and it took over thirty minutes before he found the right page. He stared at the picture. Although the object in his possession didn't quite look the same, he could confirm the proper name—binoculars.

Now he wondered also what the name of the bird was which he'd seen, but it would elude him forever, so he guessed that from now on it was a 'laughing bird.' He guessed that the bird had planned to laugh at this stupid scientist for as long as he was alive...

After a few hours, he got bored me with looking through books whose information he didn't understand. He got up, picked up his belongings, and explored more of the building. He was sure there wasn't anyone else around, but he didn't want to risk it.

He tried to open the doors that he'd found locked in the new 'alternative' opening method. He was looking forward to the process now. Although he knew also that it would leave behind evidence that someone had been here. He was uncertain what was out there, but he had theories now from the few papers he'd been reading.

The first door he found had proved too strong, even with several attempts of shooting at it with the gun. He guessed he'd need a heavy vehicle like one listed n a book in the upstairs room. After ten doors, he found one that was open. He walked into the room, and he stood staring for a while at what he saw there.

So, this must be what a real scientist does, Steven thought.

Steven walked around, feeling like a small boy again, whenever he'd accompanied his grandfather when he still lived, and looked at the many glass tubes, bowls, and other things there and he saw machines of some sort, which he assumed were used to test things. He tried the knobs and dials on a few of them, but none seem to work anymore.

25.

HE GUESSED THAT THE LIGHTS in the bunker could function still by a different means than had been the case here. He looked at every of the metal plates showing some writing and numbers on them, wondering how the people from five hundred years ago made sense of them. He was hoping to find one to give a clue about how far away the bridge was from the city. In doing this, he had ended up at the coast, and it was there that he saw the other landmass for the first time.

But he cursed when there wasn't any bridge there.

However, after getting his map out, he figured out what he saw in the distance, and worked out from it he was on the right track. He saw on the map what the people from the past had called the city next to the bridge then. When he saw another of the signs saying '6' on it, that's when he realised what it could mean.

He'd figured at first it had meant he was maybe six hours, or six days, or six weeks, or something like it, from the city. It frustrated him that there was a lack of explanation, and the map helped very little either.

Steven guessed he'd have to walk, although he'd seen people sitting in machines in books and saw a few of those types of machines around him that looked similar, and his scientific mind was wondering if he could fix one to use. But then he realised that the insides could be just as rusted as the outside. He even touched a machine to make sure he was right. Or he did it to convince himself that somehow five hundred years had done no damage to them…

Steven was uncertain how long the next part of the journey had taken him because he'd stop so often to look at buildings, or to look at the machines standing around. It was the slowest part of the entire journey and it got slower because he tried to work out how the machines might have worked, and after looking at a few, he saw that some had a key of some sort. But as much as he tried, they wouldn't work—any of them.

In the centre of the next town, was a large, somewhat square building, and Steven thought he'd found something that once was used for defence. As he walked around in the building, for odd reasons he found almost every door open. He wondered how old the building was…

Some of it gave him the impression that people had once been locked away for something, perhaps for doing something against the people who owned the building, yet other parts seemed to be decorated like he'd do in Utopus for certain celebrations. It confused the hell out of him, but he still smirked when he saw the massive bed, and then he laughed loudly as he lay himself down on it… He assumed that there was no one who'd object to it if he took a nap. But he made sure his gun was right next to him, just in case.

*** *** ***

The following morning, he was walking along a path that seemed to follow the coast. A few hours later, he discovered the outline of the bridge on the horizon, although at first, he was worried that it was the mysterious structure from Utopus somehow following me and it was rather disconcerting. Steven worried about what he might find across the bridge, and he wasn't even certain yet that the city near it was safe.

That was when he spotted something high in the sky. It was too far away to see what it was, but whatever it was it was not something Steven wanted to encounter close up. In that moment, his suspicions about Zone Zero got confirmed. But his mind immediately and rather foolishly dismissed it as 'birds.'

I guess the laughing birds are trying to find me to laugh at me, Steven thought, and he shrugged his shoulders and walked on.

Steven realised he was getting close to a city when he saw the city name listed haphazardly on a sign, though half of it was rusted away, and he cursed because it was too convenient for almost every sign so far to have the distance showing, but never any name. On a closer inspection, he noticed the bullet holes as before, and it made him frown and wonder for a moment whether the damage was by design—to make sure someone didn't know the names of these cities.

But who this someone was would remain a mystery…

When he'd seen the thing in the sky, he immediately had started thinking again about the third structure in Utopus and he didn't know why, he just had to, and he'd counted the number of the tiny towns I walked through. He thought that Utopus was doing things so much more efficiently, so he didn't think about it until he saw the thing in the sky. He rushed to a building and hurried inside it.

Once inside, Steven glanced up through the window. Being alone was getting to him seriously now, and that's why he'd looked behind himself several times, thinking there was someone in the building with him…

After ten minutes of staring from the window at the sky, and skittish as he was about his surroundings, Steven decided that resting was a better option right now, so he walked further into the current building he was in, and soon realised it was another place that had been used for buying things. But not food, as he started noticing soon enough. Steven found a metal stairway in the corner and climbed it. Then a moment later he could hear an animal growling at him then… Some sort of creature was hiding behind the cabinets, and it growled rather menacing at him.

Steven had two opposite feelings then. He was curious to know what sort of the creature was hiding there, and also, he wanted to get away from it. The creature was small, but the growling told him it would rush after him if he ran. They were having a stand-off like he'd seen in the movies that he'd watch with his father on his machine.

This stand-off became somewhat comical. A small growling creature, maybe twenty or thirty centimetres from the floor was going up against him; a man of something like 170 tall. Steven slowly knelt and tested the resolve of the creature. "Hey little fella, come here," Steven whispered, while opening his duffel bag at the same time. He reached into the bag and held out one of his father's biscuits. "That should do it," he said under his breath.

Steven carefully opened the package, and with every motion he made, and with every sound the package made, the creature growled more.

"Okay, little fella, look what I got here," he whispered then he held out part of the biscuit. The creature growled, moved forward, stopped, growled again, then backed off.

"Common—I can't kneel all day like this—come here," he said and waved the biscuit around the air somewhat.

The creature growled, then stopped the sound, and sniffed the air.

Slowly it moved forward, one tiny step after another, until it was almost at Steven's hand. It snapped at the biscuit. Steven squeezed his eyes shut and grimaced because the teeth of the creature were sharp. "Ouch, watch it, you," he said loudly. The creature rushed back. And started growling again.

Damn you, Steven, *that wasn't helpful…*

He broke off another piece of biscuit, but now put it on the floor in front of him, and not too far from his leg, so perhaps he'd be able to touch the creature. After he placed the biscuit down, he waited silently and patiently, to see what the animal might do. A repeat of the process. But when the creature ate the biscuit, Steven saw something that made him remember something that Elizabet had told him. And then the sound from the creature confirmed it.

"Ah, so you're one of them," Steven said softly, "and I'm sorry that Elizabet isn't here to see you—She would've loved you."

He held out his hand, the other one, and waited to see what the creature would do. Because he remembered that Elizabet had told him that the pets called dogs would move their tails from side to side, and this creature did that…

Steven carefully sat down, and let the dog come close to him at its own pace. He stroked it and chuckled as the creature flopped over and then he tickled its belly and realised that he'd found a female dog. "Maybe I can call you Maggie—I'm certain Elizabet would do this as well if she was here," he said. "I'm certain…"

Maggie and he played for a while, and he fed her more of the biscuits. But none of the chocolates. Somehow his mind figured that special food created for humans wouldn't be good for animals such as this dog. He didn't like the biscuits anymore anyway so gave those to the dog. The half-eaten food proved that animals hated them after tasting from it…

✳ ✳ ✳

Later, they ate the soup from two cans he still carried with me, one each though the dog's portion went into a suitable object Steven found so Maggie was able eat it easier. He didn't know if dogs were able to eat soup, and he guessed the dog had growled because she was hungry. Naming this small dog Maggie was appropriate too, because I remembered how much Elizabet had wanted a dog and said she'd give such a name if she'd found one…

Sleep came late at night for both of us, but when he woke in the morning, he was alone. Steven called out for the dog, although he wasn't sure if she'd react to "Maggie" already.

Being alone again deflated his whole being and having a dog with him changed Steven differently on that day, differently from how he might have expected. Something had changed…

When he was told that he was going into Zone Zero as the latest Subject for real he was told that there was nothing alive in this region— anymore. On the previous day, he got proof that this wasn't the case, and it had altered how his feelings about the task at hand.

"Thank you, Elizabet. Without your story about the dog in that book, I would have walked away, assuming the dog was some sort of rodent," Steven said loudly. Not that Elizabet was able to hear anything he was saying just then.

Before he would depart again, Steven ate several of the chocolates which he had deemed to be 'human food,' and then repacked all his belongings to get going again. He still needed to reach the bridge, and he didn't want it to take so long that he'd still be walking over the bridge with the next Subject hot on his heels.

Next Subject? He paused for a moment to think about what he was busy with. NO NO NO, I'm going to make certain I'm the last one ever…

* * *

An hour later, Steven walked from the building with a new purpose in his step now. He looked up at the sky and determined that he could walk for another few hours before he would need to find shelter again. Working it out from the sun's position, that he'd been good at for years, would help him determine which direction was south. He was in a town, but he didn't see any structure that could be the bridge. He was certain the structure would be large enough for me to see it from some distance.

Meanwhile, he was feeling sad about Maggie, a new friend by chance only, who he'd found the previous evening, and who had now disappeared from his life, but he guessed that she'd gone back to her own kind, similarly to how Steven had his own kind. He guessed his kind were his friends back in Utopus, and he realised that his mother, who'd walked away when Steven was thirteen, was part of it too.

He guessed that there people he was doing all this for, and these were people who had a need of the information that he was carrying, were also people he cared about, too. But none of them could surpass how much he suddenly seemed to care for an animal whom he'd named Maggie.

I'll never see the dog again, Steven thought, *but I won't ever forget her.*

Steven had looked around to figure out if the object he'd discovered high in the air on the previous day was still nearby, but the clear blue cloudless sky was devoid of anything moving. Not even any of the birds he'd seen occasionally now were in the sky just then. *They might have been sea birds of some sort*, Steven thought, *because they always came from the direction of where the ocean might be.* There was a steady warm breeze, and he could smell the sea air very well now.

There was caution in his step now while he walked towards the southern end of the town. Although he'd wanted to travel as fast as possible, caution was slowing him down. Until he knew what he had observed, he needed to go slowly as he travelled closer to his ultimate destination, and this could mean it could be weeks before he was even at the bridge. Steven remembered how he'd felt each time the third structure appeared and disappeared.

Something about it puzzled him…

* * *

Suddenly, Steven caught sight of the object in the sky, and it was there one moment, and then a few moments later he looked up again, and it was gone. He stopped walking…

It's like the dark structure, Steven thought. *How can the third structure be here?*

Steven looked around, then he lifted the binoculars and studied the sky with it and he felt now like a man who'd stood next to a machine, as described in the books he'd found. He was wearing the right clothing for it. The word next to what he'd assumed to be the man's name was the word 'soldier.' Was he, in fact, a soldier rather than a scientist…? If he was a soldier, then he needed to make sure that he was as prepared as he could get, and he had to protect the information he was carrying against any combatants, as the book called the enemies, and that could involve him killing people…

It could be, also, that someone was looking for him. And those 'people' who were looking for him could be the people that the message had warned him about. But that was one riddle solved, but there was the other riddle of who it was that needed the information I carried.

Steven had realised then that the binoculars were going to be the best method to protect himself against the people who would want to do him harm. With certainty Steven determined the object had come from an sort of enemy… his enemy… everyone's enemy.

A world, which had lost almost all its population, with relatively few people still alive, each living a destitute life from one day to the next. A few of these people were able to use the machines from five centuries ago, when the general claim was that the disease had also caused much damage to the machines that had existed back then, so they had all stopped working…

Steven wondered then who was spreading around these lies.

He'd tried to turn on some machines that stood inert in places on the road, but none had ever worked. As a scientist, who'd helped to fix machines at his father's work, he understood that some damage isn't repairable. But this didn't explain how the object that he saw, could be flying so effortlessly…

Someone out there had machines that worked, Steven thought, *and because at least one can fly around means they also could repair them too. If I encounter them I need to hide that I'm a scientists, that I understand how machines work…*

In his mind, this made such people the dangerous people that the message had warned about. They were also the people who shouldn't get the information in my rucksack…

* * *

Steven was sitting under an old bridge, taking a break from his endless walking, and he had his gun on his lap, and the duffel bag open then he removed the container in which he'd seen the bullets, and he now was picking up the bullets from the bag, and checking each for size. He smirked and shook his head every time one didn't fit.

He knew he'd feel like a real fool if none of the bullets would fit.

After checking something like a hundred of the bullets, he finally found one bullet. He approached the situation as a scientist...

"Always eliminate the parts of the test which don't work, then you'll reach the results of the test that lead to your success," my father always said.

Steven looked closer at the bullet that had fitted. There were markings on the bottom that seemed to be important, and he decided this should be representing the size or style of the bullet that he would need, so he grabbed another bullet from the duffel bag, and compared the two bullets at the bottom. They weren't the same. He put the bullet, which had fitted, down and tried the bullet he'd just taken from the bag. It didn't fit. He grabbed another bullet and noted it was different, too.

26.

STEVEN HAD REPEATED THIS PROCESS and found another bullet that didn't fit. He tried the next bullet, and he noted that the markings on this bullet was the same as the first one, and when he tried to fit the bullet, it would fit.

He looked closer at the first bullet he'd found and put it in his pocket. Then he started finding every bullet he needed to keep his gun armed. While he worked on the task, he kept looking in every direction, occasionally also using the binoculars to scan the air above him.

Except for a few birds that had arrived in the past few minutes the sky was still empty.

He did also wonder from time to time whether he'd imagined the object.

After twenty minutes, the gun was full again and he set to sorting the rest of the bullets into a pile of useless ones and the ones he now knew that he could use as spares. He grouped the useful bullets into small piles of fifteen bullets, and then he wondered how to store them. He saw some old bags of the people from long ago blow past just then. Steven got up and ran after the bags and grabbed them…

There were now five bags filled with bullets around him on the ground, and after checking the gun he realised that typically he'd need nine, so he just tore the bags in half, and he placed a pile of the bullets on each scrap of bag, then he tied the bag with a knot. He placed all the bag pouches into the duffel bag, placed the gun in his pocket, and grabbed a chocolate to eat. While he ate, he looked around again. And although the landscape was devoid of any movement, Steven felt like he was being watched. He quickly packed all the rest of his belongings, and he put on the mask, got up and started walking. He was next to a small river, and he turned left after checking the sun. He hurried along the riverbed that was stony in places and almost sand-like in others, and he decided that the white building he could see on the horizon was his next destination, and where he'd stop that night. He used the buildings along the route there to stop and to keep from being seen. At every building where people would have bought food and other items, he'd stop to investigate.

Steven began to understand from the items on display in this shop how diverse life might have been five hundred years ago.

He saw books, something made of sheets of paper showing something that brought an appreciative smile to his face, especially the pages of sparingly clothed women. He smiled at the image of two men embracing each other lovingly. There were a few people in Utopus who'd do similar actions, and kiss too. He looked for things which might be useful during the rest of his journey, and perhaps also could help me defeat whoever was pursuing him.

He was closing into the white building, which seemed much taller than he thought possible for any building. By the time he was standing in front of the building, he needed to crane his neck to look up, and he lifted the binoculars to look at the top.

Steven formulated an idea that being at the top of the building would allow him to look at the greater landscape, to not only determine where he needed to go but also to observe the land around him for the object I'd seen.

He figured that the height of this building equalled the height at which the object was flying.

He picked up the duffel bag, which he'd dropped on the ground. He climbed the stairs in front of the building and walked cautiously to the door of the building. The building was odd, almost like someone had come along and twisted the building so it stood in a skewed shape. Steven almost expected the inside to be similar. It disappointed him that the inside of the building seemed to be rather mundane in comparison.

As the building was un-powered, Steven figured he needed to climb the stairs. He guessed that by the time he was at the top he would be extremely tired.

I'll leave the exploring for when I'm departing, Steven thought. However, he did look at each floor to get an idea of what was there on each floor, trying to make a mental note of most of the floors, and what he'd observed. Most floors seemed to be places where people had been living long ago, rather than working. He also counted how many floors the building had.

By the time he was on the top floor he was panting loud, and he dropped all the bags, and then dropped too on the floor, leaning against the wall. He closed his eyes and let the tiredness wash over him and waited for his heart to stop beating so hard. He wanted to sleep, but he knew he needed to make sure he was secure in this place first. Whatever he did, it couldn't appear to anyone coming here that he'd been here…

The top floor of the building was curious to him. One person or family had lived here once. There was a separate stairway to get to the floor, rather than the stairs going all the way to the top. Steven had to pass through a door first, and he used his gun to shatter the glass as he'd done before.

The room he stood in seemed to allow views in almost all directions.

His eyes flew open when he found the bed. Three or four people could easily fit in this bed side by side and he grinned when he imagined the bed entirely filled up with a large group of people, especially the women on the papers that he'd found. He noticed this room had no curtains, so Steven decided this could be an issue. He looked around and cursed when none of the windows anywhere were covered with any curtains.

I guess five hundred years ago at this height, the people living here didn't need them, Steven thought.

He pushed against the seating, and noticed he was able to sit down on the less worn-away seating if he sat down cautiously, and then he moved them although only slowly as some of the chairs were quite heavy pieces of furniture, but he decided he needed to move them against the windows. He did the same with any of the cabinets that were free-standing rather than being fastened to a wall or the floor. He also went to the floor below and got some furniture from there.

He was uncertain what had triggered it, but when he spotted a small device, and being as curious as he was by nature, he picked it up, and pressed a few of the buttons, pausing after each, because he expected an alarm to go off for a reason. Steven jumped up when suddenly one button made its purpose clear.

How can they still work?

He pushed the button again, and the curtains opened again. He pushed the button once, and after waiting for several minutes to get a result for my actions across the entire room he put the device down, having most of the curtains shut now, which removed most ability from the people searching for him from seeing him inside this building. Although the curtains were shut, the room was still quite bright in some ways…

Now he felt a sense of safety about his surroundings, or at least a safer as he walked to the windows and lifted the binoculars, and glanced out over the landscape in every direction, until he spotted the bridge.

I'll stay here for a few days, Steven thought, *then I'll travel over that—*

Steven looked a few more times in every direction, now to check for the object, but the skies were empty. Then he nodded resolutely, then walked to the longest seat, which he hadn't been able to move. He lay down and finally relaxed for a while, then fell asleep at an undetermined time later.

He had fallen asleep and would woke up several times during the night. The last time it happened, he got up and looked out of the window. The blackness outside unsettled him. He quickly shut the curtain, lay back down, and lay staring at the ceiling for a few hours until he fell asleep once more…

This time he woke up during the next day and he guessed he'd needed the sleep. He got up and walked to the area that would have been used as a place to prepare food. He looked around for something to eat and he was certain that the people who'd used this house would eat in this place much. There wasn't anything he recognised as proper food. He wondered what the tiny round things were that some of the glass containers had in them. He put the jars back and shrugged his shoulders.

He checked then if this house had anything anywhere that was usable, and he didn't, so he decided he needed to check the three or four floors below this one. To have no food, again, was a major concern, and Steven realised that no one, living four or five centuries ago, had ever realised that a disaster such as the disease could make life tough if a person was as isolated as he was now. It made him even more aware of how detrimental his situation was. But it made him more determined to succeed. He placed his bags in a cupboard, grabbed his gun, and tiptoed down the stairs, and stepped through what was left over of the glass door, then he stopped to listen. It was quiet. He looked down each corridor for movement and anything else they might hide.

There were perhaps half a dozen doors in each of the left and right corridors on the first floor checked, and after I went into the right corridor first...

Steven knew he could kick the doors in, or he could even try to use his gun, and Steven knew to do this sparingly because he didn't know how or where to get more bullets.

The condition of the other dwellings in the building, where varied pieces of furniture either stood or lay toppled over, told him that more of this place was somewhere people had lived in a lot better condition if he had to compare it to the house, he had found days earlier.

Most of these dwellings contained nothing in them, although he was able to find food in a dwelling, including a few containers. He went back up to get the tool for opening containers. However, the dwelling where he subsequently opened a container with an awfully smelly content, which, according to the picture, was supposedly fish for human consumption, would haunt him forever...

The odour inside the container was so bad that he threw up. Steven left fast, and the building still reeked from the contents of the container when he arrived back to the top floor and he thought the odour of the container would keep spreading, and that he'd also catch wafts of it on this top floor, too. He stayed now for only as long as he couldn't breathe it in but decided he had to stay for another three days, or even four, then do the rest of the exploration, starting from around the fiftieth floor, and work his way down, and finally leave.

He would check every dwelling on every floor to make certain he missed nothing. He smirked when he realised that the odour would keep spreading, and that it could be here still if he ever was to return. And then he laughed out loud, when he realised that the odour could be 'offensive' if the people from the rogue organisation ever came here, and they would be 'defeated by the smell.'

It was such a funny thought that that I lay still for a moment, then was laughing as I lay down on the seat and laughed for the longest time. If anyone one saw him now, they would think he had become a madman.

After about fifteen minutes, he got up and walked to the cupboard where his bags were located, picked them up, and walked back to the seating. He wanted to repack, so he could get rid of the duffel bag, because he realised that having two bags was a hindrance, and if he had to defend himself, it would be easier with both my hands unencumbered.

Steven spread all the contents of the two bags over every seat. He glanced at the package in which he knew were the papers with information on them, and still he didn't know who they were meant for. It took most of the day to work on packing, but by the time the orange glow of the setting sun was shining into the room, he was down to one bag. He placed the rucksack next to the seat he was using as a bed, then he picked up the duffel bag and put all the things he didn't need to take with him in it.

He needed to hide this bag so no one could likely associate it with his presence or existence...

Steven had noticed a hatch in the wall in the food preparation area, so he walked over to it and when he opened the hatch, he looked down into a dark space. He grabbed a spoon from a drawer and dropped it in the chute. He flinched each time it would hit the sides. The sound of the bangs fast became a distant echo, and after only a minute or less, silence returned.

He waited for a few minutes to listen for other sounds.

When no other sounds came, he lifted the duffel bag into the chute, and after two minutes, he let go of it. The bag caused a lot of scraping and banging, and he flinched even more dramatically from every sound. After about two minutes, the place was silent again.

Tomorrow I will explore the rest of this place, Steven thought, *and then I will have to go.*

He lay down on the seat and looked around for a moment, and then he realised that this dwelling could have been a place that he might have been able to live in if he'd been alive about five centuries ago. He slept well on that last night there, and early the next day he started the process of descent through the building.

Steven skipped the first floors that he'd already checked, and he wanted to avoid them because he still sensed the contents from the container with his eyes, tongue, and nose, so he rushed down until the sensation had vanished.

From this point, he wanted to check every floor, and every dwelling on every floor, no matter how long it would take him. He got down by eight floors on the first day, and it was several days later when he finally got to the floor above the entrance of the building. He walked into the last room, thinking that he'd just spent a long week of looking at a boring building with sparsely decorated dwellings, but then he walked into the bedroom of the last dwelling and stopped waling, staring at the bed…

He turned his head and clenched his jaw tightly.

On the bed, tucked in under a blanket, lay the body of a woman.

From the silver-white hair, Steven could tell she had been rather old, or she would have been when she had been alive. There was an expression still visible on her face that reminded him of whenever a person might be in severe pain. She'd clawed her hands around the blanket, like she was grasping at it to fight off when the moment of death had come for her…

Steven raised his left arm and covered his mouth and nose with his sleeve, although there was no odour present in this room. And he guessed that the dry, cool air of the room somehow had preserved the body. He walked closer to the bed, and with his right hand, gently touched the partly exposed shoulder of the woman. It was icy cold to the touch. The woman's skin was like paper and parched. The ageing of the body reminded him of the body he'd found in the bunker.

Steven stared at her face and decided there was a reason for why she had died, and he was certain there was an explanation for why she lay in her bed like people had forgotten her. So, he looked around and noticed a photo in a frame, then he walked to the table it stood on.

He picked it up and stared at an older woman, with her hair bound back from her face, smiling at the person who was taking her photo. In the photo, she had a pale skin, deep blue eyes, and a slender face. He turned the photo over to see if he could find a name or date anywhere but didn't find any.

Another person who had died nameless…

Steven was about to walk from the room, then he thought it was best to burn the room if the woman had died from the disease of five hundred years ago. He had found some fire-starting tools in a room a floor higher.

27.

STEVEN KNEW HE'D NEED SOMETHING flammable. So, he looked around the dwelling and picked up a bottle and inhaled. It smelled funny, almost of flowers, but it also reminded him of a liquid that certain people of Utopus would drink.

He walked to the bed and emptied the bottle's content over the foot end of the bed.

He put his rucksack back on before executing any of his next actions, and tried to ignite the fire maker, and when he had a tall, steady flame he held the lit end against the lower side of the bed until it was on fire. He watched the flames slowly spread in a trance for a few moments, but when it became a torrent of flames, on reaching the liquid, he ran from the dwelling like the dead woman on the bed had come alive and was chasing after him suddenly.

He was outside the building in minutes and walked hastily in the direction where he'd seen the bridge and as he was walking, he was uncertain what the fate would be of the building behind him, and he was convinced with certainty that it would be a pile of rubble if he ever came back to this town. He knew that the people with their object could send it to this region to check this fire…

He realised fast that it would need had to appear that the fire had been started by light flashes from the sky, rather than by a human hand. He knew that any evidence that could tell anyone he'd been there would get destroyed by the fire.

He also knew it was best for him to be as fast away from the scene of his actions as possible and he could cope with, so he ran at the highest speed he was capable of, and then he turned onto another road, and now the bridge was in full view ahead of him. So, he thought now that he could reach the bridge in maybe two hours. He had stopped for a few moments to catch his breath and to let the pain in his sides subside and as he did this, he was looking at the sky around him for any sign of the object, but the sky was empty was before…

So, he continued his trek towards the bridge, but this time he just walked. His hand was over the gun in his pocket. Steven felt like he needed to be prepared for whatever could happen next.

When he saw a truck, it was the first definite evidence he would have, the first of many such things, that something wasn't right.

Steven might have just ignored the truck if it wasn't riddled with thousands of holes, and as he looked at them, it was reminding him of the sign along the road in the north, which he'd also used as a target practice, which had also been covered with bullet holes.

But with the truck it was so much worse. How many people with guns had there been to do this? he thought. *It resembles a vehicle I saw in Utopus, which commonly has water in it.* There were more bullet holes visible in this truck than he was able to count in a few seconds or minutes. There were so many of them. He looked around at his surroundings, and determined there was a second vehicle near him, and realised then there was even a third and fourth of the same vehicle…

Steven glanced towards the tall building where he'd been located only a few hours previously, and he was able to see a visible black trail of smoke rising from the building, which was growing in density by the minute. If he wanted to find extra clues about what had happened here, he needed to hurry.

He walked around the vehicle and found a door, and he realised it was locked, and he saw nothing to show a method to get inside the vehicle. He pulled his gun and shot at what he thought was the lock. He ducked when the shot bounced off. He determined from this that someone had made the vehicle of a material like he had encountered in the building in the previous town.

He moved back closer to the vehicle, and looked it over frantically, but he couldn't figure out how to get inside the vehicle, and he decided that the contents would only be a few boxes or similar. At least, that was his best guess. He tried to look through the bullet holes, but the inside of the truck was total darkness. He looked at the other vehicles and wondered whether he should look at them.

He had made the grey truck his second attempt for further clues, and if he found that one locked as well, he was just going to move on. He walked to the vehicle. It, too, was riddled with bullet holes. He walked to the back of the vehicle…

He had stopped and stared at the ground. He knelt at the door. It was open, and something was sticking out, so he tugged at it slightly. The blood drained from Steven's face when he realised he was holding a hand…

A hand was sticking out from behind the vehicle.

The hand was partially rotted away. A human hand as he noticed to his horror, and now Steven was curious why a person would have been inside this vehicle. And how had a human got inside a vehicle which might have been locked similarly to the others standing here? The lock showed that someone with a gun, more powerful than his own, had shot at it.

Was there a link between the bullets and this find?

Steven got up and looked up at the door. He grabbed the door and pulled at it.

It moved…

Steven pulled the door open. He was staring at the hand attached to an arm. He traced the arm visually, and he saw a torso, then a skull with a part-rotted face. The face of whoever this person had once been, was left frozen in an expression of horror. He stared further inside the truck, and saw another body, then another one, and as his eyes grew used to the darkness within the vehicle, he saw one of the most horrific scenes ever that he wouldn't forget—ever. In the truck, he saw the leftovers of a hundred, two hundred, or more people, and it seemed they all had the expression of horror on their faces.

Now he had a theory in his mind: that these people were in the truck because they were fleeing to something, or from something, or someone.

Steven looked at what would have been the top of the vehicle, and it showed that the people in the vehicle hadn't suffocated. He glanced again at the bullet holes in the surface of the vehicle, and this made him wonder if someone had wanted these people dead, and if so, why.

How long ago might this have happened? Steven thought.

He walked to the side of the vehicle with the bullet holes and examined the edges of each bullet hole. The edges had obvious rust on them.

Might all this have been done by an enemy who was active some five hundred years ago?

Steven looked at the position of the vehicles, and all of them were facing away from the bridge.

The vehicles all had been travelling in a northerly direction when an event happened that had halted their journey in this location. He returned to the back of the vehicle and quickly glanced towards the white building where he was now three hours earlier. Half of it was now engulfed now in flames.

He needed to leave now.

He ogled the cluster of body parts inside the truck and was acutely aware deep inside his soul that there might be a link between why no Subject ever returned and the evidence he had found today.

He thought it was this that was making Zone Zero so dangerous and I could tell the people, who had wanted the information he was carrying, about what he'd seen here, too. Steven felt a deep sadness and knew deep down that he would never know who these people were. But he saw a similarity between this situation, and the images he'd seen in a book. The book had used three words which had made him even more cautious: 'victims of warfare.'

These people are victims too, Steven thought. *I'll make sure they didn't die for nothing...*

Steven recalled the contents of a paper he had been reading two nights earlier, which had seemed somewhat relevant for unusual reasons:

> —From evidence gathered, we know that the place mentioned in that last globally received a message was what we know as Utopus. We've found no evidence that any valid nation or organisation connected to a valid nation sent that message. We cannot tell you how we know this because such knowledge is dangerous for everyone involved.

The reason for our actions is clear. We must safeguard this world for our few children and those who will come afterwards. I want her to be safe, and them too. The longer I search for answers here, the more I discover that shows nothing is at it appears. Nothing has been normal since this started, and it won't stop unless we fight against it. There are only a few of us who really comprehend as to what's going on still, and if the last people loyal to the rogue organisation discover that we exist, they'll most likely do everything in their power to make sure that the end would come for us all sooner rather than later.

A girl living here found a text she gave to me. It was a page from something that was called a 'magazine.' Reading it, I weep for the future we never had the chance to get. According to the same magazine, dating from 2036, Steven was reading the claim that the world would soon sustain its growing population in more efficient ways. It had claimed that poverty, which it described as someone living with no belongings, income, or any form of a good life, would soon be at its end.

It had said the United Nations that later had to defend against assassins, was, according to this text, setting up methods whereby every person on this planet would receive a minimal income set at a hundred of something.—

Steven had studied the page for the longest time to try to figure out what the shapes meant, but he was left uncertain with their meaning. But the text also had claimed that a hundred of these things would allow the poorest people to feed themselves, send their children to school, and to live better and more, but what was the other things and to Steven it had sounded much like the things they'd say in the speeches in Utopus…

He turned around once more, and he pulled at the door of the truck. He pushed the hand aside with his boot, then he shut the door of the vehicle, so making it the last resting place for the individuals within it.

When he'd decided that the door was sufficiently shut, he had glanced around once more, using the binoculars this time, and had stared at the white building for several moments with fascination as he saw a flash point, when one or more of the windows of the building would break, and after that the flames took hold faster the higher up the fire travelled through the ruined building.

He dropped the binoculars into his rucksack hastily, turned abruptly and he walked in broad strides towards the bridge, picking up a steady pace, which was neither slow nor fast.

* * *

After an hour, Steven arrived at a very long bridge of some sort, and he was certain it was the bridge on my map. He plodded along it, but steadily the sense of urgency increased, and he decided he needed to be on the other end of the bridge by the following morning.

Each step he took now had two purposes.

First it was leading him away from the evidence he had found, which might end up endangering him if the object came back, but it was also sending him to where the real dangers were, and he didn't know where that danger was awaiting him. He kept looking behind him, but then he felt compelled to look up, and he gaped as he looked at the bridge supports above him. Seeing them left him in awe at the accomplishments of the people who'd lived five hundred years ago, and who were responsible for building these tall structures.

The second day travelling over the bridge was when he ran into a snag. He was sitting for well over an hour at the edge of the bridge, with his legs dangling down, and he looked down at the broken bridge, which was hanging down only a few meters above the sea water level. He wondered at how he would get across this gap. He looked behind him to make sure he was alone, and cursed when he realised how much more skittish, he now was, although more aware of what might be going on, and more than he had ever thought possible.

He saw a metal frame on the southern side of the bridge. Steven decided he could get to the lower part of the bridge, which seemed to possess a double set of the metal tracks if he climbed down, and he did a bit of jumping around. The most tough part of the effort of getting across the bridge would be to jump from this side of the bridge to the opposite sloping, partly-collapsed part, a pillar in the past, and this part of the plan could also prove painful.

He guessed he couldn't stay sitting here forever.

Then he guessed he could read more of the pages later on, but he definitely wanted to wait with this until he was much further on the journey. Steven pulled the large map from the pocket in his rucksack and for a few minutes studied the route marked on it again and he looked at each city on the map that seemed to be where the route was passing through.

Steven looked at the names of two of the cities, Berlin and Prague, and he wondered if something was setting these two places apart from every other town in Europe. The route was avoiding every other city after the one that was located on the other side of this bridge, and he wondered if that showed that these cities were under surveillance. He looked at the area marked as the destination, and that seemed to be somewhat north of the closest of the old cities.

He wondered again why the destination was marked like such a vague afterthought almost.

He shrugged his shoulders.

Then he put the map away and glanced down again at his other dilemma below him.

He got up, pulled the rucksack off the ground, put it on his back. He walked to the metal frame and pulled at it to check its stability. Somewhat gingerly, he placed a foot on the frame, took hold of the frame above him with his gloved hand, and slowly lifted his other foot off the stone surface of the bridge.

For a few minutes, Steven hung off the side of the frame to make sure it didn't suddenly do something unexpected. Then, slowly, he climbed down.

He did this step by step, moving ever so slowly over frame. Before lowering himself below the surface of the bridge, he looked one more time toward the white building, which now just looked like a burning torch against the pale blue of the sky. The smoke from it first was drifting east, and he wondered how far it would travel, or from how far away 'they' could see it.

He continued climbing down, next clambering onto the metal structure beside the track. He then looked at the track and saw a vehicle of some sort standing on it.

I guess that explains what the tracks are for in that town which I had visited with Elizabet, Steven thought.

He looked up and saw that he'd got down by more than half of the distance from the top of the structure to the water surface. He lay down on his stomach and glanced over the edge to see what his next plan of action had to be. He saw another metal frame, and it seemed to be unstable, but it was close to a beam on the other side.

Determination set in again, and Steven knew he could travel faster once he was on the other side.

He got up again, and turned around, lowered himself over the edge, and was relieved when his foot hit something solid. He held onto a metal pole, looked down again for the next place to lower himself, and on seeing a rod sticking out from the stone he thought then that he could jump over to a small platform, and then he could try to climb up back to the top of the bridge.

He scanned the surface of the slope he needed to climb, and he noticed something that could help him. Steven placed his boot in a hole in the stone, his boot fitted in the indent much to his relief. He placed a hand in another of the holes. His relief increased when he finally stared at the surface of the bridge again. He glanced behind him when he'd climbed on top and grinned when he saw exactly how much effort the climb had been for him.

28.

WHILE HE HAD CLIMBED, HE had no time to think about falling, but now he was glad that he was able to do it without thinking about those consequences, because he was certain, suddenly, that he could easily have been lying dead some fifty or sixty meters below…

My satisfied smile about succeeding disappeared on realising that aspect of the climb.

Steven got up and started walking west, and he realised that he just wanted to get off the bridge, and he was hoping now that the bridge was 'whole' the rest of the way. He felt tired, but he didn't want to stop now until he was in the city on the other side. As he walked almost mechanically, he remembered how Elizabet and he would clamber around over the leftover pieces of the old city called Stockholm. Somehow, what he just did was a lot more dangerous.

Steven glanced back for a moment, and then he realised what had made him stop and turn around completely this time. Where previously an almost pristine white building had stood, there was now a massive cloud of dust. Shocked, Steven lifted the binoculars up and stared through them. He felt like he should be telling someone something like: "Oops, did I do… that?"

So as a twenty-two-year-old man he suddenly felt instead like a young kid just then, and he felt like his father had caught him doing something naughty, like the time when he was sitting on the roof of the building we lived in, and when he had been an eight-year-old boy— Steven cut off the thought that had entered his mind just then. Suddenly, he felt like he needed to rush. He turned, and he jogged…

His mind imagined that several of the flying objects would start chasing him at any moment and like in the movie his father had showed him on his machine, and he thought that the objects in his imagination would shoot at him with light beams, and that he would be a little pile of dust on the ground.

His imagination was making him think enemies were surrounding him, and he was also being affected by the loneliness of not having any contact with other people. This was the part of this journey which had led to the man in the bunker perhaps putting a bullet in his own head. Steven knew there was no chance of meeting anyone during the journey, so he had to learn to become resilient, and fast, too. Every step he took now had to be controlled, and he needed to learn to be strong and Steven remembered what his father would say: "You're stronger than you think."

He stopped running. He was panting loudly. Running like he had just done would only make him weaker, and he needed to do things in a way so he would ultimately succeed. *I must succeed*, Steven thought.

Steven lifted the binoculars to look ahead of him and he could see a landmass ahead of him, and he was certain it was the country on the other side of the bridge. He walked to one of the massive poles and stood in its shade, took off the rucksack and placed it down, and then he knelt beside it. He took out the map and studied the lines on it again, which he now recognised as roads based on the sign that stood swaying softly beside the bridge. There seemed to be another bridge between the major continent and the landmass that he was approaching. He knew things would get easier once he'd reached the continent, because then it was a straightforward walk to Berlin…

Steven was uncertain what he'd find there, and he was hoping it would be something useful, perhaps the people who needed the information he was carrying.

* * *

Steven spent longer in the town, he'd found at the end of the long bridge, than he'd planned, and wanted to walk around somewhere that almost looked normal. His best moments would unknowingly be established there, right beside the small statue that he found next to the water, though likely not as closely as originally intended, and which had reminded him of a story he'd read during his earlier life. The story was about something the story had called a mermaid, and it was one of the many stories he had read about these strange creatures, which all were made up by the people of the past, according to his father.

There was a large metal shape attached on the side of the statue, but he could only see traces of a name on it. Steven took out the photo from the bunker from his pocket, and compared it with the statue, and he noted the rusted statue had her own way of being in a sad pose. According to the story from the book, and she was supposedly a magical sea creature who had fallen in love with a man, but the man had ended up rejecting her. She had died when she jumped in the waves...

After a few minutes of staring at the creature's face, Steven put the photo away, then he got up and placed the rucksack over his shoulders, and simply continued with his journey. He was staring at the ground feeling a deep sadness. Then he remembered that his father had bowed his head too.

So much sadness in this world, he thought.

His journey had to get him to Berlin, and he didn't know how long it would take him.

After a few hours trekking Steven was sitting again, and then breathed in the salty air, which seemed to come from every direction. He checked the sky again for the object, walked into a building and then slept for a few hours. It was a process of walking towards where he could resume his trek into the southern continent, he'd seen in the distance that he'd repeat a little at a time for the next month, if he was counting the days correctly, and he walked over the next bridge, and then another before he was standing on soil again where he directed his journey into southern direction.

There was such boredom where every day became a repetitive version of the last day, and at the time he would rather have stopped travelling all together, and he pretended his journey was the subject of a boring book, with a reader trying to make it longer by reading it too slow on purpose and this idea in my imagination became almost like a game. But arriving at a small village, and then seeing a row of bullet-riddled vessels, designed to travel over the water, had quickly snapped him out of that somewhat sarcastic mindset. Up to this moment, he'd regarded the entire journey almost as a laughable situation and he'd decided that it was probably one of the worst ways to work out if Zone Zero was safe or not.

The eleven water vessels with the bullets in the sides of them all were facing somewhat northeast, so he checked inside them, but there were no bodies in any, so he guessed that they'd been ambushed the people who had planned to use these vessels for another purpose. He couldn't explain how he know this to be true, only just that he knew it happened that way…

The nearby village was just a shell, with all the buildings burned to a crisp. The village, or whatever was left over of it, gave Steven the first clue that World War 3 wasn't just something from five hundred years ago. *It's still happening. It still goes on*, Steven thought. *This damage is too fresh…*

The damage to the building reminded him of what he'd done to the tall white building. The small wafts of smoke made him wonder if someone had seen the fire and had done something as an act of revenge. Had he inadvertently declared war on someone out there?

Steven didn't sleep that night, and for several days he was walking only at night, letting the Moon, as he started calling it, The White Lady guide him with a knowledge of where south might be. It was during those nights he understood why some people in Utopus were calling the companion of our planet by that name. He'd been told The White Lady was a symbol of hope. He discovered, in those few lonely days, that he wanted similar, and perhaps had also needed a symbol of hope.

Steven realised he needed overdue sleep, and a lot of it, when he stumbled and fell sideways into a ditch. He got up somehow. Then he walked on, just about, until he found an old house, and inside it was a pile of dried material which would make a nice bed. He fell asleep and slept without any dreams.

* * *

Something was brushing against his face the next day and was making an odd sound. Steven opened his eyes to see a small, rather fluffy animal with a long tail that stuck up straight, and from the creature came a sound that was a mix of a buzzing sound and a rattling sound. The creature rubbed softly against his face…

Steven closed his eyes for a moment, opened them again, and he almost laughed at the creature's need to be sitting on top of him, swishing its tail from left to right over his face causing a tickle to happen. "Hello, tail swisher, I wonder what you are?" Steven whispered, then he lifted his head and grinned when in the next moment he was realising that he was recognising a cat, but the name he'd given the creature was so much more playful.

His voice had made the creature as curious about him as he was about it and the tail swisher rubbed its face against his, and each time it did this the strange buzzing sound it was making got louder.

"Are you hungry?" Steven asked though he knew the creature didn't understand him.

Steven rose upright, but the creature, which he'd called tail swisher for the lack of a proper name for it and how it moved its tail, didn't rush up my chest. It jumped off him, waited near him until I was more upright, and to show how nonchalant it was the creature sat there washing a paw with its long pink tongue…

Some its colour reminded him of my chocolate with grey and white colour in the rest of its coat, and its belly was white…

As Steven talked and made soft encouraging sounds, the creature moved to his lap, and the man found himself smiling…

He scratched the creature's head, and the buzzing sound became louder, and almost sounded like an engine. The hair of the creature was soft, it was long, and the colouring of the creature fascinated to him. It moved its tail from side to side in a curly motion.

After a few minutes, the creature, or tail swisher, curled up in his lap, and Steven decided he had to read another page of the message while he had a chance to relax there, and while he sat there, he ate one of his last chocolates. The tail swisher sniffed at his food with curiosity.

"No, that's human food," he said, and he pushed the tail swisher's face away.

Somehow Steven instinctively thought that the human food wasn't good for this creature either, just like with the dog. He scratched the tail swisher's head, and this was what it liked doing the best in this moment…

The tail swisher liked this the best it seemed. It curled over so its belly was showing. It curled, and the sound it made seemed to get louder again by the minute. Steven rubbed its head again, and he ran his hand over its belly. There was movement in the lower part of its belly. He held his hand over the rounded part of the creature's belly for a few minutes.

A memory of his mother walking away from him suddenly flashed through his mind, and he pulled his hand away. Why was he thinking about his mother now? He was thinking it with his eyes shut. There was one memory in his mind and that was of his mother. It was of her walking away. He was still uncertain why she went that day.

"She had to go."

Steven opened his eyes and looked around him in confusion. He was so certain he'd just heard his father's voice just now and he shook my head. So he guessed it was the loneliness doing that to him.

The creature rubbed its face against mine, and he guessed that its species belonged to a type that had a way to distract humans, such as him, from whenever they had a gloomy thought.

Steven looked at his rucksack and pulled the package from its pocket and grabbed out a page to read one of them. He was now certain that understanding the content of these pages would also be a way to solve centuries-old riddles of what had happened to the world of hundreds of years ago…

> —They don't want the population that remains to learn what they'd done. Here was some other information I'd uncovered recently. The person who'd orchestrated the assassination had claimed their forefather was the leader who'd done all this.
>
> I'm uncertain if any of it was true, or not.
>
> But if the information is correct, the man might likely be one of the most dangerous men alive right now. He has never shown himself in public, but some children had claimed to have seen him. Those some children also would say that he has a map of some sort inside the building where he's based. A map with a date. The map lists 2027.
> On the map, they've marked most of Europe as grey zones, and parts of the northern part of Africa were shown in the same. They'd also marked this place on the map, and had also seemingly already marked where, later, Utopus would get established, already this bridge was also marked on this map too.
>
> This was the proof we have needed all this time.
>
> If I can make sure that the others receive the information, I can prevent the leader from succeeding in whatever they're planning here. Don't worry about my safety, just make sure he is safe, just like I'm ensuring her safety. They both represent the future we're trying to create here.
> However, I must be careful, and not do anything for a while, so they don't end up suspecting something—

Steven was certain that this text gave him a clue about what was going on. He wasn't yet certain what the relevance might be between the text and what he'd seen so far. He felt like he was close now to figuring it all out. But he was aware that his life would be in danger the moment he found the answers. Steven's attention got distracted by the tail swisher. He gave it another scratch...

He smiled, then he got up, and he walked to the opening in the wall, and looked at the landscape to see where he was as he'd arrived in the dark of night, and the buildings seemed to be a place which might have been used in the past as a place his father described as a place used to rear animals for feeding humans. The tail swisher had followed him, and was brushing against his legs, and now it made another kind of sound which brought the smile back to Steven's face. The tail swisher kept repeating the new sound, so Steven walked back to his rucksack and picked it up.

He saw the creature following him around. He was uncertain if it would follow him if he left now, but he guessed it could leave just like Maggie had done, and that it would do this when it got bored with the human, and would then leave him, turn and go back to wherever 'home' is for it.

Outside the building, Steven stared a moment at the sky, but it was cloudy, so he was unsure for the first time in which direction was south. Although cloudy, nature was still being beneficial, because he noticed on which side of the building a shadow would form. It reduced the choices to two - north and south. Steven looked at the landscape in each of the two directions that he assumed to be the right choices, and he observed each direction with the binoculars. He decided that going right would be the right choice, and that he'd try to reach Berlin as soon as he was able to, although he was aware the journey would take a few months to get to the intended city was listed as someone else's choice of destiny...

But before that, he wanted to be a lot more knowledgeable about what could await him there. Maybe I should read all the pages, Steven thought as he remembered the first time, he'd heard the message when he was at the Academic Institute, when he only had his insatiable curiosity.

Damned that curiosity of mine, Steven thought angrily.

Steven realised he needed to read the messages as soon as possible, to find something suitable to write my own findings in and make an account of what had happened, and then just pack everything to leave. Later, he might be able to concentrate on writing about these findings more thoroughly, and therefore write about all of it to solve the mysteries of what he'd now found.

29.

HE WALKED BACK INSIDE THE building, and looked around for somewhere safe for him to sit while he was working and found a ladder leaning against a platform above him. He hoisted his rucksack on his back, walked to the stairs, and pushed on the treads with a boot, pulled at a few higher treads then he climbed up the stairs. At the top, he found a small suitable area, and he decided it was a perfect place for his task. The straw bales would shield me also against the nippy air…

He clambered onto the platform, then he pulled the ladder up and placed it down.

Steven wanted to control access to up here, and he checked the walls and roof and was certain he'd be able to stay here at least a week without going downstairs. He sat down and pulled the rucksack close to him.

Just as he wanted to open bag the tail swisher was back. It made him jump. Steven smiled at the tail swisher. He scratched its tail, and wonder how it had got up here, and he guessed that the tail swisher could climb up here its own way.

Steven took the pack of papers from the rucksack and put it down next to him. He had to hush the tail swisher away when he saw it was trying to get into the rucksack. He put the pack in front in front of him and untied the cords. He could now see there was a sizeable number of pages in the pile; there were well over seven hundred pages, and he doubted he could read them all in a few hours.

He read the first fifty pages, then tied all of them until he would find a book to use as a disguise, and he planned to have them all disguised so that whoever was looking for them for more sinister reasons wouldn't find them so easily. He picked up the first page and studied the words again, and he did this with every page he'd previously read. Then he picked up the next page to read. There were theories forming in his mind, and some of them were rather disturbing…

It was now obvious that the text of the pages was a continuation of the message he'd listened to at Utopus, and once again he wondered who the mysterious woman was, considering his father had behaved like he'd recognised the voice.

—This place is so strange. I got here, and it seems a place of safety. But the reality is different. I may be repeating things you already are aware of, but I miss you and him. I found a book today with numbers inside it. It's a worrying book. The numbers in it seem to be some code. Because I've had to lie low for the last month or so, I have been studying the book. I'm hoping no one knows I have it.

I've seen a similar book before, but I cannot remember where now. This book lists a date on the front page, and it's meant for some communication. I found more similar books in the building used by the leader and those who are following his orders. It seems they've been collecting these books for something.

Even more worrying is that they seem to have been doing it for a long time. While they did their prayer, one child showed me a secret way to their storage of these books. There were thousands of books in the building. If it destroyed them, it might prevent whatever they will do with the codes in them. I'm getting scared, but I must press on with this task. I'll keep sending more of these messages for as long as it takes for the information to be known to all those who work with me.

It seemed strange to me that the person who was sending the messages never was saying what they called the place, and then I realised she was possibly being overheard by someone. I wondered how they could get hold of all the books the woman mentioned. And what they were about, or how old they were?—

Steven stared ahead for a few minutes, to think about what he'd read here. One thing was certain now. There was someone around who was investigating the culprit, and he was certain that the culprit was the rogue organisation, although at that moment he wasn't certain.

—I know has been such a long time since I could send any information out, so I realised I had to be careful. I infiltrated the leader's inner circle recently, and I think I'm gaining his trust. It isn't easy to gain the trust of the people who are in this camp, but finally I've done it. He went to another building, so I carefully looked around his room today. It seems I was right about him having some plan for the world.

There's a map in that room that seems to show the entire world. On it, the region with Utopus in it marked with an outline. I'll send you a list of names next time, which you can combine to make the outline on any map you may have. Show that map to the person who'll be sent as a Subject. Show it to him…

I told her she needs to go to a safe place soon. I might have met someone who recently arrived here that I can trust, and she told me in a quiet whisper that she knows a place. They'll go next week, but then plan to come back to help me here.
I'm aware that you have always told me never to say your name, but right now I wish I could say it and that you were around to hold me.—

Steven blanched after reading this part of the message. He learnt two things from the information it was listing.

The first part was that it confirmed something about his father's behaviour. Steven remembered so vividly when his father had showed him a map, circled an area on it, then said it was Utopus, and said everything outside it was Zone Zero. This message said to show the Subject a map.

He glanced at his rucksack, reached for the small map, and dragged it from the pocket.

Was this map given to me because someone in a message told my father to do it? Steven thought, and he wondered now seriously who the 'she' was that kept being mentioned in the messages…

He wasn't certain when they had sent the messages, but the next message he read was making him worried. He tried to work out how long ago they got the message, and the first one had arrived when he was fifteen years old.

That meant that the next message he'd read was now four years old, and if all the messages were chronological up to days before he left, then he wondered how often his father had gone to listen to them. Did he receive a message every day, or several times in a day… or more? And this message mentioned a 'him' now. And 'always remember' —*was this a message about me?*

—It's been four years since I arrived here. I think I'm learning the language in which the people who run this camp speak. I can't make them realise I know what they talk about or else my life is in danger. I keep warning her to be a child that gets ignored. But she tells me always those children are normal children.

I remember reading in one of the few books they allow us to read, that they treat children so much better than this. In that book, they speak of hope. But I think hope has long abandoned this world. I think I found a message from some who lived long ago in that book. It reads, "If you forget to hope, you lose the ability to care. If you don't care, you lose the ability to be human."

I showed her that message and told her to never forget those words, no matter what. You tell him the same. Tell him to always remember. Memory is so precious. I can remember your face and his only occasionally, but it's what gives me the strength to keep going here.—

Steven had, until recently, referred to the messages as the 'voice from the past' and he wanted to know now how far in the past they really were? The sender was aware of Utopus, and how? Who were they talking to when they sent these messages?

He realised that he might have found more information about Europe of the past...

—I found a folder in the leader's room which seemed to have been discarded by them as not important enough. It was a folder with the letters UN printed on it. There were papers inside the folder... many papers of various types. I've dated some of the papers to be from 2090, and some of them have traces of blood on it. Somehow, it's linking these people here with whoever who had killed the person from the UN all that time ago. And it could be they've been hiding this information for all this time.

Also, here's the list of names that I've found recently that are listed on the map: Alaska, California, Virginia, Greenland, Iceland, Scotland, Norway, Sweden, Estonia, Russia, Finland—It lists all these places as 'cleansed' on the map. If you draw a line, you might be able to see how much they control already. Zone Zero has something to do with it, but I'm uncertain what way just yet.

I'll communicate when I know more.—

This was the message that had given Steven the information about where Utopus is. He looked at his map to check the names listed. The list and the map correlated. *But what did the message mean by 'cleansed'…? Was it another way to refer to Zone Zero?*

Steven thought back to what he knew about the origins of the word. That they might have given it to an entire country because the disease in it happened so fast that they had NO patient zero.

But this message was mentioning about a person being killed for what that person might know about a situation. Something had happened in not just the European but also in the American continent too, and in several other places too, and that it had happened fast. It seems this United Nations had had the evidence of these situations but that someone or a group of people had assassinated a person from the UN for this information, because of this information…

Steven was now absolutely certain that the killers had been from the rogue organisation…

—I heard shouting yesterday at the camp and I don't know what it's about and I think this message has to be short because of it. I might know what is going on….

The people in charge here think they've found something. It's a weapon of some sort that can fly. They're planning to send this weapon across the entire region to check it for whatever it's they're looking for in there. I'm certain they may get ready for what's coming. And they want to prevent the communication that had been established between the people who are against them.

Do not send the next one.

It isn't safe anymore.

It isn't safe for any of us anymore—

Across the entire region? Steven contemplated. *Was the object in the bunker the same sort of weapon is being mentioned here? And what are they looking for?* He glanced up and held his breath in to listen. He wanted to be certain he was alone.

The only sound he could hear was the rhythmic sound coming from the tail swisher. He was annoyed at the sound it was making, but he was in its home, so he couldn't hush the creature away for no reason. He looked down at the tail swisher. As if it knew Steven was staring at her, it curled over and stretched its body, so it stretched out in a long, thin shape.

Except for the belly…

Another memory of a woman with her belly flashed through my mind. She, too, had a protruding belly. He frowned, because he was uncertain what the significance was of the belly being in that shape might mean. "What a damned good scientist I am, don't you think?" he said loudly. The creature in his lap jumped up like I had startled it with my voice.

Steven looked at the papers again. He was certain he'd have another chance to sit down to read them later, but at least he'd found the first clue in them about what was going on, and what his own 'real role' was, and he wasn't here as some sort of stupid scientist to see if plants were growing again, or that animals like the tail swisher were thriving again.

He could go from Utopus, walk for a day, and see it, then return to Utopus and tell everyone: "I saw a bunch of birds flying," or "I saw an animal running to somewhere."

Steven thought someone out there needed the skills of science to help them with a task which was in a place which would be able to defeat the people who 'still' were doing all this—he glanced up and, in his mind, repeated the words: *—who are still doing all this? Was that what this message was about?*

The more he knew, the less certain he became of his task, and the less certain he was that things were as simple as he'd always thought they were. Steven wondered how much his father knew or understood of what was going on.

The message had said: "Do not send the next one." *Did the message mean—the next Subject? Did this person mean that his father shouldn't have sent him…?*

His scientific mind had been analysing much more of the current situation than he'd realised in this moment. He'd always assumed that his choice of being a scientist was his own, but what if he never had any choice in the matter…? What if his father made him want to do this? Did this mean that he'd never had been a real scientist? Conditioning a child to do something that could be a similar situation as the enemy might have been doing for the past five centuries…He'd seen so much already in the five months since he'd taken off on this long journey.

It proved to him definitively that the stuff they knew now as 'science' might only be a shadow of its former self…

Steven rubbed his hand over the back of the tail swisher who seemed to take a delight in arching its tail in the air each time he did this, and each time he was about to continue reading, the creature would push its face against the man's hand. "You got it so much easier," he whispered to the creature. "You just live for each day. Your day would have been just the same as always if I hadn't turned up here."

He held the pile of paper up again, but he decided that the fading light made it too hard to read them now. It was already getting somewhat darker when it was still afternoon, and if he'd been in Utopus, he would have lit up fifty or sixty thick candles to use for reading, but out here, wherever 'here' might be, he didn't have the luxury. He didn't want to be out in the open during the day and he sensed that the people sending out the first object would want to investigate inside every house for living in now for evidence of use by an unknown traveller…

Steven put all the papers back into the rucksack and closed it tightly. He lay down, using the rucksack as something to lean his head on. The tail swisher saw it as a sign that she could curl up next to him. He guessed that his body heat offered a welcome feeling for the tiny creature. He guessed it wanted the body heat, as it normally would have to feel cold during the night.

As he lay on the hard floor, Steven wondered how Elizabet was coping right now after he had to leave her behind in Utopus. He was certain that his father would take care of her. And that he'd look after the others who'd worked with his son. he wondered if he was secretly preparing any of them to be the next Subject.

"NO, I'm going to be the last ever Subject," he mumbled.

As the darkness set in around him, Steven felt more alone than ever before.

One thing certain about the information he'd probed about the events relating to the disease is that it had left the world devoid of human life, and more devoice of animal life to ascertain degree. He wondered then why everyone in Utopus thought with certainty it was the last place for humans to still exist.

If that was the case, then where had the message originated from? Steven thought, and a woman who knew where and what Utopus was, had spoken to them…

* * *

After another two months of travel and silently celebrating his birthday, Steven had arrived at a large building in a large city, and he found another of those buildings, also containing hundreds of books. While he was searching through the books, most of which would crumble to dust as he touched them, he wondered more about his father's ultimate words before he'd departed…

30.

His father had told me to 'always remember,' and comparing it to what he had found in that building, it was curious to him how the people who might have used the building could have remembered so much. In an earlier message, he'd learnt what the place where the woman was sending the message from was located, and that they had had hundreds of books, and Steven decided he was lucky the enemy hadn't discovered this location or him yet. *They haven't found me here—yet...*

After an hour of walking around, he sat down somewhere that once had seemed to have been a place where people would gather for food and drink. Although they had such places too in Utopus, this place looked different from any of them. The place looked so colourful, even after all the centuries of no one using it.

Steven placed the rucksack in front of him, and it was in this moment he got curious why his father had told him he should never lose the bag. So, he opened the bag to seek out answers that it might contain.

Before Steven commenced with his search, he looked around him just in case the tail swisher would turn up by chance. It had followed him for many days after he'd left the building with its dried grass, but then the creature was gone. He saw it two days later, one more time, but after the following day it had gone and never had returned. Steven sighed, feeling sad it had scampered off...

He looked at the papers again.

He'd recalled then how they'd heard the messages when he was working on decoding the transmissions, and two of the recordings had told them that something terrible had happened five centuries ago. The first message he'd heard, had clarified to him that someone out there had caused everything had happened as some sort of criminal act. From the second message, it became more ominous, and the Voice had warned us about a disease. However, the messages contained in his rucksack had seemed to be written texts that had told him a lot more about what went on hundreds of years ago.

One of transmissions had mentioned a coup, which had happened a little over four centuries ago. It stated this information on one of the first pages, and he'd read this information on the pages that his father had packed into his rucksack. The next page had told him more about the possible intent of those who'd been behind the coup.

—There were at least two hundred pages in the folder.

It seems they had a plan to deal with the rogue organisation and make sure that it couldn't continue with its operations. The pages give information that dates back all the way to 1992. In this year, Earth Summit was held, and although it happened according to what it says here, there was something that happened that was hushed up by the organisers.

They talked of an incident where a prominent scientist called Dr Carla Merighaver, a German scientist with a knowledge of prolonging the lifespan of seeds, and with a recent discovery involving insects, she was kidnapped and never seen again. Apparently, they never asked for a ransom, and they never found her body either. After about twenty years of her missing, her family declared her death who, for the next fifty years, spent every effort trying to locate her. The plane she was supposed to be travelling on had crashed just before they discovered her missing, and some people at the time believed she'd perished on that plane.

It states that because of security, the plane's identity was never made public, and was enroute to the airport near where the summit was due to start, went off the radar minutes after clearance to enter the airspace over Brazil was given. An investigation happened but when the chief investigator got shot on the doorstep of their house, all investigation into the attack against the plan was halted, and all they apparently handed all the paperwork related to the incident to the United Nations who archived all the paperwork and other materials away and never referenced it ever again. And then they were gone.—

Steven had felt puzzled about this message he had heard for the longest time, and his father had confirmed to him what Utopus was...

It wasn't just the northern part of they'd once called Europe that was affected by the events, but that his father had been correct when he'd drawn the line on a map and placed his palm in the centre, and had said that all that it was all Utopus being affected now, that they possibly also had planned for other places to be safe havens. At least that was what he'd worked out from the messages. He'd decided that the Earth Summit that had been listed as the possible place planned to keep people safe from the disease was also the first place at risk of an attack.

Steven shook his head. He could do all the theorising he wanted. The message was way too confusing to him, and he would have needed to see the actual papers that the woman in the message had been describing. He was only guessing now that it was the woman from the spoken message who had been conveying these messages for his father to transcribe.

There was no proof that it was... the 'her' who he'd read about in the letters. He could only assume it was 'her'—from the message he'd listened to at the Academic Institute.

It was in this moment that Steven was realising that he possessed something, which could ultimately make it dangerous for him if those within the third building were what my father was trying to warn me about. If there was a link between them and those that the messages warned about that danger became even greater...

Steven looked around inside the building with books and he also tried to memorise the words on all the pages inside his rucksack, just in case he had to leave the bag somewhere behind. He also thought it would be good to read some books there, and memorise them too, just like he had done months ago in the other building. But then another part of him thought about the people that she'd been warning about all this time, and the fact they had claimed to have wanted books...

Initially, he thought it would be best to make a fire here, and to destroy all the books that I had been reading so far.

In another paper, Steven had found information of an incident that had happened in 2001, when a scientist had got kidnapped in the south of France, and from the map that had come with the information he'd noted that it wasn't far from the place he was heading towards. It was a place where the people of this place came from where the woman had said she was located according to the recordings, and that they were planning to do something soon...

There was no information listed as to what this scientist's name was, but whoever it was hadn't lived for long afterwards. Their body had been found a month later, washed up at a nameless tiny beach in Italy. The investigators had thought he'd been killed at sea. Then something that had happened with a large boat full of people. It stated that they had come from Africa for shelter running from 'dangerous people,' but they were found on board murdered, with all their throats cut.

In this text they were claiming that there was a potential link between the two incidents, and he was wondering if the fleeing people had seen the scientist being taken, and then got killed to silence them.

Something about the text told him that there were things going on that the people in charge wanted to get investigated, such the incident where people were fleeing from one place to another getting murdered. But why would someone kill everyone in a boat, just as they kidnapped a scientist…?

It seemed the people of wherever she was, were from somewhere else.

Steven took out his map and looked it over for any potential clues. It was just a mass of features, such as mountains, roads, cities, and more. So, he had look for a map in this place of books that would help me. He found something an hour later, and he first looked if the new map had a year listed on it and he realised that the four-digit number was representing a year, and that not just books, but other things like this map, could have a year on it to tell him something about a certain year…

So, the map was listing the date of 1999, and he looked at it to find out what 'Europe' had looked like in that year. The new map was made up of lot of different colours, and rather than showing where the mountains and roads were, it showed just a few of the largest cities and the most important roads. He saw that the route someone had drawn on his copy of a map, was correlating with the long road going from Berlin to Prague, was confirming that it was the correct route to take…

The map also showing each country differently and Steven assumed that the different colours were there to show separate countries, but some of the countries seemed interesting. There were some countries, which were in a similar hue, almost the same colour, and one such country was making him curious.

He was wondering why the central region of Europe, and he noted that Berlin was inside this region, was all in the same colour, then why did it have this line drawn in the centre of it, dividing the region into two, almost trying to tell a map user that it was an area with a west and east part to it. He saw there were some places listed with the word 'former' between brackets. All of it was a giant puzzle, but Steven realised quickly he was in the right place to find answers for this puzzle. After a while he continued reading the papers with renewed eagerness…

The documents didn't go into much detail until around 2035, when an assassination attempt against the serving president of the United States. He had survived it, but according to a conspiracy making its rounds, it was only because he'd pulled one of his guards in front of him to use as a human shield…

—When the next elections had come, the population hadn't forgiven him for these actions, and they instead had elected Julia Echenka. There is a photo of her. She was someone with darker skin people who were so rare nowadays. She'd been only fifty-four when she got elected with highest historical vote count, well over 100 million, and had apparently governed from 2036 to 2044.—

The text was suggesting she'd orchestrated the organisation and planning of the idea, an event of sorts, which would have given everyone on the planet a better life, the details of which Steven had later found listed on the paper from the magazine. He had folded the magazine and placed it into his rucksack…

"Maybe this information might be useful if ever we can defeat the rogue organisation as it exists right now," Steven mumbled under his breath, "and then attempt to create the world that she had wanted…"

He decided to read on:

—It took most of her time governing the United States to organise the event. At the end of her governance over the nation, they assigned her to the UN to continue expanding her efforts. The papers say she'd died only about a year after its completion from a sudden heart attack.—

If things were different, we might be enjoying the fruits of her efforts now. She died for nothing, and unlike how most people's lifespans are nowadays, because of her efforts she would have had a long life, and Steven was kind of glad the date shown indicated that she had died before the disease had arrived.

Steven saw that the document was also claiming that, as late as in 2087, there were known descendants of Julia Echenka, living both in Europe and what had been the United States.

* * *

Leadership of Utopus comprised an equal measure of men and women.

Ninety people were in charge of the city, with his father was one of them. His father had explained that each year that ten people would leave from their posting, and each year ten others would get selected, for them as a group to govern Utopus for five years until the following year.

"It means that we maintain an egalitarian situation here," his father had added, though had never explained the meaning of his words. As he sat reading there, Steven thought about what his father had said for a moment, and compared it with what he was reading about this thing called a 'president' which Julia Echenka had been…

There seemed to also have something very special about the fact that she was a dark-skinned person and in charge of the nation listed in the article. Some people claimed it made her the 'first of her kind.' Steven had read books before about this country, and one thing he'd read in one such book was the words from a man, who'd started a speech with: 'I have a dream.'

Did this text prove his dream could have come true? Steven thought.

* * *

Steven had only ever seen maybe a dozen of those dark-skinned people himself and according to his father every person of every skin colour or hair colour had suffered equal high mortality rates.

"There are a *few* of everything only now," his father had added. "Too few…"

On telling his friend what his father had said, Elizabet had told him that her grandmother would tell her stories saying that there were more of them living in Utopus when her grandmother was a young child. According to her grandmother, they had just left for somewhere Elizabet and I had glanced at one another feeling deeply confused when her grandmother told us, "Something causes there to be fewer of them every year. They had said that they live in a secret place *not* even the people who created the disease would be able to find the place—" Then his friend's grandmother would glance around conspiratorially, and chuckle softly like she'd told the youngsters a delightful secret…

Steven had never understood what the old woman had meant with the comment, and two years later she had died, so she could never explain it anyway. The conversation had caused him to become acutely observant and always to look around him better ever since, and it had seemed she was right. He'd seen more dark-skinned people as a nine-year-old, and fewer when he finally started helping his father at the Academic institute, and even fewer just weeks before they selected me…

I guess that no one would believe me anyway if I told them that I was involved in my own bit of secret stuff, and had helped the ones I saw by carrying the little girl, Steven thought, *and I wished my father and Elizabet been as brave as them and we could have followed them… We might now be in the secret place Elizabet's grandmother had told us about…*

Steven looked back at the text and was curious *why* people had been so against a man surviving an attack against him. He wondered how different things might have been if he'd died. Would the woman have become a president at all in such a situation? He wondered why someone had tried to kill him. Someone had not liked something he had done…

Steven looked around at the many books and wondered if any of them might date from around 2035, and therefore would be able to tell him what the president of 2035 had done which had caused an attempt to kill him. He got up and went looking through the books and he found a book after searching for twenty minutes.

The cover title was listed 'Presidential Decisions 2024 - 2044.'

A perfect find for me, Steven thought.

Steven was about to walk back to the table he'd been sitting at, when he also spotted two additional books which he'd wanted to read, too. One about animals. He'd wanted to learn more of the proper names for them, and the other about plants, and he'd remembered then his earlier thought: I need to know which plants and seeds of plants might be good to eat. He sat back down at the table and smirked when he also saw that the book about plants was the same thickness as the pile of papers.

I guess I can disguise the papers with this, Steven thought as he grinned broadly, *and anyone who might look in my rucksack will think I'm walking around with a book about plants.*

Steven studied the next page and leafed through the entire book, found long ago among the ruins, and again found in a special building for storing books, then he switched books to see what it was going to tell him about these presidents...

Julia Echenka must have been the last president, Steven thought, *because nothing in this paperwork shows there were any others after her.*

He had also read earlier the United States closed its borders to keep the disease *out*, but that this country became a victim of this action. The text had stated the events had happened close to the end of 2043, and he was certain that there was a correlation between Julia Echenka being the last president, and the collapse of its economy some forty years later.

31.

IN THIS DOCUMENT, IT STATES that from 2045, Steven thought pensively, *and the country had then started being run by a committee, comprised of three individuals of each of the states… This is also perhaps what might have caused the attempt for a coup if what had been written in the documents is true.*

However, the text had quite a few sizeable gaps in the information listed within the paperwork, like a lot of missing information should be in the text. It was almost like someone had tried to erase this information before others were able to be made aware about this information.

It made him wonder again why 'they' had wanted to assassinate the UN person. Perhaps he might have wanted to destroy this information. If this was the case, what was the reason for its existence? Why would erasing all this information somehow remove the knowledge of the rogue organisation? It made little sense to me him all…

Steven found nothing in the book, which was interesting, but it did claim that the father of the almost-assassinated president had previously tried to be the president of the United States and had failed to succeed becoming the president in all three previous attempts. His son had tried four years to gain the *same* position after this man's last attempt and was selected after a hard battle.

Battle? Steven contemplated. *Did it take a battle to lead this country?*

Steven paused with reading to consider everything new he'd discovered. If it was a battle, to be a leader, it might explain the coup. The information about the last President of the United States was becoming a lot more interesting as he kept reading. The comparison between his father, who was a leader at three years older than the listed age of this woman, was also in his mind…

"Julia Echenka was fifty-four when she was elected," Steven recited verbally, "and she had only started working at the government fourteen years earlier after she'd studied law and economics at a university for six years."

Neither of these words were familiar however he did recognise *one* word. "If the person needed to be in a university to be in the role," Steven mumbled, "then might they be like an Academist, so these two…errr… skills…. are connected to leading people? So… rules? And… how to…" Steven frowned and then thought back to something Elizabet had once explained. That people would trade things. "So, a skill to show people how to trade…?" Steven had no way to get answers, so he shrugged and continued with just reading. The text stated she'd travelled to this other place when she had heard a message being told: "Anything is possible…" and no information was listed about who she'd heard saying these words.

So, a university was to learn more types of knowledge than just science, Steven thought when he read the text, a*nd maybe I should go back to Utopus when I can and tell that same message to them all over there.*

He turned to the next page, and it was a quick message listed on this page that made Steven blanch…

—Something happened here yesterday. I could hear a lot of weapons being fired, like they were defending this place from something. I'm uncertain what it was, but I don't believe I should send a message for too long or they might discover me. I'll report more when I can.—

Did the message mean the woman was taking a substantial risk in sending us these messages?

Steven wondered what had happened, because he looked at the next few pages for any clues and none were present. It seemed after the initial warning she'd just gone on to talk more about the events of centuries ago…

—She'd suggested me I should burn all the papers I found. And she said that it should be done, if that is what it said as a planned action by the UN.—

Steven now was curious what the UN had been for. *In a document, they had given the name of United Nations. If they couldn't stop the rogue organisation from doing what they were doing, then why had they existed at all?*

A document was listing the place of origin of the rogue organisation in the east of Europe, somewhere, although it also showed it either could be further to the north-east, and that the UN hadn't exactly known the correct location. It appeared that they had thought of the rogue organisation as consisting of different people, all against peace.

In a very sarcastic way, which was what was going on with Utopus, but Steven doubted it was serving the same purpose as the UN had done. Somehow, and the more he thought about it, the more wrong in some unknown way everything seemingly was. Like it was just all some pretence to lull all people into a status quo, with them controlling whether it's safe or dangerous.

That is why they put those flying machines in the air, Steven thought. *It's preventing people from going around freely.*

Steven had no idea where they had got them from, but it seemed to be 'things' that would have been used by some sort of military before. *They appear old and look like they don't belong here,* Steven thought, *and there's this specific reference of this 'she' again.* Steven frowned when he noticed the words, because now there were two people doing something dangerous. Two people whose lives could be at risk in whatever place they were doing this stuff…

Steven also was curious about the thing called the 'UN,' or as I now knew they had properly called it by the name 'United Nations.' He was also wondering, in equal measure, about the woman who'd sent this message, what it served. He'd seen references of the UN in earlier books he'd read, some of which were from fifty to seventy years ago, before the woman called Julia Echenka became a president. These books were stating the rogue organisation had already existed for many years…

He looked again through the book in which he'd seen Julia Echenka listed. According to the text, in 2042 the last nations that weren't a part of the UN had signed a document to become part of it now.

Does that mean that in 2042, all the nations on this planet worked together in a united way? Steven thought. *No wonder they were calling that other organisation who fought against them 'a rogue organisation'…*

He re-read more of the papers to see if they'd give him clues about 'who' the rogue organisation might be.

Steven leaned back to read the next page.

—There are some new people in the camp this week. I don't understand where they came from, but it didn't look like they came here by their own choice. It terrified me when the shouting started, and then one of them ran off. I don't think I'll ever forget the sound I heard next. It was horrific.

I looked over the papers while this was happening, always listening for them outside, saw on one of them something written about a capture and killing of something it called a 'terrorist.' I'm uncertain what it might have been, but it is what the people who had killed that man who ran must have been thinking when they killed him.

There were many things happening in those days between 1950 and 2020, which involved people who seemed to want to kill for no reason. I'm uncertain what this 'terrorist' word means, but it likes nothing good at all. I'm suspecting what it could be, when I place my finger over the last few letters of the word—terror. Yes, that is what it was they did when they killed that man.

I think they want to do that to all the survivors everywhere, so they can control everyone.—

Steven looked up and was feeling angry suddenly.

He was feeling an uncontrolled, furious anger. *For almost the last six centuries now, there had been people fighting against peace. It seemed now there were people who didn't want this world to be safe. Not then, and perhaps not now.*

Steven looked at the paper again: 'terror.'

The word jumped from the paper. It frightened him. He remembered about the first message, and the conclusions he'd drawn from the death toll that was stated. It had claimed that there was a 99 percent mortality across the world, and that the world had comprised of around 'eight billion people' before the disaster with the disease.

Steven had calculated from this that the population became around eighty million.

From other information, he'd concluded that the childbirth rates weren't high enough to repopulate the planet fast enough, and there were more elderly people than there are the young ones such as Elizabet or himself. *Most of the young people aren't feeling like they want to have children,* Steven thought, *because why bring a child into a world that's broken, where you cannot offer such a child any security, such as good health or a long life?*

The 'terror' that the disease had brought was still in existence. He walked for a long distance already through the leftovers of what once was Europe. He'd come across a few dogs, a few of those tail swishers, seen a few birds, seen some other animals in the distance who were so skittish they would run away from him. He concluded from what he'd seen, that the plan, the evil plan of five or even six hundred years ago, had worked—perhaps had worked better than the people who set out to execute it, had ever hoped for.

The messages on the pages he was reading, weren't a message from the past, or as he'd called them a 'voice from the past,' but were also apparently warning us, or others, of a possibility of the events of between 2072 and 2132 repeating itself. In sixty years, a disease with no name had devastated the world. It had reduced humanity to just eight million. If this got repeated, it could cause humanity to be less than a million…

Steven was reading the pages a little more, and then he would read some books he'd found. As time went by, the three tables he was using were slowly piling up with more and more books. History was being told in a very detailed text. While reading those books, he felt for the first time in his life that he was a proper scientist. He had to know stuff, learn stuff…

Somehow, Steven felt that the more he knew, the more he could teach others.

What others? Steven would think from time to time before grabbing another book. He felt so angry that history could be altered so easily by an unknown entity. The more he researched the more he was now certain that someone was trying to repeat history. In a book it even stated a stark message that resonated with him to the core: 'Those who cannot remember the past are condemned to repeat it,' although the text didn't name the person who said it anywhere in the text…

Steven felt the need to re-read these last words several times to let them sink in fully. He almost thought the people who were now doing something terrible were making these words true. If they didn't remember that only eighty million people were surviving their actions the last time when someone caused a disaster, then it would be certain we were all going to be doomed this time…

He even could see stark similarities between some images, he'd seen in the books of five or six centuries ago, and some descriptions in the messages she'd been relaying. It caused hairs to stand on my arms as he read next text…

> —The leader here called everyone to stand together at the western side of the camp. I had to go too, which is why this message is a day later than I expected. We just stood there, and even when the sun was shining was too hot and causing us all discomfort, we were made to stand there. He might have wanted to test us for something, although I was unsure what. He even got the other men to round up the children, and I watched as they stood a few hundred meters from us, also made to stand in the sun.
>
> I saw *her* among them, and our eyes locked, and ask with our eyes: "What is going on?"
>
> Without saying a word, the leader told us all to go inside, then they locked doors, and we didn't see any of them for several days, and the camp was unusually quiet. I'm getting scared now that, somehow, they've found out about me, so I'll keep doing my messages for as long as I can, then I'll attempt to get away, but if I do, she'll need to come with me. They've claimed the land north of here is the safest, and that there's a group very far north from here who uses ships to send people to the land across the sea. There's a rumour that it's the only safe place on this planet. I must try to get away and go there.
>
> I saw that woman earlier too, who'd arrived not so long ago. She placed a finger over her mouth, then motioned to me. When I got to where she stood, she said to me these three words, "Things will change." I'm uncertain who she is, and where she is from, and even more uncertain what that message means.—

Steven had seen a book a few hours before, which he went to look for when I read this bit of message. He had found the book and had paged frantically through the book until he found the photo from earlier again. It was a place in a faraway place which, according to the book, was called 'Ash Civilian Assembly Centre,' where Europeans got locked up during World War 2.

The images in the book were of people standing in the sun, and the text claimed their captors had made them to do it for hours on end. The same was happening wherever the woman was sending the messages from. The similarity was so precise between what he'd read in the message, and what the book was saying, that Steven was wondering for a moment if the message was all fake. But the moment that the theory entered his mind, he had to dismiss it.

He wondered if the message was also telling him to be cautious about where to go. But after several times re-reading it, he wasn't any wiser for it, and he just moved on to the next part of the message.

—I discovered a name today. A man called Aldric Stephanos. According to this text, he was the creator of a new pesticide, which the UN had banned a year later. This man was developing this stuff from 2039 to 2041. After the ban, he disappeared, and no one saw him after that. He had no family, was an only child whose parents died in a car crash when he was about fifteen, and here it claims that there were strange circumstances attached to it. They had considered him a loner during his youth.

And historically, it says that he kept from being photographed, and never gave interviews or anything like it. They suggest it's almost like he only existed for the few years when the pesticide was being developed, and then disappeared when it failed. The pesticide apparently had side effects on insects. It doesn't say what the effect was on the insects, but I'm wondering if there's a link between this information and the onset of the disease, especially when we know it was spread first by insects.

As it states insects had spread the disease, I think knowledge of this can be very dangerous, and I need to be careful after this. It seems, from what I read here, that various governments sent local officials to review local legislation to prepare for the disease, and that they stepped up this action by removing standing water, large areas of vegetation, and burned waste to minimise the places where the insects could spread it. I think they hoped to stop the onset of the disease, but too late discovered that food, plants, they contaminated almost everything by this time.—

This was Steven's first indicator that the person who conveyed the messages and was who got referenced in the letters was the same person. He looked at the name closer, and the name was rather odd.

The information about the insects was of interest to him a lot. Steven sat there staring blankly, just thinking about how insects could have been so interesting in so many ways. And he realised that there was one binding factor that connected all the information he'd been reading so far

- scientists were doing this stuff, either for benevolent reasons or for malevolent reasons. It was they who were ultimately responsible.

No wonder that the fucking Academist spoke about scientists with such disdain in his voice, Steven thought before he re-read the text, and traced his finger along the last line: "Almost everything was contaminated by them."

Steven looked around when he read these few words, then he looked through the windows that were located thirty meters from him, and he was curious about 'how' everything could even get contaminated. The last remnants of nature wanted to show him the answer at that moment, when he saw a fly land on the table, lift off for a while, then land again, and then was crawling over the table surface.

32.

STEVEN HAD WATCHED THE CREATURE, transfixed by what it was doing. He then watched as it flew up again and landed on another part of the table. *Insects fly everywhere*, he thought, *and they land on every surface.* Suddenly, he could see the simplicity of the method used. There was almost cruel sarcasm to the way these people of the rogue organisation used nature as the weapon of choice against the entire world… and they could do it again!

Steven realised, in that moment, that he knew the answer for why he'd seen so few animals outside. If 'everything' precisely meant that, then it also meant that the insects would have landed on animals, and contaminated them, and contaminated more animals whenever an animal ate such an insect. Some of such animals that ate insects could easily have been ones then eaten by humans. He paled when he realised that the laughing bird might have eaten such insects. But the scientist part of him also realised that 'nature' would be recovering from the disaster. In a lot of places, he saw recovery. The more south he travelled, the clearer it became. He wondered why the region south of Utopus was so desolate in contrast.

Was someone tampering with nature in this region so to create an illusion of nature being affected still by the disease…?

Steven sighed, then kept reading on.

Steven found a tiny scribble of a note among the papers, which seemed to be related to the other information, in which it stated something about a genetically changed moth, which was apparently developed between 2004 and 2021, to curb the devastation of such animals on crops. *They had meant for this technology to create a way to use fewer pesticides…*

He was uncertain why someone had listed this information here, but he was certain there should be a link somewhere. When he read the text further, he could only wonder if this information about an insect proved that the original plan had been to make insects more beneficial to humans, and that the people in the rogue organisation were working against it.

Maybe what he held in his hands might be the evidence for a conspiracy, which someone now was trying to hide, and the woman who'd sent the messages was aware the conspiracy, so went to work to tell us in Utopus this information. He could compare what the woman in the 'voice from the past' was doing with the few bits he'd read about this World War 2, in which most of Europe had seemingly been an under the occupation of Germany.

Steven realised this meant the land in the off-pink colour on the new map called Germany, and he wondered whether the line splitting the region represented them being able to be whole again after some sort of punishment against the people who'd done a crime, or that this line represented a beginning of the same things the land did in the World War 2.

He hoped the first option applied…

Steven had read in another book that there was a man who'd wanted to conquer every part of Europe, and several times would have succeeded if there weren't these people called 'resistance' doing stuff to block the efforts of the Germans. Another book suggested someone else tried similar more than eighty years later but from somewhere else. Steven never found any evidence to let him know the outcome for that attempt at conquest…

Was the woman in the 'voice from the past' part of a resistance working against the people who were planning to repeat the events of 2072?

The only way to know this information was to get to where she was right now, and then to make sure the enemy was stopped and find the people were resisting the plans to decimate humanity once again. And if those evil people were who sent the objects, he'd seen a few times in the sky above, then he had to be much more cautious.

Steven had to make sure he was travelling at night only, or if he had to travel during the day that he did it with stealth.

I wonder if there are books about military stuff here, Steven thought. *Maybe, reading such books will teach me to stay safe, but they could also give me the necessary information about how I could defeat them.*

He still didn't know who the 'them' in the text could be…

Steven ate another piece of his now dwindling supply of chocolate, while he continued reading on…

> —The information in these files from the UN is becoming less coherent, and it's like there are vast gaps in what is here. I will keep sending messages about what's in them, but the further I get with them, the less they will make sense to you.
>
> Like this idea as an example.
>
> There was an idea circulating in 2013 that they were able to introduce genetically changed babies, which would reduce the number of people who might be able to get ill. I'm wondering if those who developed the disease knew this information and therefore purposely created the disease. It seems in 2032 they had abandoned the idea.—

He frowned, and he was curious why the woman would have given this information, but then his scientific mind, which was a lot more knowledgeable now, filled in the blanks, even before he wanted to. Steven wanted to think that they had included this information as a clue as to what to do to make the world whole again.

They would need more babies, and any information on how to increase childbirth would be helpful to everyone. For that, he would need to find books about babies—he smirked when his thoughts turned to that topic. He hadn't even had a proper relationship ever with a woman, yet here he was thinking about how to get women to have babies. He found the irony of the situation hilarious.

Steven involved himself in the other task and therefore abandoned the effort of reading of the collection of messages for a while. He walked around the room until he found the specific books he now wanted, and then carried all to the tables he'd been using.

After carrying over six heavy piles, I glanced at the tables. They'd been empty when he arrived a week ago, but now they were so full that he was having trouble finding a place to place more books. He saw more tables further into the building beyond these tables and he put all the books he'd already read on these other table. Rather than placing the books on those tables haphazardly, he made them into neat piles of ten books each and started on the furthest corner. His plans had altered now, and for this plan to be executed flawlessly, somehow, he would need to dislodge the huge curtain he'd seen hanging in one of the largest rooms of the building, which he'd drape over the books to keep them out of sight from being seen from outside.

If he was able, he'd also place some bookcases in this location to make this small area on the upper floor of the building into a place that the people searching for books wouldn't find it. He'd use a type of illusion against them.

His mind started racing. He could work on getting things sorted to make it easier for the people who were fighting against that 'them' to win this war. War? He just had to do everything methodically, be as precise as he'd been while working as a scientist.

"Thanks a lot, father," he bellowed.

Steven wished his father was able to hear him right now. Because of this idea Steven's mind snapped into a realisation. His father had been preparing him for at least ten years, perhaps even longer than that.

By the time he finished with his task of moving books to the back of the room on the top floor of the building he was exhausted. When he'd started, he'd seen several cabinets which he might be able to use. And because of that, he was now walking back with something else to read, which he'd found minutes earlier. A book named 'Nineteen Eighty-Four' which sounded interesting...

It seems to be a story of some sort. Like with every book, the first thing he'd do was to look at the first page to see from when the book was created. It said '1949,' so just after World War 2 then, Steven thought, and I wonder why a person would even write about something that would happen so soon afterwards.

He found no information about the person who had written the book inside it. He sat down and read, and when he'd finished reading, he had another new take on what was going on in his own life...

Instead of three super states, we just have Utopus and Zone Zero, he thought, and this other place, which the woman in the message was describing—or that she might be from.

He wondered if the people in the rogue organisation had known about this book and had used it for their own purpose to do what they did in 2072. Steven knew the answer to this question was either in the papers he still needed to read, or if the woman who'd sent the message didn't find any such information, it meant he would never know, and neither would anyone else.

Steven looked at the pile of papers on the table, then he grabbed the next sheet...

I think the information I just read might be why they targeted UN person, he thought *He had information with him. It relates somehow to both Utopus and here...*

> —Apparently, scientists did something in around 2016 and successfully made an object disappear. They used a material with nano-size particles, which could enhance specific properties on an object's surface. It seems the technology fell into the hands of the rogue organisation when they hijacked the plane, on which the company's directors were flying, who were attending a summit organised by the UN. The company apparently stopped development and production in 2045, but there seems to be evidence here which shows the technology was still in use long after this date.—

His mind had circled back to his earlier thought. About creating an effective illusion to hide the books he'd stashed at the back of the room. Now he read a message suggesting that there was such a material in existence five centuries ago, and if he read the last lines of the message literally, it could still exist now...

It could still exist now, he thought.

His head was spinning. The words kept repeating in his mind.

It could still exist now...

If it existed still, it might be able to explain something he'd seen? Steven remembered his own earlier assertion that he'd seen the black third structure appear and disappear. He remembered all the times he was sure it was happening. He was suddenly also certain that the object he saw high above him, before reaching the bridge, was also similar, and that it, too, appeared and disappeared.

Was this proof that these nano things were still in use?

Steven stared at the book and was curious what the nano things were, and he'd found nothing in any book that had explained them, and he had to guess, and it was a wild guess, that it must have been something so new that most people who were writing books hadn't even heard about them. He looked at the next page, and saw that it, too, mentioned the technology.

According to the information he had found, there was ongoing research in its existence, until around 2093, in which the scientists were doing research into a new nano-structural material, specifically for the use in aerospace use, military use, and automotive industry. The document had claimed the technology existed as early as 2016, or even earlier than this. From around 2037, they'd combined the research to create organic computers, and they'd planned it to have organic machines, eventually.

This stuff sounds too fantastical to me, Steven thought, *and even as a scientist I cannot believe any of it can be true.*

Steven wondered what these 'computers' mentioned might be and then he remembered the door being shut at the Academic Institute. He remembered the cube from which they had extracted the message. He wondered if either, or perhaps both, was this computer that got mentioned?

Steven got up and looked around the room and down over the nearby banister. He saw nothing around that could resemble these machines. He returned to the table and looked over the last two pages again. He had to figure out what this nano stuff was, because suddenly he felt like he knew more about 'their' plans.

The plan had been deceptive in how it was put together. They had stolen much of what they would need in the rogue organisation from the proper scientists, or that they had kidnapped the people with the knowledge, or killed the people who would have been able to develop technology against the organisation. He wondered if any doctors of the time might have been working on a cure, and that they too were killed. It was all such a scary scenario, and it was one big conspiracy—except—it was still happening now. If those people referred to as 'they' had succeeded, and the aliens in some stories he'd read about as a child, or later as an adult, had really existed, the aliens might be able to come here to find the planet empty, with only the houses that everyone once lived in or that they'd used for work left over.

How and why the people disappeared, Steven thought, *and the plants and animals, would be a mystery to solve for those aliens…*

That's if the aliens existed, because some books had claimed people made them up to explain that we couldn't be the only ones in the universe.

Steven wanted to get to the roof of the building that evening, and lie on the roof, and look up at the stars above, and then try to imagine that around one of them a planet was spinning with these aliens on living on its surface, so he felt like there could still be benevolent beings somewhere out in an unknown place. And, at least, then he'd be less lonely, too…

He looked at the next page, and this page piqued his interest because of what he'd just been thinking about. He sat staring at the page for several minutes before he realised what it was talking about.

"This bit of information I find interesting," Steven mumbled under his breath, ending the comment with a loud grunt.

—There was a new technology in development in shape memory alloys, which had started with an attempt to develop equipment which could serve a new start in space exploration. Unfortunately, the program halted because of the onset of the disease. There was a link between this development, and the development of special drones, that they'd use to explore other planets. But there was an ambush which had resulted in the theft of over sixteen hundred newly developed drones.

A new legislation was subsequently introduced to curb further the use of drones, and they signed it into legislation with the participation of over a hundred countries in a new directive of the UN.

The directive came into effect in 2065.—

Not sure what a 'drone' is, but it sounds like it was something dangerous, from what it seems to say here, Steven thought, and I wonder what happened to these machines they mentioned…

Steven started thinking that he knew. He was certain he'd seen some in recent weeks and months. *In the text, it mentioned something flying*, he thought, *and I saw something fly around which might match the wording in the text. There was this highly revealing aspect to this stuff. He felt like someone was just trying to make a fool out of him…*

It felt now like he was a character from one of all the books he'd always been reading as a kid, and that this moment was like the point of no return for him in a big story he was only vaguely aware of so far where there was a beginning, middle and end… and he was soon getting to the middle part of the story of some sort. *And yes, that was makes you the fool,* Steven thought. *Someone is doing something, and here I'm sitting in this building playing a librarian. Do YOU know what a librarian even is, Steven? You saw this word written on a piece of wood in the building. A sign with the word that was sitting idly on a desk, and you wonder what such people did precisely…* But the books he had then found soon answered this puzzle…

Well, if they possessed curated books with potential answers, he thought, *then yeah, I'm foolish for sitting there and doing nothing while there are these 'drones' hunting for me.*

Steven was getting more certain that he'd walk from the building and he'd have a dozen of the black flying objects hovering at the outer door waiting for him to do something to him like the machines from a planet called Mars in a book read a few hours earlier might do to him, or as he now knew they were called, drones, all hovering about him, all with a gun aimed at him to shoot him dead.

33.

HE IMAGINED THAT PEOPLE COULD rush into the building at any moment. The shadows around him now took on the shapes of people, and he was hearing sounds which shouldn't have been there, or which couldn't be there...

So, he skimmed the next two pages, and the voice from the past seemed like she was now just rushing through information. She seemed more panicked in the way she might have spoken was shown by the shorter, more abrupt sentences written by his father. There were marks beside certain sentences that proved his father might have been concerned. The earlier sense of calmness in the word use was gone. Steven started wondering what the link between her was reading from something and what the drones doing something might be. Something was causing her to feel compelled to include the drone information.

Steven remembered his conversation with Elizabet when they were watching the eastern sea... or the lack of it. The pages he was reading now made it clear to him why the sea was as it is now. Someone had silted up sufficient parts of the seabed around the region, where he'd seen the bridge, to make sure it had dried up the sea east of Utopus. Steven wondered if that was the reason for the land being so dusty and dry.

These files from the UN seem not only to hold information about the disease, Steven thought. *They were gathering other information related to what seem to go on. I wonder really what the link was between this flood, and the information about the disease, but I guess we'll never know. It claims that they started an initiative in 2055, and that the ultimate plan was for it to be completed by around 2186...*

—Severe flooding in several places around the world had created the initiative to reclaim land from the ocean. A company in Germany started to 'grow' soil as far back as 1988. The name of the company isn't anywhere in these pages. It was producing around six metric tons of it per day by 2009. According to evidence, in 2026, they had automated the plant, and they were still actively producing this soil by as late as 2076, and the last reported information of them being active dates from 2105.

In the automated sequence, the plant would produce the soil, which got transported from the plant's location to the north-western coast of Denmark, where it was deposited into the ocean, with the view that initially the ocean would wash it away, and deposit it as silt across a large region of the North Sea. However, a news clip here states that people had protested about the endeavours of the builders, and then an accident had happened, and people had demanded the closure of the building site. It's uncertain if they ever succeeded with their demands.—

What Steven was realising, from reading the text was why the seabed, east of Utopus, had become dry. He was certain there was a correlation between that, and this described event. "Because if the region showed started silting up," Steven voiced, "less sea water could have reached the sea east of Utopus."

One concern he had now was how far from the silting process had spread. If the silting went quite far south, it would be the cause for there to be less water present between where they'd claim the water transported to the land where the sea would have been, and it made it in its current state more vulnerable to be targeted by the rogue organisation…

When he'd discerned the ships, which some sort of massive fire had burned to wrecks, there was something else which he was able to notice about them much later when it might have mattered less. He'd eyed some towers near him as he trekked to Berlin. These towers had stopped working in the middle of a task of an unknown purpose…

I'm wondering if what I'd discovered was the machines that this text was describing, Steven thought.

He was aware that he'd stumbled on perhaps the greatest conspiracy ever. One that had started in around 1910 according to some information he had read, and which was still ongoing. Six hundred years of conspiracy, and the people involved last had died four hundred years ago.

It was all one big joke, Steven thought, *and a hell of a big, laughable joke and I'm the one is solving the pun in all of it. Oh yeah, by now, I should think of all as a joke or something else to make me look a fool… and there were moments when they, that 'they' again, were succeeding…*

Steven decided that he needed to read more pages at another time. He wanted to get out of the building he'd been holed in for weeks. It felt to him he was becoming like a character in a book with stories he'd kept re-reading. Perhaps, if he was like the characters in the story who were mechanical, none of this would matter. But as human, the whole situation mattered to him.

He worked his way through the remainder of the chocolate hastily…

* * *

When Steven had set off again, he'd planned to use the methods that he'd found inside a book about the way that people had fed themselves for thousands of years - by regularly hunting and fishing, perhaps also by collecting plants and seeds to eat. Doing both only when they were hungry and not more than this. He needed to be sure he could cope with the journey as he had another seven or eight months ahead of him… it would be the most dangerous months of his life.

Especially now I've managed to solve the riddle from the past, Steven thought, wondering also how many of the enemy remained after all this time.

Before he'd left from the building with the books, Steven had moved as many books as he could carry and as fast as he could complete this task into certain areas where they'd be out of sight of the drones, because he was certain that perhaps they'd have something attached to them allowing the people guiding them to discover a place from a far distance.

Whoever is sending them out is searching for things they want banned, Steven thought, *and an enemy who wants information about things that would prove they are guilty, dangerous, out to destroy things or simply against people knowing stuff would want the things that would be these books, destroyed so no one discovers the truth… or knows how the world once was. It's like in that story really. But before you end up thinking that a book needs to be burned, you first might think it needs to be banned unfairly…*

Steven wasn't certain of it, but he knew enough now to comprehend that he might be close to the truth with this knowledge, too.

He'd repacked his rucksack once more before finally leaving. This time, he'd placed the bullets, found earlier, in the outer pocket for easy access. He realised I might end up using his gun at least once against the drones, if not more than that…

Before he left the upper floor, he went over to the curtain hanging there, and decided to just tug at it once to find out if it was there for show, or that he was able to do something with it. Steven beamed a smile when the curtain moved a moment later, and he pulled at it until it couldn't be moved any further and he looked on the other side of it after pulling it along the whole track and had a self-satisfied smile on his face when the top floor was in almost pitch darkness. He finished by moving as many chairs as possible and one table against the banister.

"It will be hard to determine with the naked eyes what's up here." Steven muttered, smirking at the thought that these books would be out of reach of the people who were searching for them. He was now feeling like a benevolent, opposite version of the person in the book whose title was mostly missing except for the '451' part of it.

Before he'd left, he'd looked around one more.

In total, he'd been there for over two months, living on a combination of the last pieces of chocolate and the tins of 'stew' that he found in a kitchen on the bottom floor. He'd spent most of his time reading, learning, researching and essentially preserving his energy reserves and therefore recovering from the first one third of the journey. He hoped that one day he'd return to this place and would be able to do this with others for them all to collect all the books there were here and take them to supposed safe place that Elizabet's grandmother had hinted at, and that there they could sorted into topics and used to fix the situation that was visible around him in the world by then.

These books and any others we find, Steven had thought as he'd worked on hiding the books, like he was burying a treasure, like in the children's book he had read as his last reading endeavour.

He'd walked to the kitchen for any further food options that might have been there that he might have been able to bring with him, but it became apparent quickly that most of the food had degraded too much from lying there rotting away for hundreds of years.

Hunting for food it is then, Steven thought and then he turned to go.

It was just after sunset when he'd left the building finally, and he'd mostly sauntered through the most-shaded parts of the streets, always checking around him.

About a kilometre from the building, Steven saw a building for buying things, and the people who'd run the place must have had to depart fast, because most of the things to buy still were standing on the pavement. He looked at each item and saw a tall stick and grabbed one and then used a nearby metal pole, which might have been a light source, to smash the stick against it and first hit it in the wrong way and laughed when it broke in three. He wanted half the stick, not three small pieces…

Steven tried a few more times, and there were just three sticks left over by the time he had a stick broken only into two. He placed all the sticks back as best as he could, because he didn't want anyone to realise that something had happened here…

He had a plan with this stick. A plan based on an idea from a book. He was certain that there would be places where the enemy had placed traps similar to those he saw in one of the many 'dangerous' books, the ones that Steven now deemed to be the type that they would want destroyed like in the 451 book, and these traps were used to catch people who were still alive, people who hadn't fallen for their lure of a so-called safe-haven, who'd ignored their lies…

The stick could help him find the traps they had set.

He'd read about it in a book that it was a trick to kill innocent people, and Steven decided this test would make it somewhat safer for him in the cities. It took Steven several days to leave the city, mostly because he was certain that during the day they could observe him, and therefore the dark of night became a new ally.

At least, he hoped so…

Steven reached the edge of the city by the following week, and now the plan was to get to Berlin as he'd found an unbroken sign there are blushed deeply when he realised he'd accidentally stopped too early in a place listed as Hamburg, and he realised he needed to get to the correct city as fast as possible. Between cities, he somehow felt out in the open, like someone could be watching him from somewhere high up, perhaps as high up as where the flashes occasionally would occur.

I understand from reading what they are now, Steven thought as he searched the early night sky for the flashes, or as the book had called them 'shooting stars' although he decided they were *too* small to be a star… and some were machines coming down not stars or rocks, one of which was likely the device they'd been studying as well in the Academic Institute.

In the past, from around 1957 to 2077, with the last machine ever sent up, the people of five and six centuries ago were using machines in space to help them with communication and a lot more. Some books he'd been reading had suggested that some of those machines were being used to spy on other countries and on people, and that was what he was fearing now. That someone out there was spying on him…

Steven walked slower, always checking in every direction for movement, and he never took the mask off because he was certain that someone could recognise his face in that way. He was certain he'd entered the toughest part of the journey, and knew, also, that this was exactly what the message had warned about.

"Why did you insist that I needed go into Zone Zero, father?" Steven mumbled somewhat incoherently.

Steven was getting delirious because he hadn't found any fresh water for a few days and didn't trust the water of the city. He mistook birds for the drones from time to time. He even shot at an animal that was just minding its own business, eating from cooked leftovers of an old time.

Once he was outside the city, Steven stopped in an abandoned building where he sat in the dark until night came. And when night came, he was imagining that the glowing eyes of animals he could see in places were something else. He wasn't sure what he thought he saw, but his mind was creating the worst sort of creatures from nothing. He saw the sign before his mind had registered what it was. It was white, and for a while he was wondering about the language. He'd heard the language a few times. One person who'd spoken this language had been Perri. Steven only remembered him by this name…

He'd acted like my father, but the opposite, Steven thought, *and told no one his last name. It was one of the last people assigned to me to work with me.*

What was so interesting about Perri was that he knew many of the different languages spoken in Utopus. He knew English, my language, and he knew also knew the old local language of the region, but he spoke at least five—or was it eight—languages almost as fluent. *No one knew how he did it, or where he'd learnt it. Or, even how…*

He'd tried to teach me some of these languages, and Steven had only managed a few words in one such language. Now he'd found a word among others on an old sign he recognised, and it was in the language that Steven been most successful in learning. He needed to visit this place, even if it was out of the way. He might have found a place where they had actually been teaching science in the past.

What he found had been a school—Steven needed to check it so he'd know what he would have had if he'd lived five hundred years ago. His pace picked up over the next few days, and he even felt in a more cheerful mood. It was perhaps four or five kilometres later when he ended up thinking that he'd made a wrong choice…

"Ohhh shit…"

The creature standing ahead of him was large. It was dark brown, well almost black, it had very thick fur. It was when it stood on the back legs Steven realised he was in serious trouble. His father had spoken about places where they would have kept animals in cages, and he told me that one of two things could have happened to such animals - they had either perished, or with certain animals, they might have escaped the place.

I guess that eventually I had to meet one of those animals, Steven thought, *but I didn't expect it to be this large…*

The animal growled as it rose. Steven now preferred the stand-off with the dog, who he'd called Maggie, over the stand-off with this animal, who seemed to be the right size to sweep me aside with one swing of one of its front legs. Steven was sure that was its intent. Slowly his hand went up to his right pocket where he kept my gun. He paused every time the animal growled, and he didn't know how long it took him before his hand was by his side again, now with his gun in it. Steven stood frozen in place, not daring to move in any direction. And to make things worse, he had an itch developing under the mask and didn't dare to reach up. For a reason, the whole situation also felt laughable.

In the previous months, all those many months that he'd been travelling so far, he'd always relied on killing birds, and a hopping creature, and creatures with weird growths on their heads.

This unknown creature appeared to be so large that it could be equal to six or seven grown men in weight, although he could only guess it by observing the creature. Its rounded facial features gave the animal an ironically 'cute' appearance, which was almost the sort of face that would entice you to want to hug it. He'd heard a term used in Utopus by some, a 'bear hug,' and Steven wondered if those people had been aware of this animal.

34.

HE WAS STARING WITH SOME fascination at the unknown creature's paws, on which he saw claws of something like eight to ten centimetres long each. He was certain that each of them could leave him with a deep gash in his body, or if it swiped him in some places, that he'd be dead.

The stand-off got annoying, so he raised my gun ever so slowly. Steven got a cramp in his right hand from holding the gun stationery for minutes at a time, and the animal was very aware of each his motions.

It stood on its hind legs for a while, then lowered to all four, then he'd lift the gun a centimetre, and on doing this the animal stood up again. He wondered if the animal would get tired after a time, but it started coming closer to him each time it had dropped to the ground. Steven needed to stand his ground, and once his gun was high enough for him to aim it, he fixed his eyes on the beast, and waited until it was standing on its hind legs again. He knew his aim had to be true and knew he only had one chance, and he had to shoot into where he assumed its heart should be.

Steven held his breath and waited.
It got up on his hind legs but dropped too soon.
He waited again.
The animal lifted again, and stayed in that position, and growled again, and this time he could see inside its massive jaw.
A shot.
In a slow-motion action, the animal toppled.
Steven saw blood welling from an area about two-thirds up on the body. It fell with a heavy thud.

The animal twitched like it was trying to hold on to life, but as Steven waited, the motions stopped, and finally the animal lay still. He didn't immediately walk over as he'd seen other animals get up, even when he was certain he'd shot them.

He aimed the gun once more.

This time, his aim was at the animal's skull. Another shot rang out.

After this shot, Steven knew that the animal wouldn't rise to its feet after that. Kneeling near its head, and he saw the glaze of the eyes go cloudy. He knew the animal was dead. He felt unhappy about having to shoot the animal, because it was such a beautiful, robust creature. He'd never seen such a creature before and vowed to check in any book he could find, to see if it gave a name for this beast. He lifted one of its paws and gazed in awe at the size of claws the creature had possessed. Each claw was as thick as his fingers; each was black. But he decided not to test the theory about the sharpness, because he was certain the claws could cause him to become ill.

Illness was the last thing he wanted.

Steven had been cautious about what he ate or drank for most of the journey so far, and he was certain that some 'food' he'd eaten wasn't so good for him. He was uncertain how bad the contents of the metal containers had been for him, but despite it, he'd eaten it despite his earlier assertion that he would skip them.

Steven thought about what he could do about the carcass. He was certain that there was no way he could drag it away, and if he left it here too long, there would be other animals which would come to scavenge it then he looked around for those animals, but the kill was still too fresh for them. He saw stacks of wooden planks in several places near the place where the animal had been killed and he got up and walked to a stack. He pushed against it with his boot. The plank sagged underfoot but stayed whole. He picked up the entire frame and carried to where the carcass lay. He placed the wood against the carcass and got the next piece. After an hour, he had the carcass covered with several layers of the planks.

Now his dilemma came. He wanted to make a fire, and so far he'd only ever done it by chance so he looked around, and saw a piece of glass lying on the ground near him and he smiled, realising it was the answer. He remembered a time when Elizabet and he were children, and we'd used pieces of glass to cause small fires to start. His father had seen us, and Steven still remembered him not being so pleased about it.

But now the small piece of glass would help. He looked up at the sun then he spat on the glass to moisten it somewhat, then he held it out so that the sun shone on it, then through it, and therefore would make a light beam on the wood. He waited, and after about ten minutes standing there, now with my left hand almost cramping, smoke was finally rising from the wood pile. After another fifteen minutes, the first flames sputtered to life.

Steven stood watching the fire as it grew bigger, then collected more planks to drop on top of the bonfire to keep it going. He wasn't certain if what he did would cook the bear meat, but it was having an effect. He could smell the distinct odour of burning hair seep into his nostrils, and he thought that after about an hour he was ready for the fire to just let itself get burned out.

Almost four hours after his encounter with the animal, he was pushing away part-burnt planks from the bonfire.

The carcass had shrunk to almost one third of its original size under the intense heat of the fire. He pulled his knife out, and stuck it into the beast's body, and made a fast, clean slit into the carcass.

The part-cooked innards spilled out onto the ground at his feet.

Steven walked around the carcass, and sliced again into the animal with the knife, and made four more similar scores. He followed this by three slits into the carcass length-ways and then started cutting to remove the meat from the body. After fifteen minutes, six slabs of rump meat lay beside him. He found a cord of some sort on the ground near where he was busy and used it to tie the pieces of meat into a temporary bundle. He wiped the knife clean on some nearby tall grasses, replaced it into the slender pocket of his rucksack, picked up the glass shard, and put that in the right pocket of his jacket.

Steven hoisted the rucksack onto his back once more, then he picked up the meat bundle and continued walking south. He left the animal where it was. It had twenty times more meat on it than he could carry, and the slabs of meat he was planning to cook more, and then copy what his father always did with meat…

His father had always placed any meat on the cover of a car in the hottest sun of the day, and the heat from the sun and reflected heat from the metal below it usually dried the meat so fast it would be about one third its original size.

Steven knew he would need to find some of those bags like his father would be using, and after drying the meat, had put them in the bags, and usually the meat would stay okay for several weeks in a row. He was wondering what flavour the meat might have but he wasn't sure where he could stop for a meal, because he was certain that someone might have noticed the bonfire. It took him four hours of walking before he found the perfect place. It was one of those food eating places he'd seen in other cities, and he walked in to see if it offered me anything useful. He smiled when he spotted something that looked like an oven in the back of this kitchen. He was familiar with the ovens like in this eating place, as he'd been in the houses of other people in Utopus who possessed such a feature. He placed the slabs of meat on the table, put his rucksack on the floor, and went out to look for wood.

Twenty minutes later, Steven had a good-sized pile of wood lying at his feet, only a meter away from the oven. He was uncertain how he could get a fire going as he was indoors, but then he picked up a piece of wood, walked outside with it and the glass shard, and stood smirking with delight as he made his second fire for the day.

After he'd repeated the earlier process with the glass shard, he walked back inside with the wood which was now burning with a good, bright flame, and he placed it into the oven in a way so not to extinguish it, just as he'd seen being done in Utopus. He pushed fifteen pieces of wood around it, and blew at it gently, to make sure that the other pieces of wood caught the flame too.

He walked to the furthest wall and grabbed one of the long spoon shapes that were leaning against the wall.

With it, he pushed the wood to the back of the oven, and he piled up more wood to push in. He knew from what he'd seen that the idea was to keep the wood feeding the flames, so the fire kept on burning, and in the stone cast oven, to make food cook…

Steven knew it would take him an hour to do everything, and then he could put the meat inside it, close the metal door, and leave the meat to cook in the dry heat inside the oven. The ovens used in this way in Utopus usually were for cooking small animals or larger fish and he was uncertain if the meat he was planning to put inside the makeshift oven would cook properly. He sat down on the table opposite of the oven while he waited, and then lay down on it, and stared up at the sky and the wisps of cloud floating past through the small roof window above him. He counted the clouds just to have something to do. He was rather bored and wanted to just get on with the rest of his journey.

I guess I can be here for a day or so, Steven thought, *and that's how long it will take for the oven to cool off. If I remember from the people in Utopus correctly that they stoked on one day and would go get the food from the oven the next day, or even two or three days later…*

By the time he could open the oven without having all his facial hair or the hair on his head singeing off, it was almost evening on the third day. He had spent most time inside the eating place because he didn't want to get seen walking through the city, and then having to rush off and therefore having to leave the meat behind. Then later, he found sheets made of strange thick material reminding him of the bags he used for his bullets but much thicker, and decided it was perfect for packing the meat once it had cooled enough.

While he waited for the remaining rumps to cool, he sat eating the sixth piece, and although it was tough, it tasted rather rich, and had a dry texture, but he was hungry enough for it to taste good…

After he'd finished eating to a level that would sufficiently replenish his body energy reserves, Steven had climbed a narrow stairway, dragging the packed meat and rucksack up there, and found himself standing in a small bedroom filled with dust and cobwebs. He dusted off the mattress that lay on the floor in the corner beside only window, then he closed the thick curtains that hung either side in streaks of rags, and used the makeshift bed for some welcome sleep…

It was already late in the day, and he'd been busy for most of the day with preparing the meat, with little sleep, for four days in a row already. He was uncertain how long it took for him to fall asleep, but he must have done so the moment his head hit the pillow.

When he woke up, Steven looked carefully past the curtains to check his surroundings. The sun was at the zenith. In the half dark of the room he busied himself with packing up all the meat, and he obsessively repacked his rucksack once more, and this time to allow some space for the meat. He didn't bother drawing the curtains by the time he felt ready to travel again, and when he entered the street with caution the street was illuminated by the orange glow of a setting sun. He walked across the street, and followed the sun's path for a while, before he turned left into a street to take him south once more, or at least southeast at first. He saw the sign for the science building again, and knew he was heading to a building which would probably fascinate him for a long time.

The street sloped downhill, and from where he walked, he could already see a silhouette of something that could be a building ahead of me. A few hours later, he walked into the shade of woodland. The first woodland he'd encountered during the journey, but not the last.

Steven looked up at the trees above me, and noted that many of them resembled the dried, shriveled trees that he'd seen in the first weeks of his journey, when he was walking south from Utopus. Compared to those trees, these ones looked healthy, and they appeared like they were thriving.

He was still cautious for the drones, which he hadn't forgotten about in the past ten days, but here in this woodland, at least, they'd have a hard time navigating past the trees in a straight line. He hoped that most of the route from here to the science place, and then to Berlin, would be among woodland, because that way most of the rest of the journey would be easy. But he'd already learnt, in this journey, that things are never as easy as you hope for them to be…

He was getting closer to his next destination a long week later, and that was when Steven realised he needed a break from this endless game of pursuit, where he was the target.

Steven wished he'd arrived already, and he was so involved in his current mindset that he didn't immediately notice the flash, and then just moments after the sign with a number on it. Then he stopped and looked behind him, thinking he'd imagined it. He continued walking, but this time he was looking up, and he noticed the flash again, and another sign with a number flashed up - it was a '2.'

It confused him what it was or what it meant. So he turned, ran for a bit, then waited until he was no longer tired, and turned and, in a brisk pace, walked towards where the second flash had happened minutes earlier. He repeated the walk. This time, a '4' showed up.
If a machine can play a game, so can I, Steven thought, smiling broadly.

He grinned and started walking at a fast pace. He wanted to see what the number would be if he saw another of the machines. It took a while, and his pace lessened, but he was laughing when the next flash revealed a '3.'

I guess that shows how limited the speed of humans can be, Steven thought, *as I've now observed so eloquently. But I do wonder how this device can work and what it was for.* Steven glanced around for clues. He saw bits of old road. —maybe to measure how many people travelled past this place in the past. He shrugged and resumed journey.

Steven remembered finding a building with Elizabet's help, filled with full of old machines. On several of the machines they'd seen something that they were sure was the speed measurement for them. They were certain that it was something for travelling in for long distances, and Steven was certain he would have gone to get one of those machines for my travel if he could have got there, but the place was in the most northern of the districts… inside Utopus, so now off limits to him.

Steven didn't find any of the two-wheeled machines anywhere near him on this old road, and he decided that people who might have used them had either gone away early, or they had hid the their machines somewhere where others couldn't find it. If such a machine was for travel, the flash he'd seen might have recorded speeds that were several thirty or forty times greater…

* * *

With a refreshed feeling of purpose, Steven increased his pace until he was jogging.

He now wanted to reach his destination that evening, and not in three- or five-days' time as originally decided. When he saw a sign with the name of the science place once more, and saw a number next to the name, Steven finally got a correlation between the numbers on the signs and how long it took to travel.

35.

IF THE '3' WAS A number related to my speed, and it said '32' on this sign, Steven thought, *then I'd be at my destination when darkness had already set in, and I've jogged for several minutes…*

He sincerely hoped to be correct in this assessment…

* * *

After running for ten minutes, Steven had to stop, because the running was causing the pains in his sides to return. He guessed that nature never designed humans to run like some of the animals as was demonstrated often enough to me by them running away when he had either tried approach them to see whether the animal was friendly, or when I approached, he had a potential food source to hunt…

The journey itself was a mind game of sorts. He was having moments during the journey when Steven felt like he wanted to give up. There were moments when he was fearing whatever unknowns lay around the next corner. He was certain that nature had never designed humans to be alone for such a long time.

That was why, for good or for bad, people would have clustered together into Utopus after the disaster.

Apart from the idea to make a person a Subject, to test his or her mettle, most people just seemed to just get on with life and worked cooperatively on varying levels of success. Steven of people in Utopus who didn't like to interact with others, and he was certain that was true also the old cities I was walking through.

If this journey taught him anything, it taught him how crucial it was for everyone to cooperate, for everyone to work towards a common goal. Humans can keep going forward if we don't stop, Steven thought, *and don't give up.*

The books he had read said that humans kept going forward for tens of thousands of years, maybe even longer than that. He had read about things called 'civilisations,' about how some almost ended, and that it was often just a single person who'd teach others not to give up or give in to adversity of the situation. That was the real intended purpose of a Subject, and he or she symbolises that same essence of not giving up.

I'm one man only, but I'm not alone. I have my father and I have my mother, Steven thought, *and, yes, I still am convinced I have her… I have Elizabet, but also my other friends at the Academic Institute who'd started helping me. There is Perri, Marcel, Jonni, Jess, and Rodrigo, who'd all ended up believing in what my father and I were doing. Maybe names of people aren't important to other people I might find, but they are to me…*

Steven wouldn't mention the other friends until long after the events that would happen in the place he was travelling towards, when in hind side things would happen there that showed he should have done so. They were just as important to him as Elizabet always has been, and she was only one of two only females in the Academic Institute, and because Steven was protective of Elizabet he was as protective of Jess, and they gave one another strength in their own friendships that only women seem capable of…

Steven wanted them all to be okay too after all this, and he hoped that we all, my father and mother included, could start a new life somewhere else away from all this stuff he saw here. Europe wasn't as it was hundreds of years ago, and the message said that most of the rest of the world was affected by the disease…

Except for that place, Steven was thinking somewhat bitterly. *Why did Elizabet's grandmother never any say more?*

* * *

But Steven had read the necessary books. In them, the people who wrote them would say that this planet, which they had called Earth just like the voice from the past would do, that Earth had a way of healing itself, to repair the damage that we humans were doing…

If that's the case, the world has been healing for the last 370 years, Steven thought, *or at least from 2072, when it all began to change. We may never have the life that the people who living five or six centuries ago had, but I'm certain we can create a better life for ourselves, one free of all the perils of the past. But I guess there are a few people even now who don't want that... This safety is my father's goal. He wants to stop those people. He wants them not to succeed... I guess now I know more I'm now also thinking along those lines. I'm uncertain who they are, but when I know where and who they are, I will make sure I stop them—*

Steven knew he'd wanted things to change ever since he was a child and he remembered being told by his grandfather that the world needed to change. Steven had told his grandfather in turn he also it wanted to change but that he didn't know how to do this. He'd told his grandson at the time that there was once a book in which it had said something Steven had never really understood until right now: "Even the smallest person can change the course of the future."

If I think about those words now in the context of what I'm attempting to do right now, Steven thought, *then I think that grandfather had meant that it just takes one person to change how this world is perceived or looked at... I'm one Subject. Can one Subject change the course of the future for this world...?*

So far, Steven had never found the book from which his grandfather had said that the words were from, but he had to admit they were probably some of the most meaningful words ever spoken by anyone, even if that someone was made up by a person who'd lived something like six hundred years ago.

There will be a change in the world, but not the type that the people that the voice from the past was mentioning would demand for the world... This change will be to make the world better, and to make it work for everyone, Steven thought, *and I think the only way to do this is for everyone to work together, and not against one another like I read in books.*

He'd been staring for a while when more thoughts entered his mind.

In the past, people would band together to help others who had ended up as a victim of a war. The message was saying that what happened to us all was because of World War 3—if that was true, then all of us should be working together, and not against each other. Life can be better, Steven thought, *and we must make it better. But there's only one thing though that I don't really understand. How can you be somewhere else if Utopus was the only place for survivors? Was it even a place for survivors to begin with?*

No person had yet ever offered Steven an answer to this last question yet, and he now wanted to certain to one. It was obvious that this was also becoming an apparent goal of his journey, and which got its first proof when he finally arrived at the science place.

As Steven walked onto what had seemed to have been a garden of some sort around the science place there were two notable features. The first feature had him almost laughing from the irony of his discovery - that the only part of the name still visible after all this time was 'Institute,' listed on a stone block in a metal that was rusting extensively. The whole place wasn't made up of a single building like the first place of learning Steven had come across, but this place had many buildings, each serving seemingly a different function, each with its own mysteries for him to solve...

The first four buildings he had entered, were listing texts from some of the books, he'd been reading, which were now coming to life. Steven saw small pots spread over many shelves and inside each container was what he assumed had been animals of some sort. Skeletons. Bits of the insides of animals, which he recognised because of his encounter with the large beast. Things that looked like plants. Insects. Other things he couldn't decipher...

The second and third building would get visited multiple times, and he needed to do it. The fourth building was probably an office by the evidence of the paperwork spread over the floor, but the mess in these buildings got him wondering why every place, which was a place for learning, for a government of some sort, or a place to heal people, why each of them was always a mess of paperwork. Steven had noticed the same thing in the bunker. Similar evidence was present in almost every place he'd visited ever since...

The fifth building he investigated got him interested. He realised from this building and the map, hanging on the wall in the first corridor, indicated to him that he was perhaps four or five days from Berlin, and he'd assumed all this time that the other big cities he'd travelled through had each been Berlin, that it would have been interesting to have explored them more and longer...

But here he was, in a school, and from the remnants of evidence in various rooms, he realised straight away what was being taught here - science. He stood staring around the room he had entered. It was a room filled with machines, with bottles, books, and a lot more...

Steven strolled through the room and was leaning over every piece of equipment or tool that appeared to have been left behind by someone and he saw a few bags on the floor in different places, and he picked one a bag, he opened it and lifted a notepad of some sort from it.

On the notepad, Steven was able to discern a few faded words, some of which he was able to recognise to be scientific equations. The writing might have been some sort of exercise that someone did to figure out other information. He wondered if he might have been studying in this room all those centuries ago. Steven sighed when he realised that this place was a place he belonged in, and not The University or even the Academic Institute.

Both those places were a pretence to give the appearance that everything was like it was hundreds of years ago, but now, more than before, it was like they had cheated him out of the life he wanted to have more than ever…

Steven threw the papers and the bag on the floor, and the contents of the bag spilled out over the floor. He stood staring at the mess for a while. He walked towards a specific item which lay in the middle of the mess. It was something that he'd seen in a book he had read before creating the secret stash.

He had found a tool to make finding his directions to his destination to be easier…

The small compass, as the book had stated, would spin for a while, then it would stop with the bright, red pointer next to the letter 'N.' He moved the device a bit, and he watched the pointer spin more, then again stop once more at the letter 'N.' Steven grinned broadly. This insignificant item was probably one of the best things any person could have given him. And likely also the most useful. He considered it to be lucky to have made it this far just by guessing directions. He put the object into his pocket next to the photo of the yellow-haired woman then I glanced again at the mess he had made.

He spotted another object. A small pale-blue tube. He picked it up and looked at it, wondering what it was then he felt at it, after which he realised that a part of the object could detach itself from the rest of it…

After a small amount of effort, Steven had dislodged the lid of the device, and he looked inside it and found something coloured brightly inside it. He wondered to 'see' what the object inside was, and he 'messed' with the object for a few minutes and felt somewhat stupid for not understanding its workings. Somehow, he got it 'to work,' and yes, he smirked over his need to curse somewhat sarcastically…

But when he saw the inside of the object, he suddenly knew what it might have been. It had the same colour as something he'd seen previously. He took out the photo of the yellow-haired woman from my pocket and compared the colour of the tiny stick to her appearance. He was certain he had found something that might have been used by women to make themselves look like the woman in the photo. He smiled at the thought of giving this tiny stick of colour to Elizabet, then showing her the photo to show her how she could use it. He could imagine her smiling with delight at the gift...

Steven saw other bags in the room, each with a more colourful appearance than the previous one. He was curious if there was a reason for the bags to be so colourful, but he guessed that all of them were perhaps the bags belonging to females, just like the one he had found the lipstick in.

Appearance was also important to these people, who could have been using this place, Steven thought, *just like it was for the mysterious woman whose last ever photo was inside the pocket of his jacket.*

Steven walked around the room, and picked up each bag, and looked inside each. All the bags had similar pads with writing on them. He thought that, in that moment, he'd discovered another mystery he would need to come back for. Now he had at least two reasons to travel to the region again...

And because of this, the mission expanded from a simple mission of just finding out whether Zone Zero could be lived into a bigger mission with a purpose to allow humans potentially to thrive once more, but only if there was no enemy to contend with. He realised that the new knowledge he was gaining meant that he would probably use it for the rest of his life.

Next, he walked to the large dark green cover on the wall, thinking at first it was just a cover, but when he pulled at what he realised then was a rusted handle, he noticed some more writing, which bore a resemblance to what had been written on the paper books. *Was a lesson of some sort in progress when everyone had to leave so suddenly?* he thought. He was certain even more than before that the things he was seeing more and more around him had directly resulted from the events relating to when the disease had happened. Now he thought that in this room, in that moment, he'd vowed to make it his lifelong mission to restore the world to something better. But the first thing that Steven needed to do urgently was to find out who had done all this. *And, no, don't give yourself other that look in the window*, Steven thought, *because you don't know such information and I need to remember my father's warning, so I won't just say what I think about it if I find my mother...*

He stayed in this old learning place for several days, just looking through people's belongings, all left behind in haste, and although it felt horrible having to dig through stuff that someone had thought of as private in the past Steven kept on with this morbid task. Steven even found a diary of someone, which he opted to take with him, and he guessed that it would give him clues about how the people had lived back then. He opted not to bring the red colour stick and decided that Elizabet's beauty was best when it was natural. In the end, Steven placed all the bags he could find in a dark corridor as a memorial to these long-dead people...

$$* * *$$

After Steven had finished inside the building, he'd finally walked from the building when he had spotted another one of the flying objects in the distance. It flew too straight for it to be a bird, so he walked in a direction that was the opposite of where it seemed to go. It was going north...

Steven was walking for most of the next three days without stopping because he thought he needed to put as much distance between himself and the latest sighting.

As he walked over the last remnants of river, then he saw another bridge a few hundred meters from him, which seemed to arch high above the water. He saw a dark area under the bridge, which he thought might offer him somewhere to sleep for the night. He was feeling tired after walking with no sleep. Then after a period of turbulent sleep, he walked to the other bridge and was surprised when he saw a stairway that seemed to lead to an even darker area under this bridge.

"I guess I want to go there I'm very curious, right?" Steven mumbled under his breath and listed with his head tilted to his voice echoing back at him. The fast ruffles made him smile as he had obviously disturbed a bird with his voice.

So, Steven decided to check it out, and he found something which looked like a doorway. He walked through the door. He found himself in an enclosed archway. He decided it was a perfect place to stay for the night. He sat down on the uneven, cold ground under the archway. It was in an interesting place...

36.

SO NOW HE WAS UNDER this bridge, contemplating what to do next. He noted the place he was using was a slope. After a few minutes he took off the rucksack and then hastily walked to the top of the slope, mostly out of curiosity, I found another archway.

Someone once had used this archway for a home because there were some makeshift beds there, mostly wet and rotting away, but it was very clear this had been someone's dwelling. He found a bench in the corner and made it to his bed rather than relying on wet mattresses after retrieving his rucksack.

Steven was wondering if this archway had since become the home of an animal because of the distinct musky odour there, which reminded him in some ways of the aroma that had been present in the cellar of where he'd lived before in Utopus. The smell took some getting used to, and he kept his sleeve over his nose for the first twenty minutes of being there… But then, he chanced it and ate something before getting some sleep. At least, that was the plan.

He'd found new papers stashed between the other papers he'd been studying. They were very thin, very flimsy paper, and it wasn't a message from the voice of the past, and when he recognised the writing and looked closer, Steven realised then that he was looking at a letter from his father, but the words at the top of the first page, showed that these pages contained a message that was meant for him:

—I'm hoping that you, my son Steven, will one day find these letters. I urge you to just read one letter every day, and once you have done that, you must destroy these letters, for no one should ever find them. Burn them, please.

Steven, I'm not used to writing letters of personal nature, especially the letters meant for my only son, so please bear with me, and don't get angry about what I say here. Know that I love you, and that I've always been very proud of you. You don't do things as I would, but it's probably for the best, and you do things for the correct reasons, and reasons that I cannot even imagine.

You're a lot braver than I ever was. I wish I didn't need to write this letter and I know you had, and probably even now have, many questions for me. I'm sorry I haven't answered them. Some were too dangerous to answer, others were ones who shamed for my own actions. I wish I could have given answers, but there's a reason, and I hope you'll find it as important as I, or at least understand why I did different things and why by the time you're done reading.

I hope you will read it all.—

What Steven was reading were words that he'd wanted to hear for so long from his father. He frowned and contemplated about what he'd read so far for the next few minutes. He'd assumed he would have been angry with his father, or angry at him, but Steven felt relief wash over him…

At long last, there were a few answers about his life, about some things that had happened in his life, and about why his father had done certain things in a certain way…

Steven continued reading his father's message. He was understanding now how sad his father must have felt when he had found out which choice his son had made, and he was certain his father didn't want me to go, even if he'd claimed in the letter, he had to do this because of the rules…

—I can tell you that the decision to make you the next subject wasn't a random act. I had to be sure I could trust the person carrying the pages in the package you carry. I'm certain you found them, or else you wouldn't be reading this letter now. I had to hide my letter among them for the safety of you, myself, and all involved. The others didn't want you as a subject. I didn't want it because you're my son. But I had to have you there because I trust you. I've told you this before, and I still mean it, so please remember, Steven, it's very important you see this through.
Once you know what is at stake, you must find the courage to keep at it, as I know you can succeed. The reason you need to see it through will be clearer later, but for now, I ask that you trust in

your own father one last time.

I understand that you often wondered why I never talked about your mother, and why I always told you to say 'father' or 'Dr Burgard' whenever we were where others were present, or whenever you talked to others about me.

There's a reason I never even told you, my son, my first name. I still cannot tell it to you, even in a letter I must stress, that you destroy after reading, and the reason for it is tied directly with the reason for your journey. I hope that is reason enough for you, and that you must continue with the journey, and travel as fast as you can to get the papers to the people who need them. Once this is over, and when we meet each other again I'll tell you my real name. I'll tell you then who I'm really am.—

In that moment, Steven was wishing more than ever that things were finally over, and soon too. He wanted to see his father again. He wanted to tell his father he never made a mistake when he had started with all the things that he had set out to accomplish. Steven hoped he would walk back towards his father holding his mother's hand, and then he would let them hug each other for the longest time possible after such a long time apart.

The sacrifice of giving up a life together. That was something I can understand after reading some books, Steven thought, *and the theme of the 451 book was that too, because the man and woman had to choose one life together or separate lives apart...*

Another story, which Steven had found in the most recently visited building, was that of a woman named Juliet who fell in love, only to be forced to choose between her family or the man she'd loved, and it moved him, and it somewhat broke his heart that they'd reunited only in death. In some ways, he supposed now that Elizabet was his own Juliet, and only because they both were a scientist. So, in that respect, he presumed his father was right about him, Steven, influencing Elizabet...

Steven hoped that, unlike the man called Romeo, he would meet with Elizabet again, and that she'd be alive and okay. He realised that there was a likelihood she'd choose someone else to spend her life with, especially if she wanted to have a child. He was certain that she'd end up with Perri if she had to choose anyone.

Steven's eyes stung as he read the next part of his father's letter...

—One of the foremost questions you have, is likely about your mother. Your mother lives as far as I'm able to ascertain, and I hope she's well. I'm confident that she's just as proud of you as I am. But I cannot go into details about her, such as what her name is, for example, because of the other things that are going on right now.

Those other things are the very important things for you to concentrate on during your journey. You must destroy this letter when you're done reading it. I cannot stop stressing it enough times. But as far as your mother is concerned, I'm not precisely sure where she is right now. I know she's somewhere out there, and it ties her safety to your success with your mission, so understand from that how much risk I take even telling something about her. I don't know how much you remember of your mother after the intervening ten years since she left, but she was like you. Or more precisely, I know why you said you wanted to be a scientist. It's because she was one, too.
I remember when you, me, your mother went to visit your grandfather before he died, and he asked you about what choice you would make when you were older, and how you said to him you would be a scientist. He and I were both academists, so we both hoped for you to be one, too. Your mother said to me later that day, "If he wants to be that he can be useful later."

I was angry at your mother for suggesting that, but I'm not anymore.—

Steven looked at the letter for a long time. Just stared at it. There were the words. They stated so starkly: "It's because she was one too." He just couldn't stop thinking now. He was upset, even angry all at the same time. *But where is she?* he thought bitterly.

Steven had so many questions for his mother right now, which he'd wanted to ask her ever since he was thirteen. He wanted to be with her right now, and not in the 'however the number of months this damned journey would still take' time span, especially now when he'd to travel so much slower and should have done it so much faster…

He re-read the page several times. He kept contemplating these words: "It's because she was one too." He stared ahead for a moment. His mind didn't want to comprehend fully what his father had written on the paper. "She was a scientist," he mumbled softly, "and why would he even be saying 'was' in this letter…?"

His mind couldn't comprehend a fact that was staring him harshly in the face. He probably couldn't have accepted it back then, yet, that he'd known something more about his mother, something that he'd known all my life. His mind had blocked out the event, the pain, the trauma, and so much more detail, and Steven now imagined that all it was a defensive mechanism to make sure he'd cope with the journey.

Had his father realised, or figured out, and only discovered years later, Steven thought bitterly, *that his son would have been the latest Subject that no one ever heard of again…?*

Instead, Steven's mind settled on a long-forgotten memory he'd pushed away from his mind, from almost sixteen years earlier, when he was only almost seven. It was a memory of his mother and him sitting opposite of one another, and he thought now that she'd been teaching him a game of some sort. He was certain it was a game.

The game had involved him holding a bundle of thin sticks, each with colours painted on them. Then his mother had told him to 'let go of them' and he did that. Their next task was to recover each of the sticks, moving none of the others, and the memory brought a broad smile to Steven's face as he recalled it was tougher than it appeared.

In the early days of us playing the game, his mother had always won, but as he grew older, he became better at the game, and he won more often. Although Steven now recalled times when he'd let his mother win instead because he loved her.

They must have played the game to distract him from what was going on around us.

A recent memory flashed through his mind, and this one wasn't a pleasant one.

It was a memory that happened during the first night in the location where he'd stopped, and he remembered it was about his father, his mother, and him too, all standing on the tiny balcony of the dwelling we lived in, and the sky showed the yellows, oranges and red of a massive fire that had raged in the north…

Suddenly, Steven was shuddering as he was remembering the explosions…

While this was happening, Steven held his mother's hand, which seemed to shake uncontrollably. He remembered looking up at his parents and they were glancing at each other, both showing a pale face and he remembered his father saying abruptly: "It has started."

What had started? Steven thought as he lay down in a tight bundle, pulling in his legs and wrapping his arms over his chest. He felt scared now, wishing more than ever he wasn't alone…

* * *

Steven had stayed under arch near the river for a whole week. Then he just got up, repacked his rucksack and had just walked south mechanically. Now days later, he saw the beginnings of another city. It loomed on the horizon as dark shapes, which was reminding him also somewhat of the dark structure appearing at times in Utopus. When he saw the first of them, he stopped, and he'd hidden behind a tree, and looked at it with my binoculars.

He waited for several minutes, but the structure never moved from the spot, and it didn't disappear either…

Steven calculated that in three days from now he'd be in the middle of this nameless city. The process of occasionally running had increased his overall progress, but he knew he couldn't sustain it, and that he shouldn't. He wanted to stop somewhere here, where he was standing right now, because he wanted to be well-rested before he was entering the city. Steven glanced in all directions at where he'd arrived at. In the past, seemingly, this had been a place for working only. He saw long, low buildings positioned in uniform rows. He saw names on them, which meant nothing to him. He selected a smaller, white building that was perhaps fifteen minutes' walk from him. He planned then to stay there for two days…

* * *

This last memory, which Steven had recalled so suddenly, was still raw in his mind. He was wondering over and over what my father had meant by the words: "It has started." Steven was aware he'd never have more knowledge about the event until he could speak again with his father.

He looked around for a shaded place to sit down and noticed a small wooden bench near the wall of a building. As he sat down, he was staring at the rather odd, metal objects next to him with two wheels on it and wondered what it was for. It was the first time he'd seen such an object, and his mind wanted to take the object apart and then try to assemble it immediately.

Steven looked around, just to check his surroundings. He grabbed his rucksack, opened it, and took out one of the meat packs, and using my knife, cut a large piece from it. He gulped the food, then decided he should move on soon…

* * *

After sitting there without moving for well over half an hour, Steven got up and walked to the white building he'd selected for a visit. It didn't look like a house to live in, not even one where people would have bought things, and the puzzle of what its intended use might have been grew as he walked through the building, craning his neck to glance past the low cabinets standing at intervals in the large room…

Steven found a table in the next room, and he sat there for a while to read more of his father's letter. He'd been ignoring the letter for a few days because it still made him angry, even when he had asked Steven not to be. He picked it up and started reading it again with a bit of hesitation…

> —Your grandfather had tried to point out that they could choose you one day as a Subject, or anyone of us. You looked at your mother at the time with some fear in your eyes, as that chance still existed, even for her.
>
> Commonly, they'll exclude people from being chosen after they're aged about forty. Your mother is fifteen years younger than I am, and I'm fifty-seven now. I was forty-seven when things changed, and I'm certain you can work out about your mother. She's forty-two now and was almost thirty-two when you saw her leave. You were always so determined about wanting to be a scientist. I didn't want to talk about it, so this is perhaps why you and I stopped talking as much as we did before. After your mother left, she became another reason I talked less to you. I decided a few weeks after she left it was best that you knew as much as possible. Even if I couldn't tell you most of the time why.—

Steven had some vague memories of his grandfather. He recalled his grandfather as a tall man with bushy grey hair, a warm welcoming smile, and two massive hands, which always seemed to cup his entire head whenever he'd hold him there.

When we'd visited 'grapa' as a young Steven would call him, although he was at a loss why he called him, that he would sit curled up on his grapa's lap, while his grandfather, his father, and his mother would be talking about 'serious stuff.' Almost all of it was too complex for him to understand. Steven now thought his grapa was an Academist like the boy's father, because he remembered hearing them use the words 'Academic Institute' several times.

37.

STEVEN WAS UNCERTAIN, HOWEVER, WHAT it was they'd talked about, —*so you can stop asking about that stuff*, Steven thought.

Setting aside this thought, Steven focused instead on the building he was in right now., and decided it was somewhere where people had collected things. In the building were dozens of shelves, all covered densely with boxes, or with pieces of wood, or with metal things, and even with things that were made of types of cloth. —*there are a lot of other things here that I somewhat recognise*, Steven thought, *and he was frowning somewhat, but I'm uncertain what the other stuff is—*

But the comparison between what he saw around him, and what the next part of my father's letter was telling him, was so stark. In the letter, his father was telling him small details, probably to trigger his son's mind to remember more details about his childhood—but he'd done a lot more than that. He'd also triggered the desire in Steven to want to have the world different from how it was now...

I guess he didn't realise that any of this shit would happen, Steven thought.

Steven walked up the stairway to the top floor, where people might have sat down for their work duties and he found some of the earlier cabinets here again, like he'd seen in the science place. He tried to turn on some of these cabinets, but none worked.

I guess they, too, relied on something to make them work which doesn't exist anymore, Steven thought as he'd to try despite making this assessment, and decided he had needed to try anyway.

Steven was standing for a long time in one spot while just staring blankly at the cabinet. It was in one of those cabinets that Steven had shot a window to pieces before. But this machine stood open, like someone had been busy with it. He was uncertain what the machine might have contained, because the colour was all faded away from the surface of the bottles inside it. However, he noted that inside each bottle might be a dark liquid, or at least it might have been in the past. He looked at the empty rows. On the bottom row, there was a singular red metal container left behind with a curly white letter. He wondered if its content might be the same as what was in the bottle. Next, he looked inside the cabinet and he saw some semi-transparent openings at the back of the cabinet. He pulled at them, but they were locked in place. Then he walked around the cabinet, and saw that someone had undone the back plate, and at first Steven was at a loss how to replicate the action.

Steven was cursing quite a few times as he worked to open the container. He was uncertain why he wanted to open it, but it might have been his damned curiosity showing its ugly head again that made him want to find out more about things from the past.

The object contained a lot of axles and cogwheels inside it. Steven recognised them from the books he had read. Steven touched different bits inside the cabinet to determine what could happen when he did this. He saw cables in the cabinet too, which reminded him of some cables he'd seen at the bunker, but most of these cables were thin…

Steven found a slightly thicker cable with an odd appendix on it and guessed that was how the cabinet would get working again. When he picked it up, he found that the prongs matched the holes in the wall, so he pushed the appendix into the wall there. Nothing happened…

He tried it a few more times, but still nothing happened.

So, Steven gave up, and he walked to a table with the metal container that he had found inside the cabinet. He placed it on the table and wondered how it could be opened. Above it was a small metal loop. Then he used his knife to lift it, and after a sharp hiss, he had it upright. He pulled the ring and was met by a strong, sweet smell. He tipped the metal container over a bowl on the table to find the contents pouring out was a thick syrupy liquid.

He had just put the can down and walked off. He wasn't even going to try drinking it.

Steven sat down next to his rucksack, and pulled the letter from his father from it, and continued to read it. He felt a tear roll down his cheeks as the reasons for the events in his life became clear. Steven wondered if his life would have been different if his father had been working as one of the people who would repair the cabinets with drinks and chocolate.

—I had my own ideas about how to get things done and I've had those ideas for longer than you have been alive. I had a hard time convincing your mother of the ideas, but she'd gone along with the ideas to be honest. In the meantime, we tried our best to make your life as normal as we could. And we tried to hide all things that could happen to either of us, or to you, from you.

You were a bright boy who always wanted to pick apart things, to put them back together again. Much of what we owned was because of this, and I did my best to make out you succeeded by helping you secretly. Your mother did, too. Your grandfather was less impressed with our efforts, especially with the old mantelpiece, which had never worked properly after you 'had played with it.'

He ended up giving me that mantelpiece, mostly to remind me of what you said to us, and to remind me of the consequences. But the fact you worked out how it worked comes from both your mother and me, but mostly from her.—

There was *that* word again. Anger welled up for a few moments, but immediately these feelings were replaced by more, deeper sadness. Now not just about the letter, but also about my grandfather, who had died a few years after that day at his house.

Steven was smiling as the letter progressed, and it made him realise how much better my father had known me. How he'd always wanted to shield his son from the dangers of this world. And the letter now made him also regret the way he'd behaved while Elizabet and I were growing up…

—However, you were also always curious about this world, and you spent too much time exploring everything, and you even got Elizabet into that habit. Both her parents and I were always despairing, when you both would disappear for days on end, when you were way too young for that. There was a time I desperately wanted you to be an Academist like I am.

But as I had trouble keeping track of a young boy and I was getting older, I considered it as a sign that something already made you choose, long before you even realised yourself, what needed to be done. You encouraged Elizabet in some ways too, with her choice of career. I'll do my damnedest to protect her from the consequences. You would go to places where most boys didn't dare to visit.

You both explored the old drains and other places, which were part of the old city that stood here once. You even went to places where children, or even adults, may not go, and I think you got that from your mother. I don't recall if you remember those places, but if you remember, make sure you always keep that knowledge to yourself, at least until things change.—

At that moment, Steven wanted things to be normal, although he was uncertain what 'normal' might feel like. He understood more of why his father had felt in the way he would show him, why he would try to warn me, and why he'd done everything possible to shield his son from later events. Suddenly, Steven felt grateful for his father to have been there for him.

If I had been going through the same sort of life of some other children in Utopus, Steven thought, *I would have grown up never even knowing either parent…*

There were people in Utopus who didn't want to have the effort of bringing up a child, so they would ask their own parents, the grandparents of a child, to bring up such a child. Perri might have been such a child, and he'd said he had first lived with his father's parents, and when they got sick, he went to live with his mother's parents. He had said he'd only seen either of his parents not much more than five times in all his life.

Steven was glad now for the time spent with his father, and realised that he had both parents with him until he was thirteen, which was more time than most people had available…

The next part of the letter was explaining his father's silence. Steven made sure that he would tell his father it was okay, and not to keep feeling guilty about those decisions he had to make. If he ever saw his father again…

He read the letter carefully, and the mention of his mother made him realise that perhaps, once he was finished with this task, he could search for her, and then perhaps bring her back with him for his parents to be reunited.

—I'm aware that you miss your mother a lot, and that you did especially in the first few years. But then, that day at the Academic Institute, told me that the feeling of loss wasn't diminished. I'm so sorry that I couldn't discuss her or her leaving more openly, but I wish I could, and realise that perhaps this letter will be the only way ever if things don't change. It isn't yet safe to talk openly about what we had discovered about what others had discovered before me. It won't be different until the change comes. I stress again that you must destroy this letter so no ever can use it against you, or stop you from your task, and if this letter gets into the wrong hands, it will mean that many people are at risk. More than you'll ever realise.—

"No, father, I realise more than you comprehend," Steven said loudly, "and I probably know more now than even you, or mother, ever knew or realised—I know what goes on, and I've seen the drones. I'll make sure we stop those people."

But stop them, how?

Steven wasn't even sure where to look for the mysterious enemy mentioned by the voice from the past. She had mentioned no location or name of a place in relation to this specific group of dangerous people. But something told him the letter was giving him clues. He stared at his rucksack for several minutes, and after five minutes he pulled the map from the bunker from the pocket, and he opened it. On the map was a line, which began at a place just south of Utopus, and led south and then southwest, towards an area circled in the northern area of what was called Spain, according to the map…

Someone was giving him a clue to help me. Someone was giving him the means to find the people he was looking for, and he was now probably about halfway to that place.

It had taken him over eight months of arduous travel so far, and he compared the distance travelled in the first half of the journey with the second half which still lay ahead. He realised that the journey had been faster despite the few mishaps so far, and smiling he realised that the biggest mishap had been the large, dark brown animal.

Steven remembered then that he still needed to know the beast's name…

He wondered for the next few days of travel as to why my father had hidden the letter between the rest of the letters. Steven assumed that his father had known that his son would become curious once he had found them. And he knew Steven would read it once the letter was found…

Eventually, Steven would have found the letters.

He re-read the first few lines again before reading the last part of the long letter…

Steven realised that his father probably had to have made one of the hardest decisions of his life when he started writing these letters. He knew his father always had tried to keep his feelings to himself, that he never outright expressed sorrow. Steven had seen him laugh, but then the day had come when a boy had woken up and he told his son that he was trusting me the most and this was the only memory Steven could find in his memories of him ever crying.

> —I'm hoping that you, my son Steven, will one day find these letters. I urge you to just read one letter every day, and once you've done that, you must destroy these letters, for no one should ever find them. Burn them, please.—

Steven looked at the last page of the letter and it was saying that he had to burn the pages. He built a small fire for this purpose, but when the moment came for him to do as his father had asked, he was having a hard time complying. Then sitting there and looking for several minutes at the flames shifting from blue to orange then yellow and back to blue, Steven had complied but only after keeping one small portion of the letter…

I'll treasure the words in this part of the letter the most, Steven thought, *because in the letter my father had acknowledged that my mother, too, had cared about me.* He read the letter several times because he wanted to have the words burnt into his memory, so that one day he could tell his mother word for word what his father had said in this letter. Somehow, that became more important than his mission for several minutes.

> —My dearest son, I hope your journey goes well, and that you can find your mother.
>
> I'm certain she left clues for you to tell you where she went, and if she did, you use those clues to find her. When you find her, tell her I think about her every day, and that I hope she'll come back to me one day. I hope she'll treasure you as much as I do. Steven, your hardest task yet will be to destroy all the pages of this letter. Do this. You'll protect so many when you do this. Keeping it isn't safe for you. I know you want to keep it, but don't. Be as careful as you can be.
>
> Your loving father—

Steven clutched the pages tightly in his two hands, and pushed them against his face, and upset overwhelmed him in that moment. Then he cried for a long time. He did most of what his father had asked and the last time he'd cried so much was the day when his mother had departed. Steven realised now how much he'd missed her.

As he sat there, with his knees pulled up, he realised again how lonely he was. Steven had tears streaming down his face. It was the first time in ten years he was crying, and he didn't bother quelling the tears either. He needed to let go of the feelings he'd been bottling up for so long. These tears were for his mother, his father, for Elizabet, for the nameless victims of hundreds of years ago…

It was four or five hours later when Steven got up in the half-dark and fumbled his way to the stairway. It took a while for him to find the table where he'd left his rucksack. He slumped over the table, and later when he woke up he was uncertain when he'd fallen asleep, but he guessed he fell asleep sitting down there.

And that was one of the more uncomfortable positions to sleep too.

Steven woke up hours later when something made a chiming sound. He looked around for a while to check what he could discover but he never found the source. After eating something, he traveled further south through the city.

The walk into the city seemed more like a victory parade, like the ones he'd seen in the books.

He imagined people standing on either side of the road, cheering him on, and the sensation gave him an unexpected spring in his step which last had happened a longest time ago. He wanted to walk on victoriously for getting this far and not having been stopped by anyone yet. He was in awe of what he was observing in this old city. Everything seemed like they designed it to be large, to allow many people to stand around, walk around, do things. He got to the large square that he'd found on the map. On the map, it was a tiny square, but it was so much larger. Steven could imagine people from five centuries ago coming to the square and holding hands to show a unity unheard of in Utopus. He could imagine them being here and declaring in one voice they affirmed something greater. He was just glancing around the square with his mouth open and staring at the openness of the place…

38.

IN UTOPUS BY COMPARISON, THE buildings were all so compacted together that it never felt like an open space, and you had to go a small old town like the one he visited with Elizabet to even get a feeling of it being an open space.

Here, the openness was by design.

Steven turned and gaped in surprise.

The massive archway, although partially ravaged by the passaging of time, was still impressive enough to make Steven stop and stare. If he was correct in his assumptions, he'd now arrived in a place once known as Berlin, so he pulled the map from his rucksack and lifted the gas mask from my face. He glanced around and I wondered what the building might have been used for in the past.

Steven discovered a mangled mass of metal on the ground and comparing it with the partial structure at the top of the building, he assumed that a statue of some sort had stood there in the past. He wondered if the building had been used in a similar fashion as an arch near The University, and that people might have gathered here to listen to speeches.

Probably, fewer boring speeches than they do in Utopus, Steven thought.

He stood there with his arms stretched out and eyes shut for several minutes, and he was just trying to imagine the whole open space in front of the archway filled up with people, perhaps with singing or music too. He knew a few people in Utopus who would sing, and they would use cups, metal containers and pieces of wood to create the rhythmic sound they would refer to as music. Steven was certain that there was a difference between their definition of music, and what the people, who might have stood here five hundred, six hundred, or more hundreds of years would count as music… or singing…

***

He remembered what his father told him in the letter, and to be careful and Steven had to assume that this was the actual reason that he'd stopped so much during the last few months of his travel, and by now he'd traversed almost all of Europe from the north to the south by now…

Each town had become another place for him to check out. He found it strange that some towns and cities he encountered were almost pristine in their appearance, while others seemed to resemble like a giant hand had come along and tumbled everything into a massive heap. The damage on the leftovers from these places indicated too often that shots were fired there. He'd arrived in the latest town, which held his interest for more than just the buildings. He found something there of personal interest to him…

Steven ran his hand over the metal beam and looked up and then recognised a type of transport from before. The metal tracks, first seen in the small town explored with Elizabet, was on a slight hill above him. However, the reason he ran his hand over this beam was instead the two numbers - the numbers 35 and 36 - carved into the metal. He glanced at the ground and spotted a thick piece of stone, and carved the number 37 into the metal, and smiled as it showed up in the dark red of the rusty metal.

Now anyone else who comes this way knows I have been here, Steven thought.

He stared at his handiwork for some time, then enhanced the scrapes somewhat more, until it had an even but still a rough appearance. The colour of the carving resembled the dark red of blood.

As he stood there, rain spattered over the surface, and as the wetness of the beam increased the appearance of the number almost seemed like blood was pouring from it. It seemed appropriate. It would become a permanent reminder that at least one Subject, numbered at 37, had visited this location—but as his father had said he needed to guard my name 'well.' So, he decided not to place his name there. He stood there in the pouring rain for several minutes, then he turned, and slowly walked south towards his penultimate destination. As he walked, he wondered if the next Subject to come this way would put their number on the beam. While he was walking, he spotted the drawing on a nearby wall, almost faded away from age, and perhaps something to mark the building. Steven wondered if this image had caused the people, who drew 35 and 36 on the beam, to copy this idea.

He stopped and stared around. He left the large square with its massive archway behind him and walked through many streets, and realised for the first time he was seeing what an actual city could have looked like...

Utopus was expansive, but it had never seemed to have been an actual city. At least not to me, Steven thought. *I can imagine people walking around this city.*

Before settling into the almost routine habit of exploring every building, Steven lifted the binoculars and checked in every direction using them. He was looking for the drones, which he was expecting to arrive at any moment. Then he spotted a building that appeared to be similar in some ways to the Academic Institute, and he wondered if it was from this where they'd once governed Germany in the past. Steven knew he had to check the messages again, and this building could be a good place to do this. And by now, he was feeling like he was doing some proper investigation of the situation as it stood. "Well, I was supposed to check the condition of Zone Zero," Steven muttered. And that was exactly what he was doing. They had wanted him to do this stuff, so he decided to 'comply.'

He walked past another enormous building, the ninth one, and now it made him wonder why this city had so many of these types of building. He checked it out like every building he'd been in, and he learnt a lot that day, but the best thing he learnt wasn't to give up on hope.

It was sometime later when Steven realised he was hearing the high-pitched whine in the air, and as it grew louder he walked faster, and then he ran.

Steven was uncertain where in the city he was when he fell.

The place where this had happened had collapsed because of the years, well centuries really, of neglect of no one looking after it and he fell into somewhere underground. Steven thought that where it had happened that the roof of the underground building collapsed after rainwater seeped in and weakened it.

Steven woke up aching over all his body because he had fallen while running from the object he saw in the sky.

The collapse of the structure, whatever it may have been in a distant past, was sudden. Steven glanced up and around for potential clues of where he was. To his mind, which wasn't capable of rational thoughts, the darkness surrounding him was ominous. He could hear crackling sounds and a wheezing whose origin he couldn't determine. He noticed the ache in his body only slowly, and as it penetrated every part of his body which he determined had come from the sudden impact, and that it had happened long before he'd woken. He immediately reached for his gun, only to find it lying among the rubble on the ground on his right. Something above him caught his attention then, and he kept still, holding his breath as he looked at the jagged edges of where he'd made his involuntary entry. He sat upright quietly and was staring at the half-blackened sky above. He remembered slowly why he had been running and determined that the black sky he was seeing was the reason. It was during the dash for cover that he had run over something that must have been so deteriorated that it instantly gave way, and he fell.

That my rucksack broke my fall and make sure I didn't die during that fall makes me lucky, Steven thought, frowning with concern. If shelter was what I was looking for then perhaps this place will have to do. This thought passing through his mind made him grasp at his head then as 'thinking' caused his head to hurt more as I considered more of the facts.

His body hurt all over, and he carefully turned to check the floor behind him for any evidence to the cause of the discomfort on the back of his skull, where the pain seemed to ooze in intervals. A spot of blood which mixed with the dust on the floor gave him all the evidence he needed that the impact was more severe than first expected.

The hood of his jacket, which he wore pulled over his head, had mostly cushioned the blow, but the blow of landing on the rubble was hard. The aches in his body were growing by the minute.

Slowly inhaling and then out seemed to settle the pain raging through his body. And after twenty times of this slow exhaling Steven felt somewhat better, and he looked around more to see where exactly he was. It was then that he was hearing a sound coming from above him, and a moment later he saw something move there. After a scramble, fighting against the pain, he took cover under the overhang of the leftover building structure near him. He looked up carefully through the holes in the overhang to see what was there. He saw the black shape from a few times before in the distance, but this time it was hovering around as if it was searching for something and Steven had to admit it made him fearful for several minutes, but then he heard a screeching sound, and it was gone.

What was that? Steven thought, *because it didn't look like a bird…*

It was a black metallic circular object with fast spinning wheels of some sort. At least, he thought they were wheels. The screeching sound came from a motor of a sort. He was uncertain how the object could be here, but it worried him. He waited and listened for the sound of the object to come back. What he observed this day didn't look like the earlier black objects. This one was larger and more menacing.

The silence, after hearing the unfamiliar sound, seemed designed to madden him. He wanted the object to come back so perhaps he could shoot it down, but then he realised that the gun was still lying where he'd seen it last after the fall, and it was several meters away from him.

They said it was dangerous out here, right? Steven thought, and he wondered why. He then looked around at where he was and decided that he should stay there for a while. He used his binoculars to search around for the black objects that he saw after my fall.

He couldn't let none of them surprise him at that moment. He didn't know what the objects were, or who controlled them, and as he'd travelled on he'd become more and more weary of his surroundings, and he was on constant lookout for them.

Steven had to admit to himself that, after a time, he mistook the few birds he spotted at times for the flying objects at times. He was uncertain where to go as he stood under the under-hang, and he was even less certain where he'd ended up. It might have been an underground place that might have been used once for transport. This was what he thought the metal bars on the ground were for, perhaps. He saw only darkness when he looked in either direction…

He heard the drone returning in the distance above him, so he decided he had to take his chances and see where the underground place would lead him. He hesitated for a few moments, because he got the same feeling, for a moment, as he experienced when he sat in the corridor at my father's work, but then it went left, and he just walked…

He waited for several minutes to listen, and when he was certain that it was all silent again, that was when he jumped down in between the metal tracks, he looked up quickly when it made a metallic sound when his boots hit the many tiny stones there. Still silent, still no drone.

Steven walked left after a few minutes, and wondered what the underground area of the city might look like.

After a ten-minute walk the track split in two directions.

Typical.

He moved right, and at the next underground walkway he climbed up when he saw something that resembled a map. This walkway had the roof intact, unlike the one next to where he'd fallen. He studied the map carefully, trying to make sense of the multi-coloured lines on it. He looked around to discover whether he was able to ascertain anything that could tell him where he was and he discovered a plaque with a name of some sort, and checked for the name on the map…

It took him an hour to search the map for the information needed, but after a time he had figured out a way out of this dark underground place. And while he worked on travelling in this unusual fashion, he kept listening also for the wheezing sound, which could announce another of the objects arriving.

The journey through the dark tunnels, walking over the metal tracks, was like entering the bowels of the planet itself. Often, Steven was overwhelmed by the uncertainty of whether he was going in the correct direction, and the multiple times he might have cursed and therefore frightened any person who might have been down there. He cursed furthermore because he was burning his thumb on the light-making object he'd found earlier up in the city. His thumb was black from the soot and burns after a time. He was about to curse again, and re-ignite the light-making object again, when he felt a soft breeze of wind flow over his face.

Instinctively, he looked up—just in case the wind was of a mechanical origin. He discovered a light source in the distance, and the fresh wind blowing at him told him he'd finally arrived at an exit of some sort.

At least, he hoped it would be an exit. After another twenty minutes of walking, he got to a rusty covering…

For a moment, he surmised that his journey underground might have all been for nothing, and in an angry act of frustration, he kicked hard at the metal cover with his boot. It broke off. After kicking the object a few more times, he made a sufficient hole through which he was able to squeeze through.

Steven shielded his eyes against the bright sun and looked around. He was crouching beside a wide river of some sort, though he wasn't certain which river he'd encountered right now. Unlike the more northern rivers he'd seen during his travel, this river still seemed to possess most of its water, and it was flowing rather rapidly. He felt lucky that he had exited in this place so precisely, and he didn't discern until later how he might have known that he was on the west side of this river. Something about how his current environmental conditions had informed him that he was on the correct side of the river by chance, and now he had travelled into a direct westerly direction for quite a significant distant, and then he'd spotted a road up ahead which headed even further west...

* * *

The next several weeks of the trek would become somewhat chaotic. He had found himself chased after by feral dogs, and because of that he needed to climb up into a tree, which turned out to have these annoying prickly leaves, which left him itchy all over for more than a week.

Steven shot at the dogs, who were circling the tree in this stand-off. These dogs weren't the friendly type like Maggie had been when he'd played with her.

After the dogs had finally departed, he had trouble getting out of the tree, as he'd been so itchy and because he'd been sitting still for days in that tree, and all this had left him with this annoying cramp in his body. He had trouble walking for a long time after, and even years later his left leg would feel bad from time to time.

But I kept soldiering on—and yes, admittedly, that was a word I had discovered in a book, Steven thought, *and I had to look in another book to find out what it could mean.* He liked the word if he was honest to himself...

* * *

In the next town, Steven's fortune had turned when he first came across a building used in the past for buying things. In this buying place he found a lot of those chocolate food things he had liked so much. He guessed then that it was turning out to be one of his more favourite things that the people from five hundred years ago had left behind for them all.

He also found more containers with the same sort of soup that his father had always brought home, and he'd walked on for a few hours more when he had discovered another much more interesting buying place.

39.

HE LOOKED THROUGH THE WINDOW, and he was rather surprised at what he had found inside the building. This place had been somewhere that the people of long ago would come to buy guns, like his weapon, and he wished now that he could go back to this place, every time he would need more bullets. He whooped so loudly that it made him jump because it had startled him. Steven had looked around to make sure there wasn't anyone near him who might have discovered him. Now the difficulty was getting inside the building, inside the cabinet where the bullets were…

He pulled the gun from his pocket and searched around him once more. He shot at the glass in the door and turned his face as it shattered. He glanced at the door. There was a massive hole in the centre of the door, and the glass that still clung in place was white, almost because of the impact of the shot…

Steven smiled broadly and he used his gun to knock all the remaining glasses from the door frame, then he had used his gun knocked on the door handle. He stood laughing at the carnage, and because his face had turned bright red as he stared at himself in the intact window before opening the door. Then he shot the door to pieces impulsively before realising this as the reason for his laughter. Yes, he felt embarrassed for not checking the door, but he was still happy with the find. The other door had been open all this time…

And now this day was probably one of the best days of the entire journey.

Further inside the building, Steven looked through the many boxes of bullets. There was more there than he'd need in a lifetime, and I just needed one specific type, and, he was already formulating a plan to come back later with other people to retrieve the entire contents of this building. If there were others to do this task with. He looked around, and he was puzzled as to why a buying place would have bullets, but no guns at all, or other shooting weapons. Steven was certain that other shooting weapons had existed because he'd seen them in books.

* * *

It was weeks later when things had changed for Steven. He had glimpsed an unfamiliar expansive landscape. First, he'd spotted a row of mountains ahead of him. Not as high as the previous ones with the snow, but these were mountains nonetheless and then not long afterwards, Steven felt the cool sea breeze, too. He realised from what he was observing in the landscape and from the occasional ruins he would pass by, that he was now close to his destination; a place that had been marked on the first map he had found…

In a much-needed lull in the journey, Steven was re-reading the letter from his father once again, just to make sure he'd sufficiently memorised its contents. It was the part of the letter where his father would mention that he was hoping that Steven would find his mother which had him both worried and happy at the same time. And the sensation was such an odd one…

—My dearest son, I hope your journey goes well, and that you can find your mother.

I'm certain she left clues for you to tell you where she went, and if she did, you use those clues to find her. When you find her, tell her I think about her every day, and that I hope she'll be able to come back to me one day. I hope she'll treasure you as much as I do. Now, Steven, your hardest task yet. Destroy all these letters. Do this. Keeping them isn't safe for you. I know you want to keep them, but don't. Be as careful as you can be.

Your loving father—

Steven looked at these last few words once more. He remembered throwing the rest of the letter into the fire for the purpose his father had requested of him after finding the letter in the last building filled with books that he'd visited. As all the final pages of the letter now also shriveled to ash slowly, Steven wondered why his father didn't want the words he'd written to be known by anyone else…

Steven had kept part of the letter all this time to hold onto the message contained within it, especially this small part that had seemingly been added to the letter as an afterthought. Now he threw the last part of the letter into the small fire in front of him. However, in his hands, he held one small piece of paper that he'd planned to keep regardless of what his father might say if he ever found out. It was saying: "I love you, son. I love more than you'll ever realise." Steven kept this small part of the letter no matter what would happen. He picked up the piece of smooth unused plastic he had found in the shop, and after seeing the dried shells of what may have been food wrapped in a similar material, he decided that wrapping up this portion of the letter similarly would preserve the letter for a long time in a similar way.

"Maybe if I wrap it similarly the paper stays dry," Steven mumbled as he folded the plastic over the fragile scrap of paper. This small scrap, so carefully preserved, was going to be the only reminder he'd to let him know that everything his father had done he had done because he loved a son...

Once Steven had read the message one more time, he put the piece of paper inside the plastic wrapping in the top pocket of his jacket, where it would remain for the remainder of his life unless he needed to show it to 'anyone' specific. Steven was certain he'd always treasure the words regardless of what was going to happen next.

The doubt about the real purpose of his journey had set in as far back as when he was still saying goodbye to his father. His father had given him 'certain warnings of caution' before he'd left Utopus behind. Then he saw the dead man in the bunker, and he had shot a hole in the side of his head. For what? It was his first clue that his journey could be futile, and just some sort of illusion of escaping a doomed fate.

Or did someone shoot him? Steven thought, now that an earlier thought re-entered his mind. He'd often thought about doing the same thing as the journey had dragged on, and now, well, now he had thought about jumping off a cliff into the water south of here. He always had so many doubts and more since his journey had started, but then something had happened...

He'd seen the flying objects at regular intervals, and they had changed his perception of his entire journey. His father's last words, and Steven's reply to him, had come back to his mind then, and he started sensing that something about the people who were being talked about wasn't right. The way the voice in the recordings had scared him or had gone on to give him the feelings that something was out to endanger him.

"Always remember," Steven's father had said, "and don't lose your rucksack, whatever happens."

"Remember? Who...? Or—what?" Steven had wondered when he'd spoken those words, "and what about my rucksack?" His father hadn't told him, and instead just held him close for a few more minutes, then he pushed me away. "Go—now—" were the last words.

There was a repetition to these thoughts until his unexpected arrival at the place that had been marked...

* * *

The morning of the last day before Steven had arrived his destination, and he'd been doubting he'd ever find the place, marked on the map, but he'd never expected that it would be a place filled with... people!

He'd been walking for so long, and passed through so many old cities and towns, all abandoned to time and the destruction by wind and rain, that he hadn't understood what he had found when he had arrived. He found a place that could easily have been from another time, like perhaps from five or six hundred years ago with all irony he could muster. He immediately wanted to ask 'them' if they were the people who'd sent the messages out that they'd been receiving in Utopus? On the morning of his last day of journey, and he was doubting he'd ever find the place marked on the map...

They had asked him more; Steven just shrugged at everything...

No, and don't just stare at each other like you don't know what the fuck I'm talking about, Steven thought angrily as he glared at the 'shapes' of people standing around him in the dark place he was now in, *and yes, we got a message, and it had warned us it wasn't safe anywhere in Zone Zero... But then I got sent out, anyway. And who had precisely sent me? You?*

Steven thought that he might have spoken then, "Everyone is in danger here actually, because if it isn't you who had selected me as Subject, and it isn't you in charge there, then someone out there's dangerous, and those people don't want you to know what goes on in Zone Zero. That place doesn't look like what you got here—" he had said to the men standing around him. When he had said these words, there was something about the men that had him worried. But at that moment, he hid the worry well and then he tried to provoke them with more comments.

"I saw one of those flying objects again. It was maybe three weeks ago, and this one had the dent on the side of it where I had tried to shoot at it, and where the bullet I'd used had just bounced off the side of the surrounding shell. Those objects are being used to search for something. I'm afraid that they may have followed me here, and that they'll find this place. When I saw this last flying object, I felt concern," Steven had almost shouted the words at them. When he saw anger on the men's faces, Steven had one thought in his mind: I know now who the 'them' are—I'm certain of it… They're claiming that I should be glad to have found this place, but I need to be wary of them, and stop possibly finding you here. Steven glanced surreptitiously towards the girl… Had he no mask on he might have smiled at her.

One reason he was doubting anything he was told since arriving was that he'd seen the dark structure near the camp, like the structure he'd seen appear and disappear in Utopus, so he knew they weren't the people who'd selected him for this damned journey of his?

"And for what? For no damned reason did I have travel here—If I sound angry, then yes, I am," Steven had shouted, "I want to know is going on—"

The girl had a finger over her mouth. Steven shut up again.

Steven's mind locked into a circular reasoning and explanation of his current situation, assuming that when he had finally arrived here, he found an origin for the bunker he'd visited a year ago, and had thought also he had found a sanctuary, and then find out that every Subject got here, but your behaviour told him he might be the only one.

If they never got to here, then where are they all? Steven thought, staring at the floor, and frowning again. *Well, I guess most of them are now dead, but I'd assume the most recent Subjects might be alive still, ranging in age from perhaps forty to eighty years, or something like this. And if you start claiming they aren't here, and never had been here at all, you'll have to tell me what happened to them…*

Where are the others?

Steven was about to ask them, but the girl was placing her finger over her lips again…

What's with the girl? Why is she here…?

Steven never thought the line on the map would lead to this place.

And honestly, the shock of discovering what he was doing was something he couldn't wait to tell his father about, if he was still living. He had expected to discover that Utopus was the ultimate place where humanity would get saved. But then he discovered all this…

His mind was all over the place, and he realised then that also he was likely delirious…

"So, please, tell me now, what's going on?" Steven demanded loudly. "I'm aware it all had started when I had arrived here and looked down at the vista below, and it left me in shock. It was so different from anything I expected to see in all the time I travelled here. I saw ruined cities and derelict land on my way, but all this looks better than anything I have seen in Utopus. It's like I've been on a journey without a purpose for all this time."

Steven rose to his feet…

"The buildings here all look so pristine, and comparing it with the buildings of Utopus, it seems like that's how that place should be. Compared to what I've observed here, Utopus seems like it's a derelict mess. It seems dull and appears to be wrong. Especially now," Steven yelled at the tallest man standing near me and then he tried to move towards the man.

"When I arrived, I could hear sounds, and my mind couldn't understand the sounds that I was hearing here," Steven screamed again not long afterwards, "and I wear the mask I've worn for the last year and a half, and I've wondered why I needed to use it at all. Was it to prevent the taint of the landscape from killing me? I just didn't know where the ones that might have been there had gone to."

Someone asked him something…

"I found the bullets that I was looking for after about an hour of searching. While I did that, I kept also looking through the window, and taking care not to be in full view of potential flying objects, which had become more frequent over the last few months, although I was at a loss why," Steven yelled again, "and I think I may have collected over a hundred boxes of bullets there. I've hidden two-thirds of them in a cave that I found some time later, a few days before I had found this place. I was planning to go back there to get those bullets."

Steven remembered now what had happened as he had arrived.

But only fragments of it.

Though, he didn't remember how long ago…

* * *

An unknown time had passed by when Steven was stood at a table and had been working on checking his rucksack. Once he had repacked his rucksack, which was by now getting overfull, and started weighing him down at each use, and he started on the last leg of the journey to the sea where he'd seen the girl rush away towards and he thought it was to a safer place, and which, he reckoned, was just a few days away, perhaps a week as most.

The heat was unbearable, and when the stench of the meat he was carrying had started, he threw it away, and therefore lived off the chocolate food, though as a melted goo in the heat, until he was at the ocean. A predator, perhaps those dogs that he'd encountered, would enjoy the rotting meat more than he would do. He wondered then for a few days afterwards if that had been what the dogs had been after.

Steven stood staring at the vast region of water ahead of him. He had finally arrived at the most southern coast of Europe and it on the eastern coast of Spain, and the water looked like the large area on the map, and seeing it in person made him appreciate even more how vast the world really was…

Then he heard the earlier screeching sound again, and he dove into the bushes beside the road. He stood up slowly, and looked in all directions to see where the sound was coming from. Then he pulled the gun from his pocket, thanking under his breath that he'd bothered to refill it. He saw the black object approach…

He lifted his gun and aimed at it. Four shots shattered the stillness of the air. The object jerked in the sky after the fourth shot and started flying erratically. He aimed once more. Moments later, the drone fell from the sky. Steven listened for several minutes to see if he could hear any others approaching, but apart from the sound of birds flying up, the air was still again once more.

Now, Steven had to find the drone before any others came flying to the region, or before any people came to search for their properly. If he was correct about their purpose, the people operating them would already know Steven had shot one down.

They know what I look like and that I was wearing a mask, Steven thought, *and that I had a gun—I need to find somewhere safe, and fast...*

∗ ∗ ∗

That was the account of the first part of Steven's journey, his arrival in this strange, southern location, at a place called the Camp, and where the first encounters with other people, after almost a year alone, had all happened. The girl, who'd been watching him silently for the better part of the last six months as Steven tried to discover why memories and thoughts about who or where he was, drifted out of his mind. He was vaguely aware of individuals around him. Some voices that were friendly. *Others who'd be shouting. Who were they shouting at...? Who was there...? Who was the girl who was always staring at him...?*

Subject 37

PART THREE

Side-Stepped

Subject 37

40.

WHEN STEVEN HAD BEEN SHOOTING at the drone, he might have made someone, out there, his enemy, acutely aware of his presence in Zone Zero, and therefore had put a target on his back because of this. He couldn't ascertain who the 'someone' was at that time, but frankly, he wished he was able to get the next bullet he shot to go into the skull of the leader of the people for all the horrible things they were planning to do…

Steven was becoming tougher in how he looked at the world, maybe even cold-hearted. He'd been alone so long that it was easier to consider their presence in this way.

The drone was lying in a ditch, and he'd noticed some sort of motion on its cover, so he raised his gun once again before he approached it. Steven aimed at the moving appendix and shot it off cleanly. He needed to wait until he was certain that nothing else was moving. Steven ambled almost leisurely towards the object that was now leaning on its side in the ditch and a few moments later crouched down beside it and stared at it with a concerned frown planted on his face.

It had a metallic sheen, and Steven was curious about what had kept it flying until he shot at it.

Somehow, he knew that the next encounter with a drone wouldn't be so simple. He was very certain that the people who were controlling these objects would now know that one of their devices had been downed somehow… by someone… He'd been walking for a few weeks, when he was certain when he saw the large water mass - again - which he'd seen a few weeks after leaving the river behind, he was getting closer to wherever they controlled the drones from.

If he'd been following the map correctly, Steven knew he'd be in what had been Spain, in the past, in a matter of few weeks from now.

This region he was traversing was somewhere halfway between Italy and Spain, what they were each called, once, in the past…

It was then that Steven got to the last page in the stack of papers left in his rucksack for him to find, and he wasn't certain what to do with the information listed within these papers. He knew his father had intended the information to be for someone out there. He found something with which to repack the papers tightly, and when he was in a building where obviously in the past, they'd sold such types of materials.

Later, during the night, which was when the plan first had hatched in his mind. If he could get in and out of Utopus unnoticed, then he could do the same thing in the place where he might end up in in a matter of weeks. There might be no one looking at where he was or anything like it. He didn't want to draw attention to himself when he'd formulated an idea of sorts, so slowly he checked where the people might be standing as he listened for the sounds of others nearby, and he needed a quiet moment to adjust to the population he was now encountering around him…

If only that damned girl wasn't making it look like she was spying on me or something.

It was the girl who had got him worried about his plan…

His exit from this dangerous place, and the subsequent escape, followed by the unexpected rescue later had been so chaotic, and it hadn't been until later he might have been able to give himself a chance to start making sense of it all. It wasn't until later, that things had appeared to be normal again. But that moment of escape, after all the interrogations, and the heat had dazed him constantly, that wasn't something he'd forget easily.

The plan now was to get out somehow, to travel north, and somehow to reach Utopus again, and to get Elizabet and his father from there to take them to safety. *Warn the others to leave too as soon as possible and hope most people would listen.* This thought left him with a feeling he was foreshadowing a dangerous part of a story of some sort…

But it seemed to Steven now, at least after talking to—well, being interrogated by and questioned by whoever had him there bound to a chair, more like it, that everywhere between here and there was some massive war zone.

And if this was the case, might anywhere be safe? And if this was the case, might this World War 3 still be going on? Somehow…

* * *

Someone nearby made random sounds a few moments later…

A muffled giggle.

Movement near him.

Someone was next to him who spoke a few seconds later, "You look so ridiculous in that mask," a youthful voice was saying softly, almost like a whisper. *More giggles.* Giggles belonging to a girl, and unusually they sounded oddly familiar. *Too familiar.*

Steven tore the mask off his face that someone, seemingly, had left on him to increase his discomfort and he did this action because of *her* laughing at him. He realised then that he was sitting in the bright sun, wearing soldier's clothing, up to a few moments before also wearing a mask, carrying the damned stupid rope, and it took him a while before he comprehended what might be going on. There were more sounds around him that he didn't understand until he would get at the bunker later. Someone had wanted him to get *there* because of a line drawn on a map. But—he sensed a familiarity about the girl who seemed to be picking at his bindings frantically, and the realisation that he had in fact been travelling deliriously with bindings in place had shocked him even more…

Steven had asked one of the people, assigned to his medical needs, as to *who* the girl might be. The answer had come from the woman going by the name of Anna, as he would find out later, who had finally whispered an answer to him, which had caused her to have some additional concern about his well-being for a while, and had explained: "She'd arrived *here* with her mother a little over thirteen years ago, when *she* was just a few months old. Her mother had never told any of us where they'd come from," as the girl had been staring at him from the nearest the tent structure, and who he now knew was apparently just thirteen, as up to that moment he had assumed to be much older…

Anna later told him more details, and it was the last conversation with her that had made him determined to leave from wherever he would end up in. He did some checking, and he'd found out that her mother had died a mere two years ago. All he was able to find out was that an accident had happened, and apparently the girl had seen it happen, and ever since that day she'd been a mute. Her mother had worked in the communications building for a while…

"She started working there around two years after arriving here," Anna had explained hastily, "and I didn't know either of their names for the longest time, although a man that I know, and who works in the building next to this particular building, had been claiming that they were sharing the same name—I'm sorry, but that's all I could find out for you."

After that day, Steven didn't see Anna anymore, and another woman had taken her place with a duty of caring for him. But this woman would never tell him a name, however many times Steven had asked her for this information. He'd just stopped talking and decided that, perhaps, it was best to behave as if he might also be a mute, like the girl he'd seen hanging around.

The presence of the girl almost became a game between the two of us. Some kind of secret game we'd only play if it was only us in the tent structure. Most times, Steven pretended not to notice that her presence, and perhaps she was pretending to be unnoticed by him. She'd laughed whenever she saw his frustration, and then he realised as *odd* as to why Anna had stated she was a mute if then she was laughing. It seemed that this game would keep going on for a few weeks, and because of that he started being annoyed about what was going on the people assigned to care for him whispered about how uncooperative he was, and that he was sullen or rude. It had caused another change in the assigned carers a few weeks later, and then Steven noticed that the girl was around again. She'd continue her game of tease just minutes after a carer had arrived. In some ways he was glad whenever she'd return because it meant that the assigned carers did less caring for him, and therefore he ended up being alone more.

However, Steven realised after enough time had gone by in his current plight that *he* cared about the girl in an odd way. He realised he was caring increasingly more about her well-being, and something about her familiarity made him realise he wanted to include her in his plan—but he couldn't.

Steven's plan was deceptively simple.

The plan had been to get to the eastern hills where he'd come from originally, and he'd wait for the right moment and make a dash for the higher parts of the hills towards the north of the location. Then he would hope for the best, and he'd travel north as quick as he could. After that, he wasn't entirely sure what he could do after this journey.

Steven wasn't sure he wanted to go back into the hell-hole that Zone Zero is…

But he needed to try to leave because something about the place he'd ended up in, this place, didn't sit well with him either, Steven thought it was his gut instinct telling him that there was more going on than he'd been told.

And the previous night they had claimed they were '*done*' with him. It was then that leaving became more urgent and that he should attempt to see if he would be able to get out of this place…

* * *

It was maybe two or three months later, when Steven was thinking that he'd get a chance of escape. The girl who'd he seen observing him seemed to be gone. Perhaps the boredom of watching a madman lying on a bed in a darkened room had driven her off.

Steven had looked around for anyone else who could be near enough to stop him, and he decided the coast was clear and he'd gotten free, collected his belongings and then had run towards the nearby hills, over which he'd arrived. He was uncertain how long had gone by since the final interrogation had started, so he assumed he'd been *there* for many weeks, or even months, or more. Prior of his escape, Steven saw his gun just lying on a table as he got close to the exit of the building, and thinking it would prove handy, he scooped it up, and grabbed his mask lying there, too. He thought about why he might want to bring it along and decided it was easy enough. They could throw something at him to cause him to become unconscious, and wearing the mask would prevent this from happening. Steven ran for at least twenty or thirty minutes in a northerly direction, but the heat exhausted him, and he stopped for a moment and leaned forward to help him to recover some of his energy reserves.

A bird call sounded out…

Then, a sound came that reminded him someone coughing, but this sound was guttural and too loud to be of a human origin, and Steven had heard many sounds, then he'd been in a sensation of complete silence, and these sounds were sudden after months of silence and it all overwhelmed him, and it became all too much for him in the next moment…

"I must be imagining all this," Steven was mumbling, and the comment caused someone near him to laugh.

No, not laugh… It was the irritating giggle of a familiar girl.

Steven jumped up then and pointed his gun around.

"You don't need *that* here, silly," a girl's voice said plainly.

These words caused Steven to think he'd gone truly mad after all this time spent travelling. Abruptly, Steven dropped the gun and it fell again to the ground with a loud clatter. Someone's arms had hurriedly wrapped around him after he collapsed once more moments later. Something wet touched his face.

Steven was feeling lost now, but it seemed that the arms surrounding him were trying to make him feel safe then someone spoke in a soft lilt. "Can you walk at all?" the voice asked him.

Steven shook his head.

Something touched his mouth, and Steven felt something cool drip over his skin. Steven's hands hesitantly reached up towards whatever 'thing' that was being held against his face, and he found a water bottle there. "Slow down. If you drink *too* fast, you'll convulse…" another voice was now saying. This voice sounded familiar now, and Steven remembered slowly where he'd discerned this voice before.

"Anna?" I asked.

"Yes, it's Anna," the voice said quietly.

For a moment, Steven wondered what identity he should be mentioning in response to her statement.

Should he say that he's Subject 37? Or tell her that he's Steven Burgard?

His mind was grappling with this conflict of decisions for several minutes. His mind couldn't to tell him what to do, and then the voice asked him something: "What are *you* called? You've never told a name in the infirmary?" and he was contemplating what to say for several more minutes.

Steven realised he might have shaken his head, trying to dispel whatever illusion he had now conjured up because of the pressing heat. He'd always been told that Utopus was the 'only place' with living people in it, and that all survivors of the World War 3 had gone there. If this was the case, how was a girl able to live out here…? And whose voices might he be hearing in the distance? Steven was certain that he was hearing the voices of thousands of people. He was certain that he gave them an answer. The person who'd spoken to him earlier didn't giggle when she found out his name a moment later: "I'm called Steven Burgard—I think—" he'd answered softly then he stared at where her voice had come from, asking now, "Where am I?"

Silence.

For several minutes, Steven wondered if he'd been imagining his entire journey, and everything that had happened to him since. If that was the case, perhaps everything he was experiencing right now was also a hallucination.

Or a dream.

That was, until now.

After some time had passed, Steven was able to discern some voices coming from another part of the structure, and he noticed among them the voice of the girl who'd spoken previously. *All talk and all giggles... again!*
Hands touched him.
Something cool sprinkled over his forehead.
When the same hands lifted him onto a bed, Steven sensed relief washing over him.
Whatever he'd endured before, until this moment, hadn't been for nothing. He was somewhere with people who'd care for him...
Steven discerned the voices again. They sounded urgent this time.
"Steven. Steven. Can you stand up at all?" Anna was asking me.
"I don't know and I'm weak like I've not eaten for days," Steven answered.
"It is all these drugs they've been pumping in you," Anna said angrily. "They're meant to keep you incapacitated and weak."
"Who?"
Silence again, then some whispering between several voices.

This was when Steven was able to remember some parts of what perhaps had happened to him during his trek through desolate Europe. The memories of the last several days came flooding back. During the journey towards the camps, he'd discovered in the southwest, towards whatever place this might be, Steven had managed to lose consciousness, because he couldn't really recall what had happened for a long length of time where he'd just sat staring ahead searching for answers. Except that each time he'd seemingly woken up and that same girl's voice had kept calling his name…

And rather than sounding all giggly as she had done before, the girl's voice sounded full of concern, like she wanted him to wake up from the unconscious state he was in. When he finally had woken up the girl was gone, but instead he'd seen two women talking, both wearing a white outfit, sitting at a table at some distance from him. When they had noticed that he was awake, one of them got up and walked off. After some time, she came back with several men. Steven was certain they had tried to ask him questions, but he still couldn't comprehend his surroundings. His ears had refused to make sense of the sounds assaulting his mind, and his mouth had refused to function.

But all this stuff was many weeks ago, he thought, and it caused him to become angry and frustrated. *Who are those people…?*

He must have spoken in a loud voice at her, because suddenly Anna's hand covered his mouth.

"Hush, or *they* might hear you down there," she said, and that's when he'd lost consciousness.

Even later, perhaps during the earliest hours of the evening, Steven woke up again, and this time he was alone. He had looked around in quick glances and found out he was in a room with yellow walls. Because he saw no one he contemplated over what he knew about Utopus. He decided he needed to go back *there* urgently to help his father and the others there, *especially Elizabet…*

Steven searched around with his right hand, and he found a needle sticking into his left arm…

41.

LEANING OVER THE SIDE OF the bed, he now saw his rucksack lying on the floor below my bed, but much as he tried, he felt too weak to reach down for it…

It might take me until winter to get back home, he thought and then he worked out in his mind that he needed to go north in a straight line. He was feeling confused. He wondered if he could get back. And would the people *here*, wherever here was, let him go back? But could I get back into Utopus? Would Elisabet be waiting for me? It will have been well over two years since I left…

Steven concluded that he wouldn't ever leave, and he'd never see his father again. He got angry and wondered then why his father had sent me away like this. *Would the girl perhaps help him to get out of this place…? If he asked her, would she help him?*

He knew that, perhaps, he could get back to the region in the north, but he didn't know if he would make it to inside the invisible boundaries of Utopus. And how would the people living there react to his return? Would *he* still be Subject 37 to them, or would they call him Steven Burgard once more?

He had realised that arriving at this southern location that he first had found out about from an old map, had caused him to have more questions than answers, because suddenly everything had changed…

* * *

As he lay in the bed contemplating his options, he suddenly heard a noise across the room. He was hearing the familiar giggle again, but now that irrational giggle was causing him much irritation every time it happened. She thought she was seeing something funny, and perhaps to her, a man in bed who couldn't do a damned thing for himself, was hilarious.

"I know you're over there," Steven said flatly. "You can stop hiding…"

Silence.

She might have assumed that it would be a funny game of some sort to laugh at the man's misfortune, before skipping away and be gone without a further word. This supposed game had repeated itself over the weeks while Steven had been recovering from his exhaustion and still-lingering injury, and a few weeks went by when he was alone again. He realised that she was near him again sometime later. And this time, after she had giggled, she spoke to him, and even though her voice and question showed curiosity, there was something about what she was saying made him wonder *who* she really was.

Much later, he sensed he wasn't alone anymore. So, he quickly looked up and noticed her sitting on the bed opposite him, with her legs folded, but the giggle was missing. She was looking at him with a typical serious 'stare' like only children are capable of, like she wanted or needed to know something from him and was perhaps hesitantly to ask him, or perhaps that's how he was perceiving her behaviour towards him…

He guessed she hadn't been around when Anna and the others had found him on the hill. He looked around one more time to be certain he wasn't back at the first place he'd found, and from the corner of his eye noted that she was matching his behaviour and movements but in an upright stature. He noted that his place seemed different. There was *no* drip in his arm here, and he saw my gun was on the table next to the bed.

There was no one anywhere them here, and strangely enough, in this place wherever it was he was feeling safe, like someone had brought somewhere him there for my safety, away from the war zone. *Or whatever was happening outside…*

Outside.

There's outside, he was screaming silently inside his mind to get him to get into action and to get up and to leave as fast as he could.

Suddenly, he realised that this place felt much like the bunker he'd been exploring so many months earlier; a place which was located not too far outside of Utopus, and he realised now what perhaps had happened there, and why the dead man was there. He had been defending it against people waging a war against their intended victims within Zone Zero. *—it was never only just a polluted place… it was a massive war zone…* The name had nothing to do with a god-forsaken disease. *It was the code name. Was that what my father had found out? Was that why thirty-seven people, including myself, had been sent so far from a supposed safe region, a city at the edge of the world that was there to keep the last of humanity—safe? As a ploy. That I wasn't selected because I was a scientist. That I was selected because I had the knowledge of how to survive in Zone Zero.*

We'd secretly been trained to do a job, if his former task done for a year, two years, or longer, could be called a job, and the people who would send them, the Subjects, weren't involved with the bunker; found so unexpectedly and spectacularly at the start of his journey. *How long have I been on this journey?* They were the people who'd been fervently resisting against their captors...

Later, the people who he was eyeing from time to time, would make clear to him why he'd seen a structure come and go so mysteriously, though he laughed first over the rather preposterous idea that it... it could fly. *But I saw those things in the night sky, they're similar?* Steven was thinking, *and I saw those devices searching.* He was able to see this same structure in the camp they'd placed him in at certain times when either Anna or the girl would pull him to the entrance and either would push aside the cloth cover and point west, before quickly dragging him back to the bed when another of the same group of rogue soldiers would arrive. Rogue soldiers who he realised could be connected to the events that had caused the destruction of Europe; both past destruction and current activities...

Current activities, Steven thought as he was again lying on the bed, *and is that maybe what I say with mother and father when they said something had begun...?*

They had pretended to enact a coup, but, had cruelly killed the world population with an unknown type of disease, and they had set out with their disillusioned idea of cleansing the world for their 'land' with this action. Whatever was really going on, it meant he had to go *back* and save the others in Utopus. The only way to *do* this would be for them to see that many people had come with him from within Zone Zero. *I must go back to my father—*

Suddenly, all my thoughts of planning the perfect rescue were being interrupted by that familiar, but annoying, giggle...

The girl spoke, and as she spoke, I stared at her in shock.

"Hi, my name is Indigo. What's yours?"

* * *

Four years later,

"Are *you* ever going to tell me your mother's name?" Steven asked the girl who'd identified now as Indigo.

"I've told you her name already," Indigo said, and she giggled again, and this was an action she knew full well would be annoying to him. "NO, you haven't. You've never said it," Steven replied bluntly, and he frowned angrily at the girl. This cat-and-mouse discussion had been going on now for a little over four years, at a minimum since the girl had revealed her first name to him.

Steven was quite aware what would come *next* in the game. She'd tell him that her mother had forbidden her from telling anyone what her mother's name was. And to Steven, the story had sounded all too familiar, because he realised that his father had done the exact thing for most of his life while he still lived in Utopus...

He had integrated well in the Bunker, as the people living inside this location, who he had met not long after arriving there, after his escape from the 'other place.' They had told him this was the Bunker and located some hundred kilometres northwest of where the camp where he'd been located, and from which he had attempted to escape from, and succeeded but only with the help of others. That *other* camp was trickery to fool any survivors into believing they were safe...

Anna was one of the individuals who would go to the camp from the Bunker to check what was going on inside the location. The occupants of the camp had discovered Steven in the hills just north-east of this place, and the people there took him to what they claimed to be their place to heal up people. It was there where Steven had met Anna initially.

Steven had 'stayed' at the camp for a while, but then someone had arrived and had led him to yet another nameless structure, and there they had forced him to tell his story. He must have been lucky that the men there had never checked inside his rucksack, or perhaps he wouldn't be sitting here right now.

Indigo, the girl who'd so annoyingly had giggled at him while he was still in *that* camp, explained she was only there because her mother had been there, too. She was annoying with her giggles, but her stubborn streak was more so. She'd ask him every other day what he was planning to *do* about what he had learnt about the purpose of the camp, and he told her outright that he couldn't do a damned thing. When she had cried uncontrollably, Steven had wondered what he'd said or done. She ran off, and after twenty minutes Anna had walked towards him, and she'd sat down beside him, and had glared at him…

"What?" he asked her abruptly.

"You don't know then," she said flatly.

"What don't I know?" he asked.

"She hasn't told you about *her* mother—even after all this time and I guess she's still complying with part of what she promised her mother she would do," Anna said bluntly, "and I needed to promise her to keep the information to myself, but now she's talking about just going back there, and be damned with it all…"

Steven frowned and was at a loss for words. "She won't even tell me what her mother was called—or where *she* is now," he replied flatly. "So far, I've never found my mother who was supposedly coming here and—"

"Actually, on the first part of your comment that's not entirely true," Anna commented softly, looking away for a moment as she seemed not capable of meeting his game, "and I've told you what happened to her mother when you were still over there."

"You did?" Steven asked.

"Yes, but I guess… you don't remember our conversation before I— had left," she replied.

Steven stared ahead of him for several minutes and stared into the empty space in front of him to contemplate over the situation then he finally replied with, "Oh…"

Anna nodded curtly.

"You remember all of it…?" she asked somewhat coldly.

He nodded to confirm.

"It traumatised her to the extreme—Indigo that is… when *it* had happened," Anna answered quietly, looking down and looking sorrowful. "She was only six—"

"That was ten years ago?" he asked abruptly.

She nodded again. "I took up the care of her. I had recently arrived there myself, from here at the Bunker, to find out why *our* feed for information ran dry," Anna said, frowning concerned as if the memory was painful to her, but Steven decided not to press on the matter.

"Feed?" he asked softly.

"I guess I need to tell you more about Indigo's mother, it seems," Anna said bluntly, "but I'd rather speak about any of that stuff in your room, where no one else can overhear what I have to tell you."

Steven nodded, and he got up, then offered a hand to Anna to help her up too. They walked silently to the small room that Steven had been assigned, located at the southern end of the complex.

They held hands to give the illusion that they were going somewhere for some 'private R&R,' which was what Anna usually would call them meeting up for their clandestine talks where others might think of it more as a more intimate endeavour such as the handsome tall new arrival sweeping a woman off her feet, but in reality their meet-ups usually would mean that she'd sit on the only chair, and he'd sit on the bed, and she'd talk about the things she knew; of how they'd run Camp X - as the people in the Bunker would call the camp from which Steven had escaped - and in such moments she'd also tell him more about the Bunker.

* * *

They had arrived in Steven's room after walking for half an hour through what was still a maze for Steven, and he'd immediately sat down on his bed, with his back leaning against the pillow there. The room was cleaner and brighter than the dwelling he'd lived in when he still lived in Utopus, but this room was just as sparse as his was there, or even sparser. It had a bed, a chair, a table, and a metal bar with these wiry things that Anna had explained were for hanging clothing on. Not that he did the task of tidying up his pile of clothing that much, and usually one of the first things Anna would do when she got to the room was to hang all his clothes over those wires. She always would whisper any information she wanted to share as she did this…

"Indigo was something like three months old when her mother had arrived at the camp, at—Camp X, and they had questioned her similarly as they did with you but because the child, she had with her, *they* were treating almost her like she'd single-handedly saved the planet," Anna said softly.

She stopped talking and walked to the outer door to lock it before she continued in a monotone.

"I've got relatively little knowledge about her mother, except for the *few* things Indigo was willing to tell me about herself, about them both, and I'm certain her mother had told her a lot of information, as she always acts like she knows more than she lets on—according to Indigo her mother had always refused to tell her daughter her own name," Anna said plainly, "and I understand you've told Indigo a similar thing about your father in Utopus. Is that right?"

Steven nodded silently.

"I'm convinced that Indigo does know what her mother's name was," Anna continued, "and I've been trying to get her to tell me it ever since she was six. I'm uncertain why but knowledge of it could be dangerous for an unknown reason that I've never figured out so far—"

"Why did you tell me *she* was a mute...?" Steven asked flatly.

"I did it to protect you both," Anna said quietly, "and I took her in my care not only because I'm uncertain if I can have children of my own but also to protect her in the meantime. Children without parents aren't treated kindly by them in the Camp. They're used in certain ways... This is my way of ensuring that I have, at a minimum, one child to be a mother for at least. I've been caring for Indigo for so long that I've noticed her personality and characteristics. Why do you never ask yourself the question of why you two always squabble like two irate siblings...?"

Steven frowned. "Siblings?" he asked hesitantly.

"Yes—and you two appear more *alike* as she gets older," Anna said bluntly, "and yes, I care for you deeply, and don't stare at me now like I'm her proper mother suddenly."

He stared down and sighed.

"If she's my sibling—my sister then was she, the woman who'd arrived at the Camp, her mother...?" Steven asked and it was a sentence his mind couldn't quite finish fully.

"What exactly do you remember of your mother?" Anna asked, sounding pensively. "You've told me many times that you can't remember anything at all, but I think deep down you know the answers already, and are either avoiding acknowledging that you know things already, or you're outright ignoring these memories..."

"I have a few vague memories of her. One memory is matching what my father has told me of why she had to go away, and in the other memories she had a swollen belly," he replied. "I thought for a while, after that happened, that she was sick and had gone to another part of Utopus to get care."

"A swollen belly?" Anna asked, then she laughed loudly.

Steven noticed for the first time that Anna giggled almost in a similar annoying way as Indigo always did.

"You call yourself a scientist when you can't even figure out *that* stuff about a woman," Anna snorted teasingly and then got up and walked to the man's bed, while she smiled at him teasingly then she pulled his pillow from behind him, which caused him to knock his head against the wall…

"Ouch, watch it," he said angrily as he rubbed the back of his head, and stared up at the woman towering over the bed somewhat angrily then glanced away because she was staring at him teasingly.

"Did her belly look like this?" Anna asked.

Steven glanced up, to find Anna standing beside his bed, with his pillow propped under her tunic, forming a swelling over her belly that now seemed so familiar that he went pale, and he knew he'd seen a woman with that shape of body before. Steven had seen his mother for a last time when he was thirteen, when he'd called after the woman…

"Mama, Mama."

"You look like you saw a ghost," Anna said, sounding concerned.
"I think I did," Steven mumbled. "I think I saw the ghost of my missing mother."

42.

"YOUR MOTHER LOOKED LIKE *HER*... or more precisely she looks like her mother, and you got a bit of your mother as well to be honest, and when did she had left your father and you, right...?" Anna asked softly, "Steven, she was pregnant when she had to leave from Utopus. And you say this happened when you were thirteen years old."

"My father would never tell me where she was going, or what she was doing," Steven replied.

"I may know *who* Indigo's mother was. She'd arrived at the camp similarly as you, and she had Indigo with her, who was perhaps three or four months old. She may have told Indigo extensively about the journey to Camp X and had told me only once, personally, that it took her a year to get there," Anna whispered, leaning forward somewhat so to lower her voice more, "and then *you* arrived under similar circumstances, around eleven years later. Indigo was ten only a half year before you had arrived here. She's now fifteen years old... and you still don't get it..."

Steven stared at his moving hands for a while which seemed to be counting the information instinctively, with him attempting to work the puzzle out in his mind. He thought that his mind did the figuring out without him even wanting it to. *If Indigo was a few months old when she and her mother arrived in Camp X, and almost eleven years later he'd arrived too, it would be too coincidental for two different people to arrive similarly at the same place. But why did they have to question him so extensively to find out where he was from? Was it that the people in the camp had noticed the similarity between the daughter of a strange woman who'd arrived ten years earlier, and a man who arrived in similar circumstances? Did the people in the camp notice that a girl living in almost feral circumstances for the last ten years resembled him...?*

"Is Indigo my sister?" he asked hesitantly.

"She is," Anna said, "and I'm certain of it. Even if I have nothing with which I could prove it to you."

"Does *she* know?" he asked even more hesitantly, too scared to look up.

"I'm uncertain," Anna said quietly. "We must find her and convince her to stay. She needs to know who you really are."

Steven nodded once, and swallowed hard and was quiet for a while before he spoke again. "But why doesn't she ever tell me her mother's name then...?" he asked.

"I'm certain she'll tell you *when* we find her," Anna answered, "and I feel that we must hurry. She has this ability to be quick when she wants to be, and if we're unlucky she may already be outside the perimeters of the Bunker."

* * *

It would take them three days before they'd found Indigo, who was hiding in a small indent in the stone structure of the Bunker, and Steven was curious at how she managed to get up there, and then Anna had pointed at the nearby pipes, which resembled a few of the pipes he had seen in the first bunker he had been exploring after finally leaving Utopus...

Steven climbed the pipes hastily to reach Indigo, and somehow had reached a metal prong sticking from the wall when he heard the familiar annoying giggle that never stopped as he finally climbed into the small indent, she was in. However, it had sounded nervous, unsure, somewhat like she'd been crying. He saw immediately she'd prepared the hiding place for a lengthy stay. There were packets of the dry biscuit stuff that he'd often eat which were stacked all around him, and it was obvious she was quite capable of find food, and water bottles, all by herself and likely without being seen...

"Move please, Steven," Anna's voice called out behind the man, and he saw that she, too, had climbed up. There was now the three of them in the small hiding space where Indigo had been living for at least the past three days, though there was evidence it had been used by her for much longer. To Steven, their current surroundings caused him to fee enclosed, like how he had felt in the shaft after seeing the second flying object...

* * *

Steven and Anna glanced at one another silently before she nodded at him and he turned to look at the girl behind him before Anna spoke, "WE need to talk, Indigo," Anna whispered after she'd recovered sufficiently from the climb up, "and especially *you* with him... please..."

"Why is *he* here?" Indigo asked angrily. "He's annoying, and he got angry at me for no reason."

"I might know the reason why I got angry like that," Steven mumbled. "If you permit me to explain, please."

"Oh, so why is that...?" Indigo snapped coldly, and then she folded her arms, straightened up in an exaggerated manner, and went on to look at him in her defiant, stubborn way that she always would do whenever she wasn't getting something to go *her* way.

Steven suddenly realised that Anna was right. *Not only does she look like me, but in she is, reality and rather obviously a female teen version of me as she sits there staring at me.* Steven contemplated about his father, and he wondered if *this* was how he had always acted out towards his father, and then he pondered for a few seconds at how his father could have ever been so patient with an at-times-unruly son with a similar sort of behaviour he was seeing now.

"My father would have told me that I was stubborn if I had behaved like *this* with him," Steven hissed somewhat angrily. "He would have this way of just being silent, and then would ignore me if I had behaved like this after he would be in this sort of mood... With me by the way... I'd know whenever he'd be angry, but at times he wasn't angry with me—"

"So, what's your father got anything to do with all this?" Indigo asked, and she sounded as angry as Steven now.

"Everything," was all Steven could say as a response, sighing sadly now.

This answer immediately replaced the stubborn frown on Indigo's face with a curious glance, first directed hesitantly at the man, and then towards Anna, then back towards to him. She glanced from me towards Anna and then repeated the motions several times before she asked, "Anna, why is *he* saying this stuff...?"

"I'm just here to make certain that the two of you talk, and that you talk properly without either of you running off," Anna said flatly, "and I'm not getting involved. Not this time."

Steven glanced towards Anna, and he saw now how she'd conveniently positioned herself at the entrance of the small indent, with both her legs leaning against the opposite wall in different places. Even if it was possible to 'run away' at nine meters above the floor below, Anna was making certain that neither of the other individuals was going anywhere. Certainly not until they'd resolved the issues between that had been building up over the past four years for various reasons…

When Steven glanced back at the girl, Indigo and he were gawking at each another with equally defiant stares.

They didn't say anything for a while.

It became a contest of who would back down first with the staring. Steven looked down first, and he did it only because of something he had remembered about something his father had said once, "Sometimes, it's better to just give in, and accept what life has given you, than to keep on being stubborn, and getting nowhere."

Steven decided that the best approach to get a resolution would be to let Indigo ask or say whatever was on her mind right now—first—and so it would allow her to say what she had always been trying to avoid telling him. She'd be who would set the pace, not him, the adult, and perhaps in the process Anna and he might find out what she'd locked away in her mind of the past events up to when she was six, but Steven realised he needed to say *one* thing to trigger her to talk, even if it meant more anger from her…

"So, you were telling me your mother's name," he whispered under his breath while not looking her in the eye.
"But I've already told you—" Was the familiar and somewhat annoying answer.

However, this time, the answer wasn't accompanied by the familiar annoying giggle. This time, Indigo had spat the reply at me with pure venomous anger in her voice. However, it seemed anger came from something other than the annoyance over a repeated question, and he was certain she was venting bottled up emotions that he knew *now* had an origin story to it. *Sad, and such tragic unnecessary reasons*, he thought bitterly.

"If you've told me then I was a fool for *not* understanding what you were saying," Steven replied as gently as he was capable of with softening the timbre of his voice, "and I'm genuinely sorry for that." Steven glanced at Anna and saw her nod encouragingly at him.

"I wanted to *know* the name because of something that had happened to me when I was thirteen or maybe a bit younger than that as well," Steven continued in a monotone, "and I've got only few memories of back then, and remember a little amount of a life with both parents present, and I was often on my own… My father and I would never speak about my mother whenever we were on our own, and there was something he would always say… He said that he didn't tell anyone ever his *first* name because it was the only thing that was entirely his."

"My mother said the same," Indigo said softly. "It's why *she* gave me my name…"

"Please, Indigo, if you tell me about *her* name, I might be able to solve some things that have puzzled me in my youth," Steven replied softly, taking hold of the girl's hand. "I've never known my father's name. He kept it from me. You, at least, knew what name your mother had used."

"She was *also*… Indigo," Steven got as a whispered answer.

Both in a state of feeling perplexed and shocked, Anna and Steven stared at one another, sensing that the other person was as confused as themselves. "Why?" they both asked, and it caused them to glance at each other again once more.

"She'd said it was the *only* way to keep safe what she was doing," Indigo answered, and a clear, sad emotion was now present in her voice.

"Keep what safe…?" Anna asked softly as she climbed closer to where Indigo and Steven were sitting as she asked the question in hushed tones.

"I can only assume that she was getting to the truth about the mean people," Indigo said angrily, "and then—" The girl's voice cut off in a hiccup sounding like she was sobbing. Steven raised an eyebrow because, for a moment, the girl had sounded more like a girl of six, and not someone almost a decade older, who had been talking to them. Anna's hand closed over his at the same time as he was scowling somewhat without him realising it until she had done this. He glanced at Anna, and he understood what she was saying with the gesture, speaking no words: "Let her talk."

"Mother said she would go to Camp X for certain purposes. Said she had to go. She would say she was there when the *first* message was received, while she was still in Utopus. She told me something about the message, but always told me afterwards to pretend that I couldn't to speak if I was over there, and especially whenever any of the evil men of Camp X were near us," Indigo explained softly. "She infiltrated the building where the leader was located and earned his trust somehow. She told me to behave like a feral child and stay near the other feral children for my safety. She also said that there was a message that my grandfather had taught everyone in the family that had prompted her to act on what they, she, had discovered..."

Steven listened silently to Indigo as she told a story and noticed quickly the similarities between her story and his own. *Something was also going on in Utopus, and people such as his father were trying their best to make sure that they were shielding the children there from the dangers it posed,* Steven thought as a few early memories flooded back, especially a specific conversation between him and his father... and it was about his grandfather. *Her grandfather too—*

"Indigo," he spoke softly, "Have you seen any dark structure in Camp X...?"
She nodded.
"Do you know what it is for?" he asked.
She nodded again.
"My mother had told me what it is for," she answered after an unrushed pause. "Every place controlled by *them* has one stationed near the camps."
"Every place—" Steven intoned in a croaky voice, "so, that means— Utopus has one, too."
"What's Utopus?" Indigo asked.
"That's what they—we—errr, they call the place I'm from," Steven replied. "You actually mentioned its name while you talked but it seemed you didn't notice it I think..."

"Why?" Indigo asked. "Why does it have that name?"

For a moment, Steven felt annoyed, but then he realised that she had as much right to know about him as he was expecting to know about her. They might be able to fill in the blanks in each other's lives if they cooperated. Also, perhaps, get enough information matching to figure out the lives of their parents.

"I'm uncertain why, to be honest, and asked my father the *same* question when I was around your age," he replied, "and my father didn't know either, or I've never figured it out either... but I wish I had."
"My mother had warned me *not* to go there and try to find answers when I was still living in Camp X," Indigo said softly.
"My father said the same about Utopus," he replied as softly.

Indigo and Steven stared at each other bemused, and suddenly they were both laughing in muffled chuckles.

"I wondered *when* the two of you were going to get along," Anna said in a mock-accusatory tone, though she was also smiling at the same time, "but, please, can we go somewhere down there that's as quiet? I'm good at pretending—I'm *not* good with heights."

Indigo and Steven glanced over at Anna, then at each other. They were both nodding at the same time.

"I recall a place where it's really quiet," Indigo quipped. "We can go there if we're careful…"

"As long as it's not more than a half meter off the floor," Anna grunted rather loudly, "and please, Steven, go find a ladder for me to climb down with."

"I will certainly," Steven replied.

Indigo was the first to climb down. Her speed getting down showed Steven that this place where they had found her was a well-frequented place for her. Steven was the next to be at the bottom of the wall, and by the time he sensed the floor underfoot he could hear the clattering of metal against stone and was surprised that Indigo knew even where to find such a thing as a ladder fast in this place. He now guessed the girl knew this place as well, or even better, than what she'd shown to know of Camp X…

When Anna was finally at ground level again, she fell into Steven's arms with obvious relief. He could see the bravery she had endured while at the height of the indent which was Indigo's little and rather useful hiding place. It took guts to do something that a person might be afraid to do. He guessed going down to Camp X to infiltrate it said it all about Anna, and before her his mother and Indigo who both did similar brave actions… That Anna had climbed up after him spoke volumes of her character, and he gained a new respect for her.

Anna glanced up at him, smiling appreciatively. Steven felt something stir deep inside him that he'd never felt before ever. Not even with Elizabet. He realised that, perhaps, he was falling in love with her. She differed from Elizabet in so many ways. Elizabet had dark hair, a tan, and a smile that always seemed sad. Anna looked at him right now like she could light up a room with her joy, and even had this quality when she had been crying. He looked closer at her, studying her features. She had her beautiful green eyes, and long eyelashes that now clung together from dampness.

She must have been crying from the fear of being alone at nine meters with her fear of heights...

Anna's expression of relief was genuine, so he figured she hadn't made up a story about being scared. He wondered if *that* was why she'd moved closer to them earlier. Had been sitting beside the exit, next to the fearful height long enough to ensure that Indigo and he would talk, then moved somewhere safer to allow her fear to settle. He glanced around and noticed Indigo standing near a door, and she smiled knowingly at him, but also rather broadly, like she saw something she liked.

Steven looked again at Anna, couldn't help himself, and lifted her chin with a finger, and kissed her on her lips. He likely surprised her because he felt her body stiffen up, then after a few moments of him kissing her, she relaxed, and then put her arms around him a moment later. He kissed her and realised it was probably the first time for her too, just as it was for him. After a few minutes, they parted and looked at each other with equal broad smiles...

 43.

STEVEN GLANCED IN INDIGO'S DIRECTION and saw her standing at the door with an ear-to-ear smile on her face, but in the next moment the teasing version of a smile came back for a few moments as she wrapped her arms around herself and made kissing motions. She giggled afterwards, then she stood with a neutral face like she hadn't seen us busy kissing, or like she had seen it but didn't care. For the first time in all the time that he'd been in the Bunker, he didn't mind her giggling. This was a giggle to tease her older brother, *not* because she was trying to annoy a strange man. He smiled at her warmly in response…

They walked towards Indigo, clasping their hands now. This time, the reason for holding hands was real, and not pretence to make it only appear to others in the Bunker that something romantic might be going between them, when before it avoided questions about why they were going to his room together.

"Finally…" Indigo said giggly as they arrived to where she stood waiting for us. Before either of them could ask her what the 'finally' was for she was walking away from them. It took them some effort to keep up.

"Wait," Indigo said as they arrived at a large open space neither of them recognised. "There's usually a bunch of guards that pass past here about now. We wait until they've passed, then wait for about a minute, then we go to *that* red door you see in the corner there."

Anna and Steven glanced at each other, and they both were equally confused as to *why* Indigo didn't want any of the guards to see them. Maybe that was why she'd said 'finally' when they caught up with her. He wanted to ask, but something about how Anna looked at him told him *not* to ask just yet, and to just follow Indigo to wherever she was leading them to. Also, both had a "why?" on our mind, made evident from how we were glancing at the other person.

"Quick, before others come here," Indigo whispered.

She rushed fast towards the red door with us following her, and with him still holding Anna's hand to help her run faster. They walked through the door that Indigo held open for us. She closed the door quietly behind her. She glanced through the small window for a moment, frowning. "Good, they didn't see us," she said. "Follow me. It's a bit of a climb up several stairs, but once we're up *there*, you'll both understand."

They had just nodded curtly. It was obvious *now* that a lot more was going on than either had ever thought possible or had wanted to realise. By the time they were at the top of the stairs, both were puffing from being out of breath. Indigo in contrast was still full of energy and kept urging us on. After an hour, we arrived in a small room, which took on an eerie similarity for Steven…

I've seen such a door once before, Steven thought.

* * *

In a small room beyond the door, Indigo sat down. "Before we go any further, I must tell you everything my mother told me… and I wasn't totally honest with you, Steven," Indigo said. "She told me about *why* father always only ever calls himself Dr Burgard…"

"How do you—?" Steven blurted out but Anna's hand stopped him.

"There's more going on than you know. More than even our parents knew, perhaps," Indigo said softly. "There's a war coming. One like *no* other before. A war that could end all of us if we're not fast enough to stop it from starting. I don't know how mother and father had ever found out about this potential war, but I do know they killed mother for finding stuff about it out."

"My mother is—dead," Steven blurted out, and forgetting momentarily that Anna had also mentioned about Indigo's mother dying, but that was before he knew they were siblings, and on hearing the words the tears rolled over his cheeks uncontrollably.

"I'm sorry—but yes, she died when I was quite young, which is how I had ended up with Anna," Indigo said plainly, "and I saw it happen. I know *who* did it. That's why Anna had also told me to pretend to be one of the feral children, like my mother had done before her. And why she had told me to be a mute?"

"You never told me that you knew that she had died," Anna whispered.

"I know but I couldn't tell you I was aware of it," Indigo said. "She told me a day would come when someone would come here, and that this someone would have information with him that would change everything."

"Who?" Steven asked but then felt stupid for asking this obvious question.

"Eh—you," Indigo said flatly.

She giggled.

Again, it was the annoying giggle of hers, but this time he deserved every bit of her teasing behaviour towards him. Steven sighed and rolled his eyes at how he got cornered by her comments. "How did *she* even know I'd come here?" he asked. "How…?"

"Mother and father had arranged all this. They are—they were aware of the truth about everything, about the possible war," Indigo answered hesitantly, "and father will be in grave danger if they find him out."

"If he's still alive we must go back to get him out of there," Steven said softly.

"If he's still alive," Indigo said, looking at him with sad eyes, "and I would hope so as I really wish that I could meet him."

"There's one problem," Steven said with a hint of panic in his voice. "I've got papers in my rucksack that 'certain people' might want to get their hands on."

"I knew that when I searched through your rucksack, during an evening at Camp X, when I was alone with you, so I took the papers out, and as a joke I replaced them with a few old books about plants," Indigo said, and she giggled again, "and I needed to make sure that I didn't laugh when I saw their faces as they looked at the books…"

Indigo chuckled for a moment after explaining her actions, then continued explaining, "and *they* put the books back inside, and put the rucksack on the table near where you slept."

"Where are the papers right now?" Steven asked. "As I think they're quite important."

As an answer Indigo simply pointed up, and Steven glanced up to see something above him, near the ceiling of the room, that looked like a metal covering.

"I put the papers up there," Indigo answered, "and I did it just after I got back here with Anna the first time after you had arrived at the camp…"

"Why didn't you tell me that you had them…?" Anna asked as she now felt a need to gently interject in the conversation between the siblings. "Why tell us now that they exist, and what are they…?"

"It's what my father had been working on most days whenever he worked in the Institute, and he did this every day before the sun was up. He listened to a message we had received and insisted I would sit in the same room when he played the recordings as he wrote them down," Steven explained flatly, "and when it was time to select the next Subject for the journey—I'm certain that someone arranged, somehow, for me to get selected. I never found out how, though. It may be a secret he'll take with him to a grave. But he said something specific, to me, before I left. He said: 'always remember not to lose your rucksack whatever happens,' before telling me to go immediately on my journey. I never understood what he meant, but now I think I do…"

"If he arranged for you go on this journey for other reasons than others intended it for, then his life is in danger," Indigo interjected softly, "and so is the life of anyone who you and he have worked with…"

"Elizabet…!" Steven blurted out loudly.

"Who is *she*…?" Indigo and Anna both asked, and Steven noted a tone in Anna's voice that showed that her immediate assessment of who this 'Elizabet' might be and discover a competitor to her newly found relationship with him somehow.

"She is—she was—someone I cared about but as a friend," Steven explained softly.

Steven glanced at Anna nervously for a moment and then after his comment she relaxed her features. He guessed she wouldn't be happy to know that he might have been in a relationship with someone else while declaring his love to her. He realised that he cared a lot more about Anna than he ever had cared for Elizabet, so he took hold of Anna's hand. She didn't pull it away…

"I made it clear how I feel about you," Steven explained softly. "She's no threat to you. I want *her* to be safe, yes, but anything like a life of growing old, or a family, that's something I'd want with you—if you'd have me."

Anna's face comically went through possibly every expression that someone's face was capable.

First, he saw disbelief. Then, a bit of fear. Then, a smile formed on her face. The fear was likely because he knew that she was several years older than him, and that she'd been alone all her life, because she'd told him this during the meal one evening. Then an expression of sheer happiness filled her face. Steven put his left hand against her cheek, somewhat wet from tears, and felt Anna lean her face into his hand…

"Somehow, I think I've loved *you* from the day when I walked into the infirmary in Camp X, and I saw you on the bed, looking so helpless," Anna said softly, "but I had to tell myself, convince my mind, every single day since then that it might be possible that you'd never love me back."

"You taught me that I *could* love someone, Anna," Steven replied gently, "and from *you* too, Indigo, of course…"

Indigo flew at them excitedly, her arms wrapping around each other person. "Now it's perfect—my brother and adoptive mother as a couple," she squealed excitedly, then after hugging us for several minutes, she moved away, asking: "Do you want those papers now?" pointing up.

"Not yet… We got a lot to organise first if there's danger ahead," Steven replied, "and we can get the papers just before we're ready to go."

"I need for you both to 'meet' the secret I've been keeping for all these years right now," Indigo said softly, glancing down shyly.

"Secret? More secrets?" Steven asked.

"Yes—and I've kept it secret from Anna, too," Indigo answered, "and *all* the feral children are keeping a secret from everyone here, well almost everyone. Most of them came either from Utopus, or from other camps. Then, they had children later. All these children, whom the people living and working in the Bunker see as feral children, are the children, grandchildren and others of the people working on trying to make the world *safe* again."

"Those are the people you were talking about when you stated that there are 'others' who should go too?" Steven asked. "When we plan on going…"

"Yes—and they hide various places, located all around the world where they keep hidden," Indigo answered. "They've recently told me that a few of the places used got attacked, and that the people in them were taken away and never were seen again."

"Is there such a place anywhere close to Utopus as well, is that what you're getting at?" Steven asked, frowning somewhat.

"Yes, there is—a boy told me that *his* grandfather and his father had escaped from there, but that his grandfather's grandfather wasn't so lucky," Indigo replied. "He told me that his family member got shot in front of his grandfather with a gun right through the left side of his skull—about here."

Steven paled when he saw where Indigo pointed with a stretched-out finger, so he whispered, "I *may* have seen the man's body, and I think I have his gun, too."

✳ ✳ ✳

They were silent as they walked through the corridors in a part of the large complex that someone had attempted to make as invisible to others living in the Bunker as they were capable of without being discovered, Steven glanced from time to time at Anna, who appeared pale, and she was biting her lip, and looked at him occasionally with glazed eyes. It was obvious to him she'd never realised that Indigo was hiding a secret as extensive or with a greater impact as this one…

Steven was sensing that Anna had regarded his sister, Indigo, as a feral child until the moment they went to search her out. He was wondering for a moment if the whole tantrum situation he'd witnessed, and which had got Anna involved too, was all a set-up of some sort on

Indigo's part. That she was working towards a goal herself and being guided by a plan set out by someone else… *her mother and his father, perhaps? Well, our parents*, if he had to be honest with himself…

Steven wondered what his role was in all the events un-raffling around him right now. *Did father purposefully expose me to as much knowledge as he could find to make me curious and, therefore, would force the idea on me to become a scientist?* Steven thought, *because that doesn't explain the many objections he fired at me, because I wanted that choice…*

Memories, long buried, invaded his mind. Steven again went through the turmoil of the memories of his mother departing when he was a boy, and him calling after her in desperation and he now realised, also, it had happened with his cheeks wet from tears: *Mama. Mama.* But now, Steven also wagered to understand his mother better in the few memories he possessed of her, still just barely, and he realised that Indigo did resemble her rather remarkably well in her features. She possessed the same pale reddish-brown curly hair, the same soft-grey eyes, and the same lips. *Even her smile seems to be the same…*

Indigo, who was walking at a high pace in front of them, was a confident, self-assured girl, who knew what she was doing. She'd been waiting for the right moment to shed off the pretence of being a feral child, and to set in motion whatever was to come next.

She had said that she understood why father always had referred to himself as Dr Burgard for reasons, Steven thought and this was something he only knew from before as he had talked to someone about the situation, *well more precisely I blabbed about the situation*, he corrected himself, during the earlier interrogation. When Steven had told Indigo more of his story of how he'd travelled from Utopus to what used to be Spain, or at least the most northern part of it, and there was a comparison he could make. He could compare himself to his mother who'd done the same travel. Like Indigo was going to tell him about her, she needed to get to know her father. *Blabbing*, Steven thought. *How dangerous is to say the wrong thing? How dangerous was it to travel while pregnant? I should tell her about what father told me…*

Generally, he noted, the explanations his sister had given him matched what Anna has said earlier in the day, though this conversation was before we'd know the consequences of the added knowledge we were getting now. It might have been a reason why she stayed with Anna and hadn't wanted to leave the woman's side, but then to be gone and reappear with no explanations, days later.

That must be what Anna is wonder about likely, Steven thought after another glance at her.

Seemingly, Indigo had realised that the time for action had come when she'd searched through his rucksack. And now, she'd gone to get it even when he'd asked: "Not yet." However, things were happening so fast that at any day it might have been found, so she hid it elsewhere and now had retrieved it and given it to him…

A lapse in judgement of people within the Bunker saved our plan, but only because we got lucky, Steven thought, *but how long will this luck last us?*

A thought from four years earlier when he was in the dark about what was really going on came to Steven's mind, when he had thought he would just arrive somewhere filled with enemies. Now, however, he realised he had found more. A sister he never knew existed. People who were working on changing the situation in the world…

Steven walked after Indigo through another door. He halted his progress into the room. He stared, realising now what the future might be like for him, for Anna, for Indigo, for all the people staring at him and for him came the realisation his father had told him about them. He knew already they existed. But he was a stranger and now he faced the toughest few minutes of his entire life. They'd have questions. Maybe one specifically.

All of them with the same one question on their faces…

✳ ✳ ✳

Six Months Later

A story that Indigo had wanted to tell later, after many other visits with this group of mysterious people, who'd been living so brilliantly and in absolute secrecy right under the noses of the enemy, would soon involve the girl telling him much more about their mother, telling him why they had worked against the enemy, and so much more…

How much more is there to discover? Steven thought as he sat down opposite his sister.

the end

HERE'S HOW TO KEEP IN TOUCH WITH ME!

My website is nathaliemlromer.com

Twitter   twitter.com/nathaliemlromer
Facebook   facebook.com/nathaliemlromer
Blog   nathaliemlromer.blog
GoodReads   goodreads.com/nathaliemlromer
Instagram   instagram.com/nathaliemlromer
Pinterest   pinterest.com/nathaliemlromer

ABOUT THE AUTHOR

Nathalie M.L. Römer was born in the Netherlands, lived there during her childhood before she moved to Curaçao as a teenager. From there, she moved to Britain to live there for twenty-five years, before moving to Sweden where she lives with her partner Anders.

In her childhood years and beyond, Nathalie has always loved to read novels. In her local library as a child, she would often borrow "adult audience" science fiction and fantasy novels, and as the bookworm, that she was (and still is), she would read them all in a few days... and go back for more, often. The genres that interest Nathalie the most is science fiction, fantasy, and historical novels. Her favourite authors include various science fiction, fantasy and historic authors that include (but limited to) Isaac Asimov, Richard A. Knaak, Jean M. Auel, and Christie Golden.

In addition, to reading novels, the other interests she pursues include needlework and crafts, archaeology, reading about various science topics, home cooking, photography, web design, and playing MMO games - mostly World of Warcraft which Nathalie credits as having directly inspired her to write stories.

www.ingramcontent.com/pod-product-compliance
Lightning Source LLC
LaVergne TN
LVHW020314200726
843507LV00012B/2089